THE DEVIL'S BIDDING

P.L. Doss

"It is always exciting to find a new author, and P.L. Doss is quite a find. The characters are sympathetic and the story is exciting. Can't wait until the next in the series!"

– Beverly M, NetGalley

"A twisty puzzle with plenty of suspects and old secrets that have far-reaching effects."

– Jen, Goodreads

BLOOD WILL TELL

"*Blood Will Tell* is a thriller with twists and turns that start from the first words and keep you going to the last page. P. L. Doss is a writer reminiscent of Patricia Cornwall or James Patterson."

– Tricia Schiro

"This book kept me in suspense from the first page. As an Atlanta area resident, I enjoyed the 'local flavor,' but even if I lived in Nebraska, this book would have kept me riveted…. The book incorporated mystery and suspense, but also family ties and divisive family issues in a very convincing way. The topics were woven together until the final, and surprising climax was revealed."

– Barbara Lee, Amazon

"7 out of 5 stars!"

– Freddie Hanrahan, Amazon

"P. L. Doss has done it again! Her second novel with Joplin and Halloran as the main characters is as much of a page turner as *Enough Rope,* her first novel. I love her attention to detail, writing style and many twists and turns as well as the character and relationship development in her novels! If you are a fan of crime dramas you will NOT be disappointed with this book!"

– bigcanoelover, *Amazon*

"I thoroughly enjoyed this crime drama. The writing built suspense and the plot was intricate enough that the final solution was not easily gleaned until revealed. The characters are well developed, believable and engaging. I look forward to more from this author."

– VixenReindeer22, *Amazon*

"Unexpected twists and turns. Great continuation from previous book. Don't have to read the previous book in order to follow the story line. Awesome characters. Everyone is so unique and brings a different aspect to solving the crime. Can't wait to read the next book to see what Joplin and Halloran get themselves into."

– Erinne Young, *Amazon*

"This book is a worthy successor indeed to *Enough Rope.* It continues to unfold the relationships between the characters, making them even more real, particularly the friendly sparring between Joplin and Halloran. It was a page-turner from the get-go, drawing me in to Doss' fictional yet very specific Atlanta—as a native, I should know! And the ending truly took me by surprise, although on a second reading I saw all the bread crumbs she dropped to lead the reader on. "

– subabysu, *Amazon*

"A good example of a crime thriller, at nearly 500 pages, which lets you get right into the story and gain background information and understand more about the characters too. Leave yourself enough time to sit and read it, as it will take a while due to its length, but you won't want to stop reading."

– Cath, Goodreads

"Absolutely engrossed me from page one to the end! The story line while complex was written and tied together beautifully! The ending was a shock to me.....never saw that one coming at all! Love the characters. I must go and get the first book to get all caught up now!"

– Bev, Goodreads

THE DEVIL'S BIDDING

A JOPLIN/HALLORAN MYSTERY

———

P.L. Doss

Mayfair
Press

THE DEVIL'S BIDDING
P. L. Doss

Edition ISBNs
Trade Paperback: 978-0-9890934-4-6
Digital: 978-0-9890934-5-3

THIS BOOK IS DEDICATED TO MY CHILDREN:

Nicole Armentrout and Clayton Doss

They are my best creations, but just like my characters,
they had minds of their own.

I can take no credit for the amazing human beings they've become.

"Zounds, sir, you are one of those that will not serve God if the devil bid you."

Iago to Brabantio
Othello: Act I, Scene I

PROLOGUE

Cautiously, the cat crept out from under the bed. It had been a long time since the frightening sounds that had caused her to hide had stopped, but she was still wary. It was dark now, the pale light from the street showing only shadows, but that was no problem for her. She padded out into the hall, head turning, eyes darting, but saw no one. The kitchen was also dark, but she saw a shape on the floor, and, as she got closer, breathed in a scent that was familiar and comforting.

The cat began to head-bump the figure, but there was no response. No petting of her head or tickling behind her ear. She tried again, and when nothing happened, moved on to the utility room where her litter box and food were kept. There was only dry food for her, a disappointment, but she was hungry and ate most of it.

After using the litter box, she returned to the figure on the floor. More head-butting still brought no response, so she curled up and put her head on her owner's back, then closed her eyes. The usual warmth she expected wasn't there, but it didn't occur to her to wonder why.

CHAPTER ONE

The first thing Hollis Joplin did when he got to the Milton County Medical Examiner's Office that morning, after Sherika had handed him a manila envelope delivered by FedEx, was head to the break room for coffee. He'd shared a cup with Carrie earlier, but it hadn't been quite enough caffeine after a late, somewhat booze-filled Friday evening at Davio's. Carrie had then gone back to bed. As an assistant ME, she had weekend duty just once a month, but Joplin worked rotating shifts with the other death investigators, and he was on for Saturday.

Making a mental note to turn down a second one of Gerry's potent dirty Martinis next time, Joplin shoved the envelope under his arm and grabbed a mug from the counter. He filled it from the large urn next to the microwave, hoping Sarah Petersen, his boss, had been the one to make the coffee that morning. She never seemed to make it either too weak or too strong, yet another reason she was held in high esteem by all the investigators. The pathologists, too, for that matter. Since becoming Chief Investigator eighteen months ago, she'd turned the unit into a well-oiled machine, leading by example whenever possible. Which meant getting to the office before anyone else and making sure she knew what the people under her needed to do their jobs.

Like decent coffee.

Joplin had been summoned to a vehicular homicide on 400 before he left the condominium he shared with Carrie, so it was after nine-thirty by the time he got to his cubicle. He'd intended to get started on his report of the scene, but decided to open the envelope first. Setting his mug on the desk, he sat down and slit the flap with a pen knife he kept in a side drawer. Inside were several eight-by-ten photographs.

The first picture was of a front door, black, with two potted plants on either side. The next showed a narrow entry hall that held only a rug and a chest of some kind, with a still-life painting of pears over it. The third picture was of a kitchen. The warm yellow walls held a pot rack and several prints of various herbs; stainless appliances and gray granite countertops made a nice contrast to them. Joplin was beginning to wonder if some realtor had heard that he and Carrie were thinking of buying a house after their upcoming wedding, when he was stopped short by the next photo.

It was of a woman lying face-down on the kitchen floor. Her head was turned to the side, but her long brown hair covered her face. She was wearing jeans and a black, fitted jacket, but her feet were bare. Joplin moved quickly to the next photo, which showed the woman from a different angle. Whoever had taken it had stood or knelt near her head this time. Two more photos were close-ups of the woman's hands, which were on either side of her, palms down, as if she'd fallen and had tried to get up. There was a wide silver ring on the third finger of her right hand and a diamond ring on the third finger of her left hand. The nails were pink and looked professionally manicured.

He was certain she was dead.

———

Sarah Petersen looked up from her computer to see Hollis Joplin standing in the doorway. His large head, thick blond hair looking a little unkempt, was cocked to one side, and his green eyes were definitely blood-shot.

"Can I talk to you?"

"Sure. What's up?"

He placed some photos on her desk and nodded toward them. "I'd like you to take a look at these."

She gave him a quick glance, eyebrows raised, then picked them up. Shuffling through them, Sarah frowned when she got to the fifth picture. "You take these?" she asked, looking up at him.

"No. According to Sherika, FedEx delivered them. I've never seen them before. But my name is on the envelope."

"Obviously, it's a crime scene, even though there aren't any labels or case numbers on the backs of the photos. The question is: whose? You didn't take these, but somebody did."

"Right. I kept the envelope they came in, but it didn't tell me much. It was labeled 'Overnight Delivery,' sent on November 8, 2013, but the ink on the sender's label was smeared, making it illegible."

"You think that might have been deliberate?"

"Sure seems like it."

The phone on Petersen's desk rang, cutting off further speculation. She was silent as she listened, but grabbed a pen and wrote something down. "We'll get on it," she said, then clicked off and handed Joplin the page from her note pad. "We'll have to figure this out later, Hollis. There's a body at that address that's more important. Why don't you leave these with me," she added, gesturing toward the photos.

"Fine with me. Maybe Sherika knows a little more about who sent them."

"If she doesn't, nobody does," Petersen said. Their receptionist had her finger on every pulse in the ME's office.

The living ones, anyway.

———

The address was in Brookhaven, which straddled both Dekalb and Milton counties. More specifically, in Historic Brookhaven, on West Brookhaven Drive. Joplin, an architecture buff, knew that Salson Stovall and Solomon Goodwin had been responsible for much of the development there, inspiring wealthy Atlantans to build summer homes in the area in the late nineteenth century, much like their Buckhead neighbors. But it wasn't an actual neighborhood until 1911, when several investors bought a tract of land they named "Brookhaven Estates" and hired Herbert Barker, a New Jersey golf pro, to design a golf course for it. The area then became the first community in Georgia to be created around a golf course.

It was something that couldn't be said about Ansley Park and Druid Hills, which seemed to please the Historic Brookhavenites. And they totally separated themselves from the newly-created city of Brookhaven, which included North Brookhaven and Town Brookhaven and was in less wealthy Dekalb County. Milton County, re-created in 2003 through a clever and calculated bit of political gerrymandering that gobbled up the choicest parts of Fulton County, had the most desirable addresses, in their opinion. Which was also what residents of John's Creek, Dunwoody, Buckhead, Ansley Park and Midtown believed. The proverbial pecking order never failed to amuse him.

He turned left off Peachtree onto Peachtree-Dunwoody, then took Winall Down over to West Brookhaven Drive. The trees in the beautifully-kept yards surrounding the Capital City Club were still ablaze with color, due to an extended Indian summer that year. Joplin turned left again and drove slowly, looking for 1452. It was directly across from the clubhouse, but he was disappointed to see that it wasn't one of the houses built by Hal Hentz or Neel Reid or even Preston Stevens, who had designed the clubhouse; he was familiar with the styles of the houses they'd created. But it wasn't new, by any means; probably built in the early teens of the twentieth century, Joplin decided. Unfortunately, whatever style it had started out with, it hadn't retained it, and seemed to be comprised of a series of lateral additions made over the years.

Sarah had told him that the body wasn't actually in the house itself, but in a carriage house at the back of the property. Joplin drove down the driveway to the right of the house and parked behind a gray Nissan sedan that he knew belonged to Ike Simmons, a senior detective with the Atlanta Homicide Unit. They had been partners for seven years before he'd left to join the Milton County ME's office. And since the APD's jurisdiction included parts of Milton, as well as Dekalb and Fulton counties, they continued to work together. They'd also been best friends. Still were, for that matter.

He grabbed his bag and slid out of the car, then walked around the other cars, which included an APD car and a blue Audi, to reach the front door of the carriage house. As it came into view, he began to walk more slowly, then stopped altogether. The door was black, with two potted plants on either side. To anyone else, this would have seemed like mere coincidence, but Hollis Joplin had an eidetic memory, and his mind retained images of anything he'd ever seen, often in three dimensions. It helped him in his work as the "eyes and ears" of the forensic pathologists who would perform autopsies on the bodies he saw at deaths scenes. But it had wreaked havoc on his ability to sleep at night since his teenage years, as well as on his relationships.

So Joplin knew exactly what he would find behind the black door with the plants on either side.

CHAPTER TWO

The door opened as Joplin was putting on paper booties over his shoes.

"Probably won't do much good," said Ike Simmons. His face, dark-complected, with broad cheek bones above a well-kept mustache, didn't look happy. "It's been like Grand Central around here."

"Who found the body?"

"Owner of the main house, Mrs. Marlow. She tried to call the victim, but couldn't get her, even though she knew she was home, since her car was here. It's the Audi out front. So she came over and knocked several times, but got no response. She heard the cat meowing—" Simmons paused and shook his head. "Actually, she said it was 'crying,' and according to her, the victim was diabetic and had some problems regulating her insulin lately, so she called 911 and then let herself in with an extra key. She went into the victim's bedroom, thinkin' she was there or in her bathroom passed out, like the last time this happened, and by the time she found her in the kitchen, the EMTs had arrived."

"Did she touch the body?"

"Said she was too scared," said Simmons, opening the door wider for Joplin. "But she let the EMTs in, and then the uniform showed up. He secured the scene after it was determined that she'd been dead for some time and there was nothing they could do, but it had already been pretty compromised."

Joplin nodded, then walked inside. He saw the rug and the chest and the still-life painting that had been in the photos and followed Simmons to the kitchen at the end of the short hallway. The body lay on the floor, dressed in jeans and a black jacket, but no shoes. Her hands were on either side near her shoulders, palms down, rings just as he remembered them. Her long brown hair covered her face, which was turned to the side. An enormous black cat with green eyes, sitting a few feet away, stared up at Joplin, as if waiting for him to do something. He took his digital camera out of his bag, set the bag on the floor, and began taking photos. The cat never moved.

"Pretty cat."

"She won't leave the body. Landlady tried to pick her up, but she wasn't havin' it. Acts more like a dog than a cat, if you ask me." Simmons looked down at the body. "She was cold, with no pulse, so the EMTs didn't turn her over or try to resuscitate her. We left her like that until you could get here."

Joplin pulled his eyes from the cat, then knelt down and opened his black bag after setting the camera down. He tugged on latex gloves, then reached out and moved the curtain of hair covering the left side of the victim's face. The first thing that struck him was the severe bruising on her neck; the second was that her face had the usual dark, bloated look of a person who'd been strangled.

The third thing that struck him was that he knew who she was.

As if reading his mind, Ike Simmons said, "Victim's name is Blaine Reynolds. Why does that name ring a bell, Hollis?"

———

Besides Carrie, Blaine Reynolds had been the only woman Joplin dated after his divorce who'd meant anything to him. He'd first met her when Lewis Minton had brought her into the Investigative Unit on a chilly Friday in March of 2007.

"I want you to meet someone," he'd said solemnly to Joplin and Deke Crawford, who was his partner that day. He'd motioned toward a petite, dark-haired woman who looked to be around thirty. She had large blue eyes and an upturned nose and was dressed in a short black jacket and tapered slacks. Her hair was straight, brushing the collar of the jacket. "This is Blaine Reynolds," said Minton, smiling, then he told her their names. "She's an investigative reporter with the *Atlanta Journal-Constitution*. The paper wants to do an article on the differences between the ME and coroner systems in Georgia."

"Ms. Reynolds," said Joplin, shaking her hand.

"Blaine," she'd said firmly. "I've asked Dr. Minton to let me observe your unit for a few days, if you'll have me. I'd like to see first-hand what death investigators do."

"I'd be happy to help," said Joplin.

"Me, too," said Deke, shyly, offering his own hand. He'd turned red as he said this, and Joplin had seen his immediate attraction to her. He wondered if his own attraction to her was as obvious.

"Blaine's going to start the first of next week," Dr. Minton had said. "I'd appreciate it if anyone on the day shift could take her out on some scenes. Would that work?"

"If possible, I'd like to go out on some night crime scenes," she'd said quickly, looking at Joplin.

"Works for me, but you might run that by Chief MacKenzie, Doc," Joplin had answered diplomatically.

"Of course. Is he in yet?"

"Not hardly," Deke had said, then looked at his feet.

Mackenzie had never actually gotten to the ME's office before ten a.m.

"I'll talk to him later then. Might as well take Blaine down to meet a few of the pathologists."

She'd glanced back at Joplin after they'd all said 'nice to meet you' and 'see you soon.' It was a look that had told him that she was attracted to him, too.

———

"Hollis?" Ike was saying, and Joplin realized he'd had to repeat it several times.

He was still crouched over the body, but he pulled himself up and looked at Simmons. "She's a reporter for the *AJC*. Was," he added, correcting himself. "I also dated her for a few months."

"Oh, lord, of course!" Ike shook his head and frowned. "How could I forget that?"

"It was almost five years ago, Ike."

"Yeah, but it was big at the time, Hollis. You know it was. I don't really read the papers, but I shoulda remembered her. You were crazy about her!"

"I was," Joplin admitted.

"Then what happened? All I remember is that you said your 'schedules conflicted,' or something like that. Which I thought was pretty lame at the time."

Joplin shrugged. "It was the truth. Mostly, anyway. Investigative reporters don't have set days or shifts. They just follow leads—whenever and wherever it takes them. My schedule changes weekly and involves day and night shifts. When she was in town and had a free night, I usually didn't. After a while, it just didn't seem worth the effort." He looked down at the body. "To her, especially."

"I'm sorry, Hollis," said Simmons, shaking his head. "And sorry you had to be the one called to the scene this morning."

"Yeah, well, I don't think that was just my bad luck."

"What do you mean?"

"I'll explain later. Right now I need to give Blaine all my attention. Something I couldn't do five years ago."

———

Twenty minutes later, as Blaine Reynold's body was being wheeled out of the carriage house, Joplin found Ike Simmons talking to the uniformed cop in the living room, arranging a neighborhood canvass.

"Ask if anyone saw a person or persons in the area on foot, too. Not just any strange cars. And find out if there were any delivery or utility trucks around yesterday. According to the landlady, she got home around five p.m. and heard the victim pull in the driveway around six, but somebody could have already been on the property by then. "

The cop finished writing in his notebook and nodded. "Will do."

Simmons waited until he'd left, then turned to Joplin. "What can you tell me, Hollis?"

"Well, first, could you tell me if the landlady is going to take care of Blaine's cat?"

"Only you would worry about a cat at a crime scene," said Simmons, shaking his head.

"You and Alfrieda took care of Quincy when I was in the hospital, Ike. You're an animal-lover, too."

"Yeah, but havin' that cat of yours at our house for three weeks almost cured me of that, Hollis. But, I'll check with Mrs. Marlow about it before I leave."

"Thanks, Ike. Did Mrs. Marlow give you any contact information about Blaine's parents? I never met them, but she told me they lived in the D.C. area. Her father's a lobbyist. Or was, when I knew her."

"She gave me a phone number for them. I'm going to call as soon as I'm through here."

"How about her fiancé? She's wearing what looks like an engagement ring."

"I got that, too. Name's Winston Avery. He's a lawyer. I'm gonna go see him after I call her parents."

Joplin nodded. "Okay, good. Thanks for telling me."

"Yeah, yeah. Now can you please tell *me* about the victim?"

"She was strangled. I could even see the hand imprints on her neck because of the bruising. Lividity shows she died where she was found; blood had settled on the right side of her face, the palms of her hands, and anterior side of her body. Rigor had relaxed completely, so I'd put the TOD at not too long after she got home. That's just an estimate, but her body temp supports it, given the ambient temperature in the house. If she's got anything in her stomach at autopsy, that could change the estimate, though."

"Thanks. CSU will be here soon, but I'm assumin' you took pictures."

Joplin nodded. "Yeah, but I almost didn't need to."

"Say what?"

"When you finish up here, Ike, I'd like you to come by the ME's office and take a look at what was delivered to me this morning. And make sure CSU bags the digital camera I saw on the kitchen counter and dusts it for prints. They also need to see what might be recorded on the camera when they get it back to the lab. Make sure they photograph it in place before they take it though."

"And you'll explain why they need to do all that when I go by the ME's office later, right?"

"Right."

"Why not now, Hollis?"

"Because you need to actually see what I'm talking about. Trust me."

CHAPTER THREE

"FedEx delivered this?" Simmons asked Sherika, one gloved hand holding the manila envelope.

"Far as I know," she said, putting a little emphasis on the "I" as she stared back at the detective. As usual, her composure was serene, and her attractive face, with its large, dark brown eyes and scarlet lips, was the epitome of competence. Sherika just reeked of competence, in Joplin's mind. It was a quality that she possessed without any attempt to make other people feel *less* competent.

They were all sitting in Sarah Petersen's office. Ike Simmons had looked through the photos, which Petersen had placed in an evidence bag, along with the envelope, on the off-chance that CSU might be able to lift some usable prints and DNA from them. After some discussion, she had asked that the receptionist be brought back there. Sherika had been with the ME's office since it opened, and knew more about the daily goings-on than anyone else. She wielded this power discreetly, but they all—pathologists and investigators, as well as office staff both above and below her—knew what was what.

Simmons immediately seized on her implication. "You mean you didn't recognize the driver?"

"Never seen him before. Which doesn't mean anything. Routes change all the time."

"What did he look like?"

She shrugged. "White guy, brown eyes, middle-aged. About your height. He smiled a lot."

"Was he wearing a company uniform?"

"Yeah. Long-sleeved polo shirt with the purple stripe on the right." She paused and added, "His left. The stripe went to his arm, then down his side, just like all the FedEx guys wear. Black pants, running shoes. Nikes. And he was wearing gloves, now that I think about it."

"Anything else you can tell us about him, Sherika," Sarah Petersen asked. Her ashy, blunt-cut hair and angular features gave her the look of a young Eunice Kennedy, and the Boston accent completed the picture.

Sherika cocked her head. "He was kinda thin, but he had a little belly on him. And I remember thinking that there was something off about his face. Like his nose didn't go with it. And his hair didn't match his skin."

"Like he'd changed his appearance?"

She nodded, then said, "But I didn't pay any mind to that. I wish I had, now, but I didn't. It was just a morning delivery, you know?"

"We know," said Petersen.

"One more thing," Sherika said.

"Yes?"

"He doesn't like black people."

Joplin stared at her. "And you know that because…?"

"Because he smiled a lot, like I told you. White people smile a lot when they feel uncomfortable around black people." She turned to Simmons. "You know what I'm saying, right?"

He sighed and said, "I know what you're saying."

———

"Why would the killer have sent you these photos, Hollis?" Simmons asked.

"I have no idea. Really. I was trying to figure that out before I got the call to go to Brookhaven. I didn't know if they were real or staged, but my gut told me I was looking at a dead body."

"Did you know it was Blaine Reynolds then?"

"No, of course not. I didn't recognize her until I brushed the hair away. It was covering her face in the photos and when I first saw the body at the scene. You know that, Ike."

He nodded. "Whoever sent—or brought you—these photos wanted you to see them before you were called to the death scene. And since they weren't in an overnight envelope, we can be pretty sure that was no FedEx driver, but Ricky and I will still check that out. I'll take them to CSU to examine, but it's a long shot. I'd also like Sherika to work with our IdentiKit artist. If they can come up with a good composite, we can show it to the people at FedEx. Since this guy seemed to have a uniform, he might have worked there at some point. And maybe that'll get us closer to finding Blaine's killer and why he— or whoever took the photos—sent them to you."

"You think someone other than the killer might have taken these photos and sent them to Hollis?" Sarah Petersen interjected.

"It's a possibility. We also need to know how this person—or persons— knew Hollis would have the morning shift today, Chief. But the most important question is this: Why Hollis? Why draw him into this? Because he once knew the victim? Was involved with her?"

Petersen turned to him. "How involved with her *were* you, Hollis?"

———

"Did you sleep with her?" Carrie asked. She speared a piece of penne pasta out of the pot and then bit into it, chewing slowly. Her long, almost black hair was gathered at the nape of her neck with what she called a "scrunchy," and her deep brown eyes looked off to the right as she was deciding whether the pasta was ready. She was wearing a peach-colored sweater he'd never seen.

And waiting for him to answer her question, Joplin was sure.

"Yes," he said finally, hands clasped in front of him as he sat across from her at the kitchen island. A black Le Creuset pot filled with Shrimp Fra Diavolo simmered in front of him. Lights from restaurants and businesses on Peachtree shone brightly through the large Palladian windows in the newly-darkened living room of the condominium, casting shadows on the brick walls. It was their favorite time of day. Usually, anyway. "Does it matter?"

He watched carefully as she turned off the gas burner and then bent down to get a colander from one of the lower cabinets behind her. First, because he was trying to gauge her mood; secondly, because he never got tired of looking at her. She had a great ass.

"Not really. It was long before I knew you. On the other hand, whoever killed her seems to want to involve you somehow, so maybe I'd better know as much about your relationship as possible. Without all the sexual details," she added as she thunked the colander into the sink.

Joplin looked at Quincy, who had heard Carrie's tone of voice and, ever vigilant, was creeping toward them. Quincy didn't like raised voices or pots and pans being banged. Neither of these things happened very often, but even once had been often enough for the cat, who had a long memory. The last time had been six months ago, when Carrie's Conservative Jewish parents had come for dinner, and the subject of Joplin's willingness to convert had come up.

He hadn't been the one to get upset. Harriet and Nathan Salinger had always been pretty great to him, especially since he was not only not Jewish, he'd also been divorced, was eight years older than their daughter, and—in their minds—was responsible for her almost getting killed by a serial killer.

Carrie had seemed to handle her parents' request well at the time, prom-ising that she and Joplin would discuss it, but after they'd left, she'd lost it. Joplin was sure the issue had more to do with what she believed her par-ents had hoped and expected for her, than just his religion—or lack of it. Since her brother's death at age ten from Tay-Sachs disease, she'd tried to be everything they wanted and needed in a child and had planned on being a pediatric pathologist.

And then, Carrie had done a thirty-day rotation as an intern at the Milton County ME's Office and fallen for Joplin's good friend, Jack, who'd later been killed. And after he, himself, had almost died, Carrie had changed her career path to forensics and applied for a residency at the ME's Office. Something which Joplin was sure must have disappointed her parents.

When the pots and pans had finally been stacked that night, and Carrie's voice had come down a few octaves, Joplin had proposed. He'd been want-ing to do so for a long time; he even had the ring, purchased a few weeks earlier, just in case the right time came up. And after seeing Quincy, who adored Carrie more than even purring could say, looking so upset, Joplin had seized the moment.

Sort of, anyway.

First, he'd had to go into their bedroom and paw through the bureau drawer where he *thought* he'd put the Tiffany box. When he'd finally found it, he'd come back into the living room, to find Carrie watching *Homeland*.

He hated *Homeland*.

Ever the romantic, Joplin had shut off the TV, knelt in front of Carrie and opened the small, aqua box.

"Will you marry me?" he'd asked.

Carrie had stared at him. "How can you ask me that now?"

"I thought it might be a good time," he'd said, a little crestfallen.

What had ensued involved crying, some apologies for her parents on Carrie's behalf, an apology on Joplin's behalf for his poor timing, several declarations of love, and a very long, tongue-involved kiss, followed by a "yes" from Carrie. Quincy, by then, was asleep, curled up on the couch.

Now, however, Quincy was in alert-mode as he leaped up onto the granite island and stared at them.

"You're scaring the cat," Joplin said as Carrie dumped the pot of pasta into the colander and then slammed the empty pot onto the counter.

"*You're* scaring *me*. Someone hates you enough to kill one of your old lovers and drag you into it."

Joplin walked over to Carrie and put his arms around her, clasping them in front of her. She was tense—rigid, actually—but he put his head close to hers and said, "We don't know that that's what happened, Carrie. I think whoever killed her wanted me to know that she was dead and that, somehow, it was my fault. But I don't think she was killed just to get me involved."

She relaxed a little, then turned around to face him. "Then why, Hollis? Why was she killed, and why would it be your fault?"

"I have no idea. Truly. I haven't even seen her since the last time we had dinner together, almost five years ago. We never even had an official break-up—just couldn't synchronize our schedules to get together. And then we sort of…stopped trying."

Carrie seemed to think about this, then said, "Who was the last one to call?"

It was something only a woman would think to ask, in Joplin's opinion, and he wasn't sure how to answer. "I was. And then, she was," he added lamely.

"What does that mean?"

"I made one last effort to try to see her, but she said she was on assignment and was going to be out of town for several days. Said she'd call me when she got back, but that never happened. Then when I was in the hospital, she called me."

Carrie frowned. "You mean a year ago? When you got rid of your colostomy bag?"

"No," said Joplin quickly. "During the Carter case. After Jack…died," he added reluctantly. It still wasn't easy to bring up Jack Tyndall. Joplin had almost been disemboweled the same night Jack had been killed, and he'd spent weeks recovering at Grady Hospital.

The color left Carrie's face, and he hated that they were both being dragged back to that time. It had taken several months for them to deal with it. Joplin had handled it at first with his usual avoidance tactics, followed by a rather severe Blue Funk, but, mostly due to Carrie's perseverance, they'd finally been able to renew a relationship that had been sidelined by Carrie's affair with Jack.

"Oh," she said, finally, as she poured the pasta back into the pot.

"It was all over the media—remember, Carrie? Blaine called when she heard I was conscious and out of danger. Just to tell me she was wishing me a speedy recovery. The call lasted two minutes, tops. Maybe three minutes."

Carrie nodded slowly. "I see. Did she ask if she could come by and visit you?"

"No. And I didn't ask her to. It was over, Carrie. Had been for a long time. And I was in love with you, even though I wouldn't admit it to myself at the time."

Tears began to form in Carrie's eyes, and she looked away from him. "Thank you for answering my questions, Hollis," she said. "Most of them anyway. The two biggest ones, though, are why Blaine Reynolds was murdered. And why those photos were sent to you."

"You're right. But I'm going to do my damnedest to find out. I promise you."

CHAPTER FOUR

Maggie Halloran raised the trunk of her car and got out her equipment. A strong wind rustled the trees surrounding the Atlanta Children's Home on Metropolitan Avenue, and she looked up, watching as they swayed colorful branches in the Sunday morning sun. The enormous stone building had once belonged to the Heyward family well over a century ago, built, so Hollis Joplin had told her, for a carpet-bagger from New York who'd made a fortune supplying railroad ties after the Civil War.

The day before, Maggie had photographed fifteen children and hoped to finish the rest today. Not because she wanted to get it over with; she was enjoying the time she spent with them. But the sooner she finished, the sooner these children might have a chance to be in permanent homes. Once a year, the Home published an online album with pictures of children waiting for adoptive families. The idea had come from a successful program initiated by the ASPCA to encourage people to adopt cats and dogs.

Children, it turned out, were a lot harder to market, but it had still been fairly successful, especially since the album came out just before the holiday season. Maggie had volunteered her services the previous November, soon after a notorious case involving a serial killer in Atlanta had opened her eyes to the plight of children in foster care. She couldn't change the world, she'd decided, but she could use her talents and abilities to help in some small way. And although her reputation as a photographer had never been stronger, Maggie had found it increasingly difficult to photograph the children of wealthy Atlantans or jet off across the country to capture the images of celebrities' families in the past few years.

"We don't need the money," Tom had told her a year ago. "Although I know that's not what your work is about. But I get the impression that you don't get the same satisfaction from it as you used to."

"I don't," she'd agreed, although she wasn't quite sure why. She'd always made it a point not to pander to her clients and had been very firm about the settings for the children she'd photographed—nothing that shouted money or was an extension of the world their famous parents inhabited. She'd tried, instead, to capture whatever she saw as the *essence*, for want of a better word, of each child. Most of the clients had liked what she'd done. Except the mother of the overweight young girl who'd tried to get Maggie to use "air-brushing" to make her daughter look thinner, she remembered now as she walked up to the front entrance of the Home. That had been a deal-breaker.

"Maggie! Hello!" said Janie Simpson, jumping up from her desk in the big entry hall. She came around to give Maggie a hug, then stood back to look at her. Janie was a youngish Junior League matron who volunteered at the Home, too, but she'd always impressed Maggie as someone who simply put in the required hours. "Betsy Talmadge told me you'd be here today. How are you? Your hair looks great! Where do you go?"

Maggie lifted a hand to her cropped auburn hair. "Jamison's," she said, wishing she didn't have to answer questions like that, and then quickly changed the subject. "Are the kids ready for me?"

"As soon as you're all set up. Just give me a call."

Happy to get away so easily, Maggie nodded, then took a right turn down the hall to a large, light-filled room that had once functioned as a solarium when the Heyward family had owned it. It was now used as a meeting place for prospective adoptive families and children, as well as volunteer groups like Big Brothers and Big Sisters. For this particular weekend, it had been turned into a photographic studio for Maggie. She'd left her Savage studio light kit in the room the day before and quickly turned everything on, then set her camera in the tripod. After adjusting the lights a bit, she called Janie, then looked at the the list of children she'd be photographing that day.

Ten minutes later, the first child appeared, a young boy around ten, who didn't quite look her in the eye. "Hi, are you Robert?" Maggie asked, smiling as she looked at her list.

He nodded shyly, and she tried to make him feel comfortable, asking him questions about himself, then telling him about her own children. Maggie continued making small talk as she directed him to sit wherever he wanted, then re-adjusted the lights to accommodate his choice. When she'd gotten the shots she wanted, she thanked him and gave him her card.

"Before these photos are published, you'll get to see them," Maggie told him. "If you don't like them, I'll come back and take some more, okay?" It was what she told each child, just as she'd told the children of her private clients. It had always been important to her that the children felt like they were involved in the process and had some control. To these children, she thought it might mean even more.

"Okay," said Robert. "Thanks," he added as he looked back at her from the door.

The next five hours were spent photographing a variety of children. Some were teenagers, and Maggie spent a little more time with them, knowing the odds of their being adopted were low, and got them to strike silly poses. Others were siblings, and she'd been told that it was likely that they wouldn't be able to stay together. Maggie made a point of posing these kids with their arms around each other's waists or their heads together, emphasizing the familial relationship. She coaxed a little boy in a wheel chair into making a "V for victory" sign, arms stretched high above his smiling face. She photographed a toddler leaping high in the air from the middle of a sofa.

It was just as Maggie had begun to pack up, thinking she was finished for the day, that Janie ushered in a little girl who looked to be around seven. Her skin and pale blue eyes pointed to a biracial background, and she looked at Maggie with a wary, almost angry, expression.

"This is Jayla," said Janie.

Instinctively, Maggie squatted down to the girl's eye level. "Hi. My name's Maggie."

"I don't want to get my picture taken," Jayla said, her lower lip sticking out stubbornly. She grabbed hold of a tiny crucifix on a delicate gold chain that was around her neck.

"That's okay. I'm pretty much done for the day, anyway." Maggie stood up and motioned toward the sofa. "But could you just sit down for a minute and tell me why you don't want your picture taken while I put up my equipment? I have to put down a reason why I didn't photograph somebody or I might get in trouble."

The child's face showed she clearly had a problem believing that Maggie would get into trouble, but she sat down on the sofa.

"That's a pretty cross you're wearing," Maggie said when it was obvious Jayla wasn't going to respond.

"It was my mother's. She gave it to me."

"I had one like it when I was a little girl," said Maggie. "And I gave it to *my* daughter." After more silence, she began to pack up her equipment, mentioning what each piece was called and how she used it to help her take pictures, hoping that might relieve whatever anxiety the little girl was feeling.

"I have a daddy," Jayla said suddenly. "And when he gets out of prison, he's going to come get me."

Out of the corner of her eye, Maggie could see Janie shaking her head, trying to get her attention. She ignored her and said, "Well, that's what I'll write down then. Do you think you could help me put some of this stuff in that big bag over there?"

———

"So why is her father in prison?" Halloran asked as he and Maggie sat at the kitchen table in their Ansley Park house having a pre-dinner drink. He'd taken the kids to lunch and a movie while Maggie had been at the Children's Home and was enjoying some adult conversation after refereeing their almost- constant bickering. The only respite had been during *Cloudy With A Chance of Meatballs 2,* although Tommy had still complained about how loud Megan was when she ate popcorn.

"His name is Will Henry, and he's serving a life sentence for murder," said Maggie looking up at him. Her deep green eyes were troubled. "For killing his wife."

"The little girl's mother?"

Maggie nodded and took a sip of her wine. "Janie Simpson, one of the volunteers, told me his name after Jayla went out to play. It was in the paper and on the national news about a year and a half ago."

"I have a vague memory of it, but that's all."

"That was right around the time Elliot was murdered, so I'm not surprised."

Halloran had found his best friend and colleague, Elliot Carter, hanging from a tree in Piedmont Park in April of 2012. It had been one of the worst times in his life, and had culminated in his almost getting killed himself—along with Hollis Joplin. Joplin and his now-fiancée, Carrie Salinger, had become good friends, especially after they'd all been involved in yet another series of deaths just a year ago.

"Wait! Is Will Henry the actor who was in that TV show filmed in Georgia?" he asked, suddenly remembering. Georgia had become a healthy contender among states where movies and TV shows were filmed in the past few years, due mostly to the generous tax cuts given by the legislature, but also because it offered what location scouts and casting agents needed: urban and rural areas, mountains and a long sea coast, and a fairly large, professional acting community. It was also home to several recording and movie studios.

"Yes. He was one of the stars of *The Undead Zone* when he was arrested. He was originally from California, but he and his wife, Daisy Bulloch, who was also part of *The Undead Zone* cast, met when they were both working on *Remember the Titans*. They were each involved with other people then, but in 2005, when Will came back to Atlanta to shoot *We Are Marshall*, their romance took off. They got married in 2006, when Jayla was born."

"But why is the little girl at the Children's Home? I mean, there must be relatives who could take her."

"Not on Will Henry's side. His parents were killed in a car accident years ago, and he was an only child. And his wife's family cut off all contact with her when she married him."

"Because he was an actor?"

"No, because he's African-American. Jeremiah Bulloch is pastor of a Primitive Baptist church. Not all Primitive Baptists believe in segregation of the races, but this particular one does."

"You're kidding."

"I wish I were," Maggie said, then took a big sip of her wine. "Family and Children's Services contacted them when Will was convicted, but they refused to come get Jayla. So she was placed at Atlanta Children's Home. Several people have tried to start adoption proceedings, but Jayla keeps turning them down, and the family court judge and child advocate assigned to her have supported her. They're hoping she might change her mind as time goes by, which is why Janie brought her to meet me today."

Halloran took a moment to digest all this. "You learned all this from Janie?"

Maggie took the last sip of her wine and stood up. "Some of it. The parts about Daisy Bulloch's parents not taking their own granddaughter in, and Jayla's refusing to be adopted. The rest I already knew from the news media, including *People* magazine, which gets a little gossipy. But I'm not apologizing for that."

Halloran raised his hands in mock surrender. "No apology needed. I'm just in awe of your expert knowledge. I may hire you as an investigator for Healey and Caldwell."

"You've never paid me for the consulting work I did on the Libba Woodridge case, as I recall," she said, referring to her analysis of the video taken of a client when she'd been drugged and helpless. "I think I need to get the money up front if I ever agree to work for you or your law firm again, Tom."

"Damn!" said Halloran. "You're right. How about a few days at The Cloister the first weekend in December? I promise I won't play golf."

"We'll see," Maggie said, in the same tone she used with the children when she didn't want to give them an immediate "no" to a request.

Halloran was sure she had something else in mind already. Something that was certain to be out of his comfort zone.

CHAPTER FIVE

The Monday edition of the Atlanta Journal-Constitution had a second article devoted to Blaine Reynolds' death, this one on the front page. Given that she'd been a well-known investigative reporter for the paper for several years, Joplin wasn't surprised. The first article had been in Sunday's Metro section, probably because the reporter hadn't been able to get many details by Saturday afternoon's deadline. But since Blaine's father was a big-time lobbyist for the NRA in Washington, airtime had been allotted to the story on all major TV networks and their local affiliates for Sunday evening. According to Ned Beeson, who'd written Monday's article, a spokesman for the NRA had contacted him and asked him to point out that, although the death was a homicide, no firearm had been used.

Cold comfort for Blaine's parents, Joplin thought as he took another sip of coffee. Carrie had already left the condominium. Although it was Veteran's Day, the ME's office was open for business as usual. He had the second shift that day, and didn't have to be in until four p.m., but he planned to get to the ME's office a little early so he could see her before she went home. He had two day shifts that week, according to the schedule—nicknamed "The Menstrual Cycle" since it was based on a twenty-eight-day rotation. The rest of the week was made up of second shifts like today and "graveyard" shifts from midnight to eight a.m. It had an impact on their relationship, but they had committed to working it out.

This thought pulled him back to Blaine, and he wondered who had let go first. Because although it was true that she'd promised to call him when she got back to Atlanta, Joplin knew that he could have—maybe *should* have—called her again anyway. Maybe she'd been waiting for him to do that.

Maybe, maybe, maybe.

Resolving to put those thoughts on hold, Joplin finished both the article and his breakfast of coffee and peanut butter-banana toast, then wondered if he should give Ike Simmons a call. Ike had been quoted by Beeson as saying that the victim's parents had arrived in Atlanta Sunday morning, and that her fiancé, Winston Avery, was cooperating with the police. Asked if said fiancé were a suspect, Ike had responded, "Not at this time."

Which meant, of course, that he was.

Joplin folded up the paper and left it on the kitchen island in case Carrie hadn't finished it. It was his turn to clean the condominium this week, so he headed into the master bedroom. Quincy was asleep on Carrie's side of the bed, partially on his back, with his paws curled in complete relaxation and his head turned to the side. Joplin let out a long sigh, wondering again how his cat had so quickly switched allegiances. It was as if Quincy, too, had realized that he'd been a bachelor too long and had claimed Carrie as his mate.

Shaking his head, Joplin went into the bathroom and began to pull out various cleaning materials from under the double vanity. In his former life, he'd always started with the vacuuming, because he actually *liked* vacuuming, but Carrie had shown him the error of his ways. Bathrooms, then dusting and polishing, *then* vacuuming, she'd told him, and although she'd grown up with housekeepers doing all of that, he'd done things her way since they'd moved in together. Hell, what did he know, anyway? His years of being single had allowed him to clean whenever the mood struck him, which wasn't very often, or when he'd invited someone to come over, which also wasn't very often. And whenever he'd had one of his Blue Funks, any hygiene rules went right out the window.

Carrie had offered to see if the cleaning lady she'd used ever since she got out of medical school was available, but Joplin had balked at that. He'd insisted on paying half the condominium's rent and utilities, but that was about all he could afford on his salary, and he wasn't going to let Carrie shell out any more. So they'd agreed to clean the place themselves. At least, he thought so. He had a sneaking suspicion that said cleaning lady miraculously appeared sometime during Carrie's week to clean and offered her services. Free, of course.

They each still clung to a few old habits, Joplin had to admit. So he never questioned the neat triangles on the ends of the toilet paper rolls on Carrie's days to clean. She, in turn, didn't seem to notice when he drank the extra Yuengling or Jim Beam every now and then. A "quid quo pro" made in heaven.

As Joplin cleaned the sink and vanity, he wondered again if he should call Ike. He hadn't talked to him since Saturday, but after considering this, he decided to give Ike a little more time before bothering him. His old partner was under a lot of pressure to deal with what had become a very high-profile case. And it would only get worse if the media found out about the photos that had been sent to Joplin.

And that he'd once been involved with the victim.

———

David Markowitz had already performed the autopsy on Blaine Reynolds by the time Joplin arrived at three p.m., according to Sarah Petersen. At the Saturday meeting with Ike in Sarah's office, they'd all agreed that Carrie shouldn't be assigned to it, given the circumstances. So he decided to walk down the hall to the pathologist's office before going to see her, and found David typing up a preliminary report.

"Anything you can tell me?" Joplin asked, coming into the room.

Markowitz looked up at him above reading glasses perched on his nose. "About life and love, or the body I just worked on?"

"I may regret this, since I'm getting married in less than six months and need all the advice I can get, but I think I'll settle for hearing about the autopsy."

"You sure, Hollis? I hear you once knew the lady."

"Did you also hear that some joker sent me crime scene photos of her before we even knew it *was* a crime scene?"

"Actually, yes, I did, and I'm sure that made the whole situation even worse for you."

Joplin sighed and put his hands in his pockets. "Much as I'd like to feel sorry for myself, Blaine Reynolds is the victim here, David, and she was a nice person. I'd like to help, if I can."

"Basically, what I found pretty much backs up what you put in your report. She was manually strangled, and from the bruising on her neck, I can tell you that she was facing her killer. He used both thumbs to crush her hyoid bone, so it was pretty quick. I found numerous black hairs on the back of her clothes, which appear to be from a cat, also mentioned in your report, but I'm going to have them tested anyway, along with other trace evidence that might be useful."

"Such as?"

"A few white threads on the front of her shirt and jacket. Under the microscope, they seemed to be cotton, but I want confirmation. I also took all the usual swabs, but I have to wait on those results. There was no overt evidence of sexual assault, though."

"Thank God for that, anyway. How about time of death?"

"Sometime between six and ten p.m., just like you thought, and closer to six. First, because rigor had already come and gone, but also because there was only coffee in her stomach, which could also explain her high glucose levels and the ketones in her urine. When I read in your report that the landlady said the victim had diabetes and had problems regulating her glucose, I tested the vitreous humor in her eyes and did a dipstick test on her urine. Did you know she was diabetic when you dated her?"

Joplin nodded. "It came up a few weeks into our relationship. We'd met for a late dinner and had been drinking some wine, so Blaine needed to test her blood sugar and told me about it. She was pretty matter-of-fact, though. Said she'd dealt with it since she was ten, and it was no big thing."

David Markowitz shrugged. "Ordinarily, that might be true, but there was something else I found that was probably having a big impact on her ability to manage her glucose levels. Simmons was present for the autopsy, so he knows about this, but he left before you got here, so—"

"What is it?" Joplin asked, immediately wary.

"She was pregnant. About six weeks along."

———

"David's right, of course," Carrie said, looking unsettled. "Hormone levels due to pregnancy can wreak havoc on glucose levels. And this can also have a very negative effect on the fetus during the first eight weeks, if the mother can't regulate her insulin."

Joplin had gone to her office after talking to David Markowitz and filled her in on the details of Blaine's autopsy. He knew she'd hear about the pregnancy sooner or later.

"The news reports last night said she was engaged to an Atlanta lawyer named Winston Avery," said Carrie when Joplin hadn't responded to what she'd said. "Have you talked to Ike? Does he know anything about him?"

Joplin shrugged. "I haven't had a chance. And I don't really want to bother him right now. He's got a lot on his plate with all the media attention."

"Well, maybe Tom knows him."

Joplin stared at her. "You're not seriously suggesting that I call Halloran, are you?"

"Why not? Blaine couldn't have been one of his clients. Unless this Winston Avery is rich and over seventy," she added, referring to the fact that Tom Halloran's reputation had been gained as an estate law litigator who often represented the young, beautiful widows of older, wealthy men.

Although Maggie and Tom Halloran had become good friends, especially over the past year, Joplin still had unpleasant memories of the times he and the attorney had been forced to work on cases together. Especially the last one, which *did* involve one of his young, beautiful clients. Halloran was one of the few—maybe *only*—attorneys he actually liked, but that didn't mean he wanted to work with him again. And even though it was highly unlikely that Blaine had been one of his clients, Joplin was reluctant to ask any favors.

"I think I'll just ask Ike about him. I'm sure he'll be looking at him pretty closely."

"You mean because most female homicide victims are killed by spouses or significant others?"

"Yes, but also because strangling someone implies not only a close, personal connection, it also means there's a lot of emotion involved. Rage, jealousy, feelings of betrayal."

"But several serial killers have strangled their victims, Hollis. You know that. Like the Boston Strangler and Carlton Gary, who killed all those women in Columbus, Georgia. They didn't have personal relationships with their victims."

Joplin nodded in agreement. "You're right. But serial killers are often acting out anger and rage against someone who abused or neglected them in the past. Anyway, Blaine's murder doesn't seem like the work of a serial killer to me."

Carrie grinned at him. "I know you did your master's thesis on serial murderers, Hollis, but how can you be so sure?"

Joplin had finally completed the courses for his master's degree in criminal justice in June, then spent the summer finishing his thesis. He would get his diploma in December. It had taken him longer than he'd originally expected, given his own brush with death the year before and the surgeries and recuperations that followed. But Carrie had encouraged him whenever he'd felt overwhelmed; she'd even suggested the thesis topic, which dealt with damage to the limbic system and its correlation to psychopathology.

He grinned back at her. "I can't, and you know it. But this seems very personal to me, not something done for enjoyment. And sending the photos to me is also very personal. He wants me to feel guilty about this in some way. Or at least connected to it."

"He?" Carrie shook her head. "I know it's difficult to break the hyoid bone, but according to you, Blaine was a small woman, and a strong, fairly athletic woman could have done it. You shouldn't rule out a woman being involved, Hollis."

"You're absolutely right, love of my life, girl of my dreams," he said, standing up and going around her desk. He leaned down, hugged her, and planted a chaste kiss on the top of her head, then swiveled her chair around and kissed her soundly on the lips.

"What was that for?" she asked, eyes narrowed.

"Isn't it obvious? Not only are you gorgeous, extremely intelligent, sexy, funny, and full of integrity, we can discuss things like how much strength it would take to strangle a small woman. I really couldn't ask for more than that in a fiancée. Or a wife," he added, raising and lowering his eyebrows suggestively.

Her eyes narrowed even more, then she smiled at him. "Get out of my office, Hollis, before I show you what a woman my size can do to the genital area of a man your size."

———

"Your ears must be burnin', Hollis," said Ike Simmons.

"You want to tell me why?" Joplin asked, leaning back in his chair.

"'Cause Blaine's parents wanna talk to you, that's why. Her father just called me. Again."

Joplin sat up quickly. "Why would they want to talk to *me*? Do they know about the photos that were sent to me? Did you tell them about that?"

"Not hardly, Hollis. You know me better than that."

"Yeah, I do. I just got paranoid for a minute."

"Don't blame you, under the circumstances. But it turns out that once some friends of Blaine's at the *AJC* got involved, your name came up. Both as the death investigator sent to the scene and someone she used to date. And it's kinda gotten around. Ricky and I talked to her editor, Mark Rawlins. Also, a few of her colleagues—Lucy Alvarez and Ned Beeson. Both the editor and Beeson thought pretty highly of Winston Avery, by the way. Ms. Alvarez seemed to think he was the Devil incarnate. You know any of them?"

Joplin rubbed his hand over his face as he processed this. "I met Lucy once or twice, the others, just by name. But nobody knows about the photos, right?"

"Right. But it's probably only a matter of time. You want me to arrange a meeting with the Reynolds? It might help keep things a little more low-profile, if you know what I mean."

"I guess," said Joplin finally. "I don't like it, but I can't come up with a better idea. Did Winston Avery want to meet with me, too?"

"He hasn't asked, but that could change."

"Let's wait till he does then. *If* he does, I mean. Listen, Ike, Dr. Markowitz told me about the autopsy. And it hit me later that Blaine only had coffee in her stomach when she died. Did you find anything to show where she got it? Or if she was with anyone there?"

"We found a receipt for a chicken salad at a Zaxby's in Alpharetta at 12:10 p.m. in Blaine's purse and a receipt for a latte at the Starbuck's in Brookhaven at 5:30 p.m. I had a uniform check both places to see if she was with anybody, with no luck either place. The latte was a take-out order, though; we found the cup in her car, too."

"Okay, thanks," Joplin said. "Markowitz also told me that Blaine was pregnant. Did Avery know about it? I mean, did he bring it up when you informed him she was dead?"

"No, and that's been bothering me. I'm gonna discuss it with him later today. It's possible Blaine hadn't told him yet for some reason. Maybe she didn't even know it herself; she was only six weeks along."

"Maybe. I guess you'll know more after you talk to him. Or maybe not. Attorneys don't like to divulge much, in my opinion."

Simmons chuckled. "I know that's right, Hollis."

"What's this guy like, anyway? I know a little about Blaine's parents, but, I've never even heard of him."

"Yeah, but I'm sure you will. He's a very up-and-coming kind of guy, if you know what I mean."

"Not really."

"Well, you remember that book that came out in the early Sixties about a white journalist who darkened his skin and traveled around the South trying to document what it was like to be black?"

"You mean *Black Like Me*?"

"That's the one. And that's the best description I can give you of Winston Avery."

Now Joplin was truly confused. "He's a white guy trying to pass for black?"

Simmons laughed again. "Naw, he's as black as I am, Hollis. But it only goes skin deep."

CHAPTER SIX

After processing all of the photos she'd taken at the Children's Home, Maggie had spent the rest of the morning pulling up what information she could from the Internet on the murder of Daisy Bulloch Henry and Will Henry's trial. Since the kids were off from school due to the holiday, she had arranged play dates for them with neighbors who owed her from several previous occasions. Tom had left an hour later than usual for the office, his only concession to Veteran's Day, which was otherwise ignored by partners and associates alike at Healey and Caldwell.

Most of what Maggie had accessed, she'd already read about or seen on various TV shows at the time the events unfolded. What struck her this time, however, were two things: that Jayla Henry had never testified at the trial, and that the Reverend Jeremiah Bulloch and his wife, Rachel, had never attended it. Despite all the speculation by various reporters in sundry newspapers and magazines and on TV about both issues, nobody really knew the reasons why.

Given Jayla's age at the time and the apparent racism of Daisy's parents, the general consensus was that Will Henry was protecting his daughter, and that the Bullochs had abandoned theirs. Just as they'd abandoned little Jayla to foster care. But Maggie wondered if there were more to it than either of those explanations. Had Will Henry been afraid that Jayla might say something incriminating about him on the stand? Had the Bullochs known something about Will—besides just the color of his skin—that made them cut off all communication with their daughter? She knew there were good, decent people who would be concerned if one of their children married out of his or her race or religion; that didn't always mean they were racist. But what Daisy's parents had done *did* appear racist, and no reporter seemed to have dug any deeper than the surface.

Then she wondered why in the world she was so hung up on what a little girl had told her—that she couldn't be adopted because her father was going to come get her when he got out of prison. The obvious answer, Maggie realized, was that it was some kind of magical thinking that many young children would probably resort to when faced with the unimaginable happening to them. Like having your mother murdered, and then being told that your father had done it.

But, still…

Understanding herself far better than the reasons she had reacted the way she had to Jayla Henry, Maggie knew she had to find out more before she could move on. She stood up and stretched, then jerked her head from side to side and up and back to work the kinks out. This done, she sat down again and pulled up contact information for Will Henry's attorney and the Bullochs' church address in Brookhaven. Next, she called her mother to ask if she could drop the kids off at her house around two that afternoon. Maggie hadn't planned on going back to the Children's Home before Wednesday or Thursday. But she needed to talk to Jayla again so she could either decide that she was reading far too much into what the child had said, or…

Whether she needed to use her IOU card from Tom.

———

Sarah Petersen didn't like the idea of Joplin's meeting with Blaine Reynolds' parents. "Why in the world would you agree to that?" she asked. "And why would Ike Simmons suggest it?"

Joplin shrugged. "He thought it might keep things from escalating. I was identified as the death investigator on the case, and some of Blaine's colleagues at the *AJC* have long memories. They knew we were seeing each other back in 2008."

She considered this, then said, "And by 'escalating' he meant?"

"I'm not really sure, Chief. I guess they're focusing on me since I knew Blaine. And they want to talk to me. Ike assured me that they didn't know anything about the photos that were sent to me."

"Did her parents know about you back then, or did they just find out?"

"I think they did. There was some talk about me meeting them when they were in Atlanta once. That was before things sort of…fizzled out between us."

Petersen frowned and shook her head, her blue eyes hooded. "You're a death investigator, Hollis," she said. "Not the detective in charge of the case or the pathologist who did the autopsy. Just because you had a brief relationship with the victim doesn't give them the right to talk to you. You did your job and turned in your report to Dr. Markowitz. If they have questions about the autopsy, they can talk to him. If they want updates on the investigation, they can talk to Ike or Rick. I don't agree with Ike's thinking on this. Meeting with you will make you *more* of a focus, not less, in my opinion."

Joplin let out a long sigh. "You're right. I know that. But even though Ike doesn't think Blaine's parents know about the photos I received, they might find out. The person who sent them, whether he's the killer or not, wanted me to be linked to her death. Somehow, he knew I'd have the morning shift last Saturday and would be here to open that envelope, whether I got called out to the scene or not. But I don't think it's going to end there."

"Do you mean this person might let the media know?"

Joplin stared back into the blue eyes. "It's certainly a possibility. Or maybe he'll find some way to let Blaine's parents know. Or the fiancé," he added.

"Are you thinking of telling them yourself?"

"Not without your permission."

Petersen considered this, then said. "We'll have the meeting here, in the conference room. See if you can get Ike to make it around eleven tomorrow morning. I'll be in charge," she added.

Joplin stood up. "Thanks, Chief."

———

Maggie had met with all the kids she'd photographed by 4 p.m. Fortunately, they'd all approved of their pictures, in varying degrees. The adolescent boys had shrugged, but nodded; the adolescent girls had needed to discuss various body parts they felt looked "fat" or "gross." The younger children had just wanted to talk to her, sitting close as they looked at the photos and giggling at their likenesses.

"You think somebody might wanna 'dopt me?" one of them asked her.

"I sure hope so," she'd said, trying to be encouraging, yet not wanting to raise too many expectations. It was a fine line to walk.

When they'd all left the conference room, Maggie packed up the photos, then went to the front office to say she'd send the digital file to the committee preparing the album for publication. After going over her contact information with the secretary, a woman she didn't remember from last year, she asked if it would be possible to meet with Jayla Henry.

"Jayla? You want to see Jayla?" The woman's expression was puzzled, and not a little concerned.

"If I could. I'm hoping I could maybe talk her into being photographed for the album. She didn't want to do that on Sunday when I was here, but maybe she's changed her mind."

"Okay," she said, her face clearing. "I'll go try to find her. I think she might be outside."

Ten minutes later, Jayla Henry walked into the office, and she didn't look happy to see Maggie. "I haven't changed my mind, Miss Maggie," she said, politely, but firmly.

"That's okay," Maggie said. "Really. But could we talk for a little bit?"

"Why?" Jayla reached up for the little cross at her neck.

"I need to go see the director about something," said the secretary quickly. "I'll be back in a little bit."

"I want to know more about your daddy," Maggie said, when she'd left.

"Why?" she asked again, a defiant look still on her face.

"I'm not really sure, Jayla. I just haven't been able to forget what you told me. That he's going to get out of prison and come get you."

"He *is*," she insisted. "I know he is!"

"I know you believe that, honey," said Maggie softly. "But tell me why."

"Because he didn't kill my Mommy! He didn't! He came to see me that night when...after I'd gone to bed. And he told me he was coming home soon. To live with us again."

Maggie's heart sank. "So he was there that night? In your house?"

"Yes! But I know he didn't kill her. Because after he left, I went downtairs to see Mommy, and she told me the same thing!"

"You mean..."

"She was still alive then," Jayla said, looking right at Maggie. "After Daddy left."

CHAPTER SEVEN

Maggie parked her car and took the elevator up to the 27th floor of the 191 Building on Peachtree Street. She rarely visited Tom at his office, but it was on her way home, and her mother was happy to have the kids a little longer. The doors opened into a large reception area where a blonde, twenty-fivish woman she didn't know sat behind the black, curved desk.

"May I help you?" she asked politely, obviously not recognizing Maggie either.

"I'd like to see my husband, if he's not too busy," she said, smiling. "Tom Halloran?"

The receptionist beamed back at her. "Of course, Mrs. Halloran! I'll just give him a quick call." This accomplished, she stood up. "May I escort you to his office?"

"Thanks, but I know where it is."

Joan, Tom's secretary, wasn't at her desk, so Maggie gave two quick taps on the door, then pushed it in. Tom had already crossed the room and gave her a hug. When he pulled away, he looked down at the fat manila envelope she was holding.

"I can't remember the last time you were here, Maggie," he said. "To what do I owe the honor?"

She tilted her head coquettishly. "Can't a girl visit her husband at his office every now and then?"

"Sure, but I have a feeling you're here to collect on that debt I owe you." He ushered her over to the sofa near the window. "And I assume it has something to do with that little girl at the Children's Home."

Halloran listened while Maggie told him about the research she'd done on the case, as well as her second meeting with Jayla Henry.

"I take it you want me to get in touch with this Damon Copeland, Will Henry's attorney, and try to find out why his daughter didn't testify?"

"Yes, but first, I'd like you to go over what I was able to download from various media sources," she said, placing the envelope on his lap.

He smiled at her. "You do know that whatever he told his attorney is protected by attorney/client privilege, don't you?"

Maggie rolled her eyes. "I got a complete tutorial from you on that subject after Libba Woodridge died, thank you."

"Then what do you think I can do?"

"I have no idea, but I have great faith in you, Tom," she said, standing up. "My mother's feeding the kids tonight, so you don't need to rush home. Go through what's in the envelope, then do a little research yourself on the case. I think you'll be as intrigued—and puzzled—as I was." She was about to walk to the door, when she turned and said, "By the way, I heard on the radio when I was driving here about Winston Avery's fiancée being murdered. I didn't have a chance to read the paper this morning, but evidently it's been all over the news because she was also Sanford Reynolds' daughter. The NRA lobbyist?"

"Yes, I did hear. Everyone in the firm has been talking about it, actually. I didn't know him well, but it's a hell of a thing."

"We met them both at the Swan House Ball this past spring. She was an investigative reporter, remember? Blaine Reynolds."

Halloran frowned, trying to remember. There had been a lot of people at the Swan House Ball.

"Small, very pretty, long dark hair?" Maggie offered.

Halloran shook his head.

"White," said Maggie finally. "She was white. They were one of the few interracial couples there that night. Maybe the *only* interracial couple there that night. Despite the fact that we live in a post-racist world these days," she added dryly.

"Of course!" he said, somewhat embarrassed that it had taken that type of anomaly to make him remember Avery's fiancée. "I do remember her now, but in my defense, we only talked a few minutes."

"I remember her because I'd read some of her articles for the *AJC*, and I was able to put a face with her byline. She was a terrific reporter, and I remember wondering what she saw in him. He was a little pompous...sort of full of himself."

"I guess he can be," Halloran said. "He's got a reputation as a very fierce competitor, almost ruthless at times. Not unusual for anyone in litigation," he added, smiling. "I was that way, once."

He might still have had that kind of reputation, if Elliot Carter hadn't become his mentor. Halloran had been an extremely driven, angry person when he'd begun his legal career. His father had gone to prison for embezzlement during his first year of law school at Notre Dame, then died, a suicide, a year later. Halloran had torn up quite a few courtrooms back then, hammering away at anyone on the stand who stood between him and winning a case. And not caring what means he used to do it. Elliot had shown him, both by example and careful coaching, that he could achieve his goal without resorting to destroying people.

"You're thinking of Elliot right now, aren't you?" Maggie asked.

"Not a day goes by that I *don't* think of him," he said softly.

Halloran walked Maggie to the elevator and waited with her until it arrived. When the doors opened, David Healey stood there, his expression revealing both surprise and wariness when he saw them. Then his usual slick, urbane mien slid back into place, and he stepped forward to give Maggie a quick hug.

"What a pleasant surprise," he said, ignoring Halloran completely. "Laura and I were just saying the other night that we hadn't seen you in too long a time. You weren't at the Legendary Party this year," he added, referring to the annual fundraising event for Shepherd's Center.

"We had to give our table to some friends, due to a conflict," Maggie said. "But I did donate a photography session for the auction."

"Yes, of course!" Healey said. "And it brought in $5,000 for the Center. But we missed seeing you…and Tom, of course."

David, the firm's managing partner, had never really gotten over Halloran's suspicion that he might have been involved in Elliot Carter's death. He had also never gotten over Halloran's being made a senior partner in the firm after only five years. And then, of course, there was the Woodridge case, which had brought Healey and Caldwell the type of publicity that David deplored. Alton Caldwell, the firm's senior name partner, had supported Halloran's handling of both cases, which had further alienated him from David Healey.

"I'll give Laura a call," Maggie said graciously. "See if we can get together soon."

"She'd like that," said Healey, and with a touch on Maggie's upper arm, which passed for warmth in his universe, he walked away from them.

Maggie's eyes followed him down the hall. "He still hasn't forgiven you, has he, Tom?"

Halloran smiled at this. "Not so I'd notice. But, then, ask me if I care. Who was it who said, 'You can judge a man by the enemies he makes?'"

"I don't really know, but if that's true, you'd look pretty darn good."

———

Halloran took a phone call from a client after Maggie had left, but opened up the envelope after that. She'd compiled articles from the *AJC* that ranged from the discovery of Daisy Bulloch's body the morning of April 14, 2012 to the jury's guilty verdict, as well as the aftermath of the trial. Included in the newspaper's coverage were interviews with Damon Copeland, press releases from the DA's office, and "leaked" information from the APD.

Maggie had also downloaded articles from *People* magazine and an investigative report in the August 2012 issue of *Vanity Fair*. The photos accompanying them showed a handsome young couple at various stages in their relationship, from courtship, to the birth of their only child, then just before and after the murder. Daisy Bulloch was exceptionally beautiful, with long, honey-colored hair and blue eyes. Will Henry had the lean, lanky build of an athlete and a charismatic smile. His eyes were grayish-blue, which added to the charisma and also showed a biracial background. In every photo of the couple, his arm was around Daisy's shoulder and seemed to show both protection and a proprietary attitude. There were no photos of either of their families.

Intrigued, Halloran turned to his laptop and pulled up whatever TV coverage he could find. He watched clips from local newscasts and some from *Inside Edition* and *Entertainment Tonight*. Most dealt with the murder and its aftermath, but some were interviews with Henry himself and coverage of the cast of *The Undead Zone*. Will Henry on camera was even more attractive and charismatic than his photos. He seemed to exude both sexuality and boyish charm. He'd also had a reputation as a player and a party guy. Stories of his exploits had dwindled after his marriage to Daisy, according to the broadcasters, then started up a few months before the murder. There were also, however, suggestions that Daisy herself had been seeing someone during the same time frame.

After digesting all this information, Halloran focused on accessing court records that could give him information on the indictment, arraignment, and adjudication of Will Henry. The latest entries showed that Damon Copeland had filed a motion for a new trial with the adjudicating court, which had been denied, and then appeals with the appellate court and the Georgia Supreme Court, also denied.

At six-forty-five, he called Copeland's office number, figuring a young defense attorney in a five-person law firm would still be working. He was, and answered the phone himself.

"Mr. Copeland, my name is Tom Halloran. I'm an attorney with Healey and Caldwell, and I—"

"I know who you are, Mr. Halloran," Copeland said quickly. "How can I help you?"

"I'd like to drop by your office some time tomorrow, if that's convenient, and discuss one of your clients with you. Will Henry, to be exact."

Copeland didn't respond for a very long time. So long that Halloran began to think he'd been disconnected.

"And why would you want to discuss Will Henry with me?" the attorney finally asked.

Halloran sighed. "Are you married, Mr. Copeland?"

Another pause. "Yes, but what does that have to do with the case?"

"Just that maybe you'll understand if I tell you that my wife has talked to Jayla Henry a few times at the Atlanta Children's Home, and she—my wife—thinks that Will Henry might be innocent."

Another long pause, then, "And what do *you* think, Mr. Halloran?"

This time, it was Halloran who didn't answer right away. He thought of all the things he might say, but shouldn't, and all the things this young attorney might want to hear. Instead, he said, "I trust my wife's judgement and instincts."

He heard Damon Copeland chuckle. "I'll listen to what you have to say," Copeland said. "But I can't say we'll *discuss* anything."

"Fair enough. Are you free around nine a.m. tomorrow?"

"I think so. Do you know where my office is?"

"550 Juniper Street, right?"

"Right. See you at nine."

CHAPTER EIGHT

Damon Copeland's office building was a two-story house between 4ᵗʰ and 5ᵗʰ streets on Juniper, which ran parallel to Peachtree Street. Most of the houses, dating to the Forties and Fifties, had been bought up by restaurants and businesses during a building boom in Midtown in the late Nineties. The market, depressed like every other area in Atlanta after 2008, had rebounded considerably in the past year. Halloran didn't know when Sibley, Pinkston and Copeland had bought the house, but it had been painted fairly recently, dark gray with white shutters. He parked his BMW on the street and went up five steps from the sidewalk to a beveled-glass door.

After ringing a buzzer, Halloran heard a click and pushed open the door. A young woman with short, stylish dreadlocks sat behind a desk to the left. She was wearing a black, cowl-necked sweater and enormous hoop earrings and looked up at him expectantly.

"May I help you?"

"I'm Tom Halloran. I have an appointment with Mr. Copeland."

"Of course. I'll let him know you're here."

A few minutes later, he was seated in a steel and leather chair facing Damon Copeland's desk, which occupied a space between two dormers. It was a sparse, yet comfortable-looking office, with a bound sisal rug over a shiny wood floor. Diplomas from Morehouse College and Howard

University Law School hung on the wall to his left over a low bookcase. A large ficus tree dominated the right wall.

"Thank you for seeing me," Halloran said. "Nice office, by the way."

Copeland smiled. He had close-cropped hair and large, wide-set brown eyes. He was a tall man, even sitting down. When he'd come out from behind his desk to usher Halloran in, he'd seemed to be only an inch or two shorter than Halloran's six-foot-four. He wore a well-tailored black suit with a lavender shirt and a paisley tie, and his expression held both confidence and a slight wariness.

"I'll pass that on to my wife," he said. "She decorated it." He leaned back in his chair and cocked his head to one side. "Now please tell me what makes *your* wife think Will Henry is innocent? And *you*, since you trust her judgement?"

Halloran flashed back to his discussion with Maggie the night before. She had been elated that he was meeting Copeland and insisted upon going with him, but he'd quickly quashed that idea. Will Henry's attorney had made it clear that he didn't plan on discussing his client with Halloran, and he knew he had a better chance of getting information if he went to the meeting alone. He'd promised to relay all of her concerns about the case though.

Now, he looked at Damon Copeland, sizing him up and trying to choose how best to engage both his interest and his trust, something he'd learned to do over the years with dozens of juries. In the end, Halloran decided to rely on what Maggie had told him about Jayla Henry—her insistence that she didn't want to be adopted and her conviction that her father was innocent.

"According to what Jayla told Maggie—my wife—her father was there in the house the night of the murder and told her that he and her mother were getting back together. She also told Maggie that after he left, she went downstairs to talk to her mother about that, and Daisy confirmed it." Halloran leaned forward in his chair. "If she's to be believed—and my wife thinks she is—then Daisy was alive after Will Henry left. So, why didn't you put her on the stand to testify to that?"

Copeland stared back at him and took his time responding. "What you've just told me is something I already knew, Mr. Halloran. And it's not enough to make me go see my client and ask for permission to talk to you about the case."

Halloran sat back and smiled. "I didn't think it would be, but at least you've confirmed a hunch I had: that for some reason Will Henry knew his daughter could give him an alibi, but chose not to have you put her on the stand."

Damon Copeland's expression didn't change, but he began to tap the middle finger of his right hand on the leather-bound blotter on his desk. "My client will never let me talk to you, Mr. Halloran."

"Please call me Tom."

"Okay...*Tom*. My client will never let me talk to you."

"That's alright. I'm still willing to offer my help. Would *you* be willing to let me read your transcript of the trial? It's a public record, so you wouldn't be violating attorney-client privilege. I know you filed a motion for a new trial, which was denied. I'm not surprised by that, considering it was Judge Morrison. And your appeals to both the Court of Appeals and the Georgia Supreme Court have also been denied. Why not let me go through the transcript and see what I can find before you file a writ? I'm sure you know the case backwards and forwards, but I'd bring fresh eyes to it. And even though I'm not a criminal defense attorney, I'm pretty conversant with the rules of evidence."

Copeland smiled and shook his head. "Why would you want to take on something like that, Tom? There were a lot of hearings to address pre-trial motions, and the trial itself lasted over two weeks. That's a lot of transcript to read and analyze, especially since you won't get any billable hours out of it." He put his hands on the desk and steepled his fingers. "Besides fulfilling some kind of…promise to your wife, what exactly would you be getting out of this? I mean, I appreciate your offer, but you have a big profile in this city, and I'm finding it a little hard to believe that you're offering to do this on a pro bono basis. I'm also not sure I want someone looking over my shoulder. We may be a small minority firm, but we've got a pretty good reputation."

"I know that. I made it a point to do a little research. And I can't guarantee that I'll come up with anything you haven't already thought of. But if there's a chance that I can, do you really want to deny that possibility to your client?"

Damon Copeland gave a small smile, accompanied by an expression that could have been either defensive or angry. Or both. Halloran was certain he was going to refuse the request outright, or dismiss it with a promise to consider it. Instead, the attorney sighed and pushed himself up from his desk.

"I'll have the transcript sent to your office tomorrow," he said. "Then maybe you'll see what I was up against. The most damning evidence came from Will's cell phone. The police got a warrant to seize it, which I argued was based on hearsay, but Georgia is one of several states that don't require warrants to obtain GPS records. They were able to connect the phone to a cell tower near Daisy's townhouse the night of the murder. The U.S. Supreme Court has granted certiorari to hear two cases—*Riley v. California* and *U.S v. Wurie*—challenging warrantless searches like this, but that won't happen until sometime next year."

Halloran stood up, too. "Again, no guarantees, but I can promise you I'll do my best to try to find something that might help."

He held out his hand, and Copeland shook it, but his expression made it clear that he wasn't going to hold his breath.

CHAPTER NINE

By the time Joplin got to the conference room, Sarah Petersen and Blaine's parents were already seated at the table. He wasn't scheduled to work until 4 p.m., but he'd gotten to the M.E.'s Office by ten-thirty so he could examine all the CSU photos sent to David Markowitz before the autopsy, as well as his preliminary report. The Reynolds had been given a copy of the report the day before, and Joplin wanted to be able to answer any questions they might have. It hadn't included the toxicological or histological results—those would take longer—but the fact that Blaine had been pregnant had been part of it, and he wondered again if they had known.

Sanford Reynolds stood as Joplin reached the conference table and extended his hand, his navy suit subtle, but expensive-looking. He was a tall, well-built man, trim without being lanky, with a full head of gray hair and eyes to match. His handshake was firm, but not too firm, and his manner was subdued, but still showed that he was used to being in charge. Joplin knew he'd been a career Marine Corps officer, reaching the rank of two-star general before retiring and becoming a key lobbyist for the NRA, when Blaine and her younger brother were still in college. She'd told Joplin she had fond memories of being a service brat and living in San Diego, Singapore and Japan, among others. At least, until she'd been forced to change high schools twice because of orders that sent the family to Parris Island, then D. C.

Blaine's mother, Nina Reynolds, didn't stand up or offer her hand, but gave Joplin a weak smile. Even from a sitting position, however, she seemed to be a fairly tall woman, which was surprising, given how tiny Blaine had been. She had dark, chin-length hair that was streaked with silver and was wearing what seemed to be a black dress with a charcoal-grey sweater and pearls. She also wore very little make-up. In fact, the only make-up he could detect was a pale pink lipstick on very full lips.

Blaine had had lips like that, and Joplin was suddenly overwhelmed by a memory of kissing her for the first time as they'd said goodbye in front of Anis, a tiny Provencal restaurant in Buckhead. He'd been noticing her lips all through dinner and wondering when he could kiss them.

"Thank you for meeting with us," Sanford Reynolds said, and Joplin was jerked out of his reverie into a sharp sense of guilt for thinking of his dead daughter's lips.

"Happy to do it," he mumbled, although he wasn't, and it was a lame thing to say.

His boss seemed to sense this and said, "Hollis, I've been explaining to General and Mrs. Reynolds the very limited role you play in the investigation of their daughter's death, and that this meeting is somewhat of...an anomaly."

"Chief Petersen has done a very good job of trying to separate that role from the fact that you dated our daughter several years ago," Reynolds said evenly. "But I have to think that the two might...overlap."

Joplin took a seat next to Sarah across from the Reynolds. "I'm not sure what you mean, sir."

"Just that perhaps you shouldn't have been sent to the scene in the first place."

"When I assigned Hollis to the case, neither of us knew the identity of the victim," Sarah interjected.

"That may be, but once you were there and…saw her, wouldn't it have been better for another investigator to take over?"

Joplin started to answer, but Sarah cut him off. "In the first place, General, I only have two investigators for each shift, and the other one was already at a scene. But more importantly, this is not the same situation as, say… a surgeon operating on a family member or a judge needing to recuse himself because he knows the defendant. I'm sure it was upsetting for Hollis when he realized the victim was someone he'd known, but it didn't affect his professionalism or competency."

"How do *you* know?" Reynolds said, glaring at her. "How the hell can you know that for sure?"

"San, please," said his wife, touching his arm. Her eyes glittered with tears. "Don't do this."

He seemed not to hear her, turning his attention back to Joplin. "Maybe you overlooked something. Something that could help find her killer! Have you thought about that! Have you? And not just *her* killer! This monster also killed our grandchild! Did you know that, Joplin? Did you know she was pregnant with our first grandchild?"

"San!" Nina Reynolds said, grabbing her husband's arm this time. She seemed both surprised and shocked by his outburst, as if she'd never seen him lose control like that.

"It's okay, Mrs. Reynolds," Joplin said. "He deserves an answer." He paused for several seconds, waiting for Blaine's father to calm down a little, knowing that the man was only projecting his fear and anger and grief onto him. "To answer your first question: Yes, I've worried that I might have overlooked something. I worry about that with every case. But with *this* case, dealing with *Blaine's* death, I was consumed by the need to do everything I could to gather information to take back to the pathologist who'd be performing the autopsy. It was the only thing I could do for her by then."

He swallowed and took a deep breath, then said, "As for your other question, sir, the answer is 'yes.' Dr. Markowitz told me Blaine was pregnant. And it made me even sadder, because *two* lives were lost. It also made me want to do anything I can to help find the person who did this." Joplin leaned closer, looking directly into Blaine's father's eyes, then her mother's. "I cared about your daughter. We weren't together that long, but it was long enough for me to know what an exceptional person she was. She was talented and hardworking and conscientious. And her work as a writer helped a lot of people. She didn't deserve what happened to her."

Mrs. Reynolds bowed her head and gave into the grief she'd been holding back, crying quietly. Her husband took out a handkerchief and blew his nose, then pocketed it and stared at the door behind Joplin and Petersen. When he finally said something, it wasn't anything Joplin expected.

"Do you think Detective Simmons can find Blaine's killer?" he asked. "I mean, is he up to the job?"

Several thoughts raced through Joplin's mind, and two of them were disturbing. He decided to ignore them for the moment and said, "Absolutely, sir. He was my partner for seven years when I was with the Homicide Unit at Atlanta PD. You couldn't ask for a better person to be in charge of the case."

"I hope you're right," said Reynolds, standing up. He nodded curtly to Petersen and then Joplin, thanking them both for their time, then ushered his wife around the conference table and out the door.

Joplin waited until the door had closed and a few seconds had passed. Long enough to be sure the Reynolds weren't within hearing distance. "Are you thinking what I'm thinking?" he asked Sarah.

"If it involves speculation that General Reynolds didn't park his racial bias at the door, then, yes."

"Funny, Blaine said once that one of the benefits of being a Marine Corps brat was being raised in a culture that made the difference between officers and enlisted more important than race or gender."

Sarah Petersen made a noise that was somewhere between a laugh and a snort. "Well, she was right about that. She was an officer's daughter, and her father was about as high up on the military food chain as you can get. I was a Gunnery Sergeant's daughter, so I felt that difference in the 'culture' as you say. But I'd be willing to bet that any soldier of color or one who was female might have a different perspective than Blaine's, too. Even if they were officers."

"Your father was a career Marine?" Joplin asked.

"And proud of it," Petersen said. "He loved the Corps till the day he died, but he trained enough ensigns and officer candidates to know that some of them would abuse the authority they were given. He told me that those who became true leaders knew how much they would depend on the enlisted men and women under them to be effective, whether they were white, black, male or female. And respect them accordingly. Hell, Joplin, why do I need to tell you any of this? You were with the APD for seven years before you came here. You can't get more para-military than that. And despite the fact that we've had a black president for five years, America is still as racist as ever."

"Yeah, I guess. I just thought a general would be a little more…"

"Politically correct? He's a lobbyist for the NRA, remember?"

"You think I should mention this to Ike?"

Petersen made the snort/laugh sound again. "I'd be surprised if Ike didn't already have a pretty good handle on General Reynolds, Hollis. If *we* can see it, I'm sure Ike didn't miss it, no matter how deferential the General was to his face."

———

Joplin's cell phone rang as he was headed to Carrie's office to see if she were free for lunch. When he saw that the call was from Ike, he debated whether or not to say anything about General Reynolds before answering it.

"Ike. I was going to call you. Sherika told me yesterday she worked with the IdentiKit officer. Have you found out anything about the man who delivered those photos to me?"

"Well, he wasn't an employee of FedEx, and the envelope wasn't sent through the company. But we figured that. They're seein' if he might have worked for them in the past, but I'm not holding my breath. I do want you to look at the composite, though. With that eidetic memory of yours, you might know who he is. Even if he was in disguise, something might ring a bell, ya know?"

"I hope so," said Joplin

"Me, too, but that's not why I called. You wanna adopt Blaine's cat, Hollis?"

"Mrs. Marlow doesn't want her?" he said, struggling to switch gears. He himself was all in, having been seduced by a pair of green eyes and the cat's devotion to Blaine. But it suddenly occurred to him that adopting his former girlfriend's cat might not sit well with Carrie.

"She's already got a cat," said Ike. "And although she didn't think it would be a problem to add another one, her cat hadn't read the playbook." There was a pause, then he said, "You think Quincy would be cool with a pretty girl cat like that?"

Joplin closed his eyes. He hadn't even thought about Quincy's reaction. "I'd better get back to you about this, Ike. I need to talk to Carrie first."

Simmons gave one of his loaded chuckles. "Yeah, you do, Hollis. Fiancées are different from girlfriends, where old lovers are concerned. And wives are even more different, if you know what I mean. You need to be thinking about that these days."

"Since I got those photographs and found out they were of Blaine, that's about all I've been *able* to think of. Carrie never knew anything about her. Now she's finding out more than she wants to know."

"The past is always present, Hollis. Didn't you know that?"

"Yeah, but I guess I needed a reminder."

"Let me know what Carrie says, and I'll call Mrs. Marlow," Simmons told him, then clicked off.

———

Somehow, Carrie managed to separate his past with Blaine Reynolds from the cat.

"It's not as if she were Blaine's child," she'd said as they sat in a booth at Taqueria del Sol. Then immediately looked down. "Sorry. That didn't come out right. But how do you think Quincy will react?"

"I really don't know," Joplin had told her. "But if you're okay with this, I guess we need to find out."

So after dropping Carrie off at the ME's office, Joplin had gotten in touch with Ike and asked him to call Mrs. Marlow. Within minutes, Ike had called back to say that he could go get the cat immediately, if that were convenient for him.

But as Joplin headed for Brookhaven, he wondered if the whole thing was a very bad idea.

CHAPTER TEN

Mrs. Marlow, a tall woman who appeared to be in her seventies, despite the obvious attempts she'd made to seem younger, looked relieved when she opened the door. She had wheat-colored hair with what Joplin had heard were called "highlights," and faded blue eyes ringed by heavy mascara. Her pink, turtle-necked sweater and gray slacks softened her almost bony frame. "Are you the person who's going to take Banshee?" she asked.

"If you mean Blaine's cat, then, yes," Joplin said.

She looked at him, frowning, it seemed, at the use of her tenant's first name. "Did you know Blaine?"

"I did. Several years ago. She wasn't living here at the time."

The landlady's face cleared. "Is that why you offered to take her cat?"

He nodded. "Yes, but I also just like cats. I have one of my own."

She opened the door wider. "Well, I hope you have better luck than I did. Mr. Whiskers just didn't take to her. Banshee, I mean," she added, leading him down the hall.

Joplin closed the door, then followed her into a large, sunny den that was at the back of the house. He could see the carriage house off to the right through the windows that faced the back yard. A fat brindle cat lounged on the sofa under the windows and stared placidly at him, its paws tucked under its chest.

"Mr. Whiskers?"

"Yes," said Mrs. Marlow. "I'm keeping Banshee in the guest room for the time being. It's this way."

She led him to a hall off the den, then opened the door into a bedroom. A queen-sized four-poster took up a good bit of the room, as well as a chair, a bedside table and lamp, and a small bureau. Several tasteful Impressionist-style paintings were scattered on the walls. Joplin also saw a litter box under the window and food and water bowls, as well as a cat carrier. There was no cat to be seen, however.

"She must be under the bed," Mrs. Marlow said, sounding a little flustered. "She likes to hide there, even though Mr. Whiskers can't get in here."

As if to disprove this, Mr. Whiskers suddenly appeared in the doorway, a gleam in his eyes as he stared at the bed skirt. Mrs. Marlow scooped him up, uttering reproaches in baby talk, then whisked him out of the room. "Try to get her in the carrier!" she called out after closing the door.

Cautiously, Joplin walked to the bed and knelt down, then pulled up the linen bed skirt. Two enormous green eyes stared up at him, the only thing visible against the background of the cat's long, fluffy black fur. "Hello, Banshee," he said quietly. "I know you won't believe me, but the coast is clear. Mr. Whiskers can't get to you now."

The cat continued to stare at him, clearly *not* believing him. Sighing, Joplin got to his feet, then picked up the carrier. There was a small rug inside it, which he took out and used to cover the carrier. Next, he opened its door and pushed it to the foot of the bed, under the bed skirt.

It was a trick he'd often had to use to get Quincy to the vet's, based on the theory that cats like to scurry into small spaces when they feel threatened. The hard part was sliding under the bed on the other side to encroach on the cat's personal space. But after a few minutes of coaxing and shooing and sing-songing to Banshee, Joplin emerged triumphant from the guest room into the den.

"You got her!" Mrs. Marlow said, clapping her hands. Mr. Whiskers, back in his lamb pose on the sofa, didn't bother to look up. "Do you want to take her special food with you? Mr. Whiskers won't eat it."

"Special food?" He was almost afraid to know.

"Oh, yes," she said, walking out to the kitchen. "I'll be right back." She returned carrying a Publix bag and some Kit & Kaboodle, then pulled a small package out of the bag. "She eats one of these broth packs twice a day, but you have to keep the dry food available, too. She's a big cat," she added. "But, Blaine sort of spoiled her, too. I think it's because she's a Ragdoll. They're called 'puppy cats,' you know."

"I didn't," said Joplin, then immediately saw an image of Ike shaking his head as he looked at the cat keeping watch over Blaine's body and saying, "She acts more like a dog than a cat." The image faded, and he said to Mrs. Marlow. "Because they act like dogs?"

"Yes! Exactly. You might want to do some research on the breed. They become very attached to their owners and follow them from room to room. Blaine told me Banshee used to cry when she went out. Or even left the room, if she didn't know where she was. And she was always pretty mopey if Blaine were on a trip somewhere and I had to feed her." She put the broth pack back in the bag and added the Kit & Kaboodle, then looked up at him. "It was pitiful."

"Sounds like it," Joplin said, hoping he hadn't bitten off more than he could chew. He took the bag from Mrs. Marlow. "By the way, any idea why Blaine named the cat 'Banshee'? It's an unusual name."

Mrs. Marlow blinked once, then said, "I never asked her."

"Okay. I better get going, but thanks for all this. I appreciate it."

"I appreciate your taking Banshee. And so would Blaine."

Joplin nodded quickly, trying not to think how Blaine might feel, and turned toward the front door. Mrs. Marlow followed him and opened it. "Has there been any progress in finding out who...who killed Blaine?" she asked.

He turned to look at her. "Not yet. It's only been three days, and there's a lot of work to do." He paused and said, "Can you think of anyone who might have wanted to hurt her?"

She frowned and didn't answer right away. "That detective asked me the same question—the black one? And I said, 'no,' because even though Blaine had to travel a lot, she had a lot of friends, and everyone seemed to like her. But *somebody* must have wanted to hurt her." When Joplin nodded in agreement, she said, "I always read her articles when they came out. She would come by and thank me when I took care of Banshee while she was gone. Bring me some kind of little present from wherever she'd been and tell me what she was working on. So I knew to look for her byline soon after." She suddenly looked at Joplin sharply and said, "She went after some pretty important people. And a lot of them ended up in trouble."

"You're right. And that's an angle that I'm sure the police are looking into. By the way, did you see anyone unusual around here the afternoon or evening before Blaine's body was found?"

"That detective—"

"Detective Simmons?"

"Yes. Detective Simmons. He asked me that, too, but I told him no." She shook her head. "There was nobody like that, and I would have noticed. I was out running errands on Friday afternoon, but I got home a little before five and turned on Fox News. I can see the driveway and the carriage house from the den. That's why I knew when Blaine got home that day."

"Right," said Joplin. But he pictured Ike telling him that Mrs. Marlow had heard Blaine's car in the driveway, not seen it. The cat began to meow; she was also much heavier than Quincy, and his left arm was cramping. "I'd better get going," he said.

"You'll let me know how Banshee is doing, won't you?" Mrs. Marlow asked anxiously. "I really do hate that I couldn't keep her."

"I'll stay in touch." He walked out the door, then turned and said, "By the way, do you happen to know who the original architect was for this house? I'm sort of an architecture buff, and I was wondering…"

Mrs. Marlow drew herself up to her full height. "It was Preston Stevens," she said proudly.

"Of course," said Joplin. "I should've known."

He smiled, then hurried to the car as Banshee began to meow again. Once he was belted in, he stared at the house for several seconds.

"Liar," he said softly.

CHAPTER ELEVEN

It was one o'clock by the time Maggie reached the Mount Tabor Primitive Baptist Church in Brookhaven, just across the Dekalb County line. She'd hoped to get an earlier start, but a meeting with a new client that morning to discuss a family picture for their 2013 Christmas card had run late. She didn't usually work on that type of sitting, but the Mainwarings were "friends of friends," and she felt obligated to see them. Luckily, she'd talked to her mother about picking the kids up from school if she had trouble getting there by 2:30. She didn't like having to ask for help with the kids again, but trying to talk to Daisy Henry's parents seemed important.

"Take your time," her mother had said when she's called her that morning. "I'm just around the corner."

Maggie's parents, the O'Connells, lived on Cherokee Road, five minutes from Christ the King Elementary School and fifteen minutes from the Halloran house in Ansley Park. The kids loved going to visit their grandparents, not least because her mother always invoked something she called "Mimi's Rules." This allowed them to eat dessert before dinner and make blanket forts in the den and the living room. It was also possible to have both popcorn *and* candy at movie outings. She'd managed to find this out only by inference, since her mother and the kids, as well as her father, who'd been the family disciplinarian when *she* was growing up, merely said,

"What happens at Mimi's house stays at Mimi's house," whenever Maggie had asked for details after a visit.

"All you really care about," her mother had told her once, "is for the children to be kept alive while they're here with us and that they're happy. Right? In return, we get to spoil them, because it's not our responsibility to raise them. We've done that and have the tee shirts to prove it," she'd added, referring to Maggie's younger sister, Bridget, called Bibbie, and her brothers, Brian and Patrick. And although her siblings also had kids, they all lived in different parts of the country, which made Tommy and Megan all the more precious to her parents. Maggie never had babysitting problems.

She was grateful for this as she turned off Dresden Drive onto Fernwood Circle. She drove past the more traditional Baptist church, which housed the Brookhaven Farmer's Market every Saturday, and the new, expensive houses that had been built to accommodate the young couples and families that wanted to live in the newish Brookhaven Village area, with its sleek restaurants and trendy shops. The Mount Tabor Primitive Baptist Church wasn't quite holding its own among all these newcomers. It was a small white building that needed a new coat of paint and seemed in grave danger of having to sell itself to the highest bidder to pay back property taxes.

There was another, smaller building beside the church, Maggie noticed as she pulled into the parking lot. She hoped it was where the Bullochs lived, since she hadn't called ahead and had no idea if either of them would be at the church. There were no other out-buildings. Maggie knew from her research that Primitive Baptists did not have Sunday schools and rejected missionary activities which might require them. There would probably be a fellowship hall inside the church building for meetings of the elders—all men—and community get-togethers, but that was it.

She'd also learned that anything that hadn't been practiced or approved or even noted during the time of Jesus wasn't accepted by Primitive Baptists. The name itself referred to what the practitioners saw as "original" in the

Christian church. Which meant that women couldn't become ministers because the Apostles were all men—a tenet of her own Catholic faith. It also meant that there was no music to accompany the *a capella* choirs that sang Sunday hymns, since music had never been mentioned in connection with Christian rituals in the Bible. And ministers didn't attend any kind of seminary; they also were never "ordained," as in other religions. Instead, when the elder who headed a particular church died, retired or otherwise left, the other elders met to elect the new one.

It was a far different religion than the one she'd been raised in, and even more restrictive and insular. Not that she had any right to judge, Maggie told herself as she walked to the doors of the church. She didn't even consider herself a good Catholic. She'd begun to pull away, at least intellectually, during the sexual abuse scandals of the Nineties, when she was still in college. But she'd been married at Christ the King Cathedral, had her children baptized there, and now, of course, they attended the school.

It had simply been easier to continue to be a member and not rock the boat. Her parents were still devout Catholics despite the problems they agreed existed in the Church; they saw the sexual abuse of children as something that was unforgiveable, but that had been done by a small number of priests. And certainly not by the ones they knew and saw at Mass every week. The global cover-up perpetrated by the Vatican was something that just hadn't penetrated the hard shell of their faith. Her siblings were divided on the issue. Brian, whose wife had converted to Catholicism when they married, remained firmly in the Church, while Patrick only went to Mass at Christmas and Easter. Bibbie had left the Church after her divorce a few years ago, upset by the long annulment process required before she could ever hope to remarry in the Church.

All in all, they were like most of the Catholic families she knew.

Turning her thoughts from an inner dialogue that had preoccupied her more often in the past year, Maggie walked the steps of the church. The wide door groaned as she opened it. There were lights on inside, but it appeared to be empty. Then, as she walked down the center aisle, a woman came out from a door on the right. She was carrying a large vase of yellow mums, which were in sharp contrast to the brown dress and sweater she was wearing. Her hair was equally drab, gathered into a loose bun at the neckline. She caught sight of Maggie and came to a halt, staring at her.

"Can I help you?" she asked uncertainly.

Maggie smiled and walked closer. "I'm looking for Elder Bulloch," she said.

"Oh," said the woman. "Just a minute." She placed the flowers on what Maggie took to be the altar, although it was as bare and plain as the wooden pews which filled the small church. "He's not here right now. Can I help you?"

"I hope so. Are you Mrs. Bulloch?"

"Yes," said the woman, her expression wary now.

"My name is Maggie Halloran. I'd like to talk to you about your granddaughter, Jayla."

Mrs. Bulloch's expression changed from wariness to fear. "I have no granddaughter," she said.

"I've met her, Mrs. Bulloch," Maggie said, moving closer to her. "She's a beautiful little girl."

"You're a reporter, aren't you? I thought by now you people would have given up! But you just keep hounding us!"

"No! I'm not a reporter! I went to the Atlanta Children's Home last week to photograph the children for an album that helps them get adopted, and I met Jayla there. I promise you I'm not trying to get a story out of you or use you in any way. I just want to talk to you. About Jayla."

"There's nothing to talk about. My daughter was dead to me the day she moved away from home and decided to live a life of sin."

"You mean...because she became an actor?"

Daisy's mother pulled her sweater tightly against her body. Her mouth twisted into a grimace that showed both disgust and pain. A lot of pain. "Among other things," she said finally.

"Like marrying Will Henry?"

"We don't believe in the races…mixing," Mrs. Bulloch said, bitterness coating her words now. "Marrying each other."

"But not all Primitive Baptist churches believe that," said Maggie.

"That's not my concern. But Daisy was raised in a God-fearing household. I knew nothing good could come of her marrying that man, and I was right." She stared at Maggie defiantly. "He killed her, didn't he? And it was God's punishment. Now I want you to leave, or I'm calling the police."

"God's punishment?" Maggie said, stunned. "You think your daughter's murder was God's punishment?"

"You don't believe in the wrath of God?" said a tall, raw-boned man who had quietly come into the church from the same side door that Mrs. Bulloch had used. His voice was calm and had none of the anger that had suffused her words. He sounded as if he were simply curious. Or maybe credulous.

"No," said Maggie. "At least, not in connection with your daughter's death. I'm assuming you're Elder Bulloch."

"I am, yes. And you are…?"

"She was just leaving, Jeremiah," Rachel Bulloch said quickly.

"My name is Maggie Halloran. I came to talk to you both about your granddaughter. Jayla. I met her at the Children's Home this past weekend."

"And how is she?"

Maggie was almost as stunned by this question as she had been by Rachel Bulloch's characterization of Daisy's murder as "God's punishment." "She's fine," she said, finally. "I mean, she's in good health and being cared for, but she needs family in her life. Especially now. I'm hoping you'll meet her, get to know her. She's a very bright, loving child who's essentially lost both her parents."

He tilted his head, his hazel eyes opening a little wider. "Is she a child of God?"

"All children are of God, aren't they?"

Jeremiah Bulloch gave a sad smile and shook his head. "Not unless the stain of sin has been washed away through baptism. And I doubt that Daisy and her...husband...saw to that."

"Well, she wears a little cross on a chain around her neck that she told me her mother gave her," Maggie said. "So maybe you're wrong about that."

Bulloch winced, as if in pain, then the expression vanished. He squared his shoulders and said, "That's unlikely. We pray for her, though. As we did for Daisy. But she refused to accept God's grace."

"So he sent His wrath down on her?" Maggie asked.

"Yes. And I have to trust His reason for doing that. It's the only way I've been able to...reconcile her death."

"My idea of God is certainly different from yours."

"There is only one God," said Elder Bulloch in the same mild tone of voice he'd been using. But his expression turned hard, as if he were finally realizing that she was a heretic. "Now, I'm not going to call the police, like my wife wanted to do, but I would appreciate it if you left." He turned to his wife and said, "Rachel, we have to finish our preparations for tonight's service."

Without another word to Maggie, Rachel Bulloch followed her husband out through the side door, leaving her alone in the silent starkness of their church.

————

Maggie barely remembered the drive to her mother's house to pick up the kids. The idea that Rachel and Jeremiah Bulloch had produced a daughter who was their polar opposite boggled her mind. How had Daisy found the courage to go against the rigid and controlling upbringing she'd experienced? She'd managed to leave both her home and religion right after high school and succeed in a tough profession that had defeated thousands of others who'd attempted to succeed in it. And without any support from her family. In fact, she decided, the Bullochs had probably rained curses down on Daisy's head as she made her escape to a life of "sin" as an actor.

But she'd not only become a successful one, she'd been, by all accounts, a loving, giving woman and a devoted wife and mother. Even if the rumors of Daisy's own affair were true, Maggie thought she might have turned to someone else out of loneliness. And if Jayla were telling the truth, Daisy had forgiven her husband and welcomed him back home.

Maggie wanted to believe the little girl. And yet, although she certainly *didn't* believe Rachel Bulloch's hateful statement that Daisy's death was "God's punishment," Daisy had been murdered. And the State of Georgia believed that Will Henry was the one who'd killed her.

CHAPTER TWELVE

Nina Reynolds picked up her Martini glass and eyed the olives impaled on a toothpick before taking a deep breath and saying, "San, what was that all about this morning at the ME's office? Talking about your grandchild, I mean. Your quote only grandchild unquote."

Sanford Reynolds looked up from his own Martini, eyebrows raised, and said, "What do you mean?"

Nina shook her head and took a long sip of her drink. "Come on, it's just us. The last thing in the world you wanted was a grandchild with Winston Avery as the father. A *black* grandchild, San. You were beside yourself when Blaine told us she was engaged to him. Have you forgotten that?"

Sanford Reynolds sat back against the cushions of the large sofa in the living room of their suite at the Buckhead Ritz-Carlton and stared at her in that *way* he had. But it was a stare that no longer intimidated her. She was long past that, although most people, especially the CEO of the NRA and the military brass, many of them friends with whom they were expected to socialize, had no idea of her sea change.

Sea change, she thought, liking the phrase, knowing how appropriate it was. She had been a Marine Corps wife for over forty years, following her husband as he went up the ranks and around the world from base to base, most of them bordering oceans and seas. She had packed up households and children, left friends and family, and learned to say just the right things to superior officers and their families, as well as—and this had been even more important, since her husband was so indifferent about it—subordinate officers and *their* families. She had missed weddings and funerals and family reunions that were important to her, either because of the time and space involved, or because of the world events that eclipsed them. But more than anything else, Nina knew she had willingly, if reluctantly, allowed her children to be sacrificed to the gods of war, unlike Clytemnestra.

That had changed three years ago, when she'd discovered that Sanford had been keeping a mistress for over five years, installing her in an apartment at the Watergate. This information had come to her via an acquaintance—not a friend, of course, because that would have been a kindness—who had mentioned meeting Sanford's "niece" at the 1789 Restaurant a few days earlier. Since Sanford had no nieces, Nina had hired a private investigator recommended by a real friend, who claimed not to know anything, but said she'd support her from hell and back. The upshot was that, when presented with the evidence, Sanford had immediately agreed to give up his girlfriend and deposit a generous amount of money in a new bank account Nina had opened. And although she hated herself for not just walking out on him, the relationship dynamics had certainly changed.

Or had they? Nina wondered as she waited for her husband to answer her. She had kept the PI on retainer to make sure that he walked the straight and narrow, but that didn't mean that San told her everything she should know. Or maybe anything, really. No new "nieces" had popped up, but he'd kept Warren's gambling problems from her, as well as the DWIs in Las Vegas, and everything he'd done to fix things. The PI had scoped that out. Now she wondered, steeling herself to pursue the current line of questioning, what else he might have "fixed." She owed that, at least, to Blaine. And maybe more.

"It wasn't until Blaine was gone, that I realized how unimportant something like that was, Nina," Sanford finally said.

She measured him. Measured the statement, measured his tone. Measured the way he looked, compared to all the times he'd lied to her. Measured the man.

And laughed. A cracked, mirthless laugh that made her thirsty. She downed half her Martini and said, "Did you drag Warren into this?"

"Into what?" he asked, hands spread.

"You know exactly what I mean. You hated the idea of Blaine marrying a black man. And you certainly would have hated having mixed-race grandchildren, San. You said so, many times. So did you send our son down to Atlanta to fix things?"

"You've been drinking too much, Nina. As usual. I haven't wanted to say anything about it, given what you're going through. What we're *both* going through. But for you to imply that I might have had something to do with our daughter's death means your brain must be thoroughly pickled by now." He stood up and gave her another withering look. "I'm going down to the bar, where I can have a drink in peace. Try not to finish off the entire bottle of vodka."

CHAPTER THIRTEEN

Halloran got to his office by 7 a.m. Wednesday so he could get some work done before the transcript of Will Henry's trial arrived. None of the secretaries was there, and, of course, none of the partners, but several of the associates' offices were lit up behind the glass walls that defined Healey And Caldwell's premises.

As well they should be, he thought, smiling a little. He, too, had burned both the midnight oil and the morning recessed lighting when he was an associate. But he'd never really had to worry about losing his job. And although the firm hadn't had to let any associates go due to the recession in a long time, the bloodletting a few years ago hadn't been forgotten. Halloran had hated that time. Most of the partners had agreed to take a cut in the firm's profits in order to stem the flow, himself included. But only a few positions had been saved before it was necessary to do it again. And again.

As he passed David Healey's office, it struck him that David had been the only partner who *hadn't* agreed to have his income reduced. He'd blustered and postured, claiming that as the managing partner he was already doing more than anyone else for the same profit share. But the truth was that, besides the time he spent hounding the associates to increase their billable hours and cracking down on what he saw as a terrible waste of time and supplies by the support staff, David did relatively little "managing." He also lagged far behind the other partners in bringing in new clients. And despite the impression he tried to give people, the "Healey" in the firm's name belonged to his deceased father, not him.

Halloran pushed these thoughts out of his mind as he passed his secretary's desk and opened the door to his office. He needed to look over a brief he'd asked Dan Jennings, one of the associates on his team, to write for a pre-trial motion he was filing the next day on the Sullivan case. But after talking to Maggie last night and hearing about her strange encounter with Daisy Bulloch's mother, he was almost looking forward to reading the Henry transcript. Finding a judicial or prosecutorial error that Damon Copeland hadn't found was a long shot, but he was willing to give it a try.

At 8:18 a.m., there was a knock on his door, and Joan came in, carrying a transcript-sized parcel. "UPS just brought this," she said. "Want me to open it for you?"

"Please," Halloran said, nodding, then, "Thank you," a few minutes later, when she returned with it.

Just as Damon Copeland had told him, it was a pretty hefty document, over two thousand pages long. Not for the first time, Halloran wondered what he'd gotten himself into. He'd assured Copeland that he could fit reading and assessing it into his schedule, but with a trial of his own coming up, as well as his usual appointments with new and existing clients, it would be a stretch. He couldn't ask one of his associates to help because he was doing this gratis, and he was certain David Healey wouldn't agree to add it to the firm's list of pro bono work.

But maybe, he decided, as another possibility occurred to him, he didn't have to involve David Healey.

Halloran picked up his phone and buzzed Joan. "Is Alston in yet?" he asked.

"I don't think so, but I'll check with his secretary and get back to you."

Halloran thanked her and began reading the pre-trial motions of *The State of Georgia v. William Aaron Henry.* The first one involved an attempt by Copeland to keep the GPS records associated with Will Henry's cell phone from being entered into evidence at trial. The detective assigned to the case had obtained the records from Verizon after some of Henry's co-workers on *The Undead Zone* had told police that he was having an affair with an actress on set, Trina Daily. When calls and texts between the two were discovered, Detective Riker then requested a warrant to seize the phone itself and was able to get GPS evidence that Henry was in or near the townhouse in Midtown where Daisy Bulloch was murdered during the estimated time of her death. Copeland argued that, although investigators may obtain access to phone records without a warrant, rumors about his client and Trina Daily didn't rise to the level of probable cause necessary to request the warrant to seize the cell phone in order to track Henry's whereabouts. He cited several cases supporting this, including *Dearing v. State* (1998), *Heidle v. New Mexico* (2012), and *Sutton v. State* (2013).

The State used *Illinois v. Gates* and *Bryant v. State* (2011) to argue that the Court must consider "the totality of the evidence," and that even rumors could be used in requesting a warrant if other evidence supported them. Detective Riker had also stated in his affidavit that there had been numerous texts and phone calls between the defendant and Ms. Daily over a period of time, and, additionally, the defendant had moved out of the townhouse he shared with the victim a few months before her death, thereby giving credence to the rumors of adultery and raising them to the level of probable cause. Copeland then argued that the phone texts between the two had contained no terms of endearment or sexual content and weren't sufficient to establish adultery, nor was the fact that he had moved. He insisted that his client's Fourth Amendment rights had been violated. Therefore, the GPS evidence was "fruit of the poisoned tree" and should be thrown out. The State then countered with *U.S. v. Leon,* contending that even if the Fulton County magistrate who signed the warrant had done so erroneously, the police had "acted in good faith" when they executed the warrant and seized defendant's cell phone.

The desk phone rang before Halloran could read further.

"Betty just called and said Mr. Caldwell is in his office," Joan told him.

Halloran looked at his watch; it was just after nine. "Can you call her back and see if it would be convenient for me to stop by and talk to him, Joan?"

Five minutes later, Halloran knocked on Caldwell's door.

Alston Caldwell was the firm's only living name partner. He'd also become Halloran's mentor since Elliot Carter's death and was not a big fan of David Healey's, although out of respect for Healey, Sr., he never voiced this. Instead, he worked whenever necessary to limit the damage "Junior," as he called David out of earshot, could do. Halloran considered an end-run around David to obtain the services of an associate something Alston wouldn't mind. He would offer—even insist—on paying the associate to work on it on his own time, but he wanted to do it with Alston's full knowledge. Anything less would open him up to David Healey's vitriol and back-stabbing. He didn't really care on his own account, but it wasn't good for the firm's morale—especially among the associates—to make himself a target.

"What can I do for you, Mr. Tom?" Caldwell asked, smiling. "Come in, come in."

Halloran sat down in one of the chairs in front of Caldwell's desk. "I need to run something by you and then ask for a favor."

"Tell me what's going on."

Quickly, trying not to take up too much of Caldwell's time, Halloran outlined the situation, telling him about Maggie's work at the Children's Home and her meeting with Jayla Henry, then moving on to what she'd learned about the trial and his own meeting with Damon Copeland. He finished up with Maggie's disturbing visit to the Mt. Tabor Primitive Baptist Church.

Alston Caldwell steepled his fingers on his desk, then nodded slowly. "And did Mr. Copeland send you the trial transcript?"

"He did. I haven't had a chance to read much of it, but—"

"You'd like to make this part of the firm's *pro bono* budget."

Halloran smiled. "Actually, no. I intend to do most of the work myself. But I think I might need to hire an associate from our criminal division to work on this, too. I'm doing this for Maggie, but, quite frankly, I'm also beginning to think Will Henry might not have gotten a fair trial."

Caldwell folded his hands and nodded slowly, as if considering the request. Then he said, "Actually, I know a little something about this case. Through my granddaughter."

"Cate?" Halloran said, puzzled. Cate Caldwell was a third-year law student at Emory. It was possible she knew Damon Copeland in some capacity, but he was certain the attorney would have mentioned that yesterday, given her connection to Healey and Caldwell.

"She's decided to go into entertainment law when she graduates," Alston went on. "And I can't say I blame her, what with Georgia's current reputation as a film, TV and music mecca. Anyway, I was able to arrange for her to have a summer internship last year with Becker and Randall, which represents Benchmark Films, the production company for *The Undead Zone*. They asked her back for this past summer, and they've made her a pretty good job offer, too, after she passes the bar."

"That's great, Alston! And I think that's a good fit for Cate. So, I take it she was in a position to know about the case through Becker and Randall. Did she ever meet Will Henry?"

"Yes, and she was pretty impressed by him. She was assigned to work with the attorney who's counsel for Benchmark Films, and she's been on set in Senoia several times, so she was able to meet most of the cast members. And I have to say, Tom, that Cate's come to believe that Will Henry didn't get a fair trial either."

Halloran sat back in his chair and took a minute to process what Caldwell had told him. Finally, he said, "Does this mean you'd support me in helping with Will Henry's appeal? Even if David Healey somehow gets wind of it and objects?"

"I don't see why he would care, since you want to hire an associate out of your own pocket."

Halloran smiled. "David would find a way, I think. He could say I was still taking an associate away from his or her primary work for the firm."

"Yes, I suppose he could," Caldwell said wryly. "But let me worry about that."

"Well, there might be a way around that," Halloran responded.

"I'm listening."

"Alston, I know Cate's in the middle of her last year at Emory, and she's probably putting in some time studying for the bar as well, but she might be the very person to help me with this case. She's not only familiar with it and has the advantage of knowing the cast members, I also wouldn't have to involve anyone from this firm."

"I can't speak for Cate," Caldwell said, smiling, "but I have a feeling she'd jump at the chance to work with you on this. Why don't I give her a call and see what she thinks? I trust her to tell me if she can't take this on right now."

Halloran stood up. "I'd appreciate that, Alston. I also appreciate your support." He turned and was about to head for the door when something else occurred to him. "By the way, who's the attorney at Becker and Randall that Cate worked with? It might be a good idea to call and see if I could talk to him."

"You might want to hold off on that for a few days, Tom," Caldwell said. "The man's got something pretty heavy going on in his life right now, as you've probably heard."

"Who is it?" Halloran asked, but almost immediately knew what Caldwell was going to say.

"It's Winston Avery, poor fellow. You know his fiancée was murdered over the weekend, don't you?"

CHAPTER FOURTEEN

Joplin had spent most of Wednesday morning at two scenes likely to haunt his dreams for several nights. The first was a vehicular homicide—homicides, actually—involving a drunk driver who'd lost control of his Jaguar and plowed into a family of four on Wieuca at 7:30 a.m., near Sarah Smith Elementary School. Apparently, Jake and Alison Meyer had been dropping their two young daughters off at school before going to work. They never made it; all four had been killed instantly. The other driver, however, had been pulled from his car very much alive. The second scene was in the Garden Hills section of Buckhead. A fourteen-year-old girl had overdosed on her mother's bottle of Xanax after two weeks of cyber-bullying by her two former BFFs. The mother had found her when she went to wake her up for school. Although she'd immediately called 911, the EMTs couldn't revive her.

Joplin stared down at the body of Peyton Henley, then retreated into watching himself go through the motions of doing his job. It was a protective device that helped to muffle the psychic pain he felt at death scenes that overwhelmed him with their extreme violence or depravity, or with the age and innocence of the victims. There had been no intentional violence or depravity in either of the scenes that morning, but age and innocence were over-represented in each. And without the armor of disassociation, he would ultimately be more vulnerable to a Blue Funk.

Joplin's Blue Funks were notorious among his friends and co-workers. They weren't simply bad moods or a form of depression or even the *weltschmertz*—world-pain—that his doctor and mentor, Dr. Aloyisius O'Brien, had explained to him was one of the side effects of his eidetic memory. It was, in fact, a combination of all three, and had almost derailed his relationship with Carrie a year ago.

So he allowed himself to bubble-wrap his heart and emotions while he processed Peyton's death scene. As if watching a replay of the memory he would later have, Joplin saw himself taking pictures of the bedside table with the empty, opened Xanax bottle, as well as the note the girl had written to her parents, and then bagging them both. The laptop on the bed next to her he also bagged; it would have a record of the pain Peyton had gone through and the "friends" who had inflicted it. This done, he watched himself checking the extent of lividity and rigor, getting a body temp, and checking the body for any abrasions, bruises or cuts.

Joplin's shadowing of himself ended as he went downstairs to talk to Detective Bob Jarmon, who had caught the case. He glanced into the living room and saw the parents sitting on a sofa, balled-up Kleenexes on the coffee table in front of them, talking to Jarmon's partner, Billy Winslow. Billy saw him and gestured toward the front door. Feeling like a coward, Joplin avoided eye contact with the Henleys.

Jarmon was on his cell phone when Joplin came out. He quickly wound up the call and said, "I figure we're out of this, right? Anything you can tell me for the incident report?"

"My best estimate of TOD is between two and seven this morning. Rigor is only in the torso, but lividity is pretty well set. She died in her bed. I got photos of the pills and suicide note and bagged them, as well as the laptop. Seems cut and dried, but the autopsy could turn up something different, Bob."

Jarmon nodded, acknowledging that what appeared to be a suicide could sometimes be a homicide, although the often deadly results of bullying—whether in person or on the internet—were seen by law enforcement too often lately. "Thanks, Hollis. Keep me posted," he said, then walked back into the house, his head down.

———

Ike Simmons called as Joplin turned onto Piedmont to go back to the ME's office.

"How'd it go with the cat?" he asked.

"Well, we found out why she was named Banshee."

Simmons chuckled. "That bad, huh?"

"Yep. I let her out of her carry case, and she ran into the master bedroom. Stayed under the bed till three a.m., then she raced around the apartment, meowing at the top of her lungs."

"What'd you do?"

"I captured her, walked around singing lullabies to her, then put her under the covers in our bed."

Simmons laughed again, louder this time. "No, really, Hollis, what'd you do?"

"That's exactly what I did, Ike. I used to have a cat like that when I was in high school, and it was the only thing that would calm him down when he got the nighttime crazies."

"And Carrie was okay with that?"

"She wasn't thrilled, and neither one of us slept well, but the cat was fine this morning. Banshee, I mean. Quincy was pissed as hell."

This time, Simmons tried to muffle his laughter and ended up making choking sounds.

"I'm glad you're enjoying this so much, Ike."

"Sorry. I'm through now. I really called to talk about General Reynolds' request that you be part of the murder investigation, Hollis. You okay with that?"

"Not really. I only heard about it an hour ago. And my boss isn't either. Hell, she didn't even want me to *meet* with Blaine's parents! And now she feels like I'm being pulled into this thing even more."

"Well, you are, and that's a fact. The question is: Why?"

Joplin sighed. "I'm still working on that. But the other question is, how do *you* feel about it, Ike? He's gone over your head."

"Yeah, I didn't much like that, and he's probably a racist son of a bitch, but I don't think that's what's going on here. You just watch your back, is all I'm sayin', 'cause Sarah's right on about you bein' pulled into this case. The only upside is that it'll be fun to be partners again." He gave another one of his deep chuckles. "Unless you think Tom Halloran might get jealous."

"As far as I'm concerned, the only upside—partnering with you again excepted—is that Halloran *isn't* involved, thank God! And speaking of attorneys, have you interviewed Winston Avery again? Did he know Blaine was pregnant?"

"I have. He claims he didn't know. Said Blaine must not have known either or she would've told him."

"Well, Markowitz said that was possible, given her diabetic condition."

"I guess. But he didn't sound too broken up about it. And he said he'd have to think about it when I asked him to submit to a DNA test to see if it was his child."

"Interesting."

"Maybe. Or maybe he's just bein' a lawyer. And maybe we'll come up with probable cause for a warrant to demand his DNA."

"Good luck with that, Ike. It would sure make General Reynolds' day if he turned out to be the killer." An image of Blaine's father, his face contorted by rage as he talked about his daughter's death depriving him of his "only grandchild," suddenly flooded Joplin's vision.

"You said it, not me," Simmons agreed. "By the way, thought you might want to know that FedEx is checking to see if the composite our guy made fits the description of a previous employee, since he was wearing one of their uniforms, but I don't hold out much hope for that either."

"That's disappointing, but not a surprise. What about the envelope and the photos themselves?"

"CSU found a few partials that didn't belong to you or Sherika or Sarah, and they're running them through AFIS, but don't hold your breath on that lead either."

"How about the digital camera?"

"Only the victim's prints were on that. If it had been wiped clean, that would have been suspicious, but it wasn't. The memory card was missing, but that doesn't really mean much. Blaine could have taken it out to have some pictures printed. We'll check around, though. See if we can find out what store she used for that. I emailed you a copy of the composite, by the way. Let me know if he's anywhere in that weird memory catalog of yours."

"I'll give it a shot, but since he was probably wearing a disguise, I don't know how successful I'll be." He paused, thinking of something Mrs. Marlow had said. "By the way, did Blaine's editor tell you what she was working on?"

"Some kind of follow-up story on the Atlanta Public Schools scandal," said Simmons.

"Well, I guess we can rule that out as a lead," Joplin said. Though the cheating scandal, involving over a hundred educators who had "coached" or even changed students' answers on the state-mandated Criterion-Referenced Competency Test had gotten national press and thoroughly trashed Georgia's educational system, he couldn't see Blaine's latest assignment as a motive for murder.

"Lotta people might feel differently about that, Hollis. The trial for the teachers and administrators who wouldn't take plea deals is set to begin in the spring. It's polarized Atlanta's business and religious communities and exposed a lot of racial tension the governor and the mayor would rather gloss over."

"Yeah, well, I'll keep that in mind," Joplin said, still not convinced. "Gotta go, partner. I need to write up my scenes from this morning, and then I plan to go to the *AJC* offices, see if I can get a little more out of Blaine's co-workers. I also want to gauge their reaction to me. I'll keep you posted."

"Okay, but do one other thing, *partner*."

"What's that?"

"Watch your back."

CHAPTER FIFTEEN

Sherika was waiting for him when Joplin arrived back at the ME's Office.
"Just the person I wanted to see," she said, standing near his cubicle, holding some papers.

"I'm honored," said Joplin, setting his black bag on his desk. "I think."

"Ike Simmons sent this. You need to look at it."

"The composite picture? He told me he was emailing it to me."

"To me, too. Case I wanted to make any changes."

"And do you?"

"Nope. That's the man who delivered those pictures."

Joplin took the sheets of paper from her. He studied the composite, then looked over the next page, which detailed Sherika's description of the man she'd seen. "Anything else you can add to this, Sherika?"

She cocked her head. "I woulda told that to the composite artist. Or you. Or Ike."

"Of course you would," said Joplin. "Thanks."

Sherika folded her arms. "You recognize him, Hollis?"

"No. Never seen him."

"Okay," she said and turned to go. "I don't like this, Hollis," she said as she walked toward the door. "I don't like this one bit."

Joplin didn't like it one bit either. He stared at the composite, then read through Sherika's description, hoping to trigger even a chance encounter with the man. Finally, he called Simmons.

"I've never laid eyes on the guy, Ike," he told him. "Unless he's a master at disguise. But even then, I'd be able to recall something. Like his ears. You can't really change ears. The nose and eye and hair color, sure, but not ears. And the description Sherika gave—six feet, paunchy, broad shoulders—all that could have been lifts and padding."

"I know," said Simmons. "It was a long shot. I'll let you know if we get lucky with AFIS."

———

After fortifying himself with coffee, Joplin wrote reports on the morning's scenes, trying not to lose the distance he'd managed to put between himself and his feelings. But as he was uploading the photos he'd taken, it became a little harder. Anything to do with children dying or being hurt had always been difficult for him, he thought as he looked away from the mangled bodies of Jenny and Abbie Meyer. Not just for him, but for most of the staff and law enforcement in general. He knew that and protected himself as much as he could, but it was part of the job. A part he couldn't avoid, unfortunately. But why had it almost overwhelmed him today? Snuck right up and tried to sucker-punch him?

Was it because of the baby Blaine was carrying when she'd been murdered? Had that almost put him over the top? Maybe, he decided. But, if so, why did it resonate so much with *him*, but apparently not so much with her own fiancé? Then again, how did he know what Winston Avery was feeling? Maybe the man was just very stoic. Or maybe Ike Simmons' gauge of his emotions was biased by his dislike of the attorney. This thought made him think of Tom Halloran, and he wondered if he should take Carrie's advice and call him. Ask him if he knew Avery and could give him any insights.

"Rough morning?" Sarah Petersen asked.

He looked up, surprised that he'd been so lost in thought that he hadn't heard her walk over to him. "Yeah, I guess. The vehicular homicide and then the teenage suicide. Maybe I'm getting too old for this."

"Huh," she said, blowing the sound out. "The day you get used to things like that is the day you'd *better* hang it up, not when it still gets to you. Have you been to any of the yoga classes I set up for the unit? You had time yesterday, Hollis. It would do you good. Viv went over the weekend. So did Deke."

"I couldn't," he said. "I had to do housework yesterday."

Petersen folded her arms and nodded, staring at him. "I'll call Viv and get her to take the scene that just got called in so you can go put some lotion on your dishpan hands," she said evenly. "You hear anything from Simmons about the photos? What CSU might have found?"

Joplin told her, then said, "We're back to square one on that."

"Pretty much," she agreed. "But maybe we'll get lucky with the prints."

"Maybe. And maybe we'll find JonBenet Ramsey's killer, too. We can always hope, right?"

Petersen tilted her head and stared at him, the blue eyes measuring his mood. She'd made it a point to check his emotional temperature routinely since his last major Blue Funk the year before. "You need a little R and R, Hollis? You've got the leave time, you know."

Joplin forced a smile and shook his head. "I'm fine, Chief. Really. I just need to make some inroads on Blaine's case. So since I don't have a scene right now, I think I'll go say hi to Carrie and then head over to the *AJC* and talk to some of her colleagues, if that's okay. Ike talked to them over the weekend, but I want to follow up on what they told him."

Petersen, a former Catholic, smiled and blessed him, making a large sign of the cross with her right hand, then turned and walked back to her office.

Joplin smiled, too, a real one this time and headed out of the Investigative Unit, then took the stairs down to the Pathology Unit. Carrie's office door was open, but she wasn't there, so he headed for the autopsy room. She was working at Table One, her back to him as she bent over a small body. Jim, one of the pathology assistants, was at the head of the steel table, holding a rib-spreader. He looked over at Joplin, his face solemn and gave an almost imperceptible shake of his head.

Joplin nodded and backed slowly through the door, hoping Carrie hadn't heard him.

———

Maggie replaced the kitchen phone in its cradle and stared out the window, trying to process what Tom had just told her about Winston Avery. They had agreed that the murders of two white women, married or engaged to prominent black men within a year of each other, could certainly be a coincidence. But the fact that Winston Avery had represented the film studio that had the first victim's husband under contract, and had also been the fiancé of the second victim, seemed to go beyond mere coincidence.

"Both murders were committed in Milton County," Maggie said after a while. "Maybe Hollis could look into this. *Should* look into this."

But Tom had been reluctant. "We've developed a nice friendship with Carrie and Hollis, but he's made it clear that he doesn't want to be involved in any more investigations with me, Maggie. If something more turns up that seems to connect the cases, I'll consider it, but at this point it's pure conjecture."

"Are you at least going to share this with Damon Copeland?" she'd asked. "He might have interviewed Avery during Will Henry's trial. I don't remember seeing his name in any news articles before or during the trial, but Damon might have talked to him at some time."

"I'll give him a call. I've also talked to Cate, and we're meeting tomorrow afternoon to go over the case. Since she's going to start working at Avery's firm this summer, she'll be a good source of information. But I have to tell you, Cate was absolutely insistent that he couldn't have had anything to do with Blaine Reynolds' death. He was, quote, completely in love with her, unquote."

"I'm not saying he killed her, Tom. I just think it's too much of a coincidence. And I don't want Will Henry to rot in jail if he's innocent."

"I know," he'd told her. "I just don't want to involve Hollis at this point."

"Okay," Maggie had said. But now, as she looked out at the brightly-colored trees in their backyard as they were rifled by a sudden breeze, she decided to take matters into her own hands.

CHAPTER SIXTEEN

Joplin parked his car in the tiered deck of Cox Enterprises on Perimeter Center Parkway in Dunwoody, headquarters for the *AJC*. He decided to see Mark Rawlins, Blaine's editor first. He'd never met the man, who was one of two senior editors who managed the investigative division of the paper, but Blaine had spoken well of him, and it was always a good idea to check in with the head honcho before talking to any of the underlings. Not that the investigative reporters he'd known over the years considered themselves underlings. Like radio personalities and TV news anchors, they were "the talent" and acted accordingly. Even Blaine, despite her professionalism, had exhibited a sort of fearless drive when it came to nailing down an interview or digging up the secrets that people—especially politicians and other sacred cows—tried to hide from her. It had seemed to him almost like a form of entitlement. As if not just her job, but *who* she was gave her license to track them down.

An image of Mrs. Marlow, her carefully made-up eyes gazing at him, filled his brain as he got on the elevator of the third parking tier. "She went after some pretty important people," he heard her saying again. "And a lot of them got into trouble."

Joplin shook the image out of his head as the elevator doors opened. After meeting General Reynolds, he wondered if some of the entitlement he'd attributed to Blaine's profession had actually come from her upbringing. Or her genes. It also occurred to him that he and Blaine had been more alike than he'd realized. He was just as driven as she had been.

———

Mark Rawlins looked close to fifty, about five-ten and trim, with thick, still-dark hair and intense brown eyes behind wire-rimmed glasses. He ushered Joplin into his small, but windowed, office at the far end of a large room filled with even smaller cubicles.

"I *did* already speak with a detective about Blaine," he said, closing the door behind Joplin and pointing him toward a chair. He was wearing a navy canvas shirt with the sleeves rolled up and tan slacks.

"I know, and I'm sorry to take up your time with more questions, but that's the way murder investigations go."

"I'm happy to cooperate in any way, but aren't you with the ME's Office?"

Joplin nodded and explained General Reynolds' request that he be assigned to the case. "I was also a homicide detective with APD for over seven years," he added.

"And you dated Blaine a few years ago, from what I've heard," Rawlins said.

"News sure gets around," said Joplin dryly. "I hope that's not the kind of news that's fit to print."

Rawlins smiled and shook his head. "Not if I have anything to say about it."

"Then I take it you weren't the one who told the General I was the death investigator on the case."

"I think that was Lucy. Lucy Alvarez. She and Blaine were good friends. Does it really matter, though?"

"Not really. I guess he would have heard about it sooner or later."

"That must have been pretty rough for you. Being at the crime scene, I mean."

"It was," he said, then moved the discussion in a different direction. "Detective Simmons said you told him Blaine was following up on something to do with the Atlanta Public Schools Scandal. What exactly was she investigating?"

Rawlins sat back in his chair and gave Joplin an appraising look. "You mentioned you were a detective with APD for seven years. Did you ever know Reginal Dukes?"

"Not directly, but I know *of* him," said Joplin. "He retired as a Detective Sargeant back in 2001, I think. Right around the time I was hired. Started a private detective agency called Phoenix Research and Investigations."

Rawlins nodded. "He did. And was hired by Atlanta Public Schools in 2006 to investigate reports of cheating at Parks Middle School."

"I thought that didn't come out until 2009," Joplin said.

"It didn't. Not until this paper reported in 2009 on discrepancies in CRCT scores that had been noticed after Beverly Hall became superintendent of APS. Blaine was one the reporters on that story. But in 2011, a reporter with 11 Alive News got wind of Reginal Dukes' investigation and report, which he claims he delivered personally to Beverly Hall in May of 2006. A report that found cheating on the 8th grade writing test at Parks. And he claims he also passed on concerns from teachers there that Parks' principal, Christopher Waller, planned to facilitate cheating on the upcoming CRCT test."

"I remember that broadcast," said Joplin, nodding slowly. He was a news junkie, and was able to draw on his memory, seeing again the interview with Reginal Dukes. "It attacked Beverly Hall's insistence that she had never heard reports or even rumors about cheating on the CRCT before the *AJC's* report and the subsequent investigation ordered by the governor."

"Exactly. And with the trial coming up soon, and Hall's doctors claiming that she can't participate in it due to her Stage IV cancer diagnosis, Blaine came to me with a proposal to re-interview Dukes, as well as the other people he said were present at his meeting with Hall."

"Who had she already interviewed by the time she died?"

"Just Dukes. She met with him last Friday. She was still working on locating the others when…" Rawlins looked down at his hands. "When she died."

Joplin took a deep breath and said, "Did she tell you if she got anything new from Reginal Dukes?"

"Not *new* exactly, but she thought it was 'encouraging,' as she put it. She said that he categorically refused to back down on his statements about what happened in that meeting. He again insisted that Ms. Hall never even looked at his report and simply asked if he had any evidence that Christopher Waller intended to cheat on the CRCT exam. Which Dukes said he didn't, at the time, just stories from the teachers. And, to date, none of the administrators at that meeting have been indicted or charged."

"Yeah," said Joplin. "That had a lot of people upset. It looked like the District Attorney was going after the low-hanging fruit. The teachers who were too afraid of losing their jobs to object to the cheating."

Rawlins sighed. "A lot of them cooperated with the investigators," he said. "Out of guilt for what they'd done. And many of those indicted pled guilty for the same reason: depriving underprivileged children of a decent education. Or at least a chance of one. And all the while, Beverly Hall was accepting accolades for being named 'superintendent of the Year' by the Obama administration in 2009, and the educators were getting bonuses that added up to over a million dollars under the 'No Child Left Behind' campaign. It was a travesty. And Blaine wanted to dig up some more dirt before the trial started."

"When was the last time you talked to Blaine, Mr. Rawlins?"

He took off his glasses and rubbed his eyes. "Friday, on her way home from her interview with Dukes. She hung up just as she was pulling into her driveway."

Joplin saw again the red Audi in front of the carriage house. He blinked and said to Rawlins, "Did you ever meet her fiancé, Winston Avery?"

"Of course," he said. "She brought him to our Christmas party last year. Not the office party. One my wife and I give every year for family and friends. And I've gotten to know him pretty well over the past several months."

"What do you think of him?"

The editor blinked again. "Why do you ask? Is he a suspect?"

"'Person of interest' is the new 'suspect' in law enforcement-speak these days, Mr. Rawlins, and Winston Avery hasn't reached that level yet. But I don't know the man, so I like to get other people's opinions."

The editor didn't reply right away. "He's an extraordinary person in every way," he said finally. "I've never met anyone quite like him, frankly, and I've met a lot of people doing this job."

"I'm glad to hear it, Mr. Rawlins."

"Please, call me Mark."

"Okay, Mark," Joplin said. If calling Rawlins by his first name would get more information out of him, that would work. "And I'm Hollis. So, can you tell me why you thought Avery was 'extraordinary'? All I've heard so far is that he's arrogant and extremely ambitious. And that he's cut himself off from the black community in Atlanta."

Rawlins smiled and shook his head. "Isn't that what a lot of people think when someone who's black is also very successful? Especially white people. And although I certainly can't speak for the black community, I know that Winston tried to set up some scholarships and mentoring programs for black students, but got discouraged by the way schools like Morris Brown mishandled their funding. But to get back to your question, I found Winston to be one of the most intelligent, accomplished, and *interesting* people I've ever met. And so did Blaine. He literally swept her off her feet, which wasn't an easy thing to do. And I know that he loved her very deeply."

Joplin found this a little hard to reconcile with Avery's attitude about the pregnancy he claimed to know nothing about, but put that aside for the moment. "You don't think he might be a little too much like her father?"

The editor folded his arms over his chest and shook his head. "Not in the way I think you mean. In their accomplishments, perhaps, and their ability to intimidate people if they want to, but Winston would never try to dominate Blaine like the General seems to dominate his wife." His face flushed, and he quickly added, "At least, that's what I noticed when I was around them."

"I did, too," Joplin assured him. "But let's get back to why you thought so highly of Winston Avery."

Rawlins sat back in his chair and seemed to consider his answer before saying anything, then said, "I guess because he refuses to accept anybody's limitations on who he is and what he can do. From what he told me about himself—and what Blaine told me—he came from nothing, but managed to get scholarships to a very prestigious college, then law school. But when he feels comfortable with you, he drops that almost imperious air and can even be a little self-deprecating."

"And he feels comfortable with you?"

"I'd like to think so. My wife and I have gone to dinner and other events with them over the past year, but Winston and I have also gone to some Hawks' and Falcons' games together, had lunch—things like that. Blaine encouraged it, because she worried that Winston doesn't have many close friends." Rawlins paused and looked down at his desk for several seconds; when he looked up, his eyes glistened. "I guess he'll need a friend now, more than ever."

"Have you talked to him since...since she died?"

"A few times. And Emily—that's my wife—and I went over to see him Saturday night. Took him some food, but I doubt he's eaten much of it. He's completely devastated. I'm going to run by to see him after I leave work tonight."

"Can you think of anyone who might have done this, Mark? Killed Blaine?"

He blinked several times, as if the realization that Blaine had been murdered had hit him again, harder this time. "God, no," he said. "I'm still having trouble believing she's gone. I can't even imagine how or why anyone could have actually…taken her life."

Joplin stood up. "Thank you for talking to me, Mark. I know this isn't easy for you. For me, either. But it'll help with the investigation."

"Anything," the editor said, but he didn't get up. "Anything you need. I'm here."

CHAPTER SEVENTEEN

"I have a confession to make," Maggie said after Tom had poured himself a pretty stiff Jack Daniels.

He turned away from the bar and smiled at her. "Let me guess: You called Carrie Salinger after you talked to me."

"How did you guess that?" she asked.

"Because I know you. I know how wrapped up you are in Will Henry's case. And in Jayla. And I know that you and Carrie are closer than Hollis and I even assume you are." He walked over to one of the bar stools in front of the island where she was sautéing mushrooms and garlic and lowered himself onto it. "So what did she say? Did she know anything about either case? Is she going to talk to Hollis about it?"

Maggie narrowed her eyes as she stared at him. "You *wanted* me to call her, Tom Halloran! You knew that if you acted reluctant to call Hollis, that's exactly what I would do!"

"Maybe," he conceded, the icy blue eyes challenging her. " Now, tell me what she said."

So she told him about the photos that Hollis had received of what turned out to be Blaine Reynolds' death scene, as well as the mysterious FedEx delivery man who didn't work for FedEx, and General Reynolds' insistence that Hollis be involved in his daughter's murder investigation. His eyes had

widened in surprise as she talked, but when Maggie told him about Hollis'
relationship with Blaine in 2008, he almost fell off the bar stool.

"Hollis dated Blaine Reynolds? *Our* Hollis?"

"Why are you so surprised?" Maggie asked. "He's very good-looking and
smart as a whip. Funny, too, which appeals to a lot of women, Tom. He
managed to get Carrie, you know."

Tom took another big sip of his drink. "I *do* know, Maggie, and if I were a
woman, I'd probably fall in love with Hollis myself. Those broad shoulders,
that big, blond head of his, those dreamy green eyes!"

"Now you're being condescending," she said, banging the wooden spoon
she was holding against the skillet to dislodge a clump of mushrooms
from it.

"Actually, I have the utmost respect and admiration for Hollis Joplin," he
said quickly. "He saved my life once, and that's something I won't forget. I
also like him and enjoy his company. I just have a hard time seeing him with
someone in the newspaper business. He's a news junkie, but he's not a big
fan of the media, especially when they're dogging law enforcement."

"According to Carrie, they met when she was doing a story about the ME's
office and followed Hollis around for a few days. They were a pretty hot item
for two or three months."

"Why'd they break up?"

"He told Carrie he didn't know. Said it bothered him for a while, and then
he stopped trying to get in touch with her."

"And then he had to process her death scene," said Tom. "That had to be
rough."

"Carrie's a little worried about him," Maggie said, adding chicken to the
mushroom mixture.

"*I'm* a little worried about Hollis, after hearing about everything he's dealing with. But the thing that bothers me the most is that someone's trying

to draw him into Blaine Reynolds' murder by sending him those photos. Maybe even trying to implicate him."

"Yeah, that's what's really upsetting Carrie, too."

"Then maybe you're right. I'd better talk to him about Winston Avery's connection to both murders."

———

Joplin lay on his back in the guest room bed, staring up at the ceiling and absently stroking Quincy, who had joined him in exile. The evening had not gone well. He'd come home to two sulking cats, one on the couch and one, according to Carrie, under their bed. Carrie, too, had seemed out of sorts, smiling too much, offering him a plate of his favorite St. Andre cheese with fig preserves, and talking breathlessly about how well she thought Banshee was adapting, when it was obvious the cat would have called the Milton County Humane Society if she knew how to use a phone.

Over a drink and a detailed description of the dinner she was cooking for him—Shrimp Fra Diavolo, one of his favorites, as well as an antipasto salad and gelato for dessert—he had become convinced that she was keeping something from him—or at least not looking forward to telling him something. He knew her well enough to know that much, but not well enough to know what that something was.

Finally, after a few glasses of wine and a few allusions to what might happen in bed after dessert—or instead of it—Carrie had told him about her phone call from Maggie Halloran.

"Winston Avery had a connection to the Daisy Henry case?" he'd said. "I never knew that, and I don't think Ike did either. It wasn't his case."

"Well, he needs to know now. This is just too much of a coincidence, Hollis. Which is why I told Maggie about the photographs and your relationship with Blaine. If he killed Blaine, he must have been the one to send those photos to you."

Joplin couldn't speak for several seconds and just stared at Carrie. Then he'd exploded, all the stress and tension and sadness over Blaine's death and its aftermath, as well as the two death scenes he'd investigated that morning, fueling a toxic mixture of fear and anger he didn't even know he had in himself. "You told Maggie about all of that?" he yelled, scaring Quincy off the couch and eliciting a series of howls from the master bedroom.

"Please calm down, Hollis," Carrie had pleaded.

"No, I won't calm down! Not only did you reveal information about an ongoing investigation, you've made it easy for Halloran to involve himself in it! Did you tell Maggie that Blaine was pregnant, too?"

"Of course not! That type of information is too personal and only for family members, Hollis. It wouldn't have been professional on my part."

"But why did you tell her anything? What were you thinking, Carrie? What in the world possessed you to do something like that? Is it because I was involved with another woman before I met you? Is that it? You just can't stand the thought that you're not the only woman I've ever cared about? Well, fuck you!"

He had never talked to her like that. Never used that tone of voice, so full of vitriol and accusation. Never used the f-word to her or even thought it where she was concerned. She had seen him in the throes of a Blue Funk, but he'd never turned on her. Not even when she'd dumped him for Jack Tyndall. Not even then. But the words had spewn from his mouth like projectile vomiting, horrifying him even as he'd said them, but making him incapable of holding back. She had stared at him as if his mind and body had been taken over by aliens, her eyes filling with tears. And then she'd whirled around and headed for the master bedroom.

Joplin had banged around in the kitchen once she'd left, cleaning up the dishes from the wonderful dinner she'd cooked. Quincy had jumped up on the island to give him moral support, and Joplin had been too heartsick to make him get down. When he'd finished, he'd gone into the guestroom, taken off his shoes, and slipped between the sheets fully clothed.

Now he contemplated his dismal future without her, convinced that she had seen him for the miserable, self-involved, mean-spirited person that he was. He was sure that he'd lost the only woman that he'd ever really loved, and through his own fault. An image of her face as she'd stared, dumbstruck and hurt beyond belief by what he'd said, came to him in the darkness. Quincy snuggled closer to him and upped his purring, but even that couldn't comfort him as it had in the past. After living alone so many years, Joplin had finally found someone who made him feel as if he were worth loving. She made him look forward to getting up in the morning, made him laugh, made him want to enjoy life in a way he never had before. He was constantly in awe of her fierce intelligence and compassion for others, her need to get to the bottom of things and find whatever truth there was to be found, her willingness to make herself vulnerable. At times, he'd found himself overcome with a happiness that was also almost eclipsed by a terrible fear that he might lose her. It was a mixture of such intense pleasure and pain that he had no words to describe it.

Slowly, Joplin rose from the bed and left the room. A light over the stove guided him as he made his way to the master bedroom. More light slatted through the space between the door and the threshold. Heart pounding, even as it crowded his throat, he knocked softly.

"Who is it?" she said after a long pause, and both tears and laughter threatened to undo him.

———

Winston Avery stood in the living room of his thirtieth-floor condominium at the Ritz-Carlton Residences like the captain of an enormous ship, the two walls of windows in his corner unit forming its prow. From that vantage point, he was able to see most of Buckhead as well as the Atlanta skyline, but he wasn't looking at either of them, his gaze turning inward instead. It was after midnight, and he was dressed for bed, but sleep had been eluding him since Blaine's death. Since before her death, really. Several days before. Because that had been when he'd first found out about her betrayal of him. He hadn't believed it, of course. Not at first. But then the evidence had become undeniable, no matter what she had told him, over and over.

He took a long sip of the neat Scotch he'd poured himself earlier. It was his fourth of the night, and it might not be his last. He would wait for that shift in his brain that meant he might be able to fall asleep—or lose consciousness, whichever came first. It really didn't matter. Everything that mattered to him had been destroyed when Blaine died. All the wealth and prestige and power that he had accumulated over the past ten years meant nothing to him now.

Avery was a big man, in more ways than just his height. "Larger than life" is how he'd often been described. Part of that was his bearing; part of it was the reputation he'd built up in the legal world as a formidable, even ruthless, adversary. He'd knocked down racial barriers and conquered anyone who'd tried to stand in his way, defying convention as well as others' expectations. And now should have been the time to enjoy everything that he'd fought so hard for.

His thoughts turned to his grandmother, who'd raised him since he was five and had lived long enough to see him graduate from law school. She'd been like an indentured servant to a wealthy white family, caring for their children and grandchildren, cleaning their houses, cooking their meals, and serving at their parties for over forty years. All the while being called "a member of the family." For his sake, to be able to move to a decent school district in Richmond or buy him good clothes or the books he read so voraciously, she'd swallowed her pride and borrowed money from her "family," working overtime to pay it off. They'd never pressured her to repay them, but it was understood that her weekends weren't her own if they needed her. And when her health and physical strength had declined, they had simply replaced her with a younger version of herself. Luckily, he had graduated from Duke by then and had worked during law school to be able to take care of her, despite the generous scholarship and stipend Georgetown had given him. It was the least he could have done.

As Avery turned and headed for the mahogany bar on the other side of the living room to fix himself another drink, he wished that he could talk to her now, even for five minutes. He'd let very few people become close to him in the past ten years and didn't regret that. But he would give everything he had to be able to tell his grandmother what had happened. She had always loved him unconditionally, as no one else had, and now never would.

CHAPTER EIGHTEEN

Joplin met Tom Halloran for lunch on Thursday at R. Thomas, a funky little
restaurant on Peachtree that was convenient to both of them. It prided itself
on its vegetarian dishes and juices, but it also served great burgers, as well as
beignets. The restaurant itself was more like an enclosed garden than a café
and was surrounded by cages of exotic birds, which chattered and squawked
and trilled in an effort to drown out the noise from the diners. They suc-
ceeded beyond everyone's wildest dreams, in Joplin's opinion, wondering
again why he'd picked this spot, convenience and burgers be damned. He
had the four- to- twelve shift at the ME's office again, but didn't order a beer
while he was waiting for the attorney. He was still a little hungover from the
night before, from both the wine as well as the lovemaking which had followed his return to the master bedroom.

Carrie hadn't awakened him when she left for work that morning, and he'd
slept until almost nine. Her scent was still on the sheets, and on him as well,
bringing back images of her as her anger had quickened into passion, and passion had subsided into tenderness. She had made sure he understood that he
couldn't talk to her the way he had, but that she also knew what his day had
been like, and she forgave him. He wished now that she'd stayed home with
him, just this once. He might have been able to convince her if he'd been awake,
but the sex had been as potent a drug as the alcohol, dropping him into a deep,
dreamless sleep that hadn't erased his exhaustion from the past few days.

"Rough night?" Tom Halloran asked as he sat across from him at the table.

"You could say that," Joplin said. "As I said on the phone this morning, I wasn't real thrilled that Carrie told Maggie so much about the Reynolds case. It's an ongoing investigation."

"And I'm a civilian, and a lawyer as well."

"You got it."

"I understand, and I can't force you to talk to me about Blaine Reynolds' murder, but maybe we can at least discuss Daisy Henry."

"I didn't handle that case, and neither did Ike. But I heard and read a lot about it at the time."

"Then you know that the circumstances of her death were very similar to Blaine's: white woman who was strangled in her kitchen, and her husband, a prominent black man, who became the chief suspect. Her daughter found her the next morning."

Joplin sighed. "How old was the daughter?"

He listened as Halloran told him about Maggie's meetings with Jayla Henry at the Children's Home, her encounter with Daisy Bulloch's parents, and his decision to help Damon Copeland with the conviction appeal.

"You really think Will Henry is innocent, Tom?"

"I know that Maggie believes Jayla Henry is telling the truth about seeing her mother *after* her father left their house. And *I* believe his Fourth Amendment rights were violated. What's puzzling is his refusal to let his daughter testify during the trial. She might have given him an alibi."

"He might not have wanted to put her through something like that because of her age," said Joplin. "And the jury might not have believed her anyway."

Their server approached, and they gave him their orders: the Thomas burger and fries for Joplin, who believed in the restorative properties of grease for a hangover, and the Ahi Tuna salad for Halloran.

"You ever just pig out, Tom?" Joplin asked when the server walked away.

"Of course. There's this restaurant on Lake Como in Italy where they mix your pasta in a hollowed-out wheel of *Parmigiana Reggiano*. It's so decadent, even Maggie wouldn't touch it."

Joplin stared at him, and Halloran had the decency to look away.

"Anyway," he said, "I agree with you on both counts, but I'm still going through the trial transcript and also looking at other possible suspects. Including Winston Avery. You have to admit it's a little too much of a coincidence that he's connected to both cases."

"Why?" Joplin asked. "Because he's the TV company's counsel of record? He might not even have met Will Henry *or* his wife. And even if he did, what motive would he have for killing Daisy Bulloch? Or even Blaine," he added. "He's not even officially a suspect at this point."

Halloran looked back at him, his gaze steady. "That I don't know, Hollis. But if someone had killed a former girlfriend of mine and was trying to involve me in the case, I'd sure want to explore that angle."

———

Cate Caldwell was a willowy blonde with her grandfather's blue eyes and a supremely confident manner. Halloran had known her since she was fifteen and had to assume that the confidence, in her case, had been a genetic trait, because she'd always been that way. She also had a great sense of humor and laughed at herself frequently, which kept her from being arrogant. Maggie had often told him to do the same. He was working on it.

"Cate," he said now, walking over to meet her as she came into his office and giving her a quick hug. "It's been too long."

"Since Elliot's funeral," she said, as he guided her over to the couch in his office. "Have you talked to Trip lately? I went to Charleston before the semester started in August and got together with him and Olivia for dinner, but haven't heard from him since then."

Trip Carter, Elliot's son, had moved to Charleston to live with his grand-mother when his parents had been murdered. Halloran, who had been Elliot's executor, and was also the trustee for Trip's trust fund, made it a point to see and talk to Trip on a regular basis.

"He's enjoying his senior year at the Porter-Gaud School," Halloran said. "*And* he's got a girlfriend."

"Wow! That *is* news! Either he didn't have her when I saw him, or he just didn't tell me."

"I think the relationship is only a few months old, actually. But he seems happy these days, according to Olivia. Still dealing with what happened, but that's to be expected."

"Yeah," said Cate looking past his shoulder. "It's a lot for a kid his age to process."

"A lot for a kid Jayla Henry's age, too," Halloran said, deciding to turn the conversation to the reason for their meeting.

"God, yes. You said Maggie met her. Talked to her. How is she?"

"Positive that her father is going to get out of prison soon and be with her. It's why she won't even consider being adopted."

Cate slowly shook her head. "I can't even imagine what she's been through in the past two years. I still can't believe there was no family to take her in."

"I couldn't either, but from Maggie's description of Daisy's parents, I think Jayla is probably better off."

"Yeah, they didn't even show up for her funeral—or the trial."

"Did you ever meet Jayla? Or Will Henry?"

"Yes, Will three or four times, but Jayla only once. Will was out on bail before the trial, and *The Undead Zone* had started filming again. I started my internship with Becker and Randall in mid-June, and Winston took me on-site to give me a feel for what a popular TV show set was like. Jayla was only five and very shy, but it was obvious that she adored her daddy. And that she was everything to him," Cate added, her expression sad. "Tom, I have to tell you I was very impressed by Will. Not his 'star quality' or his celebrity. I'm not going into entertainment law because I'm some kind of a media groupie. But I just can't see him killing his wife."

"What do you know about his relationship with Trina Daily?"

She shrugged. "At first, just what the gossip was saying: That they were involved, and that's why he'd moved out of the townhouse he shared with Daisy and Jayla. It was just gossip; no one really knew for sure. But then, Trina testified at trial that they'd been having an affair."

"Yes, I read that in the transcript, and the prosecution offered that as proof that their warrant for Will's cell phone was valid when Will's attorney took the case to the Georgia Court of Appeals. Copeland argued that the warrant was based on hearsay—the rumors you and others had heard. And the record of phone calls between the two of them wasn't proof that they were having an affair—they could have been discussing work issues. But once the police had the phone's GPS records, they were able to track Will's movements the night Daisy was murdered and placed him near the house. Copeland then argued that anything the police learned from the phone was—"

"Fruit of the poisoned tree," finished Cate.

"Exactly," said Halloran. "But both the Court of Appeals and the Georgia Supreme Court accepted the prosecution's further argument that interviews with Trina Daily were 'ongoing' both before and after they obtained the phone records, and she admitted to the affair, supporting their claim that this was information they would have obtained in the long run. A specious argument, but the court bought it and ruled that although the trial judge erred in not throwing out the evidence obtained from the phone, there was still enough evidence to merit the conviction and not enough to merit a new trial."

Cate looked dumbfounded. "You're kidding me."

Halloran shook his head. "I wish I were. Judge Sutherland dissented, essentially stating that the police had put the cart before the horse, and that it was a serious enough violation of Henry's Fourth Amendment rights to support overturning the conviction. Unfortunately, she was outnumbered."

"Well, I've already done a little research on cell phones with regard to using GPS in tracking a suspect's whereabouts, and there have been some cases lately that have attacked the validity of the results. It might be a good line of attack."

"That's great. That's something Damon Copeland needs to know about. We also need to be looking into exactly when Ms. Daily admitted to the affair and, more importantly, if they used evidence from the phone's GPS that Will was at or near the house that night to get that admission. That might be enough to amplify the position that the trial judge's decision to allow the evidence was more serious than the appellate courts deemed it."

"I'll get started on it right away."

"Good. By the way, Maggie said there was also talk of Daisy having a lover, but I didn't see anything in the transcript about that. What did Winston Avery think?"

Cate was very still for a few seconds, and her chin rose. "About whether Daisy was involved with someone, you mean?"

"That, and whether he thought Will killed Daisy."

She hesitated, then said, "He never really discussed Daisy with me. It wouldn't have been appropriate. He mentioned her once or twice, and I knew he admired her and was upset over her death. But that's all I know. I'm pretty low on the food chain at Becker and Randall, Tom. I'm not even an associate yet. I *do* know that he thought that Will was innocent. He was very vocal about that." Her chin went up again. "But why are you asking me that, Tom? What does this have to do with trying to get Will Henry's murder conviction overturned?"

Halloran didn't answer right away, trying to measure how he should answer the question. Then he said, "I know you told me that Avery was very much in love with Blaine Reynolds, but the similarities between her and Daisy Henry, as well as the circumstances of their deaths, seem to go beyond mere coincidence. If I—we—try to help Will get a new trial, we also need to look at other suspects. People the police either didn't consider or stopped considering once they thought they had their man."

"And you seriously think Winston belongs in that group?"

"It's a logical conclusion, but I can assure you I haven't already presumed he's guilty. I'm going to continue going through the court transcript and looking for any other potential errors, but in addition to researching the GPS angle of the case, I'd like you to connect me with some of the people around Will who might know more than they told the police. Or might have a motive to kill Daisy Henry. Can you do that?"

Cate looked away as she seemed to be considering this, then said, "Yes. I can call Nate Mauldin, the show's director, and set up a meeting. We can go from there. I've heard from a friend at Becker and Randall that Winston is working from home for the next few days, and I'm very reluctant to intrude."

"That's understandable," Halloran said. "We can hold off on that," he added, knowing that Joplin was going to update Simmons on Avery's connection to Daisy Henry's murder, and that Joplin intended to visit the attorney that afternoon.

"I just can't believe that he was involved in either murder, Tom—he's been a mentor to me since the day I met him. Maybe because of my grandfather, but I think he genuinely wanted to help me. So I've gotten to know him pretty well, and I can't see him murdering anyone, much less Blaine. People think he's arrogant and a little ruthless, and I can see that. But he's also extremely hard-working and devoted to his clients." Cate sighed and shook her head. "But I also don't think Will Henry killed his wife, and Winston is one of the people who convinced me of that. He couldn't actively participate in Will's defense because of his relationship with Benchmark Productions, but he believed in his innocence and did what he could."

"Did you ever meet Damon Copeland, Will's lawyer?"

"Yes. Benchmark wanted Will off the set until after the trial; the paparazzi were all over Senoia and interfering with filming. Winston was advocating to keep Will on, but the producers wouldn't budge, citing the 'morals clause' in his contract and referencing the rumored affair with Trina. He took a meeting with Damon and let me sit in. And Damon argued that it would be in Benchmark's best interests to stand by Will, unless and until a guilty verdict was rendered. He brought up the fact that the affair was only a rumor—which it was, at the time—and that Benchmark hadn't fired or suspended Trina, so doing that to Will would violate his civil rights with regard to gender. Winston was more than happy to take that back to the producers and support Damon's argument. And they agreed to keep Will on set. They did, however, get the writers to alter the plot line to reduce his screen time. Which was fine by Will. He needed to spend more time with his daughter and work with Damon on his defense."

"Speaking of which, do you have any idea why Will refused to allow his daughter to testify? I didn't have time to tell you yesterday when I called you about working with me, but Jayla told Maggie her mother was alive after her father left the house that night. Did you or Winston know anything about that?"

Cate looked surprised. "No," she said, shaking her head slowly. "I remember reading in the *AJC* that she wasn't going to testify, but I had no idea that Will was the one who quashed that. I thought maybe it was his attorney. Because she was so young."

"It might have been," said Halloran. "Copeland isn't willing to tell me anything confidential until he clears it with his client. And that will depend on whether you and I can come up with some compelling arguments for the next appeal. Or a new suspect." He stood up and walked over to his desk, then brought back a large box. "I had Joan copy both the trial transcript and Copeland's appeal. I want you to focus on the research we discussed, but would you have time to start going over them in the next few days?"

Cate stood up and took the boxes. "I'll find time," she said.

CHAPTER NINETEEN

Joplin had called Ike Simmons after leaving R. Thomas to tell him about his meeting with Halloran and Winston Avery's connection to the Daisy Henry case. Simmons was definitely intrigued, but cautioned him against saying anything about it when they met with the attorney. He was waiting in the elegantly subdued lobby of the Ritz-Carlton Residences when Joplin arrived fifteen minutes later, and nodded toward the concierge as he led Joplin to a bank of elevators.

"I told him Avery was expecting us, but he called up anyway. Said to go on up when you got here."

"Did Avery give you any flak about my being there, too?"

"He didn't sound real pleased," said Ike as he pressed the button for the thirtieth floor. "But he didn't say no. I explained that General Reynolds had asked for you to be part of the investigation."

"You think he knows I used to date Blaine?"

"Not from me. And if he does, he's not sayin.' This is a guy who plays his cards pretty close to the vests he usually wears."

But Winston Avery wasn't wearing a three-piece suit when he opened the door to his condominium. Instead, he was dressed in a dark green shawl-collared sweater and camel's hair slacks that looked more expensive than anything Joplin owned. He was at least six-feet-five, with broad shoulders, a physique like a linebacker, and gold-flecked eyes that fastened on Joplin.

His hair was closely cropped, and a neatly-trimmed beard and mustache covered the lower half of his face.

"Come in," he said wearily, then turned away and walked them into an enormous room bordered on two sides with walls of windows, motioning toward one of two gray, overstuffed sofas that faced each other as he sat in the other. "Detective Simmons I know. You must be the death investigator."

"Yes," said Joplin, feeling as if it were Avery who had summoned *them*, instead of his being asked to submit to an interview. "I'm sorry for your loss."

"And yours, too, I would imagine," Avery said. "Since you were once involved with Blaine."

It was the last thing Joplin expected the man to say to him. And as he stared back at him, he knew that was why Avery had said it. To put him off-guard, unbalance him. Whatever likeable side Mark Rawlins had found in the man was certainly well hidden.

"Yes," he responded, nodding slowly. "Blaine's death *is* a loss to me. She was a remarkable woman."

One side of Winston Avery's mouth drew up in a half-smile. Then he gave a long sigh. "Yes, she was. She was a *very* remarkable woman." He stood up and walked over to a bar on the wall between the open kitchen and dining area; a beautiful black and white Japanese kimono was suspended above it. Over that were two curved, sheathed swords, the bottom one longer than the other, with white diamond shapes on the hilts. On the right side of the bar itself was a sheathed knife with an ornate black and gold hilt, displayed on a stand. Avery went behind the bar and took down a bottle of Glenlivet. "Something to drink?" he asked

"Thanks," said Simmons, "but we're—"

"—on duty," Avery finished as he opened the bottle and poured three fingers. He walked back to the sofa and sat down again, the same half-smile on his face. "Fortunately, I'm not."

"I know you've answered Detective Simmons' questions," said Joplin evenly, "but I need to ask some of my own."

"Of course you do. Fire away, *Investigator* Joplin."

Ignoring the emphasis Avery put on his job title, which made it seem dismissive, Joplin said, "When was the last time you saw Blaine, Mr. Avery?"

Avery's unusual eyes seemed to turn inward, and he was silent for several seconds. "We went to dinner at The Palm last Wednesday night. We were there from eight until around nine-thirty."

"Did you spend the night together?"

Avery's jaw clenched, then he said, "No, we didn't, *Investigator*. It was an early evening. Blaine had to do a lot of research on a story she was working on."

"What kind of story?"

"Something to do with the public school scandal. I already told this to Detective Simmons."

Joplin ignored this and said, "What aspect of the scandal was she working on?"

"I thought you were asking some of your *own* questions, Investigator. Again, I gave this information to Detective Simmons. Don't you two talk to each other?"

"Almost every day, Mr. Avery. But if you don't like that question, here's a different one: How did you know I used to date Blaine?"

This time, both sides of his mouth turned up, but the eyes remained cold. "She told me. She told me about *all* of her old…boyfriends. I'm afraid you weren't the only one."

"I never thought I was," Joplin parried. "Did you know she was pregnant?"

Avery's face never changed, but he grew very still, like a cobra ready to strike. "Not until Detective Simmons told me," he said softly. "Did you?"

———

"Well, that went well," Joplin said as he and Ike rode the elevator to the lobby.

"Ya think?"

The interview had ended shortly after Avery's pointed question about Blaine's pregnancy, when Joplin asked him why he wouldn't submit to a DNA test to determine paternity. Avery had carefully set his drink on the enormous coffee table between the sofas and risen to his full height.

"I think we're done here, gentlemen," he'd said. "Any further questions can be directed to my attorney, John Masterson. Please show yourselves out."

"You don't think I should have asked him about the DNA test?" Joplin asked now.

"Who me? I was just a ticket-holder in that little entertaining drama, Hollis. You two went at it like two competing bachelors on Rose Night. Besides, we scored big-time."

"We did?"

"Sure did. Now we don't have to talk to the son-of-a-bitch until we ask his lawyer to bring him in, so we can put the cuffs on him. My next move is to try to get his DNA by putting someone on his tail to see if he leaves a used coffee cup or Coke can on a table somewhere when he goes out. If we try to go through his trash at his condominium, word might get back to him."

"So you think he killed Blaine?"

"Don't you? That was a first-class impression of a jealous man who would kill his fiancée and then rope her old lover into being part of the investigation, in my opinion. Or maybe in his mind a not-so-old lover. As in, what did he mean when he asked if *you* knew Blaine was pregnant?"

"Yeah, I have to admit that was pretty strange. But I have to tell you, Ike, that scenario doesn't fit in with the picture I got from Mark Rawlins. He thinks highly of Avery and insists that he loved Blaine very much. He also talked about Avery's attempts to do some good in the black community, like creating scholarships at some local colleges. And he couldn't have been the man who delivered the photos to the ME's office."

Simmons seemed to consider this, then shook his head. "Winston Avery is the kind of black man that some white people do think highly of, Hollis, because he wants to be just like them. He doesn't make them feel guilty. And as for the fact that Avery couldn't be the man who brought those photos to you, we agreed that the FedEx guy wasn't necessarily Blaine's killer. And Avery had plenty of money to hire someone to do that out. Didn't you see that view?"

"Yeah, and the Scotch he was drinking cost about $250 a bottle."

"For real? How do *you* know that? You drink Jim Beam on payday."

"Yeah, but I dream big. I Googled the ten best Scotches one night. That was twenty-five-year-old Glenlivet. It's a single malt."

"Well, hell, for that price, it oughtta be a *triple* malt!" said Simmons, shaking his head. "I believe I'll just stick to beer. Although I do like some Hennessey now and then."

"Isn't that sort of a cliché, Ike?" Joplin asked, slipping back into the one-upping banter they'd used as partners.

Simmons grinned at him. "You mean 'cause I'm black and I like Hennessey? No more so than a cracker like you drinkin' Yuengling and liking barbeque."

CHAPTER TWENTY

Halloran picked up his phone and punched in Damon Copeland's number.

Copeland answered on the third ring. "Tom," he said, his voice noncommittal. "I trust you got the transcript."

"I did. I haven't had a chance to go through it all yet, but I have a few ideas already, which I'll go over in a minute. But I wanted to apprise you of a new—at least it's new to me—twist in the case."

"Oh?"

"I just found out yesterday that Winston Avery is counsel for Benchmark Films, which produces *The Undead Zone,* and held that position at the time of Daisy Henry's death."

"Yes, he did," Copeland said, now sounding puzzled.

"And you know that his fiancée, Blaine Reynolds, was murdered last weekend?"

"Yes, I saw that on the news. I felt bad for Winston, but we don't travel in the same circles, so I haven't gotten in touch with him. I haven't even talked to him since the trial."

"Well, did you happen to notice the similarities between her death and Daisy Henry's?"

"What similarities? What are you talking about?"

"The fact that both women were strangled, and both were white women either married or engaged to prominent black men."

The silence on the phone went on for several seconds, then Copeland said, "I didn't know. I mean, I didn't know Blaine Reynolds was white. I knew she was a reporter, but her byline never gave her race, of course. She wasn't a TV reporter, so…"

"I get it, Damon. But now that you *do* know, can you see why I thought this was important?"

"I guess, but it's sort of a stretch. Interracial couples in Atlanta aren't all that rare. I know at least three in my circle of friends and aquaintances. How about you?"

"Not so much," Halloran admitted, feeling uncomfortable about that. Maybe Ansley Park, which was right across from the Piedmont Driving Club, was more of a white enclave than he'd realized. Actually, if he were being honest, it was something he'd never even thought about. Other than Ike and Alfrieda Simmons, who'd become good friends since Simmons had saved his life two years ago, he had no black friends, not in the true sense of the word. Colleagues, clients, and acquaintances, yes, but not friends.

"Do you think Winston Avery might have killed his fiancée, Tom?" Damon asked, taking him away from his uneasy thoughts.

"I just don't like coincidences, Damon. And in addition to looking for constitutional errors in the trial transcript, I'm looking at other possible suspects."

There was another long pause, then Copeland said, "I'm not so sure it's a good idea to stir things up, Tom. It's one thing to have you look over the trial transcript and the appeals, but I'm not sure my client would want that."

"Your client is sitting in a maximum security prison for at least the next twenty-five years, Damon. If 'stirring things up' helps get him a new trial, why would he object? Winston Avery was virtually invisible among all the witnesses and suspects when Daisy Henry was murdered. Because of Blaine Reynolds' death, he's now in the spotlight, and I don't think it will take long before the media makes a connection between the two cases."

Damon Copeland chuckled. "You have a different style than I do, Tom. Nothing wrong with that, it's just a little too high-profile for me, you know? I'm still trying to wrap my head around what you told me a few minutes ago. About the…similarities. Give me a day or two to process it. Right now, I'd like to just focus on the legal aspects of the case. We don't have to do the State's job for them and come up with another suspect."

The next ten minutes were spent discussing Halloran's thoughts about pressing the Fourth Amendment issue raised in the appeals, as well as the research on GPS accuracy that Cate Caldwell was working on. Copeland recalled his brief meeting with her when Benchmark wanted to fire Will Henry and expressed his appreciation for her help.

"Wow! Alston Caldwell's granddaughter. I didn't realize *that* connection either. She's a smart woman. Gonna make a great attorney."

"And she's on Will Henry's side, Damon. As I am."

"I know that, Tom. Just let me think about this, okay?"

————

Carrie Salinger dabbed some Vicks in her nostrils before carefully scrubbing her hands. Then she adjusted her visor, pulled on latex gloves and nodded to Tim Meara to begin taking photos.

"The body is that of a somewhat malnourished, white male in a severe state of decomposition," she said aloud for the tape recorder. "He has sustained an injury to the left side of the skull and face, and there is insect activity present in the wounds, as well as in his nose, mouth and ears. He is wearing battered Nike shoes, torn and dirty jeans, and a tee shirt and windbreaker, also dirty."

Carrie motioned for Eddie, the senior morgue attendant, to help her turn the body. As Meara took more photos, she noted that the clothes the victim was wearing were even dirtier on that side, and that some blood in the center of his back indicated another injury, as if he had been struck from behind.

"Okay, let's turn him back over and get the clothes off," she said to Eddie. As they were beginning to strip the body, Carrie heard the door to the autopsy room open and turned to see who it was.

"Jesus!" said Hollis as he came through the door and quickly grabbed a mask from the supply table. Holding it over his nose and mouth, he came toward her. "Thought I'd come see how your day's been and talk you into dinner somewhere. My treat, if it's relatively cheap."

"How can you resist an offer like that, Carrie?" Tim asked, rolling his eyes. "You really know how to sweep a girl off her feet, Hollis. Do you have a coupon for Wendy's?"

"Nah, he's a Mrs. Winner's guy, Tim," said Eddie.

"Don't worry, I'm going to hold out for Taqueria del Sol," Carrie said, smiling. It was their favorite Mexican restaurant and, conveniently, just down the street.

"Only if you shower first," Joplin said, pressing the mask closer to his nostrils and looking down at the body. "Man, this is a ripe one. Where'd he come from?"

"A make-shift shelter under an 1-85 overpass in Midtown," Carrie told him. "Some sewer pipes were being replaced nearby, and the construction crew found him," she added, then tilted her head as she saw the expression on Hollis' face turn serious.

"The skin slippage is pretty advanced," he said, staring down at what looked like opaque latex gloves on the victim's hands. "That usually means death occurred at least six or seven days ago."

"Usually. But Deke said the body was partially submerged in some standing water, which would accelerate slippage, and putrefaction, including bloating, is more advanced because it's been so warm lately, so that can skew things. I'll know more once I open him up, but from just the insect activity, I can tell he's been dead at least four days. It looks like he's had visits from both bottle flies and flesh flies, and Deke brought back earth samples near the body, which contain pupae. An entomologist can tell us more, but that probably means the time frame I suggested. Why do you want to know?"

Hollis let out his breath in a long sigh and looked up at her. "Because I think this is the guy who delivered the photos of Blaine after she'd been killed."

———

After finishing the autopsy on the John Doe Hollis was convinced was the bogus FedEx man, Carrie had taken a shower in the pathologists' locker room and put on the change of clothes she always kept at the office for encounters of the decomposed kind. Now she sat at her desk and took a deep, cleansing breath. Although Sarah Petersen had urged her to avail herself of the yoga class she'd arranged for her unit, Carrie hadn't felt the need; she'd been practicing meditation to reduce stress since med school. But as she went through her usual routine of visualizing her body and relaxing it from the top of her head down to her feet, she found her thoughts invaded by memories and troubling questions that had been stalking her since Blaine Reynolds' murder.

First and foremost, of course, was why the killer had taken photos of Blaine's body and then brought them or had them delivered to Hollis. Obviously, it had been to involve Hollis somehow. Maybe not to connect him to the murder, but at least to force him into being part of the investigation. The motive seemed to be revenge, but for what? For having been involved with Blaine a few years ago? And for only a short period of time? That seemed a pretty shallow reason for such an intense emotion: jealousy, to be exact. Unless, of course, what Hollis had told her about his relationship with Blaine wasn't true. Or, at least, not the whole truth.

With another deep breath, Carrie tried to concentrate on the present, not the past. But the more recent past refused to be banished. Although she'd completely forgiven Hollis for his uncharacteristic outburst the night before, it still troubled her. A lot, mainly because it *was* uncharacteristic. He had never treated her like that, talked to her like that. It made her question whether everything he'd told her about his relationship with Blaine was true, or whether he'd actually told her everything. She wasn't the kind of person who needed to know intimate details of her intimate partner's previous relationships. This situation seemed to be different somehow, but maybe that was just rationalization, she decided. Maybe it was just your average, garden-variety jealousy on her part.

Jealousy. She was back to that word again, and the circumstances of the case made her think of Shakespeare's *Othello*, one of her favorite plays as an English lit undergraduate. Winston Avery could almost be seen as a modern-day Othello, and the way Blaine had been murdered did call to mind Desdemona's death. So, then, did Hollis represent Cassio, the aide to Othello that Iago had led the Moor to believe was Desdemona's lover?

Carrie scrubbed her face with her hands and again visualized her body, attempting to relax her shoulders. This was not a sixteenth century Shakespearian tragedy, she scolded herself, ruining her concentration again. This was twenty-first century Atlanta, a mecca for affluent African-Americans. It was also a city where inter-racial relationships were common in a post-racist America led by the first African-American president.

Yeah, right, and all those Birthers who insisted Obama was a Muslim born in Africa never existed, Carrie thought as she gave up all pretense of meditating and clicked on her laptop to begin a preliminary autopsy report on the John Doe.

CHAPTER TWENTY-ONE

"That doesn't look anything like the delivery man I saw last Saturday," Sherika insisted, then immediately covered her face and mouth again. "He's younger and…different," she added in a muffled voice. "Can I go back upstairs now?"

"We assumed he'd probably changed his appearance, Sherika, but look more closely at his ears, okay?"

"They're just ears, Hollis. Yeah, they look similar, but that doesn't mean I can honestly say it was him."

Joplin sighed and said, "Okay, thanks, Sherika."

When Sherika had fled the autopsy room, he nodded to Eddie, indicating that he could roll the victim's body back into cold storage. It would have been nice to have Sherika corroborate his identification of the man, but he didn't really need that; not only were the victim's ears the same as the ones in the composite, so was the shape of the face and the placement of his eyes and mouth, even though the nose was distinctly different.

Then again, Joplin hadn't really *identified* the man. They still didn't know his name or anything about him. Now that the manner of death had been ruled a homicide—he'd been bludgeoned by an object that was both heavy, round, and covered with rust, probably an old metal pipe, according to Carrie-- a team of uniformed officers would be dispatched to canvass the houses and stores in the vicinity of the underpass where the body had been found, as well as members of Atlanta's homeless community.

Somebody would know him; Joplin was certain of that. But it might take a while, and things were heating up. General Reynolds had left a message on his cell phone asking for an update, and Winston Avery's attorney had contacted the police commissioner and accused Joplin and Simmons of "harassing" his client. They needed a break in the case, and the identity of the body in the cold room could point them in the right direction.

"I don't think he killed Blaine," he told Ike on the phone. "But he was hired by the person who did."

"You sure about that, Hollis? I mean, I hate to question that memory of yours, but all you're going by is a composite drawing of a man you didn't personally see, who was probably wearing a disguise."

Joplin sighed. "He was murdered within twenty-four hours of Blaine's death, maybe earlier, according to Carrie. And she said his organs showed years of drug and alcohol abuse. Somebody who'd jump at the chance to make some quick money. And like *you* said a few hours ago, Winston Avery had plenty of money to hire someone to deliver those photos. But whoever he was, he was a liability to the killer."

"Yeah, well, we can go with that until somethin' better comes along." There was a pause, then Ike said, "Listen, after I left you, I talked to Bill Riker, the detective in charge of the Henry case and asked if anyone had interviewed the little girl, Daisy's daughter. And he told me Will Henry refused to allow the child to be interviewed. Got his attorney to draw up some papers signed by a doctor to the effect that she was too young and would be traumatized if she had to talk to the police."

"Well, there goes that lead," said Joplin.

"Not necessarily," Ike said. "The social worker from Child Protective Services, sent to the house when the uniforms couldn't locate Will Henry right away, talked to Jayla Henry. Riker didn't get there until after she'd taken the child out of the house. And by the time they got through processing the scene, Will had been located and refused to allow them to talk to Jayla. But Riker followed up with the social worker later that mornin,' and she told him that Jayla kept crying and asking for her daddy. Said he'd been there the night before."

"And did Jayla say that she talked to her mother after he left? And that Daisy Henry was still alive, like she told Maggie Halloran?"

"No," said Ike. "She didn't. Which is probably why Riker was convinced he had his man. Even without the GPS, he knew Will had been there that night."

———

"But why would she tell Maggie that she *had* seen her mother after Will left?" Carrie asked after the server added their Margaritas and guacamole to go with the chips and salsa already on their table. It was only 5:30 on a Thursday night, but she had to practically shout to be heard over the din made by Tacqueria del Sol's happy hour patrons.

Joplin shrugged and took a long sip of his Margarita. He hadn't succumbed to a beer at lunch with Halloran, so he'd felt entitled to it. *Slippery slope*, he said to himself, vowing not to have a second one. "Maybe she just wants to believe that her father is going to get out of prison. So it's a lie she tells herself, or maybe she really believes it. Kids' minds don't work like adult minds," he added, remembering the various stories he'd told other kids about why he didn't have a father. One, in particular, that involved his father being killed in Vietnam, he'd almost believed. And it *was* true, in a way. Vietnam *had* killed Danny Joplin's soul; it just took a little longer for the alcohol to finish him off.

"But Maggie seems so *certain* that the little girl is telling the truth," Carrie insisted. "And she got Tom involved in Will Henry's appeal because of that."

"Which got me halfway believing that Winston Avery killed both women. Or at least Blaine."

"Well, that might still be true," Carrie said, frowning as she took a sip of her own Margarita. "He seems to have a lot of animosity toward you. And he knew you'd been involved with Blaine."

'true," Joplin agreed. "Look, can we not talk shop tonight? Especially anything to do with Blaine's murder. I know I brought it up, but right now I just want to be with my best girl and have a nice dinner."

"Of course," said Carrie, picking up her glass and holding it out in a toast. "To my best guy," she added, but Joplin saw an expression akin to pain, or even fear, twist her face for just a second.

———

Long after Hollis had gone to sleep, Carrie lay awake in the dark, her mind going over everything that he'd told her about his relationship with Blaine Reynolds. She was sure more than ever that he was holding something back, maybe something he thought would hurt her. He'd told her that he'd never really understood why he and Blaine had stopped seeing each other, then insisted that she'd more or less dumped him by never getting back in touch after she'd cancelled a date. *But was that true?* she wondered. If so, why would Blaine call him three years later when he was in the hospital? That showed a level of caring on her part that didn't go along with a brief affair that hadn't meant much to her.

Was it possible that Hollis had contacted Blaine after he'd gotten out of the hospital? Carrie had never really known much about what he'd been thinking and feeling during his long recuperation, other than what Maggie had told her. She'd gone to Grady every day while he was in the ICU, when he was still unconscious and in the days following, when he was awake. He had let her sit by his bed and tell him about things going on at the ME's office, but had never allowed her to talk about Jack Tyndall. Then, when he'd been released, he'd found one excuse after another to keep her from visiting him at home, even to bring him food. It had been one of the most anguished and frustrating times of her life, and she'd felt powerless to do anything about it.

Had Hollis allowed Blaine Reynolds back into his life during that time? Was that what he was keeping from her? Or was it something else? Something he was hiding even from himself?

When Hollis' last Blue Funk had overwhelmed him, and they had finally sorted things out and begun to tell the truth to each other, Carrie had made him promise that he would tell her the truth from then on about what he was thinking and feeling. That he would trust her to handle what he needed to tell her, no matter what it was, and she would do the same. It was the only way they could move forward.

But now she wasn't sure he'd been able to do that. They were engaged to be married. They were planning a wedding in the spring and a life together, with all that that promised: love, commitment, children, a strong chance for happiness and fulfillment.

Was a dead woman going to destroy all that?

CHAPTER TWENTY-TWO

The next few days were spent in an unsuccessful effort to identity the home-less man, as well as meetings with Blaine's brother, Warren, and Lucy Alvarez, Blaine's colleague and friend from the *AJC*, who'd been out in the field when Joplin had interviewed Mark Rawlins. So had Ned Beeson, one of the other investigative reporters identified as a close friend. Joplin was still playing phone tag with him.

The skin slippage made getting the John Doe's prints more time-consuming, and the results were disappointing. A check with the FBI's NGI, the Next Generation Identification program for prints, came up negative, which surprised everyone. A fairly high percentage of chronically homeless people had arrests and/or convictions for everything from vagrancy and public drunkenness to possession of illegal drugs and aggravated assault. Sometimes they could be convinced or ordered by the court to get help, but that was usually short-lived, especially in the case of men like their John Doe, who'd been living on the streets for years. For the most part, however, getting them off the streets was the priority. Especially during high-profile events that put the city in the national spotlight. Marty, the print tech, told Joplin on Friday morning he was going to check other databases, but not to hold his breath.

Joplin's meeting with Warren Reynolds on Friday afternoon didn't go much better. Although Blaine's body had been released to the family on

Wednesday and put on a private jet to be flown to D.C., along with her parents, her brother had stayed on in Atlanta to arrange for the contents of the carriage house to be packed up. He wasn't happy when Joplin called him, and only reluctantly agreed to meet him in the lobby of his hotel.

"I can only give you about fifteen minutes," he said after leading Joplin over to a corner of the elegant lounge of the Buckhead Ritz-Carlton. "I have to meet the movers at Blaine's house in half an hour."

Joplin just looked at him. Warren Reynolds' brown hair was slicked up from his forehead, but short on the sides, looking like a GQ version of a jarhead's haircut. Entitlement and privilege radiated from him like an upper-class aura. He was wearing a typical urban-chic uniform of dark, tight-fitting jeans, black tee shirt, and black blazer. He would have been considered handsome if not for eyes that seemed too small for his head, and an almost feminine mouth.

"Then maybe we should postpone this until tomorrow, Mr. Reynolds," he said. "Your parents asked me to join the investigation into your sister's murder," he added, emphasizing those two words, "and I need to ask you some questions. But if you don't have time, you can meet me at the downtown police station tomorrow. It's open on weekends."

He was rewarded by a deep flush which spread over Reynolds' face.

"Now, look here, Detective, I—"

"I'm no longer a homicide detective, Mr. Reynolds. I'm a death investigator with the Milton County ME's office. I thought you knew that."

Reynolds shook his head and said, "No I didn't. Which makes it all the more puzzling that my father wanted you to be involved."

"Maybe it was because I used to date Blaine," Joplin said, deciding to push the envelope. "Did you at least know that?"

The flush deepened, and Warren Reynolds now looked irritated. "My father *did* tell me about that when he said you were part of the investigation. I thought it was a bad idea at the time, and I still do."

"But that doesn't change anything, so tell me if you want to talk to me now or tomorrow at APD."

"I guess now. But I don't understand *why* you need to talk to me. I haven't seen Blaine much in the past few years, and I have no idea what got her killed."

"You say that as if your sister deserved what happened to her," Joplin said. "Is that how you feel?"

"No! Of course not! It's just that we weren't…close. She was five years older, and we didn't have a lot in common. We only saw each other on the occasional Christmas or Thanksgiving that we were all in the same country. My father was active military until six years ago."

"And what do *you* do for a living, Mr. Reynolds?"

Warren Reynolds' irritation graduated to a scowl. "I'm the General's aide," he said, his chin rising.

Joplin made a puzzled face. "I know what the duties of a General's aide usually involve, but as you said, your father hasn't been active military for the past six years. So what do you do?"

"Anything he needs me to do," Reynolds spat out. "For instance, he needed me to come to Atlanta last week to meet with the Georgia NRA at its headquarters to get feedback for the 2014 agenda."

"So, you were here in Atlanta when your sister was murdered."

The scowl went ballistic. "What the hell is that supposed to mean?" he shouted, causing a few other hotel loungers to look their way.

"Just that you were here when Blaine died," Joplin said. "Why should that upset you?"

"I'm through answering questions," Warren Reynolds said, standing up. "But you might have a few to answer when my father hears about this. My family has been through an enormous loss. And even though my sister had nothing but disdain for our political stance and our values, we loved her. To insinuate that we might have had a hand in her death is disgusting."

"I'll be happy to answer any questions your father might have," Joplin replied, as Blaine's brother turned his back on him and walked away.

———

"He was an arrogant prick," Joplin later told Sarah Petersen.

"Tell me how you really feel, Hollis," she'd responded dryly.

He described Warren Reynolds' off-putting appearance and attitude, then said, "It made me sick just to look at him, and that was the high point of the interview."

"Did Blaine ever talk about him?"

"I don't think they were on good terms, but that might have been because she was his big sister and kept trying to get him out from under Daddy's shadow. And his money. And although Warren talked about the family's loss, he thought Blaine was a bleeding-heart liberal who'd rejected their 'values.'"

"Enough to get rid of a blot on the family's reputation? As in, her black fiancé and a mixed racial child on the way? Or maybe because she was an outspoken gun-control advocate? Transport this scenario to the Middle East, Hollis, and you've got the perfect motive for an honor killing."

"You could be right," Joplin said, diplomatically. Sometimes, in his opinion, the chief got a bit carried away with feminist rhetoric. *Not that there was anything wrong with that*, he quickly reminded himself. "I'll take a closer look at him."

Once back at his desk, Joplin decided he'd better bite the bullet and return General Reynolds' call; maybe he could catch him before Sonny Boy ratted him out. When he answered the phone, the General seemed calm and collected, thanking Joplin for calling him and responding warmly to questions about the trip back to D.C. and the upcoming funeral. He even asked if

Joplin were planning on attending it. After a long pause, Joplin surprised himself—and possibly Blaine's father—by answering that he hoped to do so, if they got a break in the investigation within the next few days.

That, of course, led to a discussion of what little he and Simmons had been able to glean from canvassing Blaine's neighborhood and talking to her friends and colleagues. "It's early days, though, sir," he assured the General. "And we've got some leads that I can't share just yet. But we're following up on them, and I'll keep you posted."

"I hope one of them involves Blaine's so-called 'fiancé,'" he replied, contempt coating his voice. "I don't like what I've heard about that man."

"And what was that?" Joplin asked.

"That he was jealous and possessive."

"Well, I've heard that, too," Joplin said, hoping to get more out of the man. "But can I ask who told *you*?"

"Everyone I've talked to!" the General barked.

"Care to be more specific, General?" he asked.

"My son, for one," Reynolds blustered, and Joplin was sure his dust-up with Warren was about to come up. Instead, he said, "And Lucy Alvarez, who's been Blaine's friend for years."

So, "everyone" meant two people. Joplin decided it was no wonder the NRA's polls of Americans on Second Amendment rights, especially the right to bear Uzis, were always so positive.

"I'll ask her about that," was all he said, though, wondering when Lucy had become such a good friend of the General's. She'd despised him back when Joplin was dating Blaine. Then again, she hadn't been one of Joplin's admirers either. It was also possible, however, that the General had only talked to Warren, who'd passed on Lucy's comments about Winston Avery. After meeting Blaine's father, he wouldn't bet money that the man spoke the truth every time he opened his mouth.

Definitely something to check out, he decided. But to General Reynolds, he said, "I want to assure you that we're looking very closely at Winston Avery, sir. But please keep in mind that everyone's a suspect at this stage of the investigation. We haven't ruled anyone out yet. But as I said, I'll keep you posted."

The conversation had ended cordially, but the main thing Joplin had learned from it was that either Warren Reynolds had decided not to drop a dime on him, or his father didn't put much stock in what his son thought.

Only his meeting on Saturday with Lucy Alvarez yielded anything new, or at least halfway promising. The reporter was actually one of the newspaper's resident bloggers, hired soon after the 2008 recession, when most papers had lost a large percent of their cash-strapped advertisers, who provided seventy percent of their revenue. Long before that, Joplin knew, the Internet had begun to erode the public's interest in both print *and* broadcast journalism. Younger, social media-savvy journalism graduates were gradually replacing seasoned veterans like Blaine as newspapers shrank in size, content and, most importantly, subscriptions. Blaine had complained bitterly about the crumbling of an institution to which she'd devoted her life, but at least she'd kept her job.

As Lucy walked toward him, Joplin wondered again how—and why—she and Blaine had become such good friends. She was about five years younger than Blaine, with short, spiky blonde hair and a spiky attitude to go with it. He wasn't sure how she acted with other people, but the few times Joplin had been around her, she hadn't given off any warm vibes.

Sherika had directed Lucy to the conference room; he was standing just outside of it and smiled as she got nearer. "Thanks for coming here," he said, motioning her in, then to a chair at the end of the table.

Instead of sitting, she looked around her, as If checking for a mirror or cameras.

"This isn't being taped or recorded," he said, attempting to reassure her.

"If you say so," she responded, finally sitting down. She plunked a black, tote-style purse down on the table and retrieved a small tape recorder, then said, "Now it is."

Joplin smiled at her again, mentally counting to ten. "How long did you know Blaine, Lucy?" he asked, trying to diffuse the tension between them.

Color rose in her cheeks, and she looked down, then up again at him. "About five years, just around the time that—"

"I started dating her," he finished.

"Yes, if you want to put it that way."

"I could tell at the time that you weren't my biggest fan."

Now she smiled at him. "I didn't think you were her type. And I guess you weren't."

Joplin was surprised that this offhand comment could hurt him, after so many years. "I guess not," he said. "But I guess Winston Avery was. Are you a fan of *his*?"

The focus of her eyes changed, as if she were looking inward, but she just shrugged and said, "Not really. But she was going to break off the engagement."

"Did she tell you that?"

"Yes," she said, but it was with a defiance that seemed to undercut the assertion. "She was trying to decide how to tell him."

"Then she must have told you *why* she'd decided to do that."

Again the inward look. "He was very possessive. And jealous. She couldn't take it anymore."

"General Reynolds said you mentioned that to him. Mind if I ask when you talked to him?"

She shrugged. "I paid my respects to the Reynolds as soon as they got to Atlanta. At their hotel. I don't care for *him* so much, but Mrs. Reynolds is great. She and Blaine were still close, in spite of the General's relationship with the NRA and Blaine's feelings about that."

"I see," said Joplin. "So was Avery ever violent to Blaine?"

This time Lucy looked directly into his eyes and said, "If you call raping her violent, then I guess you could say he was."

CHAPTER TWENTY-THREE

"Do you believe her?" Sarah Petersen asked.

"About what? That Blaine was going to break up with Winston Avery or that he raped her?"

"Either. Both."

"I honestly don't know. Her description of Avery as jealous and possessive jibes with the way he acted toward me the other day. She told me Blaine came to work one day a few weeks ago and was very upset. 'shaken,' as Lucy put it. She said Blaine told her she and Avery had had an argument over the wedding date, and she'd asked him to leave and give her space. Instead, he pinned her down on the sofa and forced her to have sex."

"Well, that certainly sounds like rape to me," said Sarah, looking disgusted.

Joplin sighed. "Yeah, I guess. If it's true. But I got some kind of vibe from Lucy that any kind of break-up with him was just, I don't know, wishful thinking. And Blaine's not around to refute any of it."

"I'd call that pretty perceptive, Hollis. Or maybe it's your famous gut talking. "

"How so?"

"I wouldn't tell you this if it weren't pertinent, but Lucy Alvarez is a member of the LGBT community in Atlanta."

"I didn't know that," Joplin said, although he'd wondered about it. When he'd first met her, he'd even thought about asking Blaine if Lucy were gay, then decided that was inappropriate and none of his business. He usually had no idea whether someone was straight or gay and didn't care anyway. He believed individuals were who and what they realized at some point they were, whether they were attracted to members of their own sex or both sexes or knew they were trapped in the bodies of the wrong sex. It was not a choice on their part, in his mind, despite what most religions and too many countries asserted. But something about Lucy Alvarez had made him see her as a rival where Blaine was concerned, when they'd been together.

"She keeps her work life separate from her private life," Sarah Petersen said, bringing him out of the past. "I don't think she makes a concerted effort to keep it a secret, but she's very discreet. And private, which is her right. Atlanta is a great city to live in if you're not straight; that's one of the reasons I moved here. But it's also in the Bible Belt."

"I hear you. Do you know Lucy very well?"

Petersen shook her head. "Dana and I are mutual friends with some of her friends," she said, referring to her partner. "But I only know her to say hello at some of the clubs and bars we go to."

Joplin had only found out that his boss *had* a partner when she'd brought her to the office Christmas party the year before. Although she'd always been very open about her sexuality, she was every bit as private as she described Lucy Alvarez to be. "And you think my knowing she's a lesbian is pertinent to the investigation because…?"

Petersen smiled and said, "You used the expression, 'wishful thinking.' Why?"

The connection suddenly dawned on Joplin. "*She* wanted Blaine to break off her engagement to Winston Avery. Because she was in love with her."

"Wicked perceptive, Hollis. Maybe she projected her own feelings of jealousy and possessiveness onto Winston Avery. And maybe the so-called rape never happened. Or it might simply have been make-up sex after an argument, but Lucy put her own spin on it. For her own reasons. As you said before, Blaine isn't here to refute what she said."

———

Before he left the ME's office on Saturday, Joplin called Tom Halloran to give him a heads-up on what had transpired since their lunch at R. Thomas on Wednesday. He wasn't usually comfortable discussing an ongoing case, but the attorney already knew a lot, and Joplin decided to tell him about Blaine's pregnancy. Halloran seemed intrigued by Winston Avery's denial that he knew about the pregnancy and his overt aggressiveness toward Joplin, but gave more credence to Lucy Alvarez's description of Avery as both possessive and jealous.

"Even if she had a crush on Blaine and put her own spin on that rape story, it doesn't mean she was lying about Avery's jealousy," he said. "From what you just told me, he certainly seemed jealous of *you*."

"Yeah, I didn't quite understand that," Joplin admitted, then switched the subject to the decomposed body found under an expressway bridge. Halloran's excitement over this new finding was something he felt the need to rein in. "We might not be able to identify him, Tom. AFIS and NGI don't have his prints on record, and Marty now has to go to each branch of the military to get permission to access their data bases. It's going to take a while, and there's no guarantee that our guy will be in any one of them. Our best bet is the homeless community."

"But I remember your telling me once that the NGI included all data-bases, even the military."

"I did tell you that, and they should. But the various branches have been slow to comply. Especially where officers are concerned."

"You think this guy was an officer?"

"No," Joplin said. "I'm just trying to tell you that it's going to be like finding the proverbial needle in the proverbial haystack. And I've got more bad news for you," he added, then told Halloran about Simmons' discussion with the detective who'd been in charge of the Daisy Henry case.

"That is bad news," Halloran agreed. "But I'm still betting on Maggie's judgement, and she thinks Jayla Henry is telling the truth."

"Maybe she is—in her mind, at least."

Halloran gave a long sigh. "I guess I need to have another meeting with Damon Copeland and get him to fish or cut bait."

Joplin chuckled. "We have a better expression in the South, Tom, and it has nothing to do with fish and everything to do with a pot."

———

"Warren," Nina Reynolds said, when her son answered his phone, then took a sip of her Martini. It was not quite five p.m., but she had begun the cocktail hour anyway. Since they'd been back in D.C., it could never begin early enough.

"Mom! I was just going to call you."

"Well, I guess I beat you to it," she said, knowing he wasn't telling her the truth. He hadn't been doing that for a long time. *Like father, like son*, she thought, taking another sip. She was drinking alone, since San had told her he'd be home a little late. "How did the packing up go?"

"No problems. Blaine was pretty organized. Not a lot of clutter."

Tears filled Nina's eyes. "You didn't throw away anything, did you? I want to go through it all."

"Of course not, Mom. I wouldn't do that. It's all we have left of her."

"Yes!" she said fiercely, the tears flowing freely now. "It's all we have. Except for her writing. The pieces she wrote over the years. She did good work."

"Of course she did," Warren said, his voice soothing.

She knew he was trying to manage her, just like San did. Or used to. But she didn't care. Her heart was torn in two, not just broken, and being managed seemed okay for once. She needed to be comforted, even if it was all a lie. "When are you coming home?"

"I thought I'd stay here in Atlanta a few more days, make sure there are no more loose ends," Warren said, his tone changing, becoming evasive.

"What loose ends? We have the autopsy report and her...body. And you've shipped her things up to Georgetown. Your father and I need you here, Warren. We're arranging the funeral."

"I know, and I'll be there by Tuesday at the latest. I still have to finish up with the local NRA group here and in South Georgia. I was right in the middle of all that when...when Blaine..."

"Okay," she said, when he didn't finish the sentence. She didn't want to hear the word "died" again anyway. "We'll expect you on Tuesday."

"Tuesday," he repeated firmly, but Nina suddenly knew that wasn't true either.

Whatever was keeping Warren in Atlanta wasn't something he was going to share with her, but her ability to handle the truth had been all used up for the day.

CHAPTER TWENTY-FOUR

The sign announcing that they were approaching Senoia, Georgia described it as "The Perfect Setting. For Life." It was a reference to the prosperity provided by the various film and TV crews that lived and worked there, as well as the fact that the town had basically been turned into a set itself. In the 1990s, location scouts had found the old-world Southern town perfect for movies like *Driving Miss Daisy*, *Fried Green Tomatoes*, and *Pet Sematary*. But it wasn't until 2008, when the Georgia state legislature upgraded its previous incentives for the entertainment industry to a twenty-percent tax credit for production companies that spent at least $500,000 in the state, as well as an additional ten percent if they used a Georgia promotional logo in their finished projects, that things really took off. And *The Undead Zone*, where Senoia stood in for the fictional town of Sommerville, GA, provided major lift-off.

"The town has its own Hollywood-style Walk of Fame," said Cate, as they drove down Main Street, with its tree-filled grass strip running down the center of it, bordered by wide, brick sidewalks and quaint shops and restaurants. She had picked Halloran up at ten that morning after arranging meetings with the show's director, Nate Mauldin, as well as Trina Daily. Sunday, with the show's limited filming schedule, had been the best time for them. "All those plaques you see embedded in the sidewalks highlight various movies and TV shows filmed here, like the remake of *Footloose,* *Sweet Home Alabama,* and *Drop Dead Diva,* to mention just a few."

"I'm afraid I only go to movies with my kids these days," Halloran confessed. "And they're a little young for a TV show about zombies."

"Well, that's what Senoia is all about these days," Cate said, as they passed a sign that warned them not to feed the zombies. "And it hasn't stopped people from bringing their kids here. There's an *Undead* museum and a store that sells *Undead* memorabilia, and even a café called Zombie Eats. Benchmark also built facades of a Sommerville bank, a travel agency, and a bookstore."

"I hope we're not having lunch at Zombie Eats," Halloran said.

Cate laughed and shook her head. "I thought we'd go to Nic and Norman's when we finish on the set. I think you'll like it."

"As long as it doesn't serve brains."

"I'll call ahead to make sure."

———

Cate drove past a sign that read "No Admittance" to a driveway monitored by a security guard and gave her name. The guard checked a list, then handed her two clip-on visitor badges.

"Do you know how to get to Mr. Mauldin's trailer?" he asked.

"Yes, I've been here before. But, thanks."

They passed a series of catering trucks and outbuildings before reaching a group of Gulf Stream trailers that were obviously for the show's stars, directors, and production managers. Cate explained that normally, the area would be crawling with extras made up as zombies, but that only a few of the stars were on call that day. She parked her Lexus SUV in a small parking area off to the side of the trailers.

"Just a little background on Nate before we go in," she said when she'd cut the engine and turned to look at Halloran. "He's a good guy, and he believed Will was innocent, but he told me that when it came out at the trial that his cell phone put him right near the scene when Daisy was killed, he wasn't sure anymore. The bottom line for a lot of people is that the evidence obtained from the phone was true, even if the police shouldn't have been able to get it. And from what you told me last night when I called to set this up, it doesn't look like Jayla said anything about her mother being alive after Will left."

"That remains to be seen," said Halloran. "She must have been scared to death—traumatized, actually—when she found her mother the next morning. And, remember, Will wasn't charged with murder until a few weeks later, so that might not have seemed important to her. Also, the GPS settings couldn't place Will *in* the house, just near it. And from what you told me, that's not always reliable."

Cate nodded. "When you put it like that, it puts the case for Will's innocence back on track, Tom."

"It might also help to know that Maggie's going to see Jayla today to try to clear this up," Halloran said. "Plus, I'm meeting with Damon Copeland tomorrow to press him on my talking directly to Will. And there's always the possibility that we might find out something that will help Will this afternoon."

———

Nate Mauldin was about four inches shorter than Halloran and had trouble filling out the black jeans and tee shirt and button-down plaid shirt he was wearing. He looked to be in his early thirties and had thick, curly brown hair and gray eyes that looked as if they didn't miss a thing. Which was probably a good trait for a director, Halloran decided as he shook Mauldin's hand.

"Thanks for meeting with us," he said as he sat down on a nearby sofa. The trailer was comfortably, if not luxuriously, furnished and looked like a small apartment.

"Happy to do it, but I can't give you much time," Mauldin said. "We have to wrap up this season by November 22nd, and we just got some new pages from the writer. I had to call Trina and Jeremy Slater back in to film some scenes."

"Jeremy's character was created to fill the void when Will left," said Cate.

"I see. Well, I'll try to be brief, then. Could you tell me if Daisy Henry was having an affair and, if so, with whom?"

Mauldin's ruddy complexion lost color, and he stared at Halloran. "Pardon?" was all he could say.

"A lover," Halloran said. "*People* magazine and the *AJC* reported after the murder that there were rumors that Daisy was also cheating, but the police evidently never looked into that."

"How would I know something like that?"

"You were her director, Mr. Mauldin. I imagine it's part of your job to know what's going on in the lives of your actors, and I'm sure you knew more than just the rumors that were circulating about Will and Trina Daily."

"Tom!" said Cate, looking alarmed. "I don't think—"

"It's alright, Cate," said Mauldin, recovering some of his color. "I don't mind answering that." He turned back to Halloran and said, "The answer is 'no.' No matter what the gossipmongers—or the *AJC*— were saying. And the paper used the word 'allegedly,' as I recall."

"For liability purposes, of course. But you *did* know that the rumors about her husband and Trina Daily were true."

The gray eyes widened, but Mauldin said, "Yes. I had a talk with Trina a few months before…before Daisy died. I hadn't given much credence to the rumors before that—film sets become like small, insular towns, especially TV series, where the same group of actors spend most of the year, year after year, together. Deep friendships develop, along with adversarial or competitive relationships. And flirtations that sometimes turn into something else."

"And their flirtation became serious."

Mauldin nodded slowly, his eyes going off to the side, as if remembering. "I make it a practice to stay out of other people's business on set unless it has an impact on the job. A negative one, I mean. Most directors will tell you that they sometimes use what's going on in a particular actor's life to… enhance a performance."

"But this relationship didn't do that," Halloran prodded.

"Have you been watching the show, Mr. Halloran? No, I wouldn't guess so," Mauldin said quickly, answering his own question. "The relationship between Cal and Raven—Will and Trina in the show—was that of good friends, warriors together in an ongoing battle with the zombies. But there wasn't supposed to be a layer of sexual tension between them. Or an evolving romantic relationship. *That* was supposed to be occurring that season between Cal and Mona—Daisy's character. Only the camera caught the strain and unhappiness coming between Daisy and Will and the…"

"Budding romance between Will and Trina?" Halloran finished.

The director sighed, as if suddenly tired. "More like a consuming passion, by the time I finally confronted Trina. She flat out told me they were in love and that Will was going to leave Daisy."

Halloran processed this, then said, "Why did you talk to Trina, instead of Will?"

Mauldin gave a rueful smile. "This isn't my first rodeo, as they say in Texas. And in my experience—both as a director *and* a man—men think with their dicks, first, brains only afterwards. I thought I'd have more luck with Trina."

"And how did that work out?"

"Not at all. I tried to appeal to her sense of fairness with regard to Daisy, and even Jayla. Nothing. Then I told her it might impact her career. Nothing again. Then I threatened to have her character written out of the show, and she laughed at me. Said I'd be opening myself—and Benchmark—up to a nasty lawsuit, unless I was planning on getting rid of Will's character, too." Mauldin turned to Cate and said, "It was the same argument Damon Copeland used when Benchmark wanted to suspend Will, if you remember."

"I do," said Cate. "And she had you over a barrel, Nate."

"Yes. I had to let it go, hoping the affair would just burn itself out. And then Daisy was murdered."

"Cate said you believed Will was innocent until the GPS information came out at trial. Is that true?"

Mauldin seemed to pull himself out of his thoughts as he moved his eyes to Halloran's. "Yes," he admitted. "But maybe it was just wishful thinking on my part, to keep myself from thinking I should have said more or done more. Talked to Will, maybe. It was also really hard to believe that someone I knew could actually *kill* someone. You know?"

"I do," said Halloran, thinking of Elliot Carter's death and his own conflict in imagining who might have killed him. "But if you couldn't believe that he'd killed his wife, did you suspect anyone else?"

"No," said Nate Mauldin, looking first at Halloran and then Cate, as if to emphasize his denial.

———

Cate turned to look at him as they sat in the car. Their appointment with Trina Daily wasn't for another fifteen minutes. "I don't think he was telling the truth about not suspecting anyone else."

"Neither do I, but short of hooking him up to a polygraph, we can't prove it," Halloran said mildly. "He might be protecting someone or something—Benchmark, at the very least. The show has certainly been through its share of negative publicity, and it's his baby, remember."

"Publicity is publicity," said Cate. "That's one thing I've learned about this business." She let a few seconds pass. "You don't think he suspected Winston, do you?"

Halloran shrugged. "He didn't mention him when we first got here, and Blaine Reynolds' death and her engagement to him has been in the media, so that was a little weird. But I think he suspected someone closer to home."

"You mean Trina, don't you?"

"Yes. *If* Jayla Henry saw her mother after Will left, and *if* Will were really going back to Daisy, then Trina had the most to lose. Unless," he said, thinking things through to another logical conclusion, "Nate Mauldin was lying when he said Daisy wasn't involved with anyone else, which opens up the possibility of another suspect and another motive."

"Which brings us right back to Winston," Cate said, resignation in her voice.

"Not necessarily," said Halloran. "Didn't you notice Nate's reaction when I asked if he knew whether Daisy was involved with anyone? I'm no screen-writer, but a possible scenario is that Daisy went to see him when she suspected what was going on with Trina. To cry on his shoulder, so to speak. And maybe their relationship became more than director and actor." He grinned and added, "Remember, he did say that in his opinion, quote, men think with their dicks, first, brains only afterwards, unquote. He might have been talking about himself. Maybe Trina Daily wasn't the only one who was counting on Will and Daisy to get a divorce."

CHAPTER TWENTY-FIVE

Trina Daily herself opened the door to her Gulf Stream. Halloran didn't rec-ognize her or know her work as an actress, but one look at her was enough to tell him that she knew exactly how to make an impression worthy of a TV idol. She was wearing what he assumed to be her character's costume: frayed jeans with holes in the knees, a black tee-shirt, and a military-style vest with pockets bulging with ammo. She wore thick, dark dreads that had been pulled into a high ponytail to make her look like a warrior on the run, but her make-up was perfect, accentuating the fact that she was a stunning-looking woman, with wide-set ebony eyes, high cheekbones, and a very sensuous, full-lipped mouth. Besides that, however, Trina Daily had a presence that was over-the-top. Something that said she knew who she was and what she wanted.

"Hi, Cate," she said. "And you must be Tom Halloran." Her look was frankly appraising, and her expression said she liked what she saw.

"Thanks for seeing us today," he said, offering his hand.

"Not at all," she said warmly. "Please come in. But I'm afraid I'm on call and have to cut things short as soon as they have the set prepped. Did Nate tell you we're filming new pages today?"

"He did," Halloran said. "We'll try not to take up much of your time."

"No problem." She led the way into a living area that was much more elegant than Mauldin's and gestured toward a sleek leather sofa. "Nate told me this has something to do with Will," she said when they were all seated. "That you're helping with his appeal. How can I help?"

"One of the issues we're examining is the warrant the police obtained for Will's phone," said Halloran. "We think it was a violation of his Fourth Amendment rights, because it was based on rumors about his relationship with you at the time, not any real evidence that would count as sufficient probable cause."

Trina frowned and looked over at Cate, then back to him. "But I don't understand. The police told me they had the right to get his phone records from Verizon without a warrant."

"They did, but that's different from taking possession of the phone itself. They needed a warrant for that, which, as I said, didn't really provide valid probable cause. But once they had the phone, they were able to get GPS coordinates placing Will at the scene of Daisy's murder."

Tears filled Trina Daily's eyes, and she closed them, then shook her head, as if in denial of what he'd just told her. "Are you telling me that if they hadn't been able to confiscate his phone, he might not have been convicted?"

"It's a strong possibility. But, the police said they also had an admission from you that the two of you *were* in involved with each other, so they probably would have been able to get a warrant for the phone at some point anyway."

"But the second time they interviewed me, they told me that they had proof that Will was at Daisy's house the night of the murder. They said if I didn't cooperate I could be charged as an accessory to her murder! That was why I finally admitted the affair!"

"That's one basis for the appeal, Trina," said Cate. "The whole thing was like a snake chasing its tail. They had no proof of the affair when they got a warrant for the phone. But once they placed Will at the scene, they got you to admit the affair, then the prosecution used that admission to support the warrant when Will's attorney tried to get the GPS evidence thrown out before the trial. The judge ruled in favor of allowing the GPS evidence, and when the jury heard it, the damage was done."

"And as with you, the police used that GPS information to get people to talk," Halloran said. "Damon Copeland didn't succeed in getting that evidence thrown out, so it became the linchpin for all the other testimony that came out of it. Like you, the people interviewed by the police were convinced that since they'd placed him near the townhouse that night, he was guilty. But that wasn't necessarily true."

This time the tears spilled down her face, and the actress did nothing to stop them. She used the back of her hand to wipe them away and said, "And God help me, I *did* believe them! I thought that Will had killed Daisy because of…us. That maybe she'd told him she wouldn't give him a divorce or she'd never let him see Jayla again."

"It's because of Jayla that I'm involved in the appeal," Halloran said.

"I don't understand."

Conscious of the time, Halloran gave a brief synopsis of Maggie's meeting with Jayla and his decision to contact Damon Copeland. When he finished, Trina looked even sadder, her eyes downcast.

"So that's why the director of the Children's Home told me my adoption petition had been rejected," she said finally. "Because Jayla thought her father would be coming to get her."

"You tried to adopt Jayla?" Cate asked.

"Of course. She had no one. Her father had just gone to prison, and what family she had didn't want her because she's biracial. And I…I felt responsible."

"Because of the affair?" Halloran said.

Trina nodded, then her chin came up. "I know everyone thinks I broke up Will and Daisy's marriage, but that's not true. Will and I were involved when he lived in California, then he came back to Georgia for *We Are*

Marshall and began seeing Daisy. So I guess you could say that she broke *us* up. But by the time I joined the cast of *The Undead Zone,* they were having problems. And we…took up where we left off. He'd been telling me he was going to leave her, but he kept finding excuses to put it off. And then…the murder happened."

"Jayla told my wife that her daddy came into her bedroom that night and said he'd be moving back home in a few days," Halloran said gently. "After he left, she went down to the living room and Daisy confirmed that. If what she's saying is true, then—"

"Then Will lied to me," Trina Daily said sadly. "Or maybe he was just waiting to see if Daisy would take him back before he told me." She looked up at them, her eyes filling again. "But it also means he didn't kill Daisy. And that makes me happier than you'll ever know. He wouldn't talk to me after… after that night. He told me we were through, but he wouldn't say why. Just told me to stay away from him. So even before the police told me about the GPS evidence, I began to wonder if he had killed Daisy."

"But the GPS evidence *convinced* you," Halloran said. "I don't think Will got a fair trial, but if he didn't kill his wife, someone else did. And I'm looking for other suspects. Something the police should have done."

A loud banging on the door and a voice calling out, "On set in five minutes, Miss Daily," brought the interview to an end. After tearfully making them promise to let her know what she could do to help, Trina Daily hurried out of the Gulf Stream. Halloran and Cate followed her, then returned to Cate's car.

"Well," said Cate when they were settled in, "she either had nothing to do with Daisy's murder or that was an Oscar-winning performance."

"I'm reserving judgement on that," Halloran said. "And this is a TV show. She'd only get an Emmy."

———

"So, the dolls were all naked?" Maggie asked.

Tommy and Megan were in bed, and they'd taken glasses of red wine into the den. Although it was still mild during the day, with sixty-five degree temperatures, the nights were chilly, and Halloran had turned on the gas logs in the fireplace. With the kids around, they hadn't been able to talk before, but he'd just finished filling Maggie in on their trip to Senoia—including lunch at Nic and Norman's and a side trip to the Barbie Beach display on the way home.

"Yep," said Halloran. "Various Barbies and Kens in all their plastic, non-genital glory, playing volley ball. There were also some zombie dolls donated by Benchmark hovering around them. It's become quite the tourist destination."

Maggie lifted her glass. "To camp chic!" she said. "Did you take pictures?"

"Sadly, no. But the image is permanently burned onto my retinas."

"Oh, well, you had other things on your mind. Any decision as to whether Trina Daily was lying through her teeth—I mean, acting?"

"Well, I guess I know what *you* think."

Maggie set her wine glass on the coffee table and sat back. "She has a reputation for getting involved with her co-stars. Most of them married."

"And you know this…how?"

"Trust me. It's all over the Internet. And the Internet wouldn't lie, would it?"

"I think I'll reserve judgement on that, too. But to answer your question: I'm still not sure. It's times like this when I wish I had Hollis Joplin's gut instinct. He's better at reading people than I am. But just from observation of her facial expressions and body language, I'd say she was telling the truth when she said she'd only told the police about the affair when she heard about the GPS information. She also seemed genuinely happy that what Jayla told you seemed to point to Will's innocence."

"But…?"

Halloran shrugged, then took a long sip of his wine. "When I told her about Jayla's insistence that her daddy had intended to move back home before the murder, for just a few seconds she had the strangest expression on her face, like she was…stunned, is the only way I can describe it. And then it disappeared, and she said she was happy, because it meant that Will hadn't killed his wife."

"But it also meant that Will wasn't going to leave Daisy for her, and she evidently didn't know that," said Maggie, frowning.

"Or, as I've said, that Jayla only told you what she desperately wants to believe."

"I just don't believe that, Tom. When I went back to see her today, we talked about the difference between telling the truth and saying how we *wished* things could be. I asked her specifically about her father coming to talk to her before he left their house that night, as well as her going down-stairs to see her mother after he left. She looked me right in the eye and said she was telling the truth. Then I asked her if there were anything she could think of that would help prove what she'd been telling me. At first she couldn't think of anything, but then she gave this big smile and held out her wrist to show me a pink Disney Princess watch her father had brought her that night. She said he always brought her something whenever he came over to the house."

Halloran smiled and shook his head. "Will could have given that to her at any time, Maggie. It doesn't prove anything, I'm afraid. And even if we could locate a sales slip or something else to prove he *did* give it to Jayla the night of the murder, it just corroborates the State's case that he was there, not that Daisy was alive after he left the house."

"But I *believe* her, Tom," Maggie insisted. "And I don't—can't—believe that a father as loving as Will has been described would kill the mother of his child and then walk away, knowing that child would find the body the next morning."

Halloran sighed and said, "I can't either. But that's not evidence, and in the end, only facts and the evidence to support them can prove that Will Henry is innocent. Or even get him a new trial."

CHAPTER TWENTY-SIX

On Monday, Joplin had the day free, since he was scheduled for the grave-yard shift that night, but he decided to go to the ME's office anyway. Normally, he would try to sleep in a little, to prepare for a night of no sleep at all. Sarah had asked him if he wanted to work day shifts only while he was involved in Blaine's murder investigation, but he'd said no. He'd had to do that the year before, during his recuperation from both his injuries and the surgery to reconnect his bowel. He'd hated to impose on his co-workers then, and he wasn't about to do it now. So working on the investigation had to be done during his free time.

He'd spent most of Sunday going over the uniformed officers' reports of the canvassing they'd done of Blaine's neighborhood, as well as the area where their John Doe had been found, with little to show for it. The evening rush hour, when Blaine had returned home that Friday, had made any awareness on the part of her neighbors of unfamiliar vehicles in the area difficult, if not impossible. And no one recalled seeing any strangers around either. A few people in a warehouse near the expressway underpass had recalled seeing John Doe—or a raggedy-looking man, at least—emerging from the underpass now and then, but no one else. They'd assumed that he was homeless, but nobody had ever tried to talk to him. Only his death, revealed by the swarm of police cars and crime scene technicians near his make-shift home, had evoked any curiosity from them.

Frustrated, Joplin had closed his laptop and invited Carrie to brunch at Bistro Niko. The noisy, high-ceilinged main room, with its tile floors, banquettes and booths, always energized him. They'd shared mussels with frites and a Salade Nicoise, as well as crisp glasses of Macon-Villages. Carrie, who'd seemed a little preoccupied for the past few days, had been in good spirits, talking about what she planned to bring to Thanksgiving dinner at the Hallorans' house. She'd reminded him of the change in plans the night before.

Originally, they'd been invited to Carrie's parents' house for the meal, but her mother had tripped over the family dog ten days earlier and was still on crutches. When Maggie Halloran had heard about it, she'd invited them all to Ansley Park. Joplin still didn't know whether he was relieved or disappointed. Get-togethers at the Halloran household were always lively, with wonderful food and wine. He also enjoyed being around Tommy and Megan. Celebrating Thanksgiving with just Nathan and Harriet Salinger had seemed somewhat daunting at first, but it would have been an opportunity to get to know them better. A loud, crowded dining room at the Hallorans' house wasn't a good place to do that.

But Carrie was happy they were going there, Joplin had thought as he looked across the table at her. He wasn't sure what had been bothering her, hoping it wasn't a lingering effect of his outburst a few days ago. He'd made a concerted effort to be more upbeat since then, and he'd also tried not to talk about Blaine any more than he had to. He wasn't going to risk jeopardizing their future together for any reason, especially not because of his personal demons.

Now, however, as Joplin checked the cats' food dishes before leaving to go to the ME's Office, he remembered the expression on Carrie's face at Taqueria del Sol when he'd said that he didn't want to talk about Winston Avery, Blaine or Jayla Henry anymore that day. He'd promised her when they got back together a year and a half ago that he wouldn't keep things from her. That he'd talk things out, instead of letting them build up inside him. He'd failed miserably at that on Wednesday night, then sworn to her that he'd do better. And yet, the very next night, he'd clammed up and said he didn't want to talk about the case. Joplin closed his eyes and wondered, yet again, how he could keep doing the same stupid things over and over. Promising himself he would make it up to Carrie—again—he gathered his car keys and wallet from the kitchen island and left the condominium.

———

The phone rang as Joplin sat down in front of his computer.

"Found him," said Marty.

"Yes!" said Joplin, raising his fist. "Who is he?"

"Sgt. James Corcoran, an Army veteran from the War on Terror in Iraq. I had to call in some favors to get into the Army's database. He was given a General Discharge in 2004, specifically under 'Other Than Honorable Conditions,' which stripped him of any benefits, including the VA."

"You able to find out why?"

"Yep. Drug dealing. His case wasn't adjudicated because he cooperated and named names so they could break up a much bigger ring, but his rank was reduced to E-1, and he was drummed out. That would have made it pretty hard for him to go back to school or even find decent work. I knew some guys like that when I was in Afghanistan a few years later. They start out using to deal with the stress, then get pulled into dealing."

"I guess he stayed in the same line of work once he got back," said Joplin. "Which makes me wonder even more why he wasn't in the system here."

"Maybe he had family," Marty said.

"Carrie said his body showed signs of chronic homelessness. And alcohol and drug abuse."

"Well, somebody had to get him cleaned up, if not clean, for him to be able to impersonate a FedEx guy, right?"

"Right," Joplin agreed. "Thanks, Marty."

"Anytime."

Joplin was thinking of his father and his struggle with the bottle after Vietnam, when his phone rang again. The caller ID made him groan. "We're bringing a smoked salmon dip and chestnut dressing, Tom," he said, knowing that wasn't why Halloran was calling.

"I'll look forward to it, Hollis, but that's not why I'm calling."

"Of course not. To what do I owe the honor, then?"

"Two things: I'd like to read the autopsy reports on Daisy Henry and Blaine Reynolds, and I'd like to talk to the detective who worked the Henry case."

Joplin tried counting to ten, but only made it to five. "Is that all, counselor?"

"For now. Damon Copeland finally agreed to talk to his client and see if I can meet with him. If he does, Damon will make me a part of the appeals team to ensure attorney/client privilege, so I might have more questions for you after that. I won't be able to share anything I learn, though."

"The more things change, the more they stay the same," Joplin said in a lilting voice that was totally the opposite of how he felt. "My name isn't Alexa, Tom, and this isn't Amazon Prime/Law Enforcement Division. I'm not taking any orders today."

Halloran sighed and said, "You're absolutely right. Let me start over, Hollis. I interviewed the director of *The Undead Zone* yesterday and the actress with whom Will was having an affair. I think one or both of them is lying, but I'm not sure what they might be lying *about*, and I want to hear what the detective thought. Also, I need to see if dimensions were taken of the marks on both women's necks to see if they were similar. I'm having doubts about whether these cases are connected, and I'd like to rule out that possibility. At this point, I need some facts, not supposition or wishful thinking, and I'd really appreciate your help."

Joplin thought about how often the phrase, "wishful thinking," had come up in the past week and considered what Halloran was asking of him. "Tell you what," he said finally. "I'd like to compare the two autopsy reports myself. So I'll take a look and then tell you what I think. As far as talking to Detective Riker, well, I'll run it by Ike Simmons and see what he says. I have to warn you, though, once Riker finds out you're working on Will Henry's appeal, I doubt very much that he'll agree to talk to you. And I wouldn't blame him."

"Fair enough," said Halloran. "And, Hollis? Thank you for doing this."

Score one for us poor working stiffs, Joplin thought and smiled. "I'll get back to you, Tom."

———

Before going to pull the two autopsy reports from the file room, Joplin decided to call Mark Rawlins. Although he didn't believe everything Lucy Alvarez had told him, the part about Blaine and Winston Avery having some relationship problems seemed possible and was something the editor hadn't mentioned.

"No problem, Investigator," Rawlins said when Joplin apologized for bothering him again.

"Hollis, remember?" Joplin said. "I can't call you 'mark' if you don't call me 'Hollis.'"

"Okay, Hollis. How can I help you?"

"Well, I just want to see if you can shed some light on some things Lucy Alvarez told me when I met with her the other day."

"If I can. Sure."

"Lucy said that Blaine was going to break off the engagement with Avery. That he'd become very jealous and possessive of her, and that they'd had a big fight one night a few weeks ago. She said that Blaine asked him to leave and, instead, he forced her to have sex with him. Actually, she called it rape."

"You've got to be kidding me!" Rawlins said. "Where in the world would she get a preposterous story like that?"

"She said it came directly from Blaine."

"Well, I don't believe that. I can't believe that! It would be so out of character for Winston. And for Blaine, too—to tell Lucy something like that. She knew what a gossip Lucy is."

"I'm not sure I believe it myself," Joplin admitted. "But why would she say it?"

He heard Rawlins sigh. "God only knows. She's had it in for Winston ever since Blaine started dating him. But I can assure you that, as far as I knew, Blaine wasn't about to break up with Winston."

"But something was stressing her out, Mark. She wasn't taking care of herself. Not managing her insulin levels well, which was borne out by the autopsy and her landlady, who had to call the EMTs when she found Blaine unconscious a few weeks ago. She'd gone into a state of ketosis."

There was a long pause, then Rawlins said, "I guess I'd have to agree with that, too. I tried to get Blaine to talk to me about whatever was bothering her, but she just said it would all work out fine. Then one time I brought it up with Winston, when we went to a Hawks game about a week before… before the murder. But he essentially told me to mind my own business. That that was between him and Blaine. So I respected that."

"But why didn't you say anything about this last week? When Ike and I interviewed you?"

Rawlins sighed again. "I guess because I just didn't connect it to her death at the time. I mean, couples fight, then make up. There are all kinds of stresses. Blaine's father wasn't happy about the engagement, for instance. Blaine wanted to wait until the summer to get married. Winston was pushing for a Christmas wedding, or at least an earlier date. That I did know. But these are ordinary things, Hollis. Not the kinds of things that lead to murder. You have to see that."

"Hey, I'm engaged myself," Joplin said. "And it puts a lot of pressure on you."

"Then you know what I'm talking about. But despite what Lucy said to you, Winston never showed any violent tendencies, and I never saw anything that even remotely looked like a motive for murder. "

"Thanks, Mark. I appreciate you talking to me. And I'm sorry if this upset you."

"I'm not upset for me, Hollis. I'm upset about the impression this might have given you about the relationship between Blaine and Avery, that's all. And now I'm worrying that I should have tried harder to get one of them to talk to me. If only to rule out—for you and the police—that this had anything to do with Blaine's death."

Joplin had tried to reassure the editor that it probably wasn't connected, but as he headed down the hall to the file room, he wasn't reassured himself. Blaine's pregnancy, which he hadn't revealed to Rawlins, could certainly have been what was stressing her out in the two weeks before her death. Especially if she didn't know how Winston Avery would react to it. But both Carrie and David Markowitz had said Blaine might not even have known she was pregnant at six weeks along, much less four weeks, following that timeline. And Avery had told Ike that he didn't know about it.

So what had been going on between Blaine and Winston Avery?

CHAPTER TWENTY-SEVEN

Joplin stared at the two autopsy reports lying next to each other on his desk. Although he'd been briefed by David Markowitz after Blaine's autopsy, he hadn't actually read the report. Deciding to put that off, even for a little while, he picked up the blue folder containing Daisy Henry's report and began looking through the crime scene photos. He turned one over and saw that it had been taken by Jesse Potts, the assigned death investigator. Subsequent photos showed close-ups of Daisy's face, the open eyes dotted with petecchiae, and her neck, which showed the mottled bruising of manual strangulation. Jesse had also taken shots of the area surrounding the body, and Joplin could see that it was directly in front of a large, granite-topped island.

The rest of the photos had been taken by CSU. Some documented that there had been no signs of forced entry into any of the doors or windows; others revealed the first level of the house, with a spacious open floor plan that included the kitchen, dining area and great room, as well as a powder room to the right of the stairs. There was nothing to show that a struggle had taken place in any of the elegantly understated rooms. Photos marked "Master Bedroom" and "Guest Bedroom" showed the same upscale décor and almost pristine condition, as had the downstairs area. The one marked "Child's Bedroom" had the typical messiness seen in the room of an active child with an abundance of toys and books.

Joplin studied the photos of Jayla Henry's bedroom more closely. The bed, with a Little Mermaid coverlet on it, was unmade. The night table next to it held a lamp, a pile of children's' books, and a small, glittery bag with a drawstring. To the left of the bed was a louvered closet door that was open and filled with neatly-hung dresses, pants, tops and sweaters. Opposite the bed was a white bureau and a huge toy box, only partially closed. A child-sized table and chairs, painted pink, sat under a tall window facing the foot of the bed; two dolls with no clothes on were seated facing each other with plates of plastic cookies in front of them. To the right of the door was a bookcase stuffed with more books, a small pink laptop computer crowning it. It was the bedroom of a little girl who was evidently much loved by parents who had the means to spoil her.

The thought that this same little girl was now in a children's home, unwanted by the only blood relatives she had, and waiting for her father to get out of prison, filled Joplin with an almost overwhelming sadness. He knew from all his years in law enforcement that there were thousands of children in much worse circumstances, but his heart went out to Jayla and all that she had lost on a terrible night a year and a half ago: mother, father, a loving home, friends, schoolmates. In short, her life as she knew it.

Almost angrily, Joplin scooped up the photos and set them on his desk, forcing himself to move on to the report itself. But when he looked at the first page, with the name of the reporting pathologist, he was stopped short.

———

Hollis stood in the doorway of Carrie's office, carrying a blue-jacketed autopsy report and wearing a stricken expression.

"Did you assist Jack Tyndall with Daisy Bulloch's autopsy?" he asked, his voice sounding accusatory.

"No," she said. "I didn't. It was all over the news, remember? I would have mentioned it when Maggie called me last week." She felt her face flush. "Jack was my supervisor, but that didn't mean I was present at all the autopsies he did, Hollis. I was just on a thirty-day rotation here and still working in the lab at Grady then. But, why are you asking about this? And why would it be important?"

Hollis ran his hand through his hair, then sat down in one of the chairs in front of her desk. "I'm sorry. Really. Tom Halloran asked to see the reports on both Blaine and Daisy Henry, so I said I'd look through them first, and then I—" He shook his head, unable to finish the sentence.

She took a deep breath and said, "You saw Jack's name, and had a very bad moment. Then everything we've been through in the past year or so, and every bit of progress we've made in our relationship went right out the window."

He gave her a shit-eating grin and nodded. "I guess you could say that. I'm sorry, Carrie. For about the thousandth time this year. I'm also sorry I shut you out the other night at Taqueria, when you asked something about Blaine. Why don't you just give up on me and try to get on that *Bachelorette* show? You'd get a much better guy than my sorry ass."

"I've thought about that, believe me. But I didn't want to have to go through getting custody of Quincy, and now we have Banshee to think of."

To her surprise, he burst out laughing, his breath coming out in whoops of joy. It was the nicest sound she'd heard all week, and she started laughing, too.

"Maybe I should have gotten a lobotomy instead of having my guts put back together," Hollis said, when they'd both calmed down. He wiped his eyes with the back of his hand.

"Why don't you just tell me what's been going on in that *so far* unlobotomized head of yours," she said. "I'm worried about you."

He looked at her. Really looked at her and saw the fear and worry she was feeling. "I'm worried about me, too, Carrie. Something is going on inside me, just beneath the surface, that started when those photos were delivered to me. And then when I…got to the scene. There's something that I'm missing, or that I just can't get right now that's eating into me."

"Did you love her, Hollis? But didn't realize it until she was dead? Until there wasn't …a chance? Is that what this is all about?" She took another deep breath, "If it is, then, tell me. I can handle it," she added, not sure that was true.

"No," he said quickly. "I was beginning to love her, I have to admit that. And if things had gone on, I think I *would* have fallen in love with Blaine. But…it was like a curtain fell. Like I was seeing this beautiful love story beginning to play out on a stage, and then…nothing. Curtain down, play over. It truly didn't hit me at the time, Carrie. My pride was hurt, sure, but I just accepted it at the time as another one of my relationship failures. Careers that didn't fit well; personalities that didn't mesh. I was used to it."

"But it's hitting you now, Hollis," she said softly. "Is that what you're saying?"

"Yes, but not in the way you're thinking. I'm not *mourning* my relationship with Blaine. I'm just suddenly realizing how…abrupt it was. As if I'd done something or she'd heard something damaging about me that had been a deal-breaker for the relationship. And now I'll probably never know, and it's bothering me."

"But she called you at the hospital, you said. That doesn't sound like someone who never wanted to see you again. Do you think this Lucy Alvarez could have misled her in some way about you? From what you told me, she sure trashed Winston Avery, and she evidently had her own agenda."

Hollis expelled his breath in a long sigh. "It's certainly possible. But although I only knew Blaine for a short time, I know she was the kind of person who would have confronted me with something she'd heard or discussed what might have been a deal-breaker. She wouldn't have just walked away."

"I see," Carrie said, then decided to change the subject. "So did you see anything in the file that connects it to Blaine's case, other than what Maggie and Tom have pointed out?"

"Not really," he said. "They were both found strangled in their kitchens, Blaine was lying face down on the kitchen floor, and Daisy was on her side, sort of curled up in front of the kitchen island. Blaine was wearing street clothes, and Daisy was in her..."

"Daisy was in her...what, Hollis?" she asked when he didn't continue.

"Her bathrobe," he said, and, tossing a quick, "I'll be back in a few minutes," over his shoulder, he hurried from the room.

———

"What was Daisy Henry wearing when Jayla went downstairs to see her after she said her father left the house?" Joplin asked.

"And 'hello' to you, Hollis," said Tom Halloran pointedly. "But the answer to your question is: I have no idea. Why is it important?"

"Because I looked over both the Reynolds and Henry autopsy reports, and the crime scene photos do show that both women were killed in their kitchens, in the same way, but their positions weren't the same. Also, Blaine looked like she'd just come home from work, and Daisy was wearing pajamas and a bathrobe. You said Jayla went downstairs to see her after her father left, and since Jayla was still awake, I'm assuming it was still fairly early in the evening. If so, why was Daisy ready for bed?"

There was silence on the phone for several seconds, then Halloran said, "On the face of it, it doesn't make logical sense. But Daisy could have had an early call for the TV show. Or maybe Will came over later than we assumed. I haven't read all the way through the trial transcript yet, so I need to check on what the State entered according to the phone GPS. But I guess the bottom line is what Jayla remembers."

"Yes," said Joplin.

"Okay, I'll find out. It could be very important. Thank you, Hollis."

"Don't go getting all warm and fuzzy on me, Tom. Less arrogant and entitled is fine." This brought a chuckle from Halloran.

"Got it. So, what you're telling me is that your examination of the autopsy reports doesn't rule out a single killer, but you haven't found anything else to tie them together. Or that Winston Avery might have been involved in Daisy's murder."

"No. No DNA was obtained from the strangle marks on Blaine, and only a small amount was found on Daisy, but it was too degraded to develop any kind of profile. The measurements of the marks on both women's necks were roughly the same, but that doesn't tell us that they were made by the same person, just that they were similar. Also, there's never been a timeline developed for Avery's whereabouts when Daisy was murdered, because he wasn't a suspect at the time."

"But if we could get his DNA somehow, we could at least see if he's the father of Blaine's child. If he's not, that goes to motive."

"I don't like it when you talk like that, Tom, and I'm beginning to regret telling you about Blaine's pregnancy. 'We' doesn't include *you* when it comes to a police investigation. But just to let you know—"

"Then find some way to get Avery's DNA without his knowing about it!" Halloran shot back. "Go through his trash or have someone follow him around and fish his used Starbucks cup out of *their* trash."

"And Ike Simmons is doing just that, Tom," said Joplin through gritted teeth, "which is what I just tried to tell you. Because he *is* law enforcement. He's had no luck because before Avery went back to work on Thursday, he never left his condominium, and Ike didn't want to take any chances trying to go through his trash, because someone might have tipped him off. But he's got someone tailing Avery whenever he goes out now."

"So he's back at his office?" Halloran said, sounding excited.

"Yes, but he hasn't been going out to lunch or for coffee or anything, so Ike's team still hasn't been able—"

"Well, there's more than one way to kill a polecat," Halloran said. "Is that Southern enough for you?" he added, then clicked off.

CHAPTER TWENTY-EIGHT

"Son of a bitch!" Joplin said as he walked back into Carrie's office.

"I take it you just talked to Tom Halloran," she said, looking up from her computer. She listened as Hollis told her about his conversation with Tom and the way it had ended. When he'd finished, she said, "So what's the problem? If he knows a way to get Winston Avery's DNA, more power to him."

He looked at her in disbelief. "Not you, too! You know how frustrated I get when Tom tries to play detective. It's why I was reluctant to talk to him in the first place! If Avery *is* the killer, he could screw things up by obtaining evidence illegally that can't be used in court."

"Tom is a lawyer, Hollis. He's not going to do anything that would jeopardize a court case."

"Yeah, but he's willing to cut corners if it involves a client. Remember how he hid that tape the killer sent Libba Ann Woodridge? Oh, and her cell phone, too. Not to mention the kiddie porn Ann Carter said she found in Elliot Carter's bureau. It turned out to be a lie, but Tom sat on it for two weeks."

"Because he knew it *had* to be a lie, Hollis," Carrie insisted. "And he explained that he couldn't turn over the tape because Libba had refused to allow him to, and it would have violated attorney/client privilege, even after she was dead."

Joplin folded his arms and scowled at her. "You always did like Tom more, Mom, didn't you?"

"Get out of here," Carrie said, laughing. "Some of us have work to do."

"So do I," he said, standing up. "I finally got hold of Ned Beeson, and I'm meeting with him this morning. But if you talk to Maggie for some reason, ask her to try to keep Tom from playing detective. It almost got him killed the last two times he tried that."

————

Ned Beeson had agreed to come to the ME's office on his way back from a press conference at the mayor's office held to discuss a series of "smash and grab" robberies in high-end Buckhead shops. Joplin wondered why it had taken the mayor so long to publicly address the situation. For the past two months, local newscasts had been filled with stories of a group of gangs crashing cars into free-standing jewelry and electronic stores, then piling as much merchandise as they could into the vehicles before the police showed up. He assumed Mayor Reeves was going to announce the creation of a special task force to crack down on them.

Christmas decorations were already on display, despite the fact that Thanksgiving was ten days away, and Atlanta businesses were putting pressure on law enforcement to make shoppers feel safe. Another alarming crime trend involved well-heeled matrons being accosted at both Lenox and Phipps shopping malls in Buckhead and having their diamond rings pulled right off their fingers, sometimes at gunpoint. It wouldn't be a merry—or profitable—holiday season, if Atlantans and visitors who flocked to Atlanta to enjoy the festivities, were afraid to shop and go out to the myriad restaurants, museums, and activities available.

So when Beeson hadn't made it there by 11 a.m., Joplin wasn't surprised. He arrived fifteen minutes later, full of apologies, which Joplin waved away as he ushered him into the conference room. The reporter seemed much younger than Joplin assumed he'd be, looking as if he'd just finished college.

He was tall, about six-two, had dark, close-cropped hair, a very high forehead, and deep-set brown eyes. He was wearing a somewhat rumpled navy blazer over jeans and carrying an iPad Pro and his phone. True to his profession, the first thing he did after sitting down was to ask Joplin if there were any new developments on Blaine's murder and whether he could record their conversation.

Joplin smiled and said, "I can't comment on an ongoing investigation, and you're welcome to record what's said, but this isn't a conversation, Ned. It's not an interrogation either, but I need to find out as much as possible about Blaine's activities in the past few weeks."

"But I already told Detective Simmons everything I know," Beeson said, looking surprised.

"Yes, but we find it helpful to talk to people more than once. Sometimes they remember more things the second time around. Tell me how long you've known Blaine."

"Since the first day I started at the *AJC*," he said. "Two years ago. She sort of took me under her wing, you know? I graduated from the School of Journalism at UGA, then got a Master's in Journalism and Computer Science from Columbia University. But I was still pretty green, you know?"

Joplin nodded, but he thought the "you know," was more of a speech quirk than a question.

"She knew I wanted to become an investigative journalist, and she encouraged me, read some of my stuff when I was first assigned to the crime beat. She also recommended me to Mark—Mark Rawlins, our editor—when a slot opened up in the investigative section. He's pretty old-school, especially when it comes to Twitter feeds and all the other online sources we rely on—things like that. But he gets it that print journalism has changed, and seems to appreciate the digital expertise I gained in grad school. Anyway, I found out later that Blaine was instrumental in convincing the editorial staff to make that transition. And she also gave me tips on how to score points with Mark when I got the job." Beeson's eyes shifted off to the side, then he looked down at his hands. "I still can't make myself believe that she's gone."

"What kind of tips?" Joplin asked, more to give the kid a chance to move away from the emotion he seemed to be feeling than to learn more about Mark Rawlins. It was obvious that he had cared deeply for Blaine.

Beeson shrugged, then said, "Pretty much the basic stuff, I guess: Let him edit the hell out of my work the first few months so I'd know what he wants; remember that he wants good, descriptive writing as well as digital expertise; don't take his criticism personally. You know." He cocked his head. "But we actually got along from the very first. Mark's a great guy to work with; he tries to learn everything he can about cyber journalism so he can support me. And he's one of the most ethical people I've ever known. I can go to him with any kind of problem and trust him to be straight with me."

"I have a boss like that, too," Joplin said. "So, did you ever meet Winston Avery, Blaine's fiancé?"

"Yeah," he said, nodding as he smiled. "At the office Christmas party last year. He was really amazing."

"How so?" Joplin asked.

"Well, I think he was a little bored at the party, so he talked to me. Maybe because I kept asking him questions, you know? Turned out he grew up in Richmond, Virginia, where my parents are from. His grandmother raised him, and he told me he never would have amounted to anything without her. Lucy thought he was kinda pompous, you know? 'Full of himself,' she said. But I never saw that. And I know he loved Blaine."

"Well, I'm glad you got a better impression of him than Lucy Alvarez did," he said, hoping to get more of a handle on the woman who claimed to be Blaine's best friend. "She didn't have many good things to say about him."

Ned Beeson smiled and made a dismissive motion. "That's just Lucy. She's awesome, really. But she can get bent out of shape sometimes and a little gossipy. She told me once that a friend in HR had let drop that an employee tried to sue the *AJC* a few years ago, accusing Mark of racial and gender bias. I made it a point to look into it and found out it was totally baseless; it went to mediation and the arbitrator sided with the paper. Lucy's friend shouldn't have talked about it, and neither should she. But as I said, that's just Lucy. As I recall, she was upset with Mark about a story of hers he decided not to run."

That fit with what Joplin felt about Lucy Alvarez, and he nodded in agreement. "So did she ever talk to you about Winston Avery?"

"Yeah, but it's not worth repeating, for the reasons I just mentioned," he said, looking uncomfortable. "We went out for drinks once after work, and I think she'd just had a little too much wine, you know?"

"Did she ever say Avery had been...violent in any way with Blaine?"

Beeson looked him in the eye and said, "Yes, but I didn't believe her, and, as I said, it's not worth repeating."

Joplin decided not to pursue it, certain that Lucy had told Ned Beeson the same story about the alleged rape. And the young reporter's belief that it had never happened echoed his own impression of Lucy and her bias against Winston Avery. "I understand," he told him. "And I just have a few more questions, Ned, and we can wrap this up. First, when was the last time you saw Blaine?"

The young reporter's expression turned serious, almost grim. "Just a few days before she was killed. That Wednesday. She was coming out of Mark's office, and we chatted for a few minutes. Then she said she needed to return a call to Reginal Dukes. He was—"

"An investigator hired by Atlanta Public Schools, before the cheating scandal hit the news," Joplin finished.

"Yeah, too bad his report didn't go anywhere. It could've saved the school system—and the city—a lot of grief."

"And a lot of a kids, too."

"That, more than anything."

Joplin nodded, then said, "Did she seem upset about anything that last time you saw her?"

The discomfort the young reporter had shown earlier returned. He shrugged. "Maybe a little."

"Lucy did tell me that Blaine was going to break off her engagement to Winston Avery. Could she have been upset about that? Did she talk to you about it?"

"No," he said firmly. "And, as I said, I didn't put much stock in what Lucy told me. Whatever problems Blaine and Winston were having were none of my business."

"Does that mean you thought they were having problems?"

Beeson gave a little smile. "Let me put it this way: I don't know firsthand if Blaine and Winston were having any problems, so I have no idea if that was what was…stressing her out last week. But she did seem a little on edge the last few times I talked to her. Is that good enough for you?"

"Yes," said Joplin, although it didn't get him any closer to what had actually caused Blaine's stress. "Thank you for clarifying. One last question: Can you think of anyone who might have wanted to harm Blaine?"

Ned Beeson shook his head, slowly and deliberately. "I can't imagine that anyone who actually *knew* her—I mean, not just as a reporter—would ever have wanted to hurt her, much less kill her. She was nobody's fool, and she could be tough when she needed to be—it's part of the job—but, Blaine was also funny and kind and a good friend when you needed one. You know?"

"Yes, I do," Joplin said, an image of Blaine laughing, smiling and encouraging him as he told her about something that had happened on the job, flashed through his mind.

"I'm sorry," Beeson said. "Of course you do. You used to go out with her. But doesn't that make being part of this investigation kind of difficult? I mean—"

"I know what you mean, Ned. And, yes, it does."

CHAPTER TWENTY-NINE

Maggie clicked off her cell phone, but remained seated at the kitchen table as she thought about her conversation with Jayla Henry. She had called after four p.m., when she knew Jayla would be home from school. Donna Hartsfield, the Home's director, had agreed to let Jayla come to the phone, after thanking her for all the work she'd done on the photo album. Maggie was relieved that she didn't need to drive over to see Jayla a second day in a row.

Tom had called around lunchtime to tell her about Hollis' discovery that Daisy Henry was wearing a bathrobe in the crime scene photos contained in her autopsy report. Reluctantly, she'd agreed to talk to Jayla again and ask specifically about what her mother had been wearing when she went downstairs to talk to her. But she'd also told Tom that it was time to explain to the child why she was asking so many questions. She'd been very careful not to get Jayla's hopes up by mentioning that Tom was helping out with the appeal of her father's conviction, but now she believed it was time to change course. Everything that might happen next could hinge on what details Jayla could remember from that night. So, after asking her about her day at school, Maggie had gotten right to the point. Still trying to keep everything low-key, however, she had told Jayla only that her husband, a lawyer, had asked her father's lawyer if he could help.

"We don't know if he *can* help, sweetie," Maggie had said. "But he could try. And maybe the lawyer doesn't know that your daddy told you he was moving back home. Or that you talked to your mommy after he left. Did you tell him about all of that?"

"Yes!" she'd said. "And that made him happy. But then later Mr. Damon told me he'd talked to the judge, and the judge said I couldn't go to the trial."

"Well, maybe there was some legal reason we don't know about," Maggie had told her. "Maybe because you were so little."

"Yeah, that's what he said. But I'm seven now. Is that old enough, Miss Maggie?"

Maggie had gripped the phone, squeezing her eyes shut to keep from crying. "We'll have to see, sweetie," she'd answered. "But just so I'm clear on things, can you tell me again about going downstairs and talking to your mommy? Like, what was she wearing? What was she doing?"

"Well, she was just sitting on the couch," Jayla had said. "The TV was on, but she shut it off when she saw me and told me to come sit next to her. So, I did and I told her what Daddy had said to me and asked if it was true. And she said it was, but she was smiling *and* crying, which was weird."

"Do you remember what she was wearing?" Maggie had asked.

There was a long pause, then Jayla had said, "No, Miss Maggie, I don't. Is that important?"

She had taken a deep breath then, and although disappointed, said, "No, Jayla, don't worry about it."

"But I could try harder, if it is," Jayla had said quickly. "I mean, she was wearing jeans, but I can't remember what kind of top she was wearing. I think it was green, but maybe it was blue. She liked blue," she had added wistfully.

"That's great!" Maggie had said. "I mean, that you can remember *that* much. I just meant what *kind* of clothes, like, was she wearing pajamas or something. But she wasn't, was she?"

"No," Jayla had said. "I told you, Miss Maggie, she was watching TV. Remember?"

"That's right, you did," Maggie had said. "But I bet you don't remember what TV show she was watching."

"I do, too!" the child had said proudly. "It was *The Undead Zone!* That's why Mommy shut it off when she saw me, because they didn't let me watch it."

"Then how did you know that was on the TV?"

Jayla had laughed, a big belly laugh. "Because Mommy and Daddy were in it, silly. And Miss Trina, too."

"Oh, I get it," Maggie had said. "So you knew Miss Trina?"

"Yeah. She came to dinner here once, and I saw her a few times when I went to the set with Daddy. And she came out here to see me…afterwards. She's a nice lady."

"I'm sure she is," Maggie had said.

As she sat in her kitchen thinking about everything that Jayla had told her, Maggie knew, more than ever, that she was telling the truth. That the evening before she had found her mother dead in their kitchen was seared in her brain. She remembered reading an article a few years back that detailed research showing that memories that were associated with strong emotions, especially positive ones, were clearer and were retained longer. Jayla's vivid memory of her father's visit that night, and the happiness over it that she and her mother had shared later, seemed to support that. Although that night had been followed by a horrific trauma, it seemed to be what the child had clung to, despite everything that had happened since.

Jayla had insisted that her mother wasn't in pajamas when she'd gone down to talk to her. *The Undead Zone* was on the TV at the time, so maybe that would help pin down the time. Jayla had said that Daisy walked upstairs with her right after that, which meant that a little time, at least, had passed since Will Henry had left the townhouse. And that was supported by the photographic evidence that her mother had changed her clothes and was ready for bed before she'd been murdered. Evidence that could be used to build a case for Will Henry's innocence. Or at least get his conviction overturned. The police had stopped looking for anyone else once they'd focused on Will and gotten the GPS information from his phone. But this might lead to other suspects.

Maggie left a voicemail about her conversation with Jayla on Tom's cell, then set her phone on the table and went back to thinking about the significance of the bathrobe and of where that possible piece of evidence had been: in the crime scene photos of Daisy Henry's townhouse. From there, her mind went to another set of photos that Carrie had told her about. Photos that had been sent to Hollis before he'd even gone to the scene of Blaine Reynolds' murder.

She needed to see those photos. And maybe all the others, too.

CHAPTER THIRTY

Damon Copeland sat at his desk, twisting a pen back and forth between the fingers of his left hand. He hadn't been able to return to the brief he was writing since Tom Halloran's phone call thirty minutes earlier. Halloran had told him about his and Cate Caldwell's trip to Senoia, as well as the discovery that Daisy Henry had been dressed in a bathrobe when her body was found. This was something Copeland already knew from the crime scene photos. But Halloran also said that Jayla had insisted to Maggie that her mother wasn't wearing pajamas or a robe when she'd talked to her the night before, something he *hadn't* known. It hadn't come up when Copeland had talked to Jayla at length after Will told him why the phone's GPS showed that he'd been "near" his old house. It was always a tricky thing to put a young child on the stand, but he'd decided Jayla's testimony about seeing her mother after Will left would be a crucial piece of evidence in his client's defense.

He'd never gotten the chance to use that evidence.

Soon after Will's release on bail, he had come to Copeland's office. He'd been visibly upset, his voice thick with emotion, and he'd told Copeland in no uncertain terms that he was not to put Jayla on the list of trial witnesses. Copeland had tried to change his mind, then argued vehemently with him, telling Will that he was tying his hands. That if he couldn't get the judge to disallow the GPS testimony, he had to give the jury another reason for Will's being at the house. And it was the truth: Will had gone there to ask Daisy to take him back, and Jayla could testify to that. He'd already discussed it with her, so what was the problem? Copeland had asked. But Will had been adamant about his decision, telling him that he would find another attorney if Copeland didn't follow his directive.

Damon Copeland was not the kind of criminal defense lawyer who would only take a client that he was convinced was innocent. He *did* ask for honesty from his clients, telling them he needed to know whatever the District Attorney might discover, good or bad, so that he could plan a defense accordingly. He also made it clear that whatever they told him, he was bound by attorney/client privilege and would fight as hard for them as he possibly could. He would not, however, suborn perjury by putting them on the stand to give testimony that was untrue.

Will had insisted that he was innocent when he'd hired Copeland, and he'd believed him. He'd told Copeland about his affair with Trina Daily, moving out of the family home, and being on the scene the night his wife was murdered. But he'd insisted that he hadn't killed Daisy. When Will had come to his office that day in May, however, he hadn't been able to look Copeland in the eye when he suggested that their original plan, of having Will testify on his own behalf if it looked like things were going south, might not be a good idea.

Then the dominoes had begun to fall: The judge hadn't thrown out the GPS evidence; Trina Daily had proven to be a strong, if unwilling, witness for the prosecution; and Copeland hadn't been able to prove that Will was elsewhere when Daisy Henry had been murdered, without Jayla's testimony.

Now, here was Tom Halloran saying one of the crime scene photos showed that there had been a time lapse between when Jayla said her father had left and when her mother had been murdered. That Jayla had talked to her mother downstairs, and that *The Undead Zone* had been on the TV. Copeland knew the show ran on Tuesdays at nine p.m., which might help prove that Will wasn't in the townhouse then. *But what did that mean, really?* Copeland wondered. He had been convinced for a long time that his client was guilty of murdering his wife. That didn't mean he hadn't done everything he could to get an acquittal, nor did it mean he wouldn't keep on trying to appeal the conviction. Which was why he'd agreed, however reluctantly, to let Tom Halloran read the trial transcript. But it also didn't mean that the photo and what Jayla was saying now would prove that Will was innocent. Not to him, anyway.

Because Will Henry could have come back later that night to kill his wife, after Jayla and Daisy were already asleep. Copeland knew that the GPS evidence presented at trial had only shown one set of coordinates for the phone at that address, around eight p.m. But Will could have left his phone at his apartment the second time. A key to the house had been found on his key ring when he'd been arrested; he could have let himself in without calling Daisy. And his cell phone only showed an earlier call to her, around seven p.m.

If so, that meant the visit to Daisy when Jayla was still awake had just been a ploy, to establish that he intended to go back to his wife. It also meant that Will had been cold-blooded enough to use his own daughter as an alibi, knowing she'd be the one to find her mother dead the next morning. But then why would he refuse to use that alibi at trial? It made no sense.

Damon Copeland sighed and put the pen he'd been fiddling with down on top of the brief he knew he wasn't going to finish that day. He needed to call Jackson CI and make arrangements to see Will Henry the next morning. There were too many "maybes" in the scenarios he'd dreamed up. Tom Halloran had managed to make him doubt, even just a little bit, his client's guilt.

———

"I'm not playing detective, Maggie," Halloran said into the phone. "I thought about asking Cate to go to Becker and Randall and try to get a coffee cup or a soda can that Winston Avery had used, but I came to my senses in time. First of all, I didn't think Cate would do it and, secondly, even if we could establish a proper chain of evidence, any good defense attorney could challenge my 'private citizen' status. Although an exception to the exclusionary rule allows illegally obtained evidence from a non-law enforcement source, I might be seen as an agent of the police."

Maggie chuckled and said, "As much as I love it when you speak legalese to me, Tom, I'm not even going to ask what all that means. I'm just glad you came to your senses."

"Yes, I guess so, but even if we couldn't have used any DNA I could get from Winston in court, at least we could see if he were the father of Blaine's baby. That would have furthered the investigation."

"Maybe. But you'll be happy to know that *I'm* trying to further the investigation—into both deaths—in my own way."

"What do you mean?"

"I asked Carrie if she'd talk to Hollis and Sarah Petersen and see if they'd let me look at the crime scene photos from both murders, as well as the ones sent to Hollis *before* he went to Blaine Reynolds' crime scene. The ones that were obviously sent by Blaine's killer. And they've agreed I could, because I've been a sort of consultant in the past. As long as I study them at the ME's office, since it's an ongoing investigation. So I'm going over there tomorrow."

"Who's playing detective now, Maggie?"

"I am," Maggie admitted. "But looking at photos isn't going to put me in danger, Tom."

It was a statement that would come back to haunt Halloran later.

———

That night, Joplin worked the graveyard shift in a weary frame of mind. He was not only tired from the day's events, he was still plagued by thoughts of Blaine and the unknown person who had sent him the crime scene photos. He and Carrie had had a quiet dinner at home with the cats after she left the ME's office for the day, and he'd gone to their room to lie down for a few hours. Usually, Joplin could fall asleep quickly if he needed to, but that hadn't happened. At nine p.m., he'd given up and gone out to the great room.

Carrie had been sitting on the couch, watching TV, with Banshee draped across her lap and Quincy curled up beside her. "Hello," she'd said, smiling up at him. "Can't sleep?"

"Nope. What are you watching?"

"*Say Yes to the Dress.* It's a so-called reality TV show filmed in Atlanta. At a Sandy Springs bridal shop, to be exact. It's nationally syndicated, and it's a big hit."

"Why do you say 'so-called reality TV show?'"

"Because although the *people* are real enough—the bride and her attendants, as well as certain family members helping her choose a wedding dress—the show's producers script these tensions and spats between various people. The bride's mother and her future mother-in-law disagree over her choice of dress, or the bride's sister has it in for the maid of honor, or the bride's father is dying of cancer and he doesn't want to see her walk down the aisle in a sexy, mermaid-style dress. That sort of thing."

"They make up the father's cancer?"

Carrie had given him a withering look. "Very funny. No, of course not, Hollis. They make up the thing about his not liking the mermaid-style dress."

"So why do you watch it?"

"Because sometimes it's funny, and sometimes it's kind of touching. And I'm getting some ideas about what I might want for *my* wedding dress."

"I kind of like the whole sexy mermaid thing. I mean, if I get a vote."

She had smiled and said, "I'll take it under advisement," then given him a long, lingering kiss.

Now, only an hour into his shift, Joplin sat in his cubicle, alternately wishing he could be at home in bed with Carrie, then hoping that he'd get called out to a scene, just to keep his mind from being bombarded with thoughts of the Reynolds case. Five minutes later, he got a call for a vehicular homicide on Roswell Road. He grabbed his bag after writing down the address, feeling what he knew was an irrational sense of guilt, as if he were responsible for the accident.

———

By six a.m., in addition to the vehicular scene, which had cost three lives, Joplin had also gone to a homicide scene at an apartment on Piedmont and a suicide scene, involving an Afghanistan veteran, in Midtown. Deke Crawford had handled two himself and was out on yet another call; it was a banner night for the ME's office. After writing up his reports, Joplin contemplated going to the breakroom to get a cup of coffee. He could barely keep his eyes open, something that didn't happen often, even on the graveyard shift. The events of not just the day, but of the entire week had caught up with him, and he was bone- tired, as well as heart-sore. Deciding a power nap might be a good idea, he folded his arms and leaned back in his chair. He was the only one in the Investigative Unit, but the phone would wake him up if anyone needed him.

Joplin usually didn't dream during power naps; those involved light, almost conscious sleep without REM activity. But now he found himself in a cavernous, dimly lit basilica with beautiful stained-glass windows and worn, marble floors. He was standing near the altar, looking out at row after row of empty pews. The air was chilly, with a heavy, cloying smell of incense; he could see his breath plume out in front of him as he stood there, waiting. What he was waiting for, he didn't know, until the wide doors at the back of the church opened, and a woman dressed in white from head to toe entered. As she walked solemnly up the aisle, he could see that she was carrying an enormous bouquet of blood red roses that couldn't quite hide the other thing she was carrying: a child in her womb. Her long, dark hair cascaded down her shoulders inside the veil she wore, and Joplin's heart turned over at the sight of Carrie, his love and his bride. But as she came closer, Joplin saw that it was Blaine, not Carrie, who was joining him on the altar. He reached out to help her up the marble steps, but she looked up at him and shook her head at his outstretched hand, then slowly disappeared, her body becoming transparent at first, then nonexistent, as she literally evaporated before his eyes.

CHAPTER THIRTY-ONE

Maggie arrived at the Milton County ME's office at nine a.m. Carrie met her in the reception area, explaining that Hollis was off that day after having the midnight shift the night before. She led her back to the conference room, where two thick accordion folders and a chilled bottle of water had been placed on the table, as well as a yellow legal pad and a pen. But instead of leaving, Carrie motioned for Maggie to sit down, then took a chair next to her.

"I really appreciate your doing this," she said. "You were an enormous help to Hollis and Ike during the Carter and Woodridge investigations, and I'm hoping you might see something in the photos that they've missed. This whole thing is affecting Hollis more than he lets on."

"And you, too, Carrie," Maggie said. "This hasn't been easy for you."

Carrie gave an off-kilter smile. "No, it hasn't. By the way, although everything in the files needs to stay here, feel free to make copies of anything you might want to take home to study longer." She looked at her watch, then said, "I've got an autopsy to do, but let me take you to lunch around noon, okay?"

"Sounds good," Maggie said, wondering how Carrie could talk about dissecting a human being and eating in the same sentence. She smiled brightly to cover her inner revulsion, hoping they would discuss something a little less...visceral at lunch. It was one thing to know what Carrie's profession involved and to admire her for it; she'd just rather not know the gory details. Then again, she was about to look at dozens of photos of two murdered women, so who was she kidding?

"Great," said Carrie, standing up. "I'll come get you."

———

The Georgia Diagnostic and Classification Center Prison was a maximum security prison in Jackson, Georgia, fifty miles south of Atlanta, that housed around 2,100 inmates. All convicted felons sentenced to serve time were initially sent there to be assessed and classified. Some went on to other prisons, but many, like Brian Nichols, who'd escaped from a holding cell while in the Fulton County courthouse on trial for the rape of his former girlfriend and then went on a killing spree, were kept there. It was also a "death house," where over sixty executions had taken place since its creation in 1976 and others, like Carlton Gary, the Stocking Strangler who'd murdered three elderly women, awaited execution. Will Henry had received a sentence of twenty-five years to life, with the possibility of parole, but he, too, remained there, probably because of the national publicity the trial had been given. The only saving grace, in Damon Copeland's opinion, was that he was allowed to live in the prison's general population section, rather than the Special Management Unit, which housed the most violent offenders.

Copeland had made the trip to Jackson several times since the trial, although it had been well over a month since his last visit. He took exit 201 off I-75, turned left, then left again at the second light. The prison, a large, imposing white building with three rows of windows overlooking the parking lot and two watch towers, was behind high walls of barbed wire. Copeland passed through the security gate and parked, leaving his phone in the glove compartment; he'd have to leave it with Security otherwise. Once through the electronic surveillance system, he was led by a Correctional Officer to the visitors' room, which held two rows of chairs separated by a Plexiglas partition.

Copeland sat behind the barrier, waiting for Will Henry. After five minutes, during which he went over what he was going to say to his client and what he *wouldn't* say, given the monitors he was sure were in the room, the door opened, and a tall, thin, bald correctional officer brought Will into the room. He was shocked by his client's appearance. He seemed to have lost at least ten pounds, the white jumpsuit he was wearing looking two sizes too big, and he'd stopped shaving or even trimming his facial hair. Will's eyes were shrunken in their sockets, and when the CO took off his handcuffs, he just stood there and stared at Copeland. The CO put a hand on his shoulder and pushed him down onto the chair, then left.

Copeland picked up the phone on his side of the window and waited until Will did the same. "Will, are you okay?" he asked, not sure he wanted to know the answer.

Will gave a small smile. "I could use a cigarette," he said.

"Aren't you using the money I put in the account I set up for you?"

"I've been in the Special Management Unit for the past month, and my privileges were taken away."

"My God!" Copeland said. "Why didn't you call me?"

"It was my own fault," Will said slowly. "And I didn't think there was anything you could do."

"What happened? Why did they put you there?"

Will didn't answer for what seemed like minutes. His eyes filled with tears and overflowed onto his cheeks. "I got a letter," he said. "From Jayla. And I...I lost it. Just totally lost it. They tried to calm me down, but that wasn't happening. I fought them and ended up hurting one of the COs." He wiped his face with the back of his hand. "So now I'm considered to be violent, and my security level changed."

Copeland couldn't say anything for a minute. "Can I ask what the letter from Jayla said?" he finally asked. "What upset you so much?"

"The usual," Will said, but his eyes began to fill again. "That she loved me and missed me and couldn't wait till I got out of prison. But this time she asked me why I didn't write back to her anymore." He paused, trying to compose himself, but the effort was wasted when he said, "Then she asked if she had done something wrong, and was that why I didn't write to her."

Copeland sat quietly for several minutes, letting him grieve. Thoughts of his own children and how he would feel if he were separated from them filled his mind. It didn't matter that Will Henry had probably put himself in the terrible situation he was experiencing. He was a father cut off from his only child, and Copeland felt only compassion for him.

"I didn't know you were still in touch with Jayla," he said. "I didn't really understand why you wanted to give up your parental rights, but I thought that meant you would cut off all contact with her, Will."

"I wanted her to have the chance to have a new life, like I told you, with a new family. Not to have people associate her with me—with a convicted murderer. And I *should* have stopped writing to her, but I...couldn't. Not until a few months ago, when I decided I was just keeping her tied to me. Because she was refusing to be adopted, and the judge agreed to allow that and give her some time. I realized she was holding on to some kind of hope that I would get out of here."

"But why didn't you let Lena and me adopt her? We *both* wanted to, you know that."

"What kind of distance would that have put between her and my notoriety, Damon? Or between her and me? *You* would be the connection. Forever."

"Maybe not forever, Will. I'm working on your appeal," Copeland insisted. "And now I have some help. There's a chance you could get a new trial. Or even be released."

"What do you mean?" Will seemed immediately suspicious.

Copeland told him about Maggie Halloran's visit to the Atlanta Children's Home and Jayla's refusal to be photographed for the Christmas album, then Tom Halloran's meeting with him and his decision to give the attorney the court transcripts. He could see that the information agitated his client, and he hastened to assure him that no client/attorney confidences had been breached.

Will made a sweeping motion with his hand, as if dismissing the idea. "I'm not worried about that, Damon. But I don't want Tom Halloran—or anyone else, for that matter—getting involved in my case, and that includes the appeal. You're perfectly capable of handling that."

"But Halloran has uncovered some new information, Will," Copeland said. "Things we didn't know at the time of the trial. Evidence that could show that someone else killed Daisy. Jayla told Halloran's wife that Daisy wasn't dressed to go to bed when she went downstairs to see her after you left that night. But the crime scene photos show that she was in pajamas and a bathrobe when she was killed. This proves Daisy was killed much later than the time the GPS shows you were there. We need to look into that, Will. It was information I didn't have at the time."

Will Henry stared at him. "Maybe we have a bad connection, Damon, so I'll say it again: I don't want anyone but *you* involved in my case. Not Tom Halloran and not my daughter. You keep her out of this." Then he slammed his phone back into its receiver and stood up.

The CO immediately came back into the room, cuffed Will, and led him away, as Damon Copeland, his phone still in his hand, sat in stunned silence.

———

Maggie came back from the copy/fax room with copies of the photos she wanted to study further at home. She hoped it had been a profitable morning, and that she wasn't just reading too much into what she'd seen in the different sets of photos. Because of that, she also hoped that Carrie wouldn't to talk about it over lunch. Her work as a photographer had taught her that observation was only the first step in achieving what she wanted. The next part involved letting what she had observed rattle around in her brain, until she came up with elements like perspective, lighting, focal point and the tonality that was so important. The third part, of course, was execution, and that was where the subjects of her work demanded that she remain flexible. In trying to analyze photographs taken by someone else, she still needed to go through all the steps; the sequence was different, however.

Step one could be checked off. Now she needed time to think.

CHAPTER THIRTY-TWO

Joplin slept until three o'clock that afternoon, waking up only when Banshee began a soft, pitiful meowing in his ear.

"Damned spoiled cat," Joplin said, dragging himself out of bed. Banshee followed him into the kitchen and waited patiently while he tore open a pouch of the Tuna, Shrimp and Anchovy broth. Quincy, who was right behind them, looked on disbelievingly at Joplin, then slunk from the room. Making a mental note to get him a box of chicken nuggets from Chick-fil-A later that day, Joplin grabbed a mug from the counter and filled it with cold coffee, then put it in the microwave to reheat. He was rummaging around in the refrigerator when the land line rang. Carrie's name was displayed.

"Good morning, love of my life," he said.

"Good morning to *you*," she answered back, and he could almost see her smile. "Hope I'm not waking you up. I tried to be extra careful not to do that when I was dressing this morning."

"Thanks for that," he said, remembering his vivid and disturbing dream the night before, when he'd dozed off at the office. The image of Blaine in a wedding dress, with a bouquet of red roses clutched above her expanding waistline, had disturbed him for the rest of his shift. And when he'd finally gone to sleep after he'd gotten home, he hadn't slept deeply, perhaps in an effort not to experience any similar dreams. Shaking his head to dispel that image, he asked Carrie, "Anything new at the office, honey? Have traffic fatalities decreased in the past six hours? No, wait, this is Atlanta we're talking about. What was I thinking?"

"I know you had a pretty full night, Hollis. David and I, and even the Chief, have had to deal with the bodies at the scenes you and Deke covered last night. I'm sorry."

Joplin gave a long sigh. "Just Atlanta celebrating Veteran's Day, I'm afraid. Besides, *you* had to autopsy them—I just had to declare them dead and take pictures."

"Any chance we could get away for a few days, Hollis?" Carrie said. "Sarah said you've got some time off you could take, and—"

"Sarah needs to mind her own business. I'm almost longing for the old days, when I had a boss who came in late, left early, and had no idea what was going on most of the time. And she keeps pushing this yoga thing."

"You *are* her business, Hollis," Carrie said, ignoring his outburst. "You're my business, too, and I'm worried about you. Besides, did it ever occur to you that I might need a break, too?"

"I'm sorry," Joplin said, although he was sure she was saying that to try to get him to do what she and, obviously, Sarah Petersen, wanted. "You're right. And you certainly do need a break from all this. But I just can't leave town right now, Carrie. The kind of break I need is something that will turn this case around. How about if we have a staycation this weekend? Are you off?"

"Yes," she said, sounding happier. "I swapped with David, so he and Judy could go to her folks' house in Pennsylvania for Thanksgiving."

"Great! I'll make Sarah happy and ask for the weekend off, too. We could stay at the Buckhead Ritz," he added, remembering his meeting with Warren Reynolds.

"What about the cats?"

Joplin glanced down at Banshee, deciding her girth wasn't just due to her breed. "I think we can fill up those tall self-feeder/water containers I have, since we'll only be gone from Friday night to Sunday afternoon. Banshee certainly won't starve."

"Well, then, I accept! I'll even make all the reservations. Where do you want to go to dinner Friday night?"

"How about dinner in our room Friday and at Davio's on Saturday? It's right across the street."

"Perfect. I like the way you think."

"And guess what I'm thinking with," Joplin said.

Carrie laughed, then clicked off the phone, leaving him with several thoughts swirling around in his brain. He let them swirl for several minutes, then pulled up the Contacts list on his phone and punched in a name.

"Mrs. Marlow?" he said when she answered. "This is Hollis Joplin."

———

"Joan," said Tom Halloran, standing next to his secretary's desk. "I hate to ask you to do this so late in the day, but could you make two copies of this transcript and then send the original back to Mr. Copeland?"

"Of course, Mr. Halloran," she said, standing up and taking the box from him. "There's plenty of time. Do you want me to call a courier service before I start copying it?"

"No, FedEx Overnight is fine. And thanks," he added, as she smiled and headed for the copy room. Luckily, the firm had two high-speed copiers that could each print out several copies and collate them in record time. They were indispensable in even a mid-size law firm like Healey and Caldwell. He was sure Damon Copeland wouldn't be happy if he knew copies were being made, but Halloran hadn't been especially happy when he'd gotten the phone call from Copeland telling him to pack up the transcript and send it back.

"My client has directed me to tell you that he doesn't want you involved in his case, and that includes helping with the appeal," Copeland had said tersely.

"What's going on, Damon?"

"I'm sorry, but I'm not at liberty to discuss anything with you," he'd replied, although less tersely.

"I see," Halloran had said, although he really didn't. But he did understand Copeland's position; he couldn't go against a client's directive, even if he thought it was a bad idea.

"I appreciate everything you've done, Tom. I mean that," he added before the line went dead.

But, evidently Will Avery *hadn't* appreciated what he saw as interference in his case. Halloran hadn't been able to ask Copeland if his client had been upset simply because he and Cate were helping with the appeal, or by the idea that they were focusing on other suspects for Daisy Henry's murder. Whatever the reason, it didn't seem to be a logical one. Why would a man convicted of murder and languishing in prison not want every bit of help he could get to get him out of said prison? It made no sense at all.

Until it did.

———

Joplin stopped by Mrs. Marlow's house to get the key to the carriage house. Today, she was dressed in a Burberry jacket and black slacks. He knew it was a Burberry jacket because Carrie had once pointed out the distinctive plaid to him in front of a window at Saks when they were walking back to their cars after dinner at Davio's. He had been impressed by the price tag, less so the design. He answered Mrs. Marlow's questions with more patience than he felt. She, in turn, answered a few of his, such as whether she had ever met Warren Reynolds before he'd come over to pack up Blaine's belongings. He learned that she had met Blaine's brother only once in the three years she'd been a tenant, and that had been about six months earlier.

Joplin also learned, without having to ask, that Mrs. Marlow hadn't been impressed by Warren, nor did she think that Blaine had been happy to see him. He had shown up at her door around six p.m. on a Friday, in *jogging* shorts, without *calling first*, which seemed to bother Blaine *no end*, she told him. She knew this because Blaine had cut short her visit with her, apologizing as she ushered Mrs. Marlow out the door. Afterwards, as Mrs. Marlow was walking back to her house—evidently very slowly, Joplin was sure—she'd heard Blaine asking just what the hell Warren thought he was doing, showing up like that.

"He didn't really have a good answer," Mrs. Marlow said. "Just stammered out that he was in town, staying at the Buckhead Ritz, and decided to go for a run before he met some clients for dinner and drinks. He even asked Blaine if she wanted to join them, but she wasn't having any of *that*," she added, her voice lowered conspiratorially. "No, sir. She told him flat out that she didn't want to meet, much less have *dinner* with, anybody from the NRA, which I think was pretty narrow-minded, if you catch my drift. I mean, Fox News says they're just trying to protect our Second Amendment rights, you know."

"I know," Joplin said, nodding solemnly.

"I loved Blaine like a daughter," Mrs. Marlow said. "But she had some pretty way-out ideas, if you know what I mean." When Joplin nodded again, she said, "Like thinking Obama was one of our *best presidents*! Yes! She even said that to me! Of course, her *fiancé* was black. I about *fainted* when I met him, but I didn't let her know how I felt about it. I mean, to each his own, but I figured it wouldn't last."

"Why not?" Joplin asked, encouraging her.

"Well, I don't know," Mrs. Marlow said, looking around, as if the answer might appear on a tree or the side of his car. They were standing at her front door. "I just thought that maybe…I don't know. That maybe her *family* would get her to come to her senses. I mean, they're so *prominent*. I see General Reynolds on Fox News all the time!"

"How did Blaine come to rent the carriage house?" Joplin asked, suddenly curious about that.

"Oh, through a friend of a friend who knew I had decided to rent it out," said Mrs. Marlow airily. "I really didn't want to after John died—John was my husband," she added. "But everyone said I should, because it meant that someone else would be around at night. In case anything happened."

Before Joplin could help himself, he said, "What did you think might happen?"

"Well, you know—somebody might try to break into my house. There's a lot of crime around here since they put in that MARTA station right around the corner on Peachtree. Or I might have fallen and broken my hip. Of course, it would have been better if I'd rented to a man, but then Blaine asked to see the carriage house and absolutely fell in love with it, so it seemed like it was meant to be. Although it turned out that I was the one who helped *her* when she needed it. Like with Banshee or when she had problems with her diabetes. How is Banshee, by the way?"

"She's doing great. My fiancée loves her, and Quincy has accepted her better than I thought he would. He's used to being an only cat."

"Well, that's grand! It eases my mind a lot to know she's happy."

"I think she is," said Joplin. "By the way, Blaine's co-workers have told me that she seemed sort of stressed out a week or so before she died. Did she talk to you about that? Tell you about any problems she was having? Sounds like she felt pretty close to you," he added, hoping that might encourage her to prove that to him.

Mrs. Marlow seemed to think about this a little, then said, "Well, I can't be sure, but I think she was upset with him," she said. "Winston Avery. She seemed a little down, but when I asked if she felt okay, she just said she was fine. But after Blaine fainted that time, I wasn't taking any chances, so I… stayed close by. Checked on her when she was home."

And probably listened outside a window or her front door, Joplin thought. "So did you find out anything?" was all he said.

"Well," she said, raising her eyebrows and drawing the word out. "One time when I happened to be outside—gardening," she added quickly—"I overheard her saying in a very loud voice, 'We have to talk about this! We can't go on like this!' She was really upset. And then I heard her say his name a few times—you know, 'Winston! Winston!'—like maybe he'd hung up on her. But I never found out what it was all about."

Not for lack of trying, I'm sure, Joplin thought. Then he turned, hearing a car in the driveway. He held up the key Mrs. Marlow had given him, then gestured toward the CSU van. "Guess I'd better get going. I'll get this back to you as soon as we're finished. And thanks again," he added. "For letting us into the carriage house and for telling me about what you accidently overheard. It might be important."

She beamed at him. "You're so welcome. I want to do anything I can to help you find out who killed Blaine."

———

Joplin walked Marty Raeford and Bobby Dilling to the carriage house, going over what and where he wanted them to dust for prints. He'd already explained to Marty that he was hoping to get Warren Reynolds' prints, if possible, as well as anyone else's who might have gone into the property after it had been released by APD. Mrs. Marlow told him she'd never had a chance to have her housekeeper to clean up after Blaine's furniture and other belongings had been taken by the moving company Warren Reynolds had hired, which was a piece of luck. He'd also asked the two forensic techs clean up after themselves, since she'd been kind enough to let them in without a warrant.

"Sure thing, Hollis," Marty said. "If I don't get a hit, do you want me to get into the military databases again to see if he's there? His daddy being a Marine Corps general and all, he probably wanted him to serve at some point."

"Good idea, Marty," Joplin said, opening the door. "I'm going to hang around, get the key back to Mrs. Marlow, but I'll wait in my car and make some phone calls. Let me know when you're through."

CHAPTER THIRTY-THREE

"He's guilty," Halloran said to Maggie as they had a glass of wine after din-ner. "That's why he didn't want to put his daughter through testifying, and that's why he gave up his parental rights. And that's also why he didn't want to hear about any new evidence Cate and I might have found. It all comes down to Occam's Razor, in the end."

"The simplest solution is the best one?" Maggie asked.

"That's what *most* people think," he said. "But it's really just a problem-solving principle that advises you to choose a solution with the fewest assumptions when you're dealing with competing hypotheses. That's because a simpler solution is more easily tested, but it doesn't rule out other possibilities."

"Then you admit that there *are* other reasons for Will's actions?"

"Sure. One, he's protecting someone. Or, two, if his conviction gets overturned—whether he's guilty or not—he doesn't want his daughter to get her hopes up, and he *still* doesn't want her to testify, because it would be traumatic. But neither one of these other possibilities makes any sense. If he actually knows who killed his wife, why wouldn't he tell the police, so Jayla wouldn't be put through what she's experienced the entire last year? And why wouldn't he let her testify? Weren't his life and being with his child more important than protecting a killer? As for the second possibility, Jayla already has her hopes up, and she's older now and more *able* to testify at a new trial. But, besides not letting Jayla testify, there's also another reason I think Will Henry is guilty: Damon didn't put him on the stand."

"A lot of lawyers don't do that, Tom. You've told me that's a really risky thing to do."

"Yes, but in this case, if Will Henry is innocent, it would have been a chance for him to tell the jury his side of the story. In fact, it was almost necessary after all the damning evidence the prosecution was able to introduce. But if Damon thought his client was guilty, he couldn't let him get on the stand and tell lies. It's called—"

"Suborning perjury," Maggie finished.

"Exactly."

Maggie seemed to consider this as she took a long sip of her wine. But then she shook her head and said, "I think you're wrong. I don't think it's any of those possibilities, especially that he's guilty. Occam's Razor be damned."

"You know, you and Hollis are so much alike when it comes to gut feelings, Maggie, my dear," Halloran said, smiling at her. "And once you get something in your head, you don't let go."

"Those 'gut feelings' are based on keen observation, Tom, not just some kind of emotional reaction. Speaking of which," she added, as she stood up, "I want you to look at something."

She was gone for a few minutes, returning with some photos, which she handed to him. "These are three photos from the Blaine Reynolds case, taken by Hollis, the Crime Scene Unit, and the person who sent Hollis the photos before he even *went* to the crime scene. Tell me what you see. Or, more importantly, what you *don't* see."

Halloran spread the photos out on the coffee table and studied each one carefully. Then he studied them all again. Finally, he shook his head, bewildered. "Other than a slight difference in angles, I don't see any difference in them."

Maggie smiled triumphantly. "This is just one of the things I saw when I looked over all the crime scene photos shot at Blaine's house. There are others, but I need time to process everything." She stabbed a finger at the second and third set of photos. "See the camera there, on the countertop next to the refrigerator?"

"Yes," said Halloran, still bewildered.

"It's not there in the first photo, which was among the set of photos sent to Hollis that morning, before he got the call to go to the crime scene."

Halloran looked at the first photo, then the other two, then at Maggie, the importance finally dawning on him. "The killer used Blaine's camera to take the photos he sent to Hollis. Which means the decision to do that and bring Hollis into the whole thing, might not have been premeditated. And maybe the murder wasn't either."

———

"Carrie says you need time to look over the crime scene photos a little longer, but I thought I'd see if there's anything you can tell me right away, Maggie," Joplin said. He had the day shift that Wednesday, but had waited until ten a.m. to call Maggie. It was either that or bug Marty again at CSU.

"Well, I wanted to be able to give you everything at once, but since I've already talked to Tom about this, I may as well tell you, too, Hollis." Joplin listened as she told him about the camera that was present in Blaine's kitchen in the photos he and CSU had taken, but not the ones sent to him. "I can't believe I didn't notice that myself," he said. "I guess I'm losing my eidetic memory."

"Didn't you tell me once that it doesn't help you with remembering dreams, only actual events and conversations? Maybe it's the same thing with photos."

"Maybe so. But I'm glad we have your photographer's eye."

"Do you agree with Tom that it might mean that the killer didn't plan on taking those photos and sending them to you until he saw the camera? Or that even the murder itself might not have been premeditated?"

"I agree more with the first possibility than the second. It's more likely that the decision to kill Blaine was premeditated, but seeing the camera gave him—or her—the idea to photograph the crime scene. The reason for sending them to me is still the biggest unknown."

"Well, I'll keep examining the copies of the photos I brought home with me and see if I can find anything else."

"Thanks, Maggie. I think what you've found already is important. I just don't know why yet."

"I'm happy to do it," she said. "Especially since it looks like the Daisy Henry case is going nowhere. Damon Copeland asked for the trial transcript back and said Will doesn't want Tom involved with the appeal or to reinvestigate the case itself. Now Tom's decided Will is guilty and he's pretty much washed his hands of the whole thing."

Joplin gave a long sigh. "Well, he's probably right, although I hate to think of that little girl waiting for her father to get out of prison and come get her."

"I do, too, Hollis. It's what started me down this path, but it looks like it's not leading anywhere."

———

Joplin headed for Sarah's office as soon as he got off the phone with Maggie. The door was open, and Sarah, dressed in a black pantsuit and a crisp white shirt, was studying something intently on the screen of her computer. She looked up and smiled at him when he knocked discreetly on the door jamb.

"I hear you and Carrie are going to the Ritz this weekend," she said. "Great idea."

"Word travels fast around here," Joplin said, but he smiled back at her.

"I'm glad you approve, because I need to take a vacation day on Sunday. I'm already off on Saturday."

"I think we can spare you. Anything new on the Reynolds case?"

Joplin told her about Maggie's discovery, and they discussed Tom Halloran's theory that the murder might not have been premeditated. Then he said, "Talking about those photos reminded me that Ike thought it would be a good idea to find out how the killer seemed to know that I would be here when they were delivered. Any luck with that?"

She brushed some hair off her forehead and said, "I wish. The monthly schedule is sent out to everyone here, even the autopsy techs and the secretaries. It's also sent to the various police departments, so they can call whoever's on duty directly during the evening and graveyard shifts when a death is reported. That means a lot of people would have had access to it, Hollis."

"But that seems to rule out any of the people we've been looking at who might have murdered Blaine," Joplin said. "Even the people who knew Blaine and I used to date for a while. How would any of them be able to access the schedule?"

She shrugged. "I don't know, unless one of them is an IT wizard or best friends with a hacker. But the killer would have had to know ahead of time that you'd be here Saturday morning or there wouldn't have been any point in taking the photos in the first place, and that, of course, *does* mean premeditation. But it still doesn't explain *why* he sent them to you."

"Now you're making me feel very paranoid, Chief."

"Why is that?"

"Think about it: Who are the people who would either know or have access to the Investigative Unit's shift schedule *and* know that I used to date Blaine Reynolds. Forget motive for right now."

He could see the realization hit Sarah Petersen as her expression changed from puzzled to dismayed, maybe even horrified. "Everyone who works in this office," she said slowly. "And at least a few homicide detectives at APD, since Ike Simmons knew."

"Yeah, and because of Jack Tyndall, I don't have the luxury anymore of not suspecting my friends and co-workers."

CHAPTER THIRTY-FOUR

Joplin was no sooner back in his cubicle when his phone rang.

"I think I've got something for you, Hollis," said B. J. Reardon, the head of CSU.

"That might improve my day, B. J. Lay it on me. Did Marty and Bobby find some good prints at the Reynolds' crime scene?"

"Marty's processing them now, but that's not why I called. It's about some evidence we found on the victim's clothes. Human tears, to be exact. On the jacket she was wearing. "

"Does this mean you were able to get some DNA?" Joplin asked excitedly.

"Unfortunately, no," B. J. said in his usual formal manner. "There are no cells in human tears. Unless, of course, the person has dry eye disease. Then some cells are present."

"But not in these tears, I take it."

"Again, unfortunately, no. But we were able to determine that the tears were psychic in nature, which might point you in the right direction, in terms of suspects."

"Tears can be 'psychic?' You mean, like, have ESP or something?"

B. J. Reardon made a noise that passed for laughter and said, "Good one, Hollis. No, in this case, 'psychic' means emotional or weeping tears. There are three types of tears; basal, which lubricate the eye; reflex, which occur when the eye is irritated by something like an onion or tear gas; and psychic, which stem from high emotional stress. That can cover a lot of emotions, including happiness, but, under the circumstances, I would think more negative emotions, like anger or sadness, were involved."

"And you could tell all this from some tear stains?"

"Well, it'll be up to you and Ike Simmons to determine what *kind* of emotion was involved, but we could differentiate these tear stains from basal or reflex stains due to their chemical components. Psychic tears have more protein-based hormones, like prolactin, adrenocorticotropic hormone, and Leu-enkaphalin, than the other types."

"Well, thanks, B. J.," Joplin said. "I think. And you said Marty is processing some good prints?"

"As we speak. I'll make sure he calls you when, and if, he gets some hits."

"I appreciate that, B. J."

"Not at all, Hollis."

Joplin slowly replaced the phone in its stand as he thought about what Reardon had told him. It wasn't much, but it did seem to support the profiling theory that manual strangulation implied a very personal connection between killer and victim. The person who killed Blaine was in the grip of an extremely strong emotion. The obvious one would be anger, but then why would he—or she, he reminded himself—be weeping?

An overwhelming image of Winston Avery, his powerful hands around Blaine's neck, his face streaked with tears, surged through his brain. The conflicting emotions of love and hate, as well as anger and sadness, played across his face. With his question about whether Joplin had known about Blaine's pregnancy, Avery had suggested that he thought he and Blaine were cheating on him. That was no justification for strangling Blaine, but it certainly was a motive for photographing her after he'd killed her and then sending those photos to Joplin. In fact, it made perfect sense—or, from Tom Halloran's perspective, it was logical.

Joplin's phone rang again, pulling him away from the logic of it all.

"You're gonna like this, Hollis!" said an excited voice.

"I hope that's you, Marty and not some perv trying to get his jollies," Joplin said.

"You're a laugh a minute, Hollis," Marty retorted. "I got some good prints. Most of them belong to Warren Reynolds, some to the movers, we figure, but some also belong to the landlady."

"Mrs. Marlow?"

"If that's what she's calling herself these days. And Warren Reynolds was in the Army and sent to Iraq the same time as Sgt. James Corcoran. But he's also got a record. I had to get it on a state-by-state basis since it involved misdemeanors, but he's had at least two arrests for DWI, involving drugs, in Nevada. I talked to someone in the Las Vegas PD, and he told me the arrests just 'disappeared,' probably because of the General's influence. He also said Warren was 'quite the player' at the casinos and racked up a lot of debt, which was always paid off."

"Wow! I *do* like this. Though it kind of blows my mind to think that a brother might kill his own sister."

"You mean you never saw any of the *Halloween* movies or *The Amityville Horror?*"

"'Movies' is the key word here, Marty. Not real life."

"Yeah, but *The Amityville Horror* was based on a real story, Hollis. Ronald De Feo was convicted of killing his entire family. And don't forget about all the women in the Middle East who've been murdered by family members— often brothers—for causing dishonor to them by marrying the wrong men."

"Have you been talking to my boss, Marty?" Joplin asked.

"What?"

"Nothing. So, what did you find out about Mrs. Marlow? Blaine's landlady."

"Well, for starters, she was born Aline Louise Norton in Darien, Georgia, in 1942. And in 1995, her second husband, John Murphy, died under quote, suspicious circumstances, unquote. He drowned in their swimming pool, even though he was said to be an excellent swimmer by family members, who weren't buying the widow's story. He left her pretty well-fixed, but the authorities could never pin anything on her. The only reason I was able to find her in the system is because Roswell PD got everyone's prints on record to rule out an intruder."

"What about the first husband?" Joplin asked. "He still alive?"

"Nope. His name was Donald Walters. He died in 1975, of heart failure. But that could mean anything, especially if a coroner or the family doctor filled out the death certificate. She married John Murphy five years later, in June of 1980."

"Well, she mentioned her first husband's name was 'John,' but where does the 'Marlow' come from?"

"No idea. There's no record of her marrying after her second husband died."

"Okay, Marty, this is good stuff. Thanks." Joplin had known Mrs. Marlow didn't always tell the truth when she'd said that Preston Stevens had been the architect for her house. He was very familiar with Stevens' work, and 1452 West Brookhaven wasn't an example of it. At the time, Joplin had thought she was just making her house—and herself—seem more important. But the possibility that she had a checkered past hadn't occurred to him.

"No problem, Hollis. Let me know if you need anything else."

But the only thing Joplin needed right then was for his head to clear. Since he'd gotten to the ME's office, his brain had been overloaded, beginning with Maggie Halloran's information about the digital camera, moving on to B. J.'s revelations about the tears found on Blaine's clothes, then Marty's discovery that Warren Reynolds had been in the Army, had perhaps known James Corcoran and had also at one time had a substance abuse and gambling problem. And then the stunning news that Mrs. Marlow might have killed a husband or two.

At least two people could have had the opportunity to kill Blaine, Joplin knew now, since Mrs. Marlow had admitted to being at home when Blaine returned that evening, and Warren Reynolds could have walked—or run—there from the Buckhead Ritz, as he'd done once before. As for motive, maybe Blaine had learned about her landlady's husbands' suspicious deaths or discovered that her brother had a new arrest or conviction that the General didn't know about. He couldn't see Blaine as a blackmailer—she was too straight-forward for that—but she might have confronted one or both of them and gotten killed for it. Why Mrs. Marlow would be crying as she strangled Blaine, however, made no sense. And she didn't seem to have a reason for wanting to involve him in the investigation. At least, no apparent one. But, for that matter, Warren Reynolds also didn't have one.

And neither one of them, Joplin realized, would have known that he'd be at the ME's office the next morning, or have had access to the monthly schedule for the Investigative Unit.

Joplin had come around full-circle to the uncomfortable—no, devastating, really—possibility that someone he knew, probably someone with whom he worked, had hated him enough to drag him into the investigation of Blaine's murder.

If so, it would mean that lightning had struck twice in the same place.

Before Elliot Carter's death, and everything that happened afterwards, Joplin would never have believed that someone he saw almost every day, who was also a close friend, could betray him. More than that, could try to kill him. He had known Jack Tyndall even before he started at the ME's office, and they'd become friends within a few weeks after Lewis Minton hired Joplin as a death investigator. Although they were very different—Jack was already on his third wife and quite the womanizer—Joplin had thought of him as the brother he'd never had. He and Ike had a friendship forged by their relationship as partners, from years of watching each other's backs and constantly dealing with the unrelenting bureaucracy of law enforcement. There was nothing he couldn't tell Ike Simmons, or do for him, and he knew Ike felt the same way.

With Jack, Joplin had experienced—or thought he had—a friendship based on a common, small-town, somewhat narrow-minded upbringing that had pushed both of them to expand their horizons. But Joplin had never known the real Jack Tyndall.

And Jack Tyndall had not even been his real name.

The man who'd almost killed him a year and a half ago had been a sociopath whose addict mother had given him to her dealer to pay off her debts. But to this day, Joplin didn't even know if *that* story were true. He had believed in his gut, in his ability to know, or at least *sense*, when someone was telling him the truth or just plain bullshitting him. Joplin still felt on solid ground with Ike Simmons, who had saved his life the night Jack had tried to end it. And he'd returned the favor six months later, in the basement of a house in Sandy Springs where Ike and two FBI agents—and Carrie, as well—were being held captive by someone else whose childhood had also been a living hell.

But finding out that his second-best friend had been lying to him during the entire time he'd known him had made Joplin doubt everything he'd thought to be true, for several months after the Carter case. Ike and Carrie and Maggie—even Tom Halloran, for that matter—had helped him see that he could still trust his own judgement where most people were concerned. So had Sarah Petersen.

"Not everyone is a sociopath, Hollis," she'd said to him before he'd walked out of her office a little while ago. "Try to remember that."

"I know," he'd said, mustering up a smile. "But they're so good at hiding in plain sight among all of the rest of us."

Whom did he know, Joplin wondered, who might be hiding in plain sight *now*?

CHAPTER THIRTY-FIVE

On Thursday morning, Winston Avery sat and stared at the black and white kimono hanging on the wall over the bar in his condominium, drinking coffee and trying to decide whether to go to Blaine's funeral. He knew her parents wouldn't want him there, her father especially. Nina Reynolds had been warm and welcoming to him when they'd all met for dinner at The Palm several months ago. The dinner had been his idea, at what Blaine had said was her father's favorite restaurant whenever they came to Atlanta. But Sanford Reynolds had been displeased when the manager and the maitre'd had paid more attention to his daughter's new fiancé than to him. He had quickly found fault with the table given to them, then the server, who was not the one the General always requested.

"San, we're here to celebrate Blaine and Winston's engagement," Nina had said, her hand on her husband's arm. "And we're Winston's guests."

"Then he should have gotten a better table," the General had said.

"Dad—"

"They know me very well here, sir, so I'm sure we can get any table you'd like," Avery had said, smiling at him in what he'd known was a very patronizing way.

They'd stared at each other for several seconds, then General Reynolds had smiled back at him. "I don't think the ladies would like that, *son*," he'd said, making it obvious that he'd meant "boy."

"Good, because I'm starving," Nina Reynolds had said, opening her menu.

Later, he and Blaine had laughed about the whole thing, even though she'd been angry at her father.

"But you put him in his place," she'd said, turning to look at him as they'd sat out on his balcony after they'd Ubered her parents back to the Ritz.

"Not without a price, I'm sure," Avery had said, and knew that price would be exacted if he tried to go to Blaine's funeral. If he'd been her husband, he would have been the one planning her funeral. But he hadn't been her husband, and he was also a prime suspect in her murder. The bottom line, however, was that, suspect or not, he wouldn't be allowed to attend the funeral, not if General Reynolds had anything to say about it. Avery had gotten his hopes up on Monday when Nina Reynolds had called him, but it had simply been a courtesy call to tell him that she was returning Blaine's engagement ring to him by courier. When he'd asked that Blaine be buried with it, she had said she was sorry, but that wouldn't be possible, "under the circumstances." Her last words to him, though, urged him to take care of himself.

With a sigh, he picked up his cell phone and tapped the contact number for Buckhead Flowers. Luckily, Jeannette, who usually handled his flower orders, answered, and Avery asked her to use the best florist she could find in the D.C. area. He placed an order for an arrangement of white chrysanthemums in a large crystal vase to be delivered to the funeral home given in Blaine's obituary, which he'd found online. He asked that no note be sent with it, which probably surprised Jeanette. He didn't want to take any chances, in case the General might decide not to allow even his flowers at Blaine's funeral.

This accomplished, Avery sat back against the couch cushions and once again stared at the kimono. Doing this had been a form of meditation for him since he'd brought it home with him from Japan. His grandmother had died not long after his graduation from law school, leaving him a life insurance policy of $100,000. He had been speechless, then sightless, as the tears poured down his face. According to the attorney, who'd looked a little teary himself, "Miz Mary" had been paying twenty dollars a month on it for almost eighteen years.

It had been her last gift to him, after a lifetime of gifts. And love. He used $5,000 of it to go to Japan during the two weeks he had free before he would start his job as an associate with Grady and Berryman in Atlanta. It had been the first time he'd ever been out of the country, and he wanted to get as far away from the States, both literally and figuratively, as he could. When he'd landed in Tokyo, unable to speak a single word of Japanese, he'd hired a driver/translator highly recommended by his hotel's concierge named Haruto Takata. Haruto had driven him all around Tokyo, as well as Kyoto and Yokohama on side trips.

The days had flown by, filled with glimpses of a culture that was so unlike his own that he had thought seriously of chucking it all—the new job and apartment waiting for him in Atlanta, the girlfriend in Richmond thinking of moving in with him—and staying in Japan. He had loved the aesthetic importance that its people placed on everything around them—food, flowers, clothing, landscapes—as well as their devotion to art and music and nature. But what had fascinated Avery most was the way in which they interacted with each other. The exquisite politeness and deference shown to each other was more alien to him than anything else he'd seen. But when he had expressed his wonder and even admiration of this several days into the trip, Haruto had surprised him with his response.

"Japanese people are, as you said, very polite," he had said, smiling. "We have to be, in a country so small, yet so crowded. We are trained from birth that society as a whole is more important than any individual, and respect for others is what keeps our society functioning. But everything is based on status and power. When two Japanese people who don't know each other talk, they start out using a very formal way of speaking. Once it becomes apparent who has the higher position, tone and inflection change accordingly. It's a way of maintaining order and balance in our world."

Even now, as he sat looking at the kimono, bought in Kyoto as a gift for his girlfriend, Avery remembered that conversation as a sort of epiphany for him. Instead of giving the kimono to the girlfriend, he had brought it with him to Atlanta and hung it on the wall of the living room in his first apartment there. He'd taken it with him wherever he'd moved, making it the first thing to be hung on the most visible wall in his home. It was to remind him that he would never again allow anyone to size him up as anything but a strong, powerful man in a society that placed little or no value upon black people. He knew that most people saw him as arrogant and overly dominant; he had never cared about that. The few people to whom he was close had seen a different side of him over the years, but he knew whatever friendship or loyalty he had counted on from them would probably come to an end soon.

Winston Avery had never been one to feel sorry for himself. Despite whatever discrimination and difficulties he'd experienced in his life, he knew that he'd also been extremely fortunate. Most of that good fortune had come from his own hard work; the rest had come from the love given to him by two extraordinary women. But he felt utterly and completely alone now. He had abandoned the religion of his childhood, instilled in him by his grandmother, yet he wished with all his heart that he could turn to a merciful and forgiving God for comfort.

Avery closed his eyes and tried to summon that long-lost God. Minutes passed, but he felt nothing, and when he opened his eyes, the kimono hanging on the wall, that had always inspired him, looked like a shroud. His shroud. His eyes shifted to the aikuchi daggar on the bar. He longed for the day that he could use it to put himself out of his misery, and perhaps redeem himself in the eyes of whatever god accepted a life for a life these days. But not yet. Not yet.

Not until Hollis Joplin was dead.

CHAPTER THIRTY-SIX

"I can't believe this!" Cate Caldwell said after the server had brought their food.

They had met for lunch at Murphy's in Virginia Highland, since it was close to the Emory campus, due to Cate's class schedule. Halloran had decided to wait and tell her in person about Damon Copeland's phone call on Tuesday, and she seemed to be as mystified as he had been. He nodded as he took a bite of his chicken pesto burger.

"It's not making Will look innocent, as far as I'm concerned," Halloran said, after wiping his mouth. He went on to give her the same reasons he'd given Maggie the night before, as well as Maggie's opinion about Will Henry's guilt.

Cate took a bite of her seafood salad as she considered what he'd told her. She was wearing a long, open sweater over black jeans, with a woolen scarf wound around her neck; the weather had turned more seasonably cold in the past few days. "I understand why you feel that way," she said, "and if I didn't know Will, I would agree with you. Just as I understand why you consider Winston Avery to be a prime suspect in Blaine Reynold's death. But like Maggie, I can't believe that Will is capable of killing Daisy and leaving Jayla to find her body. I also can't believe that Winston would kill Blaine, for whatever reason—jealousy, possessiveness—the reasons you and this Hollis Joplin are giving as motives."

Halloran smiled, trying not to look arrogant or condescending. And the memory of his own disbelief that a close friend such as Elliot Carter could have been guilty of any kind of heinous act urged him to be open to what Cate was saying. But the reality that Hollis Joplin had been completely wrong about *his* close friend, when it came to murder, came to mind. Besides, Cate hadn't known Will Henry all that well. Her relationship with Winston Avery, however, seemed to be much closer. It suddenly occurred to him to wonder *how* close.

"Have you seen Winston lately?" he asked.

"No, but I…I called him," she said hesitantly. "Just to let him know I was thinking of him."

"How did he seem?"

"Pretty depressed. Can you blame him?"

"No, of course not, Cate. I can't even imagine what he's going through. Do you think he'd talk to me? Maybe give me his opinion as to why Will Henry doesn't want to know what new evidence we've turned up? I have no intention of asking him anything about Blaine, I promise. But part of me still wants to believe that Will might be innocent."

Cate took a deep breath, then let it out. She was obviously stressed out at the thought of even broaching such a thing with Avery. But she said, "Let me think about it, okay, Tom?"

"Of course. There's no rush. I'm not even involved with the case anymore. I'm sorry I even brought it up, Cate. You've got enough going on anyway. Aren't exams coming up soon?"

"Right after the Thanksgiving break. Then I've got the whole month of December off, thank God."

"Well, as I recall, the last semester of law school is pretty low-key."

"Yeah, mainly the ethics and professionalism seminars. Nothing important, right?"

"I'm sorry, I didn't mean—"

Cate smiled at him. "It's okay, Tom. You're one of the most ethical attorneys I know—after my grandfather, of course. But I'm also on law review, remember? So I don't really get to relax much next semester. And I have to work on the article I'm editing over the Christmas break."

"Really? What's the subject?"

"Same-sex marriage. *United States v. Windsor* and the substantive due process issue, to be exact. It's a great article."

"I bet it is. I'll look forward to reading it."

They chatted some more while finishing lunch, then Cate looked at her watch. "I've got to get to my next class, Tom, but let me split the bill with you."

"Not a chance. Just get back to me about meeting with Winston Avery, if you decide to ask him."

"I will. Don't get up," she added as she stood up and blew him a kiss. "I need to run, but I enjoyed it. Thanks, Tom."

Halloran watched Cate walk quickly away, then motioned for the check. He paid it and wandered into the wine shop. He'd promised Maggie to get the wine for Thanksgiving, and Murphy's always had a wonderful selection. He bought two bottles of Billecarte-Salmon Blanc de Blanc to toast the holiday, as well as two each of a nice Vine Cliff Chardonnay and an Altesino Brunello Riserva. Maggie was doing her famous Turducken, which involved putting a deboned chicken into a deboned duck, then into a deboned turkey and filling it with a sausage stuffing. The variety of wines should make everybody happy, he decided. And there was always Jameson and port for after dinner.

He walked back to his car, thinking of his appointment at three that afternoon with Mason Andrews, opposing attorney in the Sullivan case. He was fairly certain Andrews wanted to talk about a settlement, given his client's disastrous deposition. Halloran's clients, Brian Sullivan and Eileen Sullivan Mayhew, were suing their brother for taking advantage of their mother's advanced dementia to loot her bank accounts and get her to turn over an expensive piece of property to him. In the past few weeks, Halloran had deposed the woman's doctors, caretakers, and financial advisor, as well as Brian and Eileen, all of whom painted a pretty damning picture of Neil's greed and Mrs. Sullivan's incapacity to know what he gave her to sign. And at Neil's own deposition, two days earlier, he'd lied repeatedly about things that Halloran could use to impeach his testimony at trial. Andrews had called him that morning for a meeting to "get this whole thing resolved," and he was looking forward to it.

Halloran truly enjoyed his work, despite the fact that it frequently exposed him to the greed and mendacity of a lot of people. But he especially enjoyed the opportunity to confront those people in a court of law and get justice for their victims. He knew he had a reputation as a litigator who represented the young widows of much older, wealthy men, but those were the cases that got the most publicity. The Sullivan case was under the media's radar, but he would take great pleasure in negotiating a settlement that would give his clients some peace of mind. He might not be able to recover all the money Neil had been able to get his hands on, but he could make sure the property went back into his mother's name and have someone else be given power of attorney over her finances and medical decisions.

As he headed downtown to his office, however, Halloran's thoughts turned to a little girl waiting for her father to get out of prison. He hadn't been able to do anything to help *her*, and it didn't look like he'd able to in the future, unless Will Henry had a change of heart.

CHAPTER THIRTY-SEVEN

Maggie sat at the conference table at the Milton County ME's office and shuffled through the three sets of crime scene photos one more time, making sure she'd gleaned every bit of information from them that she could. She had called Hollis around eleven a.m. to ask if she could get access to the original photos again, and he'd readily agreed. What little she had wasn't going to do him much good with regard to finding Blaine's killer, but if he and Ike Simmons zeroed in on a prime suspect, it might add to the evidence against him. Or her, she reminded herself. Finally satisfied that she could add nothing more to what she could tell Hollis, she grabbed her cell phone and called him, asking if he could join her.

He was there in less than a minute. "I sure hope you've found something more in those photos, Maggie," he said, sitting down next to her.

"Well, not as important as discovering that the digital camera was missing in the set of photos sent to you, but I hope my observations might be of some help."

"They always are, Maggie."

"Thanks, Hollis. But first, tell me if it will upset you to look at all the photographs again. I can just tell you my findings without having to show you."

"I appreciate your asking, but nothing's as bad as actually *seeing* Blaine dead. And I've been through all three sets a few times anyway. Besides, if it helps find her killer, I'd do it several more times."

"Okay, then. Here goes: I looked specifically for differences between the photos sent to you and the ones you took when you were called to the scene." She pointed to the first and second stack of photos on the conference table. "A global comparison of the two sets shows differences in the number of photos taken and perspective, as well as distance from the camera to Blaine's body. And from that I can analyze, to a certain extent, intent and emotion."

Hollis give a long sigh. "I'll take your word for that, Maggie. I just see images when I look at photos."

"Then I'll try to keep this simple. Let's take your photos first. Your intent, given the number and type of photos, was to capture the important elements of the scene from a forensic perspective. You took twelve photos, and they contain what you wanted the pathologist who'd be doing the autopsy to see. Most of them are very objective, especially the first five, which I'm assuming you shot when you first got there." Maggie picked up the second stack and laid out the first five photos side by side. "See, you took some shots from what I assume is the door into the kitchen to show the body's placement, which also show the counter where the camera should have been. Then a couple that were just of the body itself, including one that showed the back of Blaine's head and shoulders, with her hands on either side. But there's still a lot of distance between the camera and the body."

"Well, that's because I was preserving the scene for the pathologist, showing what I saw when I first got there."

"Of course," Maggie said, nodding. Then she scooped up the five photos and dealt out the final seven. "But look at these, taken after you realized that it was Blaine. There's a huge change in both the distance from the camera and the perspective—the emphasis you're placing on a particular object being photographed. And that's where intent and emotion come into play. And where the photos become more subjective."

Hollis blinked several times and rubbed his chin. "And you can tell this… how? I mean, I'm not disputing what you're telling me, but I need more information. How are you able to compute the distance from the camera to the…body, for example?"

"I can tell you, but then I'd have to kill you, Hollis, because it's a trade secret." Maggie was gratified when he laughed and shook his head. "No, really," she said. "It's a lot of photographer-speak, involving the number of pixels between objects and the camera lens, and something called 'depth of frame.'"

"Oh, God, no! Not pixels again!"

"Yep. Your eyes glazed over when I explained about pixels after you asked me to look at those photos during the Carter case, remember?"

"I'll never forget," Hollis said, still smiling. "So skip the explanation. I'll take your word for it."

"I appreciate that. Okay, next, you took a close-up of Blaine's left profile, with her hair moved to one side," Maggie went on, tapping the sixth photo. "That was right after you realized that it was her, right?"

"Right. I mean, Ike and I talked about it for a few minutes; he remembered who she was. That I had gone out with her for a few months. And I guess I was in a state of shock, but then he left the kitchen, and I…I took that photo."

"Would you have taken a shot like that if you hadn't known the victim, Hollis?"

He didn't answer right away, as if he were thinking about it. Then he said, "No, I guess not. I would have had Ike help me turn the body over, so I could take a full-face photo. But I didn't want to touch her again. Not right away, I mean. Her skin had felt so cold when I brushed her hair away from her face. And I kept having flashbacks of times we'd spent together. So I bent over her and took that photo, and then I gave myself a few minutes before I turned her over."

Maggie pointed to the seventh photo. "And then you stood up and backed away and took a full-length shot of her, right? As if you were putting some distance between yourself and the body."

Hollis took a deep breath. "Yes, I guess you could say that now."

She directed his line of vision to the five remaining photos. "And then you got angry, and snapped four shots just of Blaine's face and her neck, to show what someone did to her. How that person had taken a beautiful, living person and squeezed the life out of her. Made her face look ghastly, like something out of a horror movie. And then you took a picture of her bare feet. To show how vulnerable she was. How defenseless."

Hollis took a deep breath, let it out. "Yes. Jesus, Maggie, this is harder than I thought it would be."

"I know. And I hated to put you through that, but in order to show you what Blaine's killer was trying to do when he or she took the first set of photos, I needed to demonstrate that I could analyze the photos that *you* took. Does that make sense?"

"Yes, it does," he said, nodding. "So tell me what you see in that set."

Maggie moved Hollis' photos to the side. "There are only seven in this set," she said, laying them out on the table. "When you first saw them, you didn't know what you were looking at—or whom. The photographer starts with the front door, leading you through that into an entry hall, then to the kitchen. It's almost like a video, in a way, making you anticipate what you'll see next. And that's the body on the floor. So now you're intrigued, wondering if these are crime scene photos and, if so, who took them? And why were they sent to you? Then there are three shots of Blaine's head and shoulders, showing her hands on either side of her head, but not her face, which is covered by her hair." She paused and looked at Hollis, to see how he was handling this. "You okay?"

He nodded, his expression grim. "Keep going."

"Okay. Now here's where it gets particularly interesting. Do you see any differences between the three photos?"

She watched as Hollis studied each one carefully. After a few minutes, he started shaking his head, then suddenly stopped and said, "It looks at first as if each photo is the same, but there's a slight shift in the first and third ones."

"Exactly. What kind of shift?"

"In the first one, there's more space between Blaine's left hand and the edge of the photo, but in the third one, it's the opposite. There's more space between her right hand and the edge. Yet in the middle photo, the second one, the hands are equidistant from the edges."

"Yes!" Maggie said. "It's very subtle, but it's definitely a shift in perspective. The photographer was directing the viewer's eye first to Blaine's left hand, then to her right hand. In the shots taken by you and CSU, there's no emphasis on the hands at all."

Hollis turned to look at her. "But, obviously, I wasn't perceptive enough to see what the photographer was emphasizing, Maggie, so what was the point?"

"We might never know that, Hollis, but there's a message there. An expression of something the person who took these photos was feeling. It's saying, 'Look closely at this hand, with the engagement ring on the third finger.' Then the message is, 'Now look at *this* hand, with the simple silver band on it.' So the questions we need to ask are: What ring is that on Blaine's right hand? Has she had it for a long time, or did someone just recently give it to her? Or was it placed on her finger after she was dead?"

CHAPTER THIRTY-EIGHT

Joplin was in luck. Nina Reynolds answered the landline instead of the General. After finding out from Darius Gamal, the ME's office manager, that all of Blaine's personal effects had been released to the family with her body, he had decided to call that number, rather than General Reynold's cell phone.

"I know this is a bad time to be bothering you, Mrs. Reynolds," he said, after identifying himself, "but I need to ask you about a ring that was sent back to you with Blaine's…with Blaine."

"You mean the engagement ring? I've already sent that back to Winston. Mr. Avery."

"No, not that ring. I'm talking about a wide, silver band that she was wearing on her right hand when she was…found." Joplin hadn't realized how difficult it would be to talk to Blaine's mother about this. He wished now that he'd had Sarah Petersen call her. It might have been easier on Nina Reynolds as well.

There was a pause, then she said, "Yes, I remember that now, although I had never seen Blaine wearing it. It must have been something new. Something she bought recently."

"Did Winston Avery ask about it when you talked to him? Maybe he gave that ring to her, too."

"No, it never came up, actually. He asked if Blaine could be…buried with the engagement ring. I had to tell him no, of course, but he never said anything about the other ring. Is it important?"

"It might be. I wish I could explain, and I hate to ask this of you right now, but do you think you could overnight it to me? To the ME's office, I mean."

"Certainly," she said, but she sounded very uncertain, as if the request was the last thing she would have expected.

Which, of course, it was. Even Sarah had questioned the importance of the ring, or rather the slight differences in the three photos of Blaine's upper torso and hands.

"Couldn't that have just been an accident, Hollis?" she'd asked when they'd discussed what Maggie Halloran had seen in the photos.

"I asked her that myself," he'd said. "But she pointed out that there wouldn't have been a reason to take three, almost identical, pictures of the same thing unless the variations were somehow important, and I have to agree with her."

So here he was, bothering Mrs. Reynolds over a lead that might go nowhere, two days before her daughter's funeral. "I appreciate that," Joplin said now to her. "And, again, I really hate to intrude at a time like this."

"I was her *mother*," she said, almost fiercely. "I'm happy to do anything that could help." Joplin heard her take a deep breath. "By the way, San mentioned that you might come up for the funeral. Is that still a possibility?"

"I wish it were, Mrs. Reynolds," he said, feeling guilty that he was going to be spending the weekend at the Ritz-Carlton with Carrie instead of paying his respects to Blaine and her family. When he'd said that, it had been totally impulsive. And totally thoughtless, since he'd known that he would never have been able to explain to Carrie why he'd felt a need to go. Or explain to himself, for that matter.

"I understand," Nina Reynolds said quietly, breaking into his uncomfortable thoughts. "Blaine cared a lot about you, Hollis. I want you to know that.

She told me so. She really regretted that…that the two of you…didn't make a go of it."

He couldn't speak. The silence stretched out too long, and she finally said, "If you'll give me the address, I'll contact UPS right now."

Joplin managed to give her the address, then stammer through some awkward assurances that he would be thinking of her and the General on the day of the funeral, before he finally said goodbye.

———

Maggie picked up the kids from school and listened as they told her about their day on the way home. After getting them each a snack, she settled them at the kitchen table with their homework, then went into the den to call Tom.

"Do you have a minute?" she asked when he answered.

"Sure. What's up?"

"I want to invite Jayla to spend Thanksgiving with us, Tom, but I thought I better run it by you first."

She heard him give a long sigh. "Have you thought that through, Maggie? We got her hopes up about helping her father get out of prison, but I'm off the appeal now, so what can we possibly say to her? The truth—that her father doesn't *want* our help, even if it means he can get his conviction over-turned—isn't something I want to tell her. And I'm not going to lie. That wouldn't do any good."

"I know, I know," Maggie said, near tears. "I've thought of all that, believe me. But I can't bear to think of that child without any family on Thanksgiving. Or Christmas. Or any other day, for that matter! She lost her mother, and now she's been abandoned by everyone who should be there for her. Including us!"

"Maggie! Honey, how in the world can you say that?"

"Because you've given up, Tom. You believe Will Henry is guilty, so you've washed your hands of the whole thing! Don't tell me that isn't true."

She heard him sigh again. "What do you want me to do? I can't insist that Damon Copeland let me help with the appeal, for God's sake! He's been given a directive by his client, and I have to respect that. Not just respect it—abide by it. The Bar Association doesn't look too kindly on attorneys who look like they're poaching clients."

Maggie took a deep breath, knowing she would be asking Tom to do something that might look exactly like "poaching." But she couldn't stop herself. "Then just keep on doing what you've been doing, Tom: Find out who killed Daisy Henry. That's not like trying to stay involved with the appeal, and you don't need Damon Copeland's permission—or Will Henry's either. And if what you find out proves that Will is guilty, then so be it. I won't say another word. But in the meantime, we can have Jayla on Thanksgiving and truthfully tell her that we're trying to help her father."

The silence on the other end was deafening. She held her breath, knowing Tom was considering every angle of what she was proposing, as well as any ramifications.

"Do you even know if the Children's Home will let her come to us that day?" he finally said.

She let her breath out. "No, but I'll find out."

CHAPTER THIRTY-NINE

Sarah Petersen had switched Joplin's shift from that Friday evening to the day shift, so he would have the entire weekend for his and Carrie's "staycation." He got to the ME's Office by 7:50 a.m., but Sherika was already there, so he didn't need to use his key. There was no package from UPS and Nina Reynolds on her desk, however, which disappointed him.

"Don't you ever go home, Sherika?" Joplin asked.

"I won't even bother to answer that, Hollis," she said, giving him one of her looks. Then she smiled and cocked her head to one side. "I hear you and Dr. Salinger are going to the Buckhead Ritz this weekend. Are you celebrating anything special?"

"Yes, getting away from people who know way too much about our personal business," he said. "Word sure travels fast around here."

"It stops when it gets to *me*," Sherika said. "'Cause I heard it right from Dr. Salinger, if you need to know."

"So if she told you about our weekend plans, why don't you call her 'Carrie' instead of 'dr. Salinger?'"

"Wouldn't be right, Hollis, and you know it."

"But you call me 'Hollis,' not 'Investigator Joplin.'"

"Yeah?" she said. "What's your point?"

Joplin stared at her, then said, "No point. No point at all."

———

The package from Nina Reynolds arrived at 8:30. Sherika brought it to his cubicle, handed it to him, then curtsied, a sly smile on her face. "For you, boss," she said, then walked quickly out of the room.

Joplin stared at the empty doorway and smiled. If reincarnation were actually an option, he wanted to come back as one of Sherika's friends, no matter who either one of them was in the next life. The thought made him question why he had never socialized with her outside of the office. It might have been because he was single, and that would have seemed inappropriate. Then again, she'd been a single woman when he'd been a single man, so why hadn't he ever thought of dating her? That might have been inappropriate, too, he decided, but he'd never thought twice about asking Carrie out. He was wondering if the fact that he'd never considered dating Sherika made him a snob or a racist, when his phone rang.

"You get the ring from Nina Reynolds yet?" Ike Simmons asked.

"It just got here. Listen, Ike, did you ever wonder why I never asked Sherika out before I started dating Carrie?"

"What the hell are you talking about, Hollis? You smokin' something I need to know about?"

"Why is that such a strange question?" Joplin protested. "She's a smart, beautiful woman who was right under my nose? Why didn't I ever think about dating her? Am I a closet racist or something?"

He heard Simmons sigh. "If you're askin' something like that, Hollis, it usually means you're not. As for why you never thought to ask Sherika out, I have no idea. But, I know for a fact that Sherika would never have gone out with you if you *had* asked her."

"Why not?" Joplin asked, his ego ruffled.

"Because she's too smart to make the mistake of dating someone she works with."

"You mean, like Carrie and me? As I recall, you encouraged me to ask Carrie out."

Simmons chuckled. "Well, you got me there, Hollis. The truth is, Sherika just doesn't date white men. Alfrieda tried to set her up with one of the ADAs in her office—a white guy who saw her when he was at the ME's office to meet with one of the pathologists—and she said no. Said she didn't cross that line."

"Well, that makes me feel better, but doesn't that make Sherika a little racist, then?"

"This is the stupidest conversation we've ever had, Hollis! No, it doesn't make Sherika racist—it's just a personal preference on her part, for God's sake! Which is probably why you never thought to ask her out. And, now, if you don't drop this whole damn subject, I'm gonna hang up."

"Okay, okay, Ike," Joplin said. "But you're my best friend. If you and I can't have a conversation about stuff like this, who can?"

He heard Simmons sigh again. "You're right, Hollis. I don't know why this makes me so uncomfortable, and I'll try to figure it out. But could we just focus on the ring Nina Reynolds sent you for now? I promise we'll talk about this another time."

"Sure, Ike. I'll bring it over to APD within thirty minutes."

———

Joplin stopped by Sarah Petersen's office to let her know where he was going. But when she looked up at him from her desk, the first thing he said to her was, "Would you ever date a black woman? If she were a lesbian, I mean?"

Petersen blinked twice, then said, "I would, if I weren't already involved with someone. And, I already *have* dated a black woman, not that it's any of your business, Hollis. Where's this coming from?"

"It just occurred to me that even though I've always found Sherika to be extremely attractive, I never thought about asking her out when I was single. It's bothering me."

"Do you think maybe it has something to do with the fact that your former girlfriend was engaged to a black man?"

"I'm sure it does," Joplin admitted. "I mean, I wasn't shocked or anything—just surprised. But knowing Blaine, I figured he must be a pretty special guy, no matter what color he was."

"And yet, you've heard some pretty disturbing things about the guy."

"Yeah, that bothers me, too. I hate to think that she was unhappy because of him."

"Maybe she wasn't unhappy. And maybe, as we discussed earlier, a lot of what people like Lucy Alvarez told you springs from jealousy. And not just the romantic or sexual kind of jealousy: Winston Avery has made himself a pretty big target. He's a very successful black man, but he also seems to have distanced himself from the black community."

Joplin nodded, remembering Ike's comment that although Avery was black, it was only "skin deep." But there had also been positive feedback about Avery on that issue. Sort of. "Well, Mark Rawlins said he'd tried to give back to the black community, set up some scholarships, but it hadn't worked out." When she didn't respond, he held up the UPS package and said, "Listen, I promised I'd get this over to Ike, so I'd better get going. But I have my phone, so I'll be on call."

"Okay," she said. "But, Hollis? Try not to spend time worrying about why you never asked Sherika out while you're at the Ritz with Carrie this weekend, okay?"

He grinned and said, "I think I can manage that."

———

They took the package right to B. J. Reardon in the Crime Scene Unit. Joplin told him that they suspected that Blaine Reynolds' killer had placed the ring on her finger after she was dead and needed to find out whatever CSU could tell them about it, including any partial prints or DNA they might find.

"I doubt that the killer was that careless, and it's been handled by several people," Joplin said. "But it's worth a shot. We'd also like some photos taken first, so we can show them around, see if any of her friends or coworkers ever saw her wearing it. Or ever saw it on anyone else, for that matter. And we plan to take them to some local jewelers and see if any of them recognizes the manufacturer."

"We'll do our best, gentlemen," B.J. said in his measured, almost formal, manner. He evidently didn't believe in the idea of Casual Fridays, because he was wearing a tweed jacket over gray slacks and his usual bow tie. Today's was a red plaid. "Although I agree with you that we're not likely to find much in the way of latent prints or DNA, Hollis. I'll have someone take the photos you requested first and get them down to Ike within the next hour, though."

They thanked him and took the elevator back up to the main floor. Joplin asked Ike to assign some uniforms to take the photos around to several major jewelry stores when he got them, but said he wanted to show them to Blaine's coworkers himself.

"I want to check that off my list today," he said and went on to tell Ike about the upcoming weekend with Carrie. "Except for dinner at Davio's, we're not planning on leaving the room. Can you get someone to run a few of the photos over to me when you get them?"

"Happy to. And I'm also happy you and Carrie are taking some time for yourselves. You don't wanna lose that lady, Hollis."

"No, I don't, Ike."

Simmons looked at his watch. "I'll leave word about the photos, then I need to head to the airport and pick up my in-laws. They're getting in from

Jersey a little early for Thanksgiving." He rolled his eyes and said. "Then all of my family get here from Macon next Wednesday. I almost wish we coulda taken the Hallorans up on their invitation to go to their house this year. It's gonna be a zoo."

"I wish you were going to be there, too, Ike. My *future* in-laws will be there with us, and we're having something Tom called 'turducken.'"

———

Joplin was just about to head back to the ME's office when he got called to a vehicular scene on Johnson Ferry. Although it was Friday, it was only a little after ten a.m., so the traffic wasn't too bad on I-85 North, which he took to Georgia 400. He got off at Exit 3, then took Peachtree-Dunwoody to Johnson Ferry. The accident scene was in the residential section of the street, away from the congested grouping of hospitals and medical offices nearby. A small crowd had gathered around a late-model, pewter Mercedes 350 that had gone off the road and straddled the sidewalk. Next to it was an EMS van, and both technicians were standing near the rear doors. Ahead of it was a Sandy Springs police car.

He parked behind the van and quickly got out, carrying his bag. The uniformed officer briefed him on the situation, which involved an elderly man who had evidently had some kind of cardiac "event."

"The EMTs got him out and onto a gurney, then started compressions, but couldn't revive him after twenty minutes," the officer, a tall, blond man with a military haircut told him. "They kept going, but then one of them called the ER doc on duty at Northside Hospital and was told to stop. It was pretty obvious the guy was long gone," he added. "He was eighty-five. I retrieved his wallet, and I'll go notify next of kin when you get done."

"Thanks," Joplin said, then stepped up into the van to do what little he could for the dead man.

CHAPTER FORTY

Tom Halloran walked Eileen Mayhew and Brian Sullivan to the bank of ele-vators and pushed the "Down" button. He had invited them to the Driving Club for lunch to celebrate after they'd agreed to the settlement he'd negotiated with their brother and his lawyer, but they'd both needed to get back to work. After again thanking him profusely for all he'd done, they disappeared behind the closing doors of the elevator car. He looked at his watch, saw that it was only a little after noon, and resisted the urge to go back to his office and write up his latest billable hours. Instead, he called Joan on his cell and told her he was going out, but would return in time for his two o'clock appointment with Granville Dennison, a new client.

Once in his car, Halloran headed north on Peachtree Street for Midtown, more specifically, Broadchurch Square, where Daisy Henry had been murdered. He turned right on 6th Street, crossed Juniper, then left on to Piedmont Ave. The condominiums, three-story, red-brick townhouses, were on Piedmont Place, a quiet street about two blocks north. There were eight of them, lining the right side of the street; each had a two-car garage and brick steps leading up to the front doors. Will and Daisy had leased Number Eight, on the far right end, a corner unit. Halloran drove past it to the complex's entrance and turned in. The balconies and patios of the units looked out on a pool and tennis court that took up most of the grounds. It

was all extremely well-kept and showed both taste and money, two com-
modities that didn't always go hand-in-hand in Atlanta.

Halloran pulled his car into a small visitors' parking lot next to the tennis court, but didn't get out. His main reason for being there was simply to
see the complex and get a feel for where the murder had occurred. If Jayla
Henry were telling the truth, then her father would have parked right where
he was. There would have been no reason for him to hide the fact that he
had gone to see his estranged wife. It wasn't a gated complex, so no one—
except, perhaps for neighbors or passersby—would have noted his presence
or prevented him from coming in. But that would have held true for anyone
else who might have come to see Daisy Henry, after Will had left.

He looked over to Number Eight. The crime scene photos hadn't been
included with the trial transcript that Damon Copeland had sent him, but
Maggie had discussed them in detail the other night, after studying the ones
at the ME's Office. So Halloran knew that the large, open living area, con-
sisting of the entry hall, kitchen, living room and dining room were on the
first floor. Jayla's bedroom and the master bedroom were both on the second floor; a game/recreation room with a bar took up the third floor. He
couldn't actually see the patio door of Number Eight, but he assumed it was
like all the other seven and opened into the kitchen.

Was that why Daisy had been murdered in the kitchen? Halloran wondered. *Because she had let someone in through the patio door?* Then, again, if
Will Henry had parked in the visitors' area, he would have gone to the patio
door as well. No new clues there, he decided. But, regardless, whether Daisy
had let someone else in that night, it had to have been someone she knew.
Someone she either trusted or, at the very least, wasn't alarmed by.

It occurred to Halloran that Hollis had never gotten back to him about
being able to talk to the detective in charge of the Henry case—Riker, that
was his name. He picked up his phone from the passenger seat and found
Joplin's number.

"Did I get you at a bad time?" he asked when Joplin answered. "You sound like you're in the car."

"I am. I'm on the way to the *AJC* offices in Sandy Springs. By the way, would Maggie ever consider a career in law enforcement? She spotted some things in the crime scene photos of the Reynolds' case that we're following up. Although I guess it's a case of *déjà vu* all over again, since she helped us out with the Carter and Ridgewood cases, too. She's got a real gift, Tom."

"I know," Halloran said. "She told me a little about your meeting at the ME's office yesterday. About the two rings? Is that why you're going to the *AJC*?"

"Yeah. Nina Reynolds doesn't remember ever seeing Blaine wear the silver band. Which doesn't mean she couldn't have gotten it recently. But I agree with Maggie that whoever sent those photos to me was sending some kind of message by focusing on the rings. So if we can rule out that she'd worn the ring before the murder, it could mean that the killer put it on her finger after she was dead."

"Good luck with that, then. But I'm calling to see if you or Ike ever got in touch with Detective Riker to see if he'll talk to me."

"But Maggie told me you'd been kicked off the appeal," Joplin said, sounding surprised. "She also said you think Will Henry is guilty."

"I was, and I still do—until otherwise convinced. But if you think she's gifted when it comes to analyzing photos, she's even better at persuading a husband to do her bidding. And, as said husband, here I am, back on the job of trying to get Jayla Henry's father out of prison. But not by helping with his appeal. That's out of my hands."

"Actually, I totally forgot to ask Ike about talking to Bill Riker, Tom. A lot's been going on. And then when I heard you were off the case—"

"No need to apologize, Hollis. But if you could get in touch with him, I'd appreciate it. I mean, I know you and Carrie are going to the Ritz for the weekend, so I don't want to pressure you, but—"

"Jesus Christ!" Joplin said. "Is there anybody in this town who *doesn't* know we're spending the weekend at the Ritz?"

"That I can't tell you, Hollis," Halloran said solemnly, trying to keep the amusement out of his voice. "I'd keep the curtains drawn, if I were you, though."

But after Joplin had clicked off, Halloran's mood turned solemn for real. He felt chilly all of a sudden, and saw that a strong wind was rifling through the trees surrounding the condominium complex. More leaves had fallen since the day before. Various news outlets had tried to predict the weather for the upcoming Thanksgiving holiday, and the consensus was that the Indian summer they'd been enjoying was fast coming to an end. For the first time in a long time, he felt an uneasiness, a sense of foreboding, that clashed with his ordinarily logical and pragmatic nature.

Halloran looked up at the sky. A few minutes earlier, it had been fairly clear and blue, but now clouds had moved in, and the light around him had dimmed.

CHAPTER FORTY-ONE

It began to rain as Joplin turned onto Perimeter Parkway and headed for Cox Enterprises. He parked in front of the building, after placing his Milton County Medical Examiner sign on the dashboard. After going up to the 10th floor, he was told that Mark Rawlins was "away from his desk," by the receptionist, but both Lucy Alvarez and Ned Beeson were on deadline and working. She was reluctant to let Joplin through to the large, open room that housed the reporters' cubicles. Finally, she agreed to call each of them to ask if they had time to see him. Joplin had wanted to show them the pictures of the ring Ike Simmons had sent over to him separately, but he took what he could get. Luckily, they didn't come out to the reception area together.

"You needed to see me?" Ned Beeson said, looking puzzled.

"Just for a few minutes," Joplin said and motioned toward a nearby sofa in the lobby. When they were seated, he took the photos out of the manila folder he was carrying and showed the first one to the young reporter. "Did you ever see Blaine wearing this ring?"

Beeson's eyes left Joplin's face slowly and focused on the photo. When he didn't answer right away, Joplin sifted through the others that showed the ring from various perspectives—top view, side view, and next to a ruler to show its relative size. Finally, Beeson said, "No, but I don't know if that means anything. I didn't see her every day. Or she could have worn it when she went out. Got dressed up, I mean. It's a beautiful ring. Simple, but elegant, as my mother would say."

"What is?" Lucy Alvarez asked. Joplin hadn't heard her walking over to them.

"A ring that Blaine had," Beeson said. He turned to Joplin. "Or at least I assume so, since you asked me if I'd ever seen it on her."

"Well, I've never seen it before," Lucy said, looking down at the top photo Joplin was holding. "Who told you it belonged to Blaine?"

"Nobody," Joplin said. "She was wearing it when she was found. Along with her engagement ring," he added, looking pointedly at Lucy.

The doors to one of the elevators opened, the dinging sound making all of them glance at it. Mark Rawlins came out, looking surprised when he saw them.

"Am I invited to the meeting?" he asked, walking over to them.

Joplin stood up. "It's not really a meeting, Mr. Rawlins. I came by to see if any of y'all had ever seen her wearing this ring." He handed the photos to the editor.

Rawlins took them and shuffled through them, then gave them back to Joplin. "Well, I haven't. She wasn't really big on jewelry. In fact, the only ring I ever saw her wearing was her engagement ring."

"That's true," Lucy said. "She didn't like bracelets either."

"It looks like a wedding ring," Ned Beeson had also stood up and was leaning over Joplin's shoulder as he studied a close-up of it. "One that a woman would wear by itself, without an engagement ring, I mean. Was there an inscription inside? Maybe it belonged to Blaine's grandmother or another relative."

"Actually, there was an inscription," Joplin said. That was the only thing Simmons had gotten out of CSU, other than the photos. "The word, 'Always.' But her mother said she'd never seen it before, so it couldn't be a family piece."

"Have you asked Winston about it?" Ned Beeson asked. "I would think he'd know."

"Maybe. But he didn't say anything about it when Mrs. Reynolds told him she was returning the engagement ring to him."

"Jesus!" said Ned, shaking his head. "That was kind of a low blow. I mean, couldn't she have waited until after the funeral?"

"I guess not," Joplin said. "By the way, any of you going to the funeral?"

All three of them nodded, looking solemn. Only Mark Rawlins broke the silence. "I spoke to the managing editor, asking for time off for anyone who wanted to attend. Blaine was one of our own, and it's the least we can do."

"Anybody else going?"

"Actually, several staff members, including those at our Washington bureau," said Rawlins.

Joplin knew Blaine was well-liked and respected by her peers, but the cynical side of him wondered just how much the power and influence of General Reynolds factored into the equation. Especially where the Washington bureau was concerned. "Well, I know y'all have deadlines to meet, so I'd better let you get back to work," was all he said, however.

"Speaking of the funeral," said Mark Rawlins as the other two turned to go back to the reporters' room, "will we see *you* there?"

It was a question Joplin probably should have expected, given that several people at the paper knew he had dated Blaine, but it took him aback. "I wish I could," he said, hoping the lie didn't show on his face. "But I think it's more important for me to be here in Atlanta, working on the case."

"I think you're right," Rawlins said, his expression turning sad. "And I think Blaine would appreciate that." It looked as if he were going to say something else, but he just shook his head and walked away.

Joplin watched him as he left the reception area, then pushed the "Down" button. As he waited for the elevator, it occurred to him that he should at least send flowers to the funeral parlor handling Blaine's funeral. Then he wondered if businesses like that in D.C. called themselves "funeral parlors." Maybe that was just a Southern thing. Whatever, he decided. The florist would know, and while he had them on the phone, he could also have some flowers sent to his and Carrie's room at the Buckhead Ritz. Then, the irony of ordering flowers for both his old girlfriend and his new fiancée washed over him. A flashback to the dream he'd had a few nights ago, with Carrie turning into Blaine as she walked up the aisle to meet him, made him freeze as the doors to the elevator opened. He made himself get into it, but as the doors started to close again, Joplin flung his arms out to stop them and squeezed out of the elevator, wondering if the sudden feeling of claustrophobia that had gripped him was because of the elevator or the memory of the dream.

The receptionist looked at him strangely as he headed for a door marked "Stairs," but didn't say anything. Which was just as well, because he wouldn't have been able to explain why he was going to walk down ten flights to the lobby.

CHAPTER FORTY-TWO

Carrie had reserved a small suite on the 17ᵗʰ floor of the Ritz-Carlton that overlooked Peachtree Street and Lenox Square Mall. It was not quite 6:30 p.m., but it was already dark, and the view, as Joplin stood looking out the window, was full of colorful, seasonal lights. The enormous Christmas tree atop Macy's wouldn't be lit until Thanksgiving night, but he could see its outline against the sky. He usually loved this time of year and had looked forward to doing some Christmas shopping with Carrie on Saturday, but he couldn't seem to shake the sense of oppression he'd felt since leaving Cox Enterprises.

Determined not to ruin the weekend with his negativity, Joplin turned away from the window and went to the small bar set up near the wide-screen TV. He poured two fingers of Jim Beam into one of the hotel's glasses and added ice from the bucket. They had reversed their dinner plans, deciding to go to Davio's that night and order room service on Saturday, and Carrie was still in the bathroom, getting ready. Joplin was already dressed, in khakis, a white dress shirt and a navy blazer. Their reservation was for 7:00, early for most Buckheadians, but he wanted to be back in the room by 8:30 for what he considered to be the main event, and it wasn't dinner. Given the day he'd had, with two more scenes after his visit to the *AJC*, heavy rain and even heavier Friday traffic, he wasn't sure he'd be at his prime if that event took place too late.

As he turned on the NBC Nightly News, Joplin wondered if he were getting too old. He used to be able to party half the night and still function at top speed on the job. But he'd turned thirty-six in February, which was too close to forty to feel young. And Brian Williams' first words made him feel even older.

"Good evening, from Dallas, Texas," the news anchor said. "We're in Dealey Plaza, just across from the sixth-floor window in the Texas School Book Depository building where three shots were fired fifty years ago today that changed the course of American history. And here in the shadow of that very building, it was a perfectly awful day. Thirty-five degrees, rainy and windy, perfectly matching how it felt to be here today and going back fifty years ago. By this time of night, right now, Air Force One had just landed back in Washington, carrying the president's casket, his widow Jacqueline Kennedy and the new president, Lyndon Johnson. Most Americans were home for the day, schools and offices had let out early, and millions were huddled around their TV sets, where they would remain transfixed, watching the coverage off and on for the next four days. Here now is David Brinkley, who started off this broadcast on this very night, fifty years ago. "

The screen went from being in color to black and white. "Good evening," Brinkley said, his expression grave. "The essential facts are these: President Kennedy was murdered in Dallas, Texas. He was shot by a sniper hiding in a building near his parade route and was dead within an hour. Lyndon Johnson is president of the United States."

"Oh, my God," Carrie said as she came into the small living room. "I remembered that the anniversary was coming up a few weeks ago, but with everything going on, I'd totally forgotten."

"Well, neither of us had even been born when it happened, so I guess it shouldn't mean as much to us," Joplin said. He quickly shut off the TV, afraid it would put a damper on the evening, and stood up. "Wow! You look amazing!"

Carrie stared at him. "You know you don't mean that, Hollis. About the Kennedy assassination. I've heard you talk about the impact it had on American history and politics several times. Why don't you want to watch the show? We can push our reservation back, if you're worried about that."

"I know, but I'd rather concentrate on my beautiful fiancée tonight," he said, going over to Carrie and wrapping his arms around her. She held her face up to him, and they enjoyed a long kiss that was passionate enough to make Joplin forget about any performance worries later on. When they finally broke apart, he held her out at arms' length and said, "When did you get that dress? I've never seen it before."

"I stopped at Phipps after work last week, when you had the four-to-midnight shift, so I could get a few new things for the holidays. Like it?" She twirled around so he could see the back of the burgundy sheath that fit her like the proverbial glove. Her long, almost black hair looked sleek and shiny, and she was wearing strappy high heels that made her only a few inches shorter than he was. Sparkly, dangling earrings and dark lipstick completed the picture. "It's not actually red, but it's close enough, especially for a nice Jewish girl like me."

"I like it so much, I wish you could take it off right now," he said. "I think we should stay in tonight, like we originally planned."

"Not a chance," she said, smiling as she walked over to the desk next to the TV armoire and scooped up a small, black purse. "You're going to buy me a Dirty Martini and a very expensive dinner first."

———

They eased into a soft, leather banquette and gave their drink order to the server, then settled back to look at the menu. Ten minutes later, Gerry, their favorite bartender, brought their Martinis to the table himself.

"I just wanted to see for myself if you were still engaged to this guy," he said to Carrie in his soft Irish brogue, jerking a thumb toward Joplin.

Carrie laughed and held up her left hand, palm turned inward, to show him her engagement ring. They had celebrated there with a Champagne dinner the night after Joplin had proposed, back in May, but Gerry still acted as if he couldn't quite believe it. It was a running joke between him and Carrie, but Joplin sometimes wondered how much of a joke it was on Gerry's part.

"I'm just glad he's willing to make an honest woman of me," Carrie said.

"Sure, and if you were an honest woman, you'd admit that you could do better, love," Gerry said. "Didja know that Joplin's an *English* name? And that the English have been major players in the oppression of good people the world over?"

"I'm willing to take that chance, Gerry. Hollis has promised to quit oppressing after we're married."

"Word," said Joplin, raising a finger.

Gerry shook his head. "Then I'll be prayin' for you, love. Two rosaries a night, or I'm a heathen."

They laughed as he walked away, Carrie a little more heartily. When their server approached, they gave their orders: a shared plate of Oysters Rockefeller, two chopped salads, the scallops for Carrie and the braised short ribs for Joplin. Within minutes, another server had placed what Joplin called "puffy bread," along with some butter, in front of them.

"The calories don't count tonight," Carrie said firmly. "In fact, I think we should order some Parmesan Truffle Fries for the table. Doctor's orders," she added.

"Can I watch you eat them?" Joplin asked, placing a hand over her right thigh, then pushing her dress about two inches toward her mid-section.

———

The oysters, though an unproven aphrodisiac, proved to be a sure thing.

Carrie was either in a very frisky mood or feeling the effects of the Dirty Martini and a wonderful Sangiovese that their waiter had suggested. Or both. She insisted on doing a very amusing striptease for Joplin in the living room of their suite that involved her taking off her jewelry and her panties first. Somehow, she made taking off her earrings even sexier than taking off the black thong she was wearing. Next came the dress, after she'd asked Joplin to unzip her and unhook her lacy, black bra. She freed her arms from both, then stood there and let him look at her breasts for what didn't seem to Joplin like a long enough time. After that, she turned her back to him, slowly pushed the dress down to her ankles, bending as she did, then stepped out of the dress with the raised-arms flourish of an Olympic gymnast.

"I'd give that a fifteen," Joplin said, clapping.

She grinned at him and walked toward him, a little unsteady on her feet after the dress dismount. "Oh, you ain't seen nothin' yet," she said confidently.

"Really? What else is there to see?" he asked.

Instead of answering him, she crooked her index finger at him and beckoned him into the bedroom. The maid had turned down the bed and put what appeared to be chocolates on each pillow. Carrie snatched up one of the chocolates, slid between the covers, and unwrapped it. With her mouth full of chocolate, she stared up at him and said, "Now, it's your turn. Strip."

———

They did almost everything they'd ever done in bed during the past year, as well as a few things they'd never tried. Midway, Joplin raided the mini-bar, bringing back an assortment of nuts, potato chips, and Oreos, as well as two tiny Champagne bottles. They ate and drank everything, giggling as they guessed how much the hotel would charge them for it. At one point, Carrie placed an Oreo between two potato chips, scarfed it down, and announced that it contained enough *umami* to please the chefs at Momofuko. She had a little trouble pronouncing "Momofuko," and it sounded much sexier than she probably intended. Joplin didn't recognize the name of the restaurant anyway, but her pronunciation roused his already building desire to renewed heights. He swept the empty bags of chips and cookies and nuts from the bed, rolled on top of her and entered her missionary-style, the only position they hadn't tried that night.

Afterwards, they spooned, Joplin's arms around her tightly, his knees tucked into the crook of hers. "Let's not wait too long to have children," he said. "My biological clock is ticking."

"Mmm," said Carrie, sleepily. "I thought that was your heart."

"Couldn't be," he said. "I gave that to you a long time ago."

She didn't respond to that, and a few seconds later, she began to snore.

CHAPTER FORTY-THREE

Joplin's cell phone woke him from a deep sleep, brought on by cumulative fatigue, alcohol, and expended passion. He didn't catch the call, but saw that it was from Ike Simmons and that it was almost ten o'clock on Saturday morning. A terse message directed him to call ASAP. He got out of the bed quietly, stepped over the pile of clothes he'd stripped off to the sound of Carrie's whistles and cat calls the night before, and went into the bathroom.

Simmons answered right away. "Hate to bother you, Hollis, but I thought you might want to know that Winston Avery was taken to Northside Hospital fifteen minutes ago with a knife wound to the stomach. He's not expected to live. I'm at his apartment. You wanna join me?"

"I can be there in twenty minutes," Joplin said, clicking off. He picked up the hotel phone next to the shower and punched the valet icon, asking for his car to be brought up right away, then got into the shower and turned on lukewarm water, hoping it would shock his brain into a more alert state. Carrie was awake when he went back into the bedroom.

"It's a little late for modesty, I think," she said, eyeing the towel he clutched around his waist.

"I didn't want to risk arousing you to uncontrollable lust when I can't do anything about it," he said, going over to kiss her.

"Oh, I think you're underestimating yourself," she said, coyly, cupping his balls under the towel.

Joplin grinned, but stepped back a little, allowing his balls to flop out of her hand. Then he filled her in on Ike's phone call as he walked over to the right side of the bureau under the bedroom's TV. He pulled underwear from it, then a shirt, pants and wool jacket from the closet. Dressing quickly, he grabbed his badge, wallet and keys, and kissed Carrie again before heading out.

"Call me as soon as you get a chance," she said.

"I will," he said over his shoulder. "Order some breakfast for us. I'll try to be back in an hour."

The car was waiting for him when he got outside. He made it to Avery's condominium in six minutes and left it with another valet there. Waving his badge at the concierge, Joplin hurried to the elevator and rode it to the thirtieth floor. A uniformed cop opened the door and gestured toward the living room when Joplin identified himself and said he was meeting Simmons.

Ike was wearing latex gloves and standing near the large gray sofa closest to the bar area. Joplin saw bloodstains on both the sofa and the Persian rug, as well as the medical trash left behind by the EMTs. The enormous glass coffee table that separated the sofas had been pushed aside to allow them to place Avery on the floor and have better access to him as they worked on him. A bottle of Glenlivet and a smeared crystal glass sat on it.

"Who found him?" was Joplin's first question.

"His cleaning lady. Her usual day was Friday, but she had to take her husband to the doctor yesterday, so she asked Avery if she could come today instead. That could be why he's still alive. She got here at nine, used her own key when he didn't come to the door, and had the presence of mind to phone 911 before she called the concierge to get Security up here."

"Where is she now?"

"I let her go home after I took her statement. She held it together until the EMTs wheeled Avery out, but then the shakes set in."

"How bad is he?"

Simmons jerked his head toward the bar. "You remember seeing a knife displayed on that stand when we were here last week?"

The image in Joplin's mind was exactly as he had seen it then: a knife with a black-lacquered sheath and gold decorations, attached to a matching hilt and resting on a curved, black, wooden stand.

Simmons pointed to an object on the coffee table. "There's the hilt," he said, "but the knife itself was still in Avery's stomach when they took him to the ER. The doc they called said it would be safer to remove it during surgery. If he made it that far," he added. "The guy was barely breathing when they got here, but he still had a heartbeat, so they got some IVs in him to stabilize him and took him. Last report I had was about five minutes before you got here. They said he was in surgery and still alive, but they weren't makin' any bets that he'd stay that way."

"Did you find a note?"

"Nope. That woulda made our jobs a little simpler, of course. CSU should be here any minute, and I'll have them dust for prints and pay special attention to the hilt and the Scotch and the glass, but I doubt they'll find anything other than Avery's prints. I think the guy tried to off himself, Hollis, but we'll have to leave that open for now. Without a body, there's nothin' for you to do here, but I wanted you to see the scene anyway."

Joplin nodded as he looked around. He wished he had his camera, but he knew he could remember everything. "I guess there's not enough blood for Jimmy to work with," he said, referring to Jimmy Hernandez, APD's bloodstain analyst.

"No, but I asked the ER to preserve Avery's clothes. Might be something Jimmy can tell from them. I'm also gonna write up a warrant for a DNA profile on his blood. The suicide attempt should give us probable cause, and we can at least determine if he fathered Blaine's baby. If he didn't, that may help us with motive."

"Well, that's one good thing out of this anyway. But, if he *did* father the baby, that might change things, Ike."

"Maybe. But if he didn't even know Blaine was pregnant, what difference does it make?"

"I guess. But have you talked to Security or the concierge? Did he have any visitors last night?"

Simmons shook his head. "The concierge checked last night's log, and there were no visitors listed. Security is getting us the tape made by the lobby cameras last night. I'm doin' everything by the book, Hollis, including requesting a search warrant for some things that might connect him to Blaine's murder, and I think we'll be able to wrap this case up. Avery killed Blaine Reynolds for reasons we may never know—rejection, jealousy, revenge for something he felt was a betrayal—take your pick. And then he killed himself out of remorse."

With a long sigh, Joplin looked around the room once more. "I can't argue with you, Ike." He glanced at his watch. "Blaine's funeral is this morning. In fact, it'll start in just a few minutes. If he killed her, Avery might not have been able to face that."

"Go back to the Ritz, Hollis, and enjoy the rest of your weekend. Carrie's probably gonna have my ass for dragging you over here, but I knew you'd never let me hear the end of it if I didn't."

"You're right, buddy. I mean that. Just keep me posted, okay?"

"Any new developments, I'll call you," said Simmons. "But don't hold your breath. If Avery *doesn't* die, I doubt he's gonna tell us squat."

———

"Well, Othello killed himself—and with a knife, too," Carrie said, as she spread some scallion cream cheese on half of a pumpernickel bagel.

They were enjoying a leisurely room-service brunch of mushroom omelets, a basket of bagels with lox and three different kinds of cream cheese, fresh fruit, and Bloody Marys. Carrie had greeted him in one of the hotel bathrobes, looking freshly showered and shampooed, then ushered him over to the table in front of the window. They had sipped their drinks as Joplin told her about his visit to Winston Avery's apartment and Ike's belief that he'd tried to kill himself.

"You mean the character in the play?" he asked now, puzzled by the reference.

"Yes. Ever since I heard about Blaine's death, I've been thinking about the similarities to the play. I mean, she was a beautiful white woman, daughter of a General, who was strangled by her fiancé, a powerful, prominent black man. Desdemona's father was a Roman senator and Othello was a general, but you see what I mean." Carrie shook her head as she speared a piece of smoked salmon onto her plate. "I even worried that you fit the role of Cassio, with whom Desdemona was alleged to have betrayed Othello. You know—because of the photos that were sent to you? They were meant to cast some kind of blame on you, like Iago having one of Desdemona's handkerchiefs placed in Cassio's rooms."

"Carrie, honey, you are totally out of my league in many ways, and one of them is your liberal arts education," Joplin said. "I know *about the* play, of course, but I've never read it, so I'll have to trust you on the similarities. But don't you think that's a bit of a stretch?"

"Yes, I decided I *was* taking things a bit too far. But you have to admit, if Winston Avery *did* kill Blaine and *did* try to kill himself, it's a little too coincidental. Are you going to eat that last piece of lox?"

"You go ahead," Joplin said absently, thinking about what she'd said. "Are you saying the case is like real life imitating art? Is that what you mean?"

"No," said Carrie, adding the second piece of salmon to her bagel. "I'm saying that even if Winston Avery *did* kill Blaine and tried to kill himself, maybe you should still look for Iago."

"Now *him* I remember. He was Othello's second-in-command or something, who convinced him that Desdemona was cheating on him, right?"

"Actually, third-in-command. Cassio was promoted over him by Othello. But Iago also suspected Othello had slept with his wife, Emilia, so he had two reasons to be jealous—and to want revenge. So he manipulated the other characters' underlying racism against Othello and their jealousy of all that he'd accomplished."

Joplin took a bite of his omelet and considered this. "Other than Othello and Desdemona, I don't think that fits the Reynolds case."

"No, it doesn't, but maybe some of the attitudes and emotions do. Like racism and envy. And, of course, jealousy." Carrie gave a twisted smile. "Jealousy is a pretty powerful emotion. I should know."

"Yes, you should," Joplin said, remembering the grip it had had on him when Carrie was involved with Jack Tyndall. "I wasn't very good at hiding my feelings when…you and Jack were seeing each other, was I?"

Carrie looked at him in surprise. "Hollis, I wasn't talking about you. I was talking about *me*. For the past two weeks, since all this began, I've been jealous of a dead woman. Of Blaine. Of what she might have meant to you at one time, and maybe still did. And you've been so distant at times, so preoccupied. I've felt like there's something you're not telling me, and it's eaten away at me. Can you understand that?"

Joplin dropped his fork and grabbed both of her hands. "Of course I can. And I'm sorry. So sorry you've been feeling this way. The bottom line is that if I'd really loved Blaine, or was even beginning to, I wouldn't have let her get away. But even more important is the fact that I love you more than I've ever loved *anyone*. And if I haven't made you know that—*feel* that—it's my fault, not yours."

Carrie's hands gripped his back, but her face relaxed, and she smiled. "I do know that, Hollis. It's just a matter of getting my head and my heart on the same page."

Joplin smiled back at her. "Now, I wasn't an English Lit major like you, honey," he said, "but isn't that what's called a mixed metaphor?" But before she could answer, he lifted her left hand to his lips and kissed it. He felt the engagement ring brush his lips as he did, and something stirred at the back of his mind. But instead of chasing it, he turned her hand over, palm up, and kissed that, too. *This weekend is for Carrie*, he reminded himself, and even though part of his mind was envisioning the funeral—the Reynolds family would probably be at the grave site by now—he pushed all thoughts of Blaine away, as well as what might be happening with Winston Avery.

For as long as he could, anyway.

CHAPTER FORTY-FOUR

Ike Simmons called around four-fifteen while they were in the Lenox Square
Williams-Sonoma. Joplin had agreed to help Carrie set up a gift registry
for a couple's bar shower the Hallorans and the Simmons were giving them
in January. He was still in shock over how much the various Reidel wine
glasses and decanters cost and was about to suggest that they register elsewhere, when his cell phone rang.

"Tell me," was all he said when he answered it. He'd heard nothing from
Ike since he'd left Avery's condominium that morning.

"He just came out of surgery. The doc says he's stable, but still critical. The
knife perforated his bowel and lacerated the abdominal aortic artery. He
said the only reason Avery didn't bleed out is that something called a pseu-
doaneurysm formed over the nick, which kept him alive until they could
repair it. But he was already septic by then. If he lives, it'll be miracle. And
maybe one he wouldn't want anyone to pray for."

"What do you mean? Is he going to be a vegetable or something?"

"No, but he'll probably be a convicted murderer. CSU found the memory
card from Blaine's digital camera in a desk drawer in his home office. I put
that on the list of things to look for when I requested a search warrant. It has
all the photos that were sent to you on it."

Joplin sighed. "Well, I guess you were right then."

"I guess I was," Ike said, his voice tight.

———

Maggie rushed into the kitchen from the garage, calling his name, then stopped short when she saw Tom sitting at the island, watching CNN. The headline read, "Breaking news from Atlanta."

"I take it you've heard about Winston Avery," she said.

"Cate called me after you left to go to the Children's Home," said Tom. "She had just heard about it from a friend and was almost hysterical. Said she'd met him for a drink at F & B around eight last night to ask if he'd talk to me, and he was very down about Blaine's funeral. I told her I'd try to find out what I could and get back to her. I left a message for Ike Simmons, asking him to call, but I haven't heard back. I'm sure he's pretty busy though. How did you hear about it?"

"It was on the WABE news when I was coming back from the Children's Home."

"Well, this sure shakes things up, doesn't it?"

"Yeah, it does. I'm surprised Hollis didn't let you know about it. I mean, I know he and Carrie are taking a mini-vacation at the Ritz, but I'm sure he knows about this."

Tom gave a short laugh. "*I'm* not surprised he hasn't called me. It's like pulling teeth to get anything out of Hollis. Although he did call me yesterday and tell me that the detective who was in charge of the Henry case is willing to meet with me tomorrow. But I had to ask him twice to arrange it."

"I wonder if Avery's suicide attempt will have an impact on that case," Maggie said.

"There's no telling, at this point. But I can bring it up when I see Detective Riker." Tom looked at his watch. "It's 4:40. Do you still want to try to make it to Mass, Maggie? I don't think I'll hear back from Ike any time soon. But we'd better get the kids cleaned up if you do."

The 5:30 p.m. Mass was an option they frequently chose on a Saturday night when they had no plans. The kids were bribed by the pizza afterwards at the nearby Fellini's on Peachtree Street, about a half-mile from Christ the King Cathedral. And nobody had to cook or clean up.

"I think that's a good idea," she said, feeling an overwhelming sense of sadness over the news. "Maybe Winston could use some prayers."

———

"So, the Children's Home is going to let Jayla spend Thanksgiving with us?" Tom said, after they'd found a booth. Fellini's was already crowded, and they'd had to wait in line to place their order.

They had agreed not to discuss Winston Avery until they got home, although Maggie had checked her phone after they left Christ the King to see if there had been any update on his condition. WSB News was reporting that he was out of surgery, but still in critical condition.

"Actually, they're letting me pick her up on Wednesday afternoon and have her spend the night here, since everybody's coming to the house at noon," she said. She had allowed both Tommy and Megan to bring an iPod Touch into the restaurant, and even though it made her feel guilty, it gave them a chance to talk. "It'll make things a little less hectic, and she and the kids can help me with the pies."

"Does she know about this yet?"

"Of course! I went to see her after I discussed the whole idea with Donna Hartsfield, the director. Donna's hoping that eventually Jayla will agree to be adopted, and being with a family for the holidays might help with that. Plus, she knows me and feels comfortable with it. And Jayla seems to be excited about it, too—especially the part about making pies. She said her mom used to let her play with a piece of dough when she made pies. And she asked me to tell her about Tommy and Megan."

Neither of the kids looked up when their names were mentioned, and Maggie regretted her decision to allow electronics at the table. *What kind of a mother am I?* she wondered, for the millionth time that year. *They're totally oblivious to their surroundings.*

"Okay, good," Tom said, although she was sure he still wasn't wild about the whole idea. Just like agreeing to continue to investigate Daisy Henry's murder. She knew he was just doing it for her, and she loved him for that, but she wished he could see beyond logic and probabilities. "I'm looking forward to meeting her," he added, and Maggie decided to believe him.

"Let's put the kids to bed a little early," she whispered, one hand cupped over her mouth, although she knew Tommy and Megan weren't paying any attention to them. When she saw the server approaching with their salad and pizza, however, she said, "Time to put the iPods away, kids," in what John Rosemond, the anti-Spock pediatrician and columnist she followed regularly, called the "alpha voice."

CHAPTER FORTY-FIVE

Detective Bill Riker was waiting for him when Halloran arrived at the Starbucks on Peachtree Center Avenue a few minutes before the appointed time of 11 a.m. the next day. He was sitting at a table in the far left corner of the café with his back to the wall, and even though Halloran had never met him and didn't even have a description of him, he knew the man was law enforcement. Riker looked to be in his late forties and was dressed in a navy sweater and jeans. He had dark, graying hair and a long, thin face with a scowl on it. Halloran nodded in his direction, then went to the counter to order a black coffee. The detective was still scowling when he walked over to the table.

"Thanks for agreeing to talk to me," Halloran said, although Joplin had told him Riker was only "returning a favor" and not to expect much from him. He didn't, but it was worth a try, and Maggie seemed to appreciate it. "I'm Tom Halloran," he added, offering his hand to the detective.

After squeezing Halloran's hand a little harder than necessary, Riker said, "I know who you are. I've got fifteen minutes, and then I have to be somewhere. What's your stake in the Henry case?"

Halloran had already decided not to play any legal angle. He smiled, took a sip of his coffee and said, "Just a favor for a friend, actually. My wife," he added, when he saw Riker's eyes narrow.

"Your *wife*?"

"It's a long story, but I'll keep it short," he promised, then briefed Riker on everything that had happened since Maggie had met Jayla Henry, except for anything to do with Damon Copeland or Hollis Joplin. He did, however, tell him about Winston Avery's connection to the Henry and Reynolds cases.

"You mean the lawyer who was engaged to Blaine Reynolds?" Riker asked, leaning forward and looking a little more engaged. "Who tried to kill himself? The media's having a field day, calling the case 'a modern-day Othello,' and today's paper says he's a major suspect in her murder. I haven't had a chance to talk to anyone on the case yet, but as far as I'm concerned, he's guilty as hell."

Halloran began to regret asking to meet Detective Riker. "He might be," he said, "but, other than the obvious similarities in the cases, I haven't come up with anything that connects him to Daisy Henry's murder. Did you ever talk to him when you were investigating the case?"

"No. I didn't even know about him. But we *did* know who killed Daisy: her husband." He held up his left hand and ticked off the reasons why with his right index finger. "He was having an affair with that actress, Trina Daily; his wife wouldn't give him a divorce; he was at the scene; and he had no alibi. Bingo! I heard the story about his daughter seeing him that night, but all it was was more proof he was the killer. We didn't need her testimony at the trial because we had the GPS evidence."

Halloran decided not to bring up Henry's 4th Amendment rights. "Yes, but if Jayla Henry is telling the truth, her father was there earlier that night, not when the ME says Daisy died. And she says he told her he was coming home. For good." Halloran leaned in across the table. "The crime scene photos show Daisy was dressed for bed, which puts time of death at the later end of the ME's estimate, not at 8:30, when the GPS shows that Will Henry was there. Jayla also said her mother was watching *The Undead Zone* on TV, when she went downstairs to see her, which comes on at nine o'clock."

Riker seemed at a loss for words, but then his eyes narrowed again. "What crime scene photos?"

Halloran didn't answer right away. If he told Riker that Hollis Joplin had described the photos to him, he might be getting him into trouble. But telling him that Maggie had been granted access to them by Joplin would do the same thing, and might even be worse. Instead, he decided to tell the detective something that was true, but not the whole truth. "Will Henry's attorney, Damon Copeland, received copies during discovery," he said, although the attorney had never shown those to him. "Up until last week, I was helping Copeland work on the appeal of Henry's murder conviction."

"What happened last week?"

"Copeland's client didn't want me involved with the case."

"Because he's guilty as hell," Riker said with a smug grin.

"That's what I think, too," Halloran said, deciding to shift tactics. "But my wife is still nagging me to keep trying to find a way to get Will Henry out of prison. Because of what the little girl said, although I think she was too young to know what time her father was there. But I need to be able to tell Maggie I've ruled out anyone else who might have killed Daisy. And that's where you can help me. Get her off my back, if you know what I mean."

"Oh, I know what you mean," Riker said, nodding his head. "I got one like that at home, myself. What do you need from me?"

"Did you follow up on the rumors that Daisy was having an affair? Was there any truth to that?"

"We did, and I can assure you there wasn't a shred of evidence to back up the rumors. Not like with Will. We talked to everyone on the set, same time we asked about the rumors about him and Trina Daily. But even if it had been true, it woulda been one more nail in Will's coffin, as far as I'm concerned."

"You mean because it would have been another motive for killing his wife?" Halloran asked.

"Exactly. Might have been an even bigger motive. In my experience, men don't handle cheating the same way women do. A wife might forgive her husband, especially if there are children involved, but unless a man is totally pussy-whipped, he's not gonna get over something like that. Even if he's stepped out himself."

Halloran nodded solemnly, although he had a feeling Riker was speaking from personal experience. "I totally agree. So you never got any vibes from, say, Nate Mauldin, the show's director, that there might have been something going on between him and Daisy, right?"

"Right," Riker said.

"And you never talked to Winston Avery, because he wasn't on your radar, right?"

The detective's chin came up, but he stared back at Halloran. "Right. We certainly didn't know he was gonna kill his fiancée a year and a half later."

"Of course you didn't," Halloran said. "And even if he and Daisy *were* involved, that would have given Will Henry an even stronger motive to kill her. As I said, I totally agree. And I think I can finally convince my wife that you got the right man, Detective."

"Glad I could help, Counselor," Riker said, smiling broadly now.

"You really did," Halloran said, standing up and offering his hand again. "And I appreciate it."

"Anytime," Riker said, taking Halloran's hand, but not trying to crush it this time.

But Halloran doubted there would be a next time, especially if the idea he got while talking to the detective panned out.

———

Joplin and Carrie were once again at Bistro Niko having lunch, after checking out of the hotel an hour earlier, when Ike Simmons called with an update. Joplin had managed to keep himself from initiating any contact with Simmons, despite the breathless reporting on the local news—and the only slightly more subdued tone on the national news—of Blaine's funeral and Winston Avery's "alleged suicide attempt" the night before, but it had been tough. Now he listened intently as Ike told him that Avery's heart had stopped during the night, but he'd been revived and taken back into surgery, due to worsening sepsis. He was holding on, but still not conscious.

"But that's not the big news," Ike said. "His DNA results came back and—are you ready for this? He *was* the father of the baby Blaine was carrying."

"I'm not as surprised as you sound," Joplin said.

"Yeah, but it doesn't really change anything, despite what you said, Hollis. There's still the memory card from Blaine's camera we found in his apartment. Besides, Avery said he didn't know she was pregnant, and Dr. Markowitz said it's possible even *Blaine* didn't know, because of the diabetes."

"You're probably right, Ike. Was there anything on the security tapes from the lobby?"

"Nothin' conclusive. Avery is shown coming out of the elevator around 7: 15 last night and going through a side door that leads to F & B, the French restaurant in the building. I'll tell you about that in a minute. Anyway, he comes back into the lobby around 8 p.m. There are a couple people there at the same time, but they're not near him, so it looks like he was alone. The valet guys on duty said he didn't call for his car, and tapes from the garage show that it was parked there all night."

"But he *did* go into the restaurant."

"Yes. According to the bartender, he sat at one of the tables in the bar area, and a quote pretty blonde woman unquote joined him. He'd never seen her before, and Avery paid for their drinks, so she's an unknown. The woman left first, and the valet said she gave him a claim check for a gray Lexis SUV. We're having a shot of it on the garage security tape enlarged, so we can get the license plate number."

Joplin sighed. "Okay, Ike, thanks for the update. We're about to have lunch, but I'll be home in a few, so call me if anything comes up."

Their server came with their bottle of wine, then opened it and poured a small amount in Joplin's glass to taste. Joplin obliged him, but thought the whole ritual was silly; he'd never been served a bad bottle of wine. Or maybe he had, but never realized it. He wasn't a big wine drinker.

"Very good," he said of the Steel Chardonnay that Carrie had suggested would go well with her Duck Confit and his Skate Wing. Like Davio's, this was one of their favorite restaurants, and even though they'd been there just a few weeks ago, they never tired of it.

When the server had left and they'd toasted to their wonderful weekend, Carrie set her glass down and said, "Okay, tell me what's happening." When he'd finished recapping his phone call with Ike, she said, "It's all so sad, Hollis."

"I know. I hope...I hope she *didn't* know she was pregnant. And that he didn't either, if he did kill her." He sighed again and said, "I guess that doesn't make a lot of sense."

Carrie reached out and put her hand over his. "Sure it does. I know exactly what you mean."

CHAPTER FORTY-SIX

"Did you learn anything new?" Maggie asked when Halloran returned from his meeting with Detective Riker. She patted the seat next to her on the sofa in the den.

"Not really," he said, sitting down. "But Riker did confirm my belief that the police focused on Will from the very beginning and looked for anything that would support their theory that he killed Daisy because she wouldn't give him a divorce. He insisted that he and his partner asked the cast and crew about rumors that Daisy was having an affair, but claimed no one could support that. But in the next breath, he said that would have been an even bigger motive for Will to kill her, if she had. Something about men being less willing to forgive cheating than women. I think they just discounted any leads that might have led away from Will."

"As in, the show's director, Nate Mauldin?"

"Exactly. And while I was listening to Riker blather on about the different attitudes men and women have about infidelity, I kept thinking about the way he was able to place Will at the crime scene the night of the murder."

"You mean his cell phone?"

"Yes."

"But what good is that going to do, Tom?" Maggie asked. "The investigation was closed over a year ago. The police aren't going to try to get a warrant for the director's cell phone records at this point."

"True, but they might try to get one for Winston Avery's to see if *he* were near Blaine's apartment the night she was murdered, and then they could also see if he were in contact with Daisy in the months before she died. At least we could rule him out as the person she might have been seeing. I went over to Daisy's condominium complex in Midtown on Friday afternoon, just to check it out. The parking area is in the back and not well-lit. The neighbors all said they never saw Will that night, which is why the police went after his phone. But anyone else could have gone unnoticed, too—after Will had left."

"Okay, but let's say Hollis or Ike Simmons would go along with that. If Avery had no involvement in Daisy's murder, we're back to square one."

Halloran nodded. "I know. So then we have to try to access the information from the other end."

"Which is?"

"Daisy's cell phone. I don't know if they ever got her phone records or just focused on any contact with Will that night, if they did, but the phone has to be somewhere. Either in an evidence box or with her other possessions. Or maybe we don't even need the phone itself to subpoena the records. I guess I was just remembering how Ike Simmons was able to get a lot of information from Libba Ridgewood's phone. I haven't heard back from Ike yet, so I think I need to give him a call, and I'll bring it up then. I also want to tell him about Cate's meeting with Avery on Friday night."

"Why not just ask Detective Riker about Daisy's phone?"

"I think that door is pretty much closed. He was very defensive when I asked whether he'd followed up on the rumors about Daisy. So I let him believe that I thought Will was guilty, too, and I was just trying to get my busybody wife off my back. I'm afraid threw you under the bus, Maggie."

"Maybe," Maggie said, frowning. "Or maybe what you said to him is the truth. Do you still think Will is guilty? That's what you said last week, when Damon Copeland told you Will didn't want you involved with the appeal."

"I know I did. But I also think Will didn't get a fair trial. And Detective Riker overlooked things that I don't think Ike or Hollis would have. So I'm reserving judgement for the time being."

———

The cats had evidently missed them, Joplin decided, as Quincy twined between his ankles and Banshee meowed loudly when he and Carrie let themselves into the condominium that afternoon. They hovered around them as they unpacked bags and checked mail and returned calls, then needed lots of brushing and petting after dinner as the four of them watched TV.

The local news programs had fairly buzzed with coverage of Blaine's funeral and Winston Avery's apparent suicide attempt. When he and Carrie had seen enough, she pulled up Friday night's *Say Yes to the Dress* on Comcast Demand. They both enjoyed a segment that showed the bride's mother and future mother-in-law at odds over the bride's choice of wedding dress, although Carrie warned him again that it was all orchestrated by the director and producers.

"Speaking of dresses, have you decided what kind of dress you want?" Joplin asked during a commercial. "That mermaid style is pretty sexy, but you might want something a little more 'Audrey Hepburn,' like the groom's mother wants. She's a piece of work, isn't she? And the bride's mother just wants the kind of wedding *her* mother didn't let her have."

Carrie stared at him. "Hollis, there's nothing real about 'reality TV.' I keep trying to tell you that! I watch it for style ideas, but it's pure entertainment."

"I know that," he said a little sheepishly. "But I enjoy it anyway. And, just in case you're wondering, I like the 'fit and flair' style dress. You'd look like a dream in it."

She threw a couch pillow at him.

But the evening ended sweetly, with the four of them moving to the king-sized bed. He and Carrie snuggled, while Quincy and Banshee, who had finally succumbed to being part of the family, settled into their chosen spots on the bed. Joplin was asleep in five minutes, exhausted from a weekend of sex, food, wedding registries, and the drama of Winston Avery's suicide attempt.

———

Joplin's dream that night wasn't disturbing; in fact it was almost comical. There were several brides in this one, but Blaine wasn't one of them. They all walked down the aisle, each one in a different dress, as strains of Mendelssohn's Wedding March filled the church. But when they reached the pews holding family members, several people stood up and began criticizing the dresses, each one reminding a particular bride that she hadn't chosen the right one. A loud, authoritative voice admonished them all to be quiet, and Joplin, who was sitting at the back of the church, looked up at the altar, where Winston Avery, dressed in a priest's vestments, stared down at the congregation from a tall pulpit.

"This isn't about you!" he shouted at them. Then he looked directly at Joplin and said, "Don't listen to them. Think of what this would be like if you didn't listen to them."

And then he slowly faded away, leaving no one else on the altar except a faceless groom, hands stiffly at his side as he waited for his bride.

CHAPTER FORTY-SEVEN

Winston Avery was still alive on Monday morning, according to The Morning *Show* on the local CBS channel, but still not conscious. As Joplin fed the cats, then poured some Grape Nuts and milk into a bowl, he remembered the ten days he'd spent in the same condition after being almost disemboweled in May of 2012. He had felt as if he were constantly sinking and rising in a bottomless ocean, occasionally getting close enough to the surface to hear voices, then disappearing beneath the waves. He didn't wish the experience on anyone, even the person who had probably killed Blaine Reynolds. Or the recuperation that would follow, if Avery survived.

That thought reminded him of last night's dream, which still puzzled him. Avery fading away seemed straightforward; he still wasn't expected to live. But why was he a priest, instead of the groom, and what was it that he didn't want Joplin to listen to? Blaine's family members and their dislike of Avery? Deciding to think about that later, he concentrated on giving his jaws a work-out with the Grape Nuts.

After waking up Carrie with a cup of coffee, Joplin quickly showered, shaved and dressed. Carrie didn't have to be back at the ME's Office until 9:00 a.m., but he wanted to get in before 7:30 so he could go over everything with Sarah Petersen and call Ike.

"Take your time, honey," he said to Carrie, after giving her a lingering kiss.

"It's still early. Stop by and see me when you get to the office, okay? Avery's still alive, but I'll probably have an update by then. If I don't get called out to a scene, of course."

"Mmm," said Carrie sleepily, but she smiled and took a sip of the coffee. "I wish I were back at the Ritz. Room service around here is going to suck."

"Well, I left the Grape Nuts out," Joplin said, then gave her another quick kiss.

With all the City of Atlanta schools out for Thanksgiving week, the drive to work took less time than usual. There were only two cars in the parking lot, one belonged to Viv Rodriguez and the other to Jeffrey, one of the overnight techs. Even Sarah Petersen hadn't arrived yet, which meant he'd have to make the coffee himself. The main entrance was still locked, since Sherika also wasn't in yet. Joplin let himself in, then headed for the Investigative Unit.

"You and Carrie have a good time on your weekend?" Viv asked, looking up from her computer. She was dressed in dark slacks and still wore her navy ME jacket.

"Better than perfect," he said. "Busy night?"

"Not too bad, but I got called out to a pedestrian hit about two hours ago, and I'm just finishing the report. Deke was gone when I got back."

"You want some coffee?"

"No way. I'm gonna crash as soon as I get home. Besides, I've had your coffee before, Hollis."

Joplin laughed and headed for the break room, but paused when he saw December's "Menstrual Cycle" on the bulletin board. Sarah always put it out before the end of the month, in case they needed to reschedule certain days. It reminded him that he still didn't know how someone, other than his co-workers and various law enforcement personnel, would be able to access the schedule.

Sarah had suggested a "hacker-for-hire," which was something Winston Avery, with all his money and connections, would be in a position to use. *If so, did that mean that that person would be in danger?* he wondered. But since Joplin's former relationship with Blaine and the fact that fake crime scene photos had been sent to him weren't public knowledge, a hacker hired by Avery might never have made the connection to her murder. Then again, someone who would murder a homeless drug addict as a precaution wouldn't have counted on that. And Winston Avery would have made sure he tied up any loose ends. The problem was, he didn't know any hackers, so there was no way of telling if one had been murdered recently. But then, another possibility occurred to Joplin as he headed down the hall. He shook his head to dismiss it; it was far-fetched, went against everything he held dear, and the motive was still extremely hazy.

Or was it?

As if in answer, images of *Say Yes to the Dress* flooded his brain. He saw again the father who had cancer and the two mothers-in-law arguing over the bride's dress, as well as the feuding bridesmaids. He heard Carrie say, "It isn't reality, Hollis." He also heard her say something that might be even more important.

"I'm saying that, even if it turns out that Winston Avery did murder Blaine and tried to kill himself, you should still try to find Iago."

———

Ike Simmons clicked off his cell phone for the second time in ten minutes. The first time was after Hollis had called him, wanting to see the security tapes from Winston Avery's condominium; the second was after a strange conversation with Tom Halloran about Daisy Henry's cell phone. Halloran had also told him that Cate Caldwell, who'd been working with him on Will Henry's appeal, met Avery for a drink Friday night, so the mystery of the blond woman at F & B was solved. Her connection to the Henry case and to Avery took a few minutes for the attorney to explain. Simmons said he'd contact her.

Hollis wouldn't get to APD for at least fifteen minutes, so he decided to humor Tom and go to the Evidence Room to see if Daisy's cell phone was in one of the boxes. He doubted he would do any more than that, though; the Henry case had been solved, or at least closed, for over a year. And although Simmons could certainly believe that a black murder suspect might not have gotten a fair trial, his priority was the Reynolds case.

There were several boxes of evidence in the Henry case, and both Will and Daisy Henry's cell phones were in one of them, along with Daisy's pajamas, bathrobe, and slippers. He would have to check out the homicide investigation file, however, to see if Riker had gotten phone records for Daisy's phone. Riker was a good enough detective in Simmons' opinion, but he sometimes took shortcuts and overlooked avenues of investigation that Simmons himself wouldn't. He just didn't go that extra mile that top-notch detectives did, and it showed on the witness stand.

Simmons remembered too many times that Riker had groused about being "raked over the coals" by defense attorneys who questioned his expertise or, sometimes, his attitude toward ethnic suspects. Daisy Henry's murder had happened just before Elliot Carter had been found hanging from a tree in Piedmont Park, along with all the fallout from the discovery that one of their own had killed him, so Simmons excused himself for not knowing more about the case. But Hollis had let him know that Tom Halloran was reinvestigating it, and that there might be a connection to the Reynolds case through Winston Avery. They hadn't gotten the records from Avery's cell phone yet, however, and the odds that they'd be able to access Daisy's phone records at this point were pretty low. He'd need to just find out what he could from the investigative file.

But Hollis was sitting at his desk when he returned, so Simmons put that on the back burner as he led his former partner to a conference room with a TV and DVD player available. After sliding the disc into place, he sat next to Hollis to walk him through the tape. He fast-forwarded it to the section showing Winston Avery walking out of the elevator into the lobby. The time stamp was 7:11 p.m.

"See. He goes right past the concierge into the lobby for the corporate section of the building. We got the security tape from that, too, but it just shows him walking toward F & B. It does show the young blond woman the bartender identified as joining Avery in the bar, though, so I'll show that to you later." Simmons again fast-forwarded the tape to where it showed Avery coming back into the condominium lobby. "There's nobody with him, and the only other person in the lobby is here, with his back to the camera, heading for the bank of elevators," he said, pointing to a figure wearing a long hooded jacket.

"Did the concierge know him?" asked Hollis.

"He said he didn't see him. You can see the concierge talking to someone on the phone, so I guess that's why."

"*I* can hardly see him, Ike. In fact, I can't even tell if that's a man or a woman because of the hood."

"It was a cold, rainy night, Hollis. That doesn't mean this guy was trying to disguise himself. And Avery walks behind him over to the elevators, but doesn't say anything to him, and then they both get into the elevator on the right. It doesn't look like he knew him."

"Maybe. Didn't Security have a camera pointed at the entrance? I mean, don't they need to see who's coming in, even if the concierge misses them? Or *especially* if the concierge misses them?"

"They just sent us this one. Maybe the uniform I sent to talk to them didn't ask for it, because we were ruling out whether anyone had visited Avery. But I'll check." Simmons sat back in his chair. "What's this all about,

Hollis? You think Avery didn't try to kill himself? That someone wanted him dead?"

Hollis gave a long sigh. "I'm not sure what I think yet. This whole scenario reminds me of Elliot Carter's death. We thought *he* died of autoerotic asphyxia, remember? And it didn't look like anyone had gone to see him at his apartment either, but then—"

"You found out that the concierges at his condominium only noted when a visitor asked to see a resident and was either sent up to their apartment when the resident admitted them or turned away if the resident wasn't home. The length of time spent by the visitor wasn't recorded, so Carter's killer was able to go to his apartment unnoticed, after he'd visited someone else in the building."

"Right," said Hollis. "I don't think that happened in this case, but my point is that even the best security system can have a blind spot"

"We'll check it out." Simmons ejected the disc and replaced it with another. "Here's the security tape from the commercial lobby showing Avery entering it and crossing over to the restaurant." He ran it forward a little, then pointed to a young, very attractive blonde coming in from valet parking and also heading for the restaurant. "Tom Halloran just gave me her name. You recognize her?"

Hollis closed his eyes for several seconds, then opened them. "I don't know her name, but she was in the video we shot of Elliot Carter's funeral at St. Phillip's, remember?"

Simmons smiled and said, "Not like you do, evidently. Halloran says her name is Cate Caldwell, Alston Caldwell's granddaughter. She's a law student at Emory and was helping him with Will Henry's appeal."

"That I knew, but I didn't connect the name with the woman at the funeral."

"I'm gonna call her when you and I finish," Simmons said. "Halloran said she'd be willing to talk to me. He also wanted a favor," he added, then told Hollis about the attorney's request.

"I hate to put more on you, Ike, but maybe you should follow up on this. If Avery's phone number shows up on the phone's logs, that might connect him to both murders. And, if not Avery's, then maybe another number might show that Daisy was involved with someone. If Halloran's still pursuing this, he must have changed his mind about Will Henry's guilt."

"I'll add it to the list," Simmons said wearily. "But let's get back to *our case*, okay? You haven't told me what caused you to think Avery didn't try to kill himself."

"Have you ever watched *Say Yes to the Dress*, Ike?"

"Say what?"

Simmons listened as Hollis talked about a dream he'd had the night before and a television show about brides trying to find wedding dresses. As if that weren't enough, Hollis ended up by asking him if he'd ever read Shakespeare's *Othello*.

"Remember when I said our conversation about why you never dated Sherika was the strangest one we'd ever had?" he asked, after letting it all sink in. "Well, I was wrong. Totally, fuckin' wrong. 'Cause *this* conversation is bat-shit crazy and stranger than that."

"Just listen, Ike," Hollis said, his voice rising. "What if a lot of the things the people around Blaine—her father, her brother, her editor, her colleagues—told us about her relationship with Winston Avery were wrong? What if the whole thing was orchestrated by someone who wanted us to *think* that? Like the directors and producers of a show like *Say Yes to the Dress* do. They create a lot of drama about the bride and her family or the bride and her bridesmaids that's just to make the show interesting, but it's not true or it's really hyped. And what if Winston Avery himself was fed a bunch of lies—like that Blaine was being unfaithful to him—maybe with me? That would explain why he was so hostile to me."

Simmons nodded slowly. "It's possible," he said. "Still pretty wild, and there's no evidence to support it, but it's a theory. But how do we either prove or disprove it?"

"I have a few ideas," said Hollis, and Simmons shook his head.

"I was afraid of that."

CHAPTER FORTY-EIGHT

Halloran got a call from Ike Simmons around noon. He was both surprised and glad that Daisy Henry's phone had been found so quickly and was also quick with his thanks.

"Don't get too excited," Simmons said. "The contract she had with AT&T expired a long time ago. It's dead as a doornail, in other words, and I won't be able to access any records without a subpoena. But I don't really have probable cause to request either one at this point. This is a closed case, with a conviction and a defendant in prison. And you haven't actually discovered any new evidence, right, Tom? It's all just conjecture at this point."

"Yes, but there might be a way around that," Halloran said, trying to think of one. He wasn't the attorney of record, and had been ordered off the case by the man who was, so he had no standing. He couldn't very well ask Damon Copeland to request a warrant, for the same reason. And what they were trying to get from the phone records *was* new evidence. "I'll give it some thought."

"In the meantime, I can put in a request to look at the investigation case file, which might already have the phone records. Give me a day or two."

"Sure. I know you've got a lot going on, Ike, and again, I appreciate your help with this."

"Me, too. You saved us some time by letting us know about Cate Caldwell. I'm meeting with her in about an hour."

But that meeting had to be postponed. Simmons was no sooner off his phone when it rang again, with the news that Winston Avery had died. After telling his partner what had happened and asking him to call Cate Caldwell and cancel their appointment, Simmons rushed out of the Homicide Unit.

———

Joplin got the news as he and Carrie were eating chicken and avocado sandwiches that he'd picked up at Einstein's after he'd left APD. "I'll see if Carrie can do it," was all he said when Ike had finished giving him the details. Then he'd clicked off. "Winston Avery died a little while ago. Ike's on his way to Northside."

Carrie set down her sandwich. "Wow. I can't believe how sad that makes me feel. I mean, despite the fact that he…"

"Probably killed Blaine?" Joplin said. "Yeah, I know. But I've decided that you could be right in thinking that Avery had an unseen 'partner in crime,' so to speak—an Iago to feed him lies about Blaine and stoke his jealousy. If he *did* kill her, that's no excuse, but it's a mitigating circumstance. And that same person may also have tried to convince him that *I* was the person involved with Blaine, for some reason."

"But what can you do about it, now that Avery is dead?"

"Well, for starters, I've already gotten Ike to believe it's at least a possibility. I was about to tell you about going over the security footage from Avery's condominium with him this morning, when he called just now. He's going to follow up on a person in the footage who seemed suspicious and get phone records for Avery's cell phone, among other things. And I'm going to look more closely at the rumors circulating about his relationship with Blaine and try to determine the source. But there's also something you can do, Carrie."

"The autopsy, right? But wouldn't you rather have someone like Dr. Minton do it? He's the Chief ME, Hollis, with way more experience than I have. Or David, for that matter. My feelings won't be hurt."

"I know, and if he thinks that's best, I won't argue, but I have every confidence in you. Besides, Ike wants to attend, and so do I. Would that bother you?"

"It would help, actually. Since Avery wasn't dead when he was found, there was no death investigator, and the scene wasn't preserved. But you both saw it, albeit with Avery gone, and Ike saw him with the knife still in him. I'll use the photos CSU took, but I also might have some questions during the autopsy. Especially if you're thinking that this wasn't a suicide. Is that what you're thinking, Hollis?"

"It's just a possibility, Carrie. And manner of death is your call, not mine. I don't want to influence *your* thinking."

"As if you could," she said, folding her sandwich back in its wrapper and looking him in the eye. "What is it that B. J. Rearden always says? 'science should never be—"

"The handmaiden of the law," Joplin finished.

"Exactly," She stood up and said, "I'll go talk to Dr. Minton. Can you get CSU to send over their photos from the scene?"

"I'm on it," said Joplin, standing up, too.

———

Joplin called CSU about sending the photos, then asked to speak to Jimmy Hernandez, hoping he'd have at least a preliminary report on the bloodstains on Avery's clothes and the rug area between the couch and coffee table in his apartment.

"I can't give you anything conclusive yet, Hollis," Jimmy told him. "The EMTs had to cut open his shirt to examine him, so that compromised the spatter from the wound, and the blood on the carpet got there when they set him down to work on him, so it wasn't pertinent."

"*But?*" said Joplin, to encourage him. "I know there's a 'but,' or you wouldn't have said 'anything conclusive.'"

He heard Hernandez sigh. "It's his hands, Hollis."

"What about his hands? You couldn't have seen his hands, Jimmy. He was rushed to Northside, and any blood on his hands would have been washed away."

"Right. But I talked to both EMTs right after I got Avery's clothes, and they said when they arrived, he was sitting on the couch with his hands on either side of him, palms up. But the photos CSU gave me didn't show any blood on the couch. His prints were on the hilt of the knife, but if he'd stabbed himself, there would have been blood on the sides of his hands, from spatter when the knife was plunged in and also when his hands made contact with the shirt covering his abdomen. So there should have been transfer stains on the couch when his hands fell to his side. I even went to the apartment myself to see if there were some faint bloodstains that the camera hadn't captured, but there weren't."

"Okay," Joplin said. "I'm getting the picture now. But why do you think this isn't conclusive, Jimmy? It sure seems like it's proof Avery's wound wasn't self-inflicted."

"Because I haven't had a chance to test it yet," Hernandez said. "And it's not a scientific conclusion until I do. You know that. But I haven't been able to work on it since Saturday because of the Cogburn case," he added, referring to a double murder in DeKalb County that had happened on Saturday night. "That had to take priority, especially since Winston Avery was still alive."

"Yeah, I get it," Joplin said. Jimmy Hernandez was famous for his meticulous recreation of scenes using bloodstains, which had built his national reputation and made him much in demand as an expert witness. It also frustrated the hell out of homicide detectives and prosecutors who needed information on a time schedule to which Hernandez couldn't—or wouldn't—conform. "Carrie's doing the autopsy as soon as we get the body. Maybe we'll get something more conclusive from that."

"I'll try to make some time for it tomorrow, Hollis. It's the best I can do."

After thanking him, Joplin called Sherika to ask her to notify him the minute the photos from CSU arrived, then headed over to Sarah Petersen's office to bring her up to speed.

CHAPTER FORTY-NINE

Tom Halloran had heard the news of Winston Avery's death on the radio as he drove back to Healey and Caldwell. Although he hadn't known Avery well and still considered him a suspect in Daisy Henry's murder, he'd felt a strange sense of loss. Not a personal loss…more like a loss to the community. The legal one, at any rate, if not to the black community. From all accounts, the attorney had cut himself off from any connection to those who might have benefitted from his prominence or given him their support in return. According to Cate, Avery had gone to bat for Will Henry when he was in danger of being fired from *The Undead Zone*, but that may simply have been part of his business dealings.

After checking in with Joan and learning a client had cancelled a two o'clock appointment, Halloran decided to call Cate, hoping he could break the news to her himself. He was too late; she'd heard it from Ricky Knox, who'd called to tell her that Ike would have to reschedule her appointment with him that afternoon. Compared to her reaction on Saturday, after hearing about Avery's suicide attempt, Cate seemed relatively calm, but Halloran thought that was either due to numbness, or the fact that she'd been resigned to his death due to the gravity of his injury. Or both. With a promise to update her on anything he might learn, he clicked off, then headed to Alston Caldwell's office. Whatever her feelings for Avery had been, Cate could use her family's support.

———

The body of Winston Avery arrived by ambulance a little after three p.m., accompanied by all his medical records, including the EMT report, the ICU charts, x-rays, a list of the surgical and resuscitation procedures performed, and the doctor of record's final report. By that time, Carrie, who'd been given a green light to perform the autopsy, had already pored over the death scene photos. She'd also listened carefully as Joplin recounted his conversation with Jimmy Hernandez.

"Take that into consideration, Carrie," he said as they sat in her office waiting for Simmons to get there. "It's conclusive enough for me, but you know Jimmy."

Carrie nodded. "I will. But right now I need to read through all the medical records Northside sent before I even look at the body. Let me know when Ike gets here, though."

Joplin nodded and stood up, then quietly left the room so she could get started. Sarah had taken him off the afternoon rotation as soon as she heard of Winston Avery's death, and he planned to use whatever time he had before the autopsy to tie up some loose ends.

———

Even dead, lying on a steel table and only half covered by a blue-speckled hospital gown, Winston Avery looked like a warrior from some long-ago battle, Carrie decided. His eyes were closed, but his face didn't look peaceful. His long, muscular arms lay by his sides, but his hands were clenched, as if he were prepared to defend himself. As if there were still some kind of kinetic energy left in his body.

Carrie looked up, as she always did before an autopsy, at the sign above the door leading into the storage room that said, "Mortui Vivos Docent," the Latin words translating to: "This is where the dead teach the living." She was already suited and gloved, as were all the others in the room: Ike, Hollis, Eddie, and Tim Meara. Pulling down her Plexiglas visor and clicking on her recorder, she gave a description of the body and then announced, for the record, that, for obvious reasons, she was skipping an examination of the body or hospital gown for fibers or trace evidence. After removing the gown, she then directed Tim to take photos, made x-rays of her own, and took parings of the fingernails, which she placed in an evidence bag.

From the hospital records and documentation, Carrie knew that Avery had been operated on twice, first to try to repair the damage done by the knife, then to try to deal with the sepsis and peritonitis that almost killed him twelve hours later. The surgeon had reopened the original site, but had widened it to allow for more of the bowel to be excised. She made note of this and had Tim take close-ups of the long incision that ran from the diaphragm to mid-belly.

"Before I open him up, I'm going to get ocular fluid," she said, looking over at Hollis and Ike as she picked up an 18-gauge needle attached to a 10-ml. syringe that she'd laid out earlier. "I'm doing this out of the usual order because I consider it the most crucial part of this autopsy. And I'll tell you why in just a minute." Ignoring their puzzled looks, Carrie inserted the needle into the globe of the left eye, at the lateral canthus, and slowly withdrew two milliliters of the vitreous humor, then placed it in a sterile tube which already had sodium fluoride preservative in it. She got another syringe, then walked around the table and withdrew fluid from the other eye. After that, too, was placed in a tube, she put both tubes in an evidence bag. Before finally turning to look at Hollis and Ike again, Carrie picked up one of the hospital x-rays and snapped it onto a viewing lamp near the autopsy table, then retrieved a stack of photos from another table.

"The attending surgeon, Dr. Malcolm Wright, had photos taken while the knife was still in Winston Avery," she said, passing them to Hollis and Ike.

"Then he took x-rays from various angles. This took a few minutes, but Avery had been stabilized by then, and Dr. Wright needed to know exactly what the knife had hit before he pulled it out of the abdomen. We're lucky he did this, because the subsequent surgeries make it impossible for me to determine the trajectory of the knife." She then turned back to the nearby table and picked up the knife, in the shape of a miniature sword, that had been in Avery's abdomen.

"Jesus!" said Ike. "That thing looks even more deadly than when it was in a stand on the bar in Avery's apartment."

"It *is* deadly," Carrie agreed, "because it's what killed Winston Avery, even if peritonitis and cumulative trauma ultimately stopped his heart. But the hands that plunged it into his body weren't his."

"I believe you, Carrie, but how can you tell that for sure?" Hollis asked.

"Because before you two came in here, I took measurements of Avery's arms and hands," she said, "as well as the distance between his shoulder and the middle of the surgical wound, where the knife went in. I had already noted the angle of the knife in the photos, and it sent up a red flag for me. That was later confirmed by the x-rays taken before the initial surgery and photos of the couch on which he was sitting. The bottom line is that Winston Avery, if he were sitting on that couch when the knife went in him—and there's no blood evidence to show differently—in the position in which the EMTs saw him, according to Jimmy Hernandez, he couldn't have done it himself."

"You mean because of what Jimmy said about the absence of transfer stains on the couch?" Ike asked. "Hollis told me about that while we were waiting for you."

"No," said Carrie. "It's pure math." She turned to Eddie and said, "Can you bring over a chair and help me demonstrate something, Eddie?"

"I guess," Eddie said, eyeing the knife nervously.

"Thanks. Now turn the chair so Hollis and Ike can see you from the side," she added. "That's good. Now take the knife and hold it with both hands in front of your body, as if you were going to stab yourself." When Eddie had reluctantly done as she asked, she turned to look at Ike. "See the difference between the angle here and the one in the photos and the x-ray?"

"Yeah, I do," Ike said. "But that doesn't mean Avery held it just the way Eddie is. What if he were holding it more upright, with the knife pointing downward?"

"Then it wouldn't have hit the exact spot in his abdomen that it did. It would have been lower. But—" and here Carrie went over to Eddie, took the knife from his hands and then stood behind him—"if someone came up to Avery behind the couch holding the knife and leaned over him like this, *then* plunged the knife in, look at the angle. As I said, I factored in all the measurements—the height of the couch seat, which I got from Jimmy, the length of Avery's torso and arms, the exact spot the knife went in, and the angle and trajectory of the knife in the x-ray. And just to make sure, I took the knife and the pertinent photos and x-rays to Dr. Minton's office and went over the whole scenario with him and David Markowitz. They agreed with me," Carrie added, looking both of them in the eyes.

"Which is why Jimmy was so troubled by the absence of blood on Avery's hands and the couch," Hollis said. "The killer must have washed the blood off his own hands, wiped the hilt of his fingerprints, and then placed Avery's hands around the knife hilt to get *his* prints on it."

"And *then*," Carrie said pointedly, "He carefully washed out the two glasses Avery mixed drinks in, refilled Avery's glass and pressed his right hand around it, put his own back in the cabinet and left, certain that Avery was either dead or dying. And even if he survived for a while, the killer was also certain that he wouldn't remember anything that had happened."

"Because he put roofies, or something like it, in Avery's drink?" Hollis said.

"Yes. Which is why I took the ocular fluid. It's only been three days since Avery was stabbed, and trace amounts of drugs like flunitrazepam—Rohypnol—or GHB—gamma-hydroxybutyrate—can remain in the body that long. Vitreous fluid is separate from the blood system, so the drug is less likely to be compromised there. And since the body can make its own GHB, even post-mortem, which would show up in a blood tox screen, it's a more accurate medium for assessment. The hospital's tox screen showed a blood-alcohol level of .1—high, but not enough to render a man his size unconscious. There were no other prescription or illegal drugs in his system either, but the doctor didn't request tests for GHB or flunitrazepam. This was framed as a 'suicide attempt,' not a date rape murder, remember."

"Wow," said Ike. "You did good, girl!"

"You sure did," Hollis said, smiling at her.

"Thanks, but I'm not finished," Carrie said. "I'm going to complete a full autopsy, and we'll have to wait on the lab for the vitreous analysis, but I wanted y'all to be able to get going with this. If further analysis or evidence proves I'm wrong, I'll be the first to admit it, but I don't think I am. Manner of death is homicide, as far as I'm concerned. There's the possibility that Avery did actually kill Blaine, and this was revenge for it, but I'm doubting that at this point. I think the killer was our Iago. And I also think he killed Avery to keep him from revealing the role he played in Blaine's death."

"And to plant the memory card from Blaine's camera in Avery's apartment," added Ike.

"Right," said Carrie. She watched as both men turned to look at the body on the steel table, their expressions hard as stone.

CHAPTER FIFTY

Joplin and Ike Simmons walked slowly and silently to the elevator on the ground floor of the ME's office. Joplin wondered if Simmons were experiencing the same gamut of emotions that he was, but knew his former partner well enough to know not to ask; he would talk about it when he wanted to. So they made it to the Investigative Unit without saying a word to each other. Simmons had dropped a folder onto his desk before they'd gone downstairs for the autopsy, and Joplin used that as an ice breaker.

"You didn't have time to tell me what this was," he said now, picking up the folder.

"Phone records from Blaine's cell phone, like you requested. I woulda sent them to you, but, as I told you a few weeks ago, we didn't find anything that sent up a flag, except for a sorta cryptic text from her brother and another one from Avery that didn't seem like much at the time, so I—"

"I know, Ike. I knew you had it. I just want to look through it. Especially now."

"Yeah, I hear you," said Simmons, nodding. "Guess we thought we had our man. At least, *I* did. Had him tarred and feathered at the get-go." He gave a long sigh. "I'm no better than Riker."

"The hell you are!" Joplin said. "And why would you bring him up anyway?"

"Because I'm beginning to doubt he ever checked Daisy's cell phone records out like he told Halloran he did. He had his sights on Will Henry from Day One and didn't pursue any other leads or suspects. I saw Winston Avery as a black man who was trying to be white, and my attitude towards him influenced the way I handled this investigation."

"I don't believe that, Ike. You and I both thought the evidence pointed to him, but we've done things by the book, following every lead we got, and you were willing to listen to me when I thought Avery might have been framed. And that was *before* we found out he was murdered."

Simmons gave him a pained smile and shook his head. "If you say so, buddy. Best way to make it up to him is to find his killer, so I'm gonna head over to the Ritz-Carlton Residences and go through every security tape they've got from Friday night. I'll let you know if I see anything, and you do the same," he added, nodding towards the folder.

When Simmons had left, Joplin decided he'd better let Sarah Petersen know about Winston Avery's suicide turning into a homicide. Although surprised, she agreed with Carrie's ruling and applauded the steps she'd taken to reach it. She also listened carefully to Joplin's Iago theory, but stopped him cold when he started talking about *Say Yes to the Dress*.

"I have great respect for your gut, Hollis," she said. "And I've seen your eidetic memory in action, but I prefer not to think that your insight comes from reality TV."

"That's my whole point, Chief," he protested. "There's very little reality in reality TV. Which is why—"

"Spare me," was all she said, holding up her palm for emphasis. "Just go find the guy. And keep me posted."

———

Blaine's phone records consisted of information gleaned from the phone itself—contacts, text messages, various apps, and emails—as well as a list from AT&T, her carrier, detailing all the calls made by Blaine or to her in the weeks before her death, with dates, phone numbers, and their duration. Simmons had cross-referenced the numbers with Blaine's contact list and identified most of them: her parents and brother, Winston Avery, Lucy Alvarez, Mark Rawlins, Ned Beeson, her doctors, her hairdresser, Mrs. Marlow, her vet, and various friends.

And him.

Joplin didn't know whether he felt shocked, surprised, or happy about that. Finally, he decided it was all three, but the last bothered him. Why did he feel happy that Blaine had kept his phone number after all these years? Pushing on, he looked at the emails she hadn't deleted, which were from *AJC* readers, as well as the text messages, and saw the two Ike had mentioned: a text from Avery the Tuesday before the murder agreeing to meet with Blaine and one the next day telling her he'd made a reservation at The Palm for eight p.m. that night. So maybe, he decided, he'd been right about a few things anyway: Someone had poisoned Winston Avery's mind about Blaine, and she'd uncovered something about her brother and confronted him.

The call record also seemed to prove that Simmons had been right when he'd told him a few weeks ago that there was nothing conclusive on it. There were calls to and from Reginal Davis in the week before the murder, ending around 3 p.m, on Friday, November 8th, when she would have met with him. Her mother had called several times that week, and her brother once on that Friday morning. Lucy Alvarez and Ned Beeson had also called Blaine in the early afternoon on Friday; there were several calls to and from Mark Rawlins that week as well. The most calls to and from Blaine, however, were with Winston Avery; many that she made lasted only seconds and seemed to be times when she couldn't reach him, and had either left a short message or hung up. They had increased in frequency the week before her death.

Joplin closed the folder and shoved it away from him, frustrated over what seemed to be a dead end. He leaned his elbows on his desk and massaged his temples. Something was nagging at him, but he couldn't pinpoint what it was. He closed his eyes, trying to give his right hemisphere time to come up with the answer; it usually helped. And after a few minutes, it occurred to him that he *hadn't* seen a call logged that he'd expected to see. Puzzled, he dragged the folder back to him, opening it to the day of the murder. When he saw that he was right, Joplin at first tried to think of reasons for its absence; he couldn't come up with anything. Images and conversations with various people—Mrs. Marlow, the General and his son, and Blaine's colleagues—began to overwhelm his brain. Some were chronological, others flashed back and forth in time. So he focused on ordering them and then calling up images of only one person: Ned Beeson. And Joplin watched and listened again as the young reporter answered his questions, both in the ME's conference room and at the *AJC's* headquarters.

Then Joplin finally knew who had killed Blaine Reynolds and, more importantly, why. He also thought he knew why the killer had pulled him into the investigation, and why no one had been seen going into the carriage house on Mrs. Marlow's property when Blaine was murdered. His theory explained both the brutal, personal way she'd been killed, as well as the tears that had fallen on her as she was dying. And the way she'd been posed, with the platinum ring on her right hand.

But it was only that—a theory. And unless Simmons found something in the security tapes from the Ritz-Carlton Residences, there would be no evidence to prove it. He would have to come up with an idea to force the killer's hand. And as Joplin sat there, his hand on the folder as if it were a Bible on which he was swearing an oath, an idea *did* come to him. But he would need help to pull it off. He was pretty sure Simmons would go along with it, but Mark Rawlins might need some convincing. Before talking to them, however, Joplin needed to make a few other calls.

The first would be to Mrs. Marlow, to ask her exactly what she'd seen in the driveway the night Blaine was murdered.

———

Ike Simmons didn't like the plan at all.

"I thought you learned your lesson about being a hot dog when you pulled that crazy stunt trying to catch Eliot Carter's killer!" he shouted into the phone. "Insteada being a *death* investigator, you're gonna end up a *dead* investigator, you keep doing this kinda wild-ass shit, Hollis."

"You got a better idea, Ike?" Joplin asked. "You just got through telling me you couldn't find another image of the guy walking near Avery on the Security tapes or anyone who saw his face. We've got zip on the ring we think the killer placed on Blaine's finger, other than the fact that it's platinum and probably very old. And we have no forensic evidence, no connection to James Corcoran, and no way to trace whatever Carrie might find in Avery's ocular fluid back to him. But we both know he killed three people. And might kill more to cover his tracks, if we don't stop him."

"No, *you* know he killed three people, Hollis. It's still just a theory as far as I'm concerned. And a crazy one at that."

"Then help me prove it. If I'm wrong, I won't be in any danger. You can even bring Ricky in on this, if you think we need back-up. And if it'll make you feel better, I'll run it by Sarah. I have to anyway. She told me last time I decided to ask for forgiveness instead of permission that she'd take my badge if I ever pulled that kind of stunt again, so if she says no, that's it."

The phone was silent for several seconds, then Simmons said, "You promise?"

"I promise."

He heard Simmons give a long, frustrated sigh. "Okay, but I call the shots, and we pull the plug if it goes south. No hot-dogging."

Joplin grinned and said, "None whatsoever. Now all we have to do is get Mark Rawlins on board."

CHAPTER FIFTY-ONE

After a long meeting in Lewis Minton's office that also included Sarah Petersen, Ike, and Carrie, Joplin finally received permission—albeit reluctantly, especially from Carrie—to go ahead with his plan. Simmons called his captain and the DA's office to address legal and tactical issues that might come up and got a green light to go ahead, along with several caveats. Then they all tried to anticipate the problems and contingencies they might encounter. But all of it, of course, depended on Mark Rawlins.

Joplin waited until six p.m. to call him, hoping he would be home by then. The editor sounded both curious and surprised when Joplin asked if he could stop by his house that night, whenever it would be convenient.

"Can't this wait until tomorrow, Hollis? I'm pretty down about Winston's death. It's really hit me hard. But I could meet you at my office first thing in the morning."

"I know it's an inconvenience, sir, and I wouldn't ask, if it weren't important. The fact of the matter is, this is *about* Avery's death, and I need your help."

Rawlins didn't answer right away. "Then I guess you'd better come over. It's my wife's bridge night, and I'm just finishing an early dinner, so come anytime."

After a brief meeting with Sarah and a slightly longer meeting with

Carrie, Joplin called Simmons and told him where to meet him, then headed for his car.

———

The Rawlins' house was a large, two-story, brick Georgian on Redfield Drive, just off Peachtree-Dunwoody. It looked like a house where Christmas parties should be held, and it occurred to Joplin as he walked up the steps to the door that if he and Blaine had stayed together, he probably would have been to one of them. Rawlins opened the door after he rang, wearing jeans and a shawl-collared navy sweater and holding what appeared to be a glass of whiskey.

"Come on in," he said, then ushered Joplin into a wide foyer dominated by a blue Persian rug and an imposing grandfather clock. "I'm having a stiff drink. It's been a long day. Are you still on duty or can you join me?"

"As a matter of fact, I'm *not* on duty, but I'd prefer a beer, if you have one."

"Glass or bottle?" Rawlins asked, walking towards the back of the house.

"Bottle's fine," Joplin said, following him. He came to an open door on the right that went into what looked like a study. Rawlins gestured to it and told him to make himself comfortable. An ornate desk holding an open laptop and a phone in a charging stand sat in front of a wall of book shelves on the left. There were two leather chairs on opposite sides of a window facing the door, with a table and lamp between them. A fireplace, gas logs glowing, was on the wall to the right. What Joplin assumed were various awards for journalism covered the mantel. It was the most comfortable room Joplin thought he'd ever seen.

"You have a beautiful house," he said, when Rawlins came into the room.

"I have to give Emily all the credit for that," Rawlins said, smiling. He handed Joplin his beer and sat down in the other leather chair, the smile gone. "Now what is all this about my helping you in some way? You said it had to do with Winston. I still can't get over his sudden death. I thought he was holding his own, from the reports I've gotten."

Joplin took a long sip of his beer, then set the bottle down on the table next to him and leaned forward. "I think we all did. And yes, it does have to do with him. The autopsy was performed today, and his death has been ruled a homicide."

It was evidently the last thing Mark Rawlins expected to hear. His face lost its color, and he took a large mouthful of his drink. "How can that be? I mean, I just assumed that…that—"

"That he'd killed himself," Joplin finished, picking up the beer bottle and taking another sip. "We all did. We also assumed he'd killed Blaine, and that the remorse was too much for him."

"But the police report we obtained stated was that he stabbed himself. How did the autopsy determine that he didn't?"

"The angle of the knife was wrong. And Dr. Salinger took ocular fluid to have it tested for something like Rohypnol or GHB. She thinks that's how the murderer was able to subdue a man as large as Avery."

"And was it? Present in the ocular fluid, I mean?"

Joplin shrugged. "It'll take a day or two to find out. But in the meantime, the *real* killer is still at large. We know who he is, but we don't have enough evidence. Not yet, anyway. And that's where you come in. If you'll help us, anyway."

"Me? But, how? How in the world can I help you?"

"Because he works for you: Ned Beeson."

Rawlins' jaw went slack with what was either shock or disbelief. "You've got to be kidding. Ned Beeson isn't capable of doing something like that! And why would he?"

"That's what I thought, too," Joplin said. "Or I did, until today. But he's also a human being who's capable of being overwhelmed by feelings of love and jealousy and intense possessiveness. And that's why he killed Blaine Reynolds, and had to get rid of Avery."

"Wait a minute," Rawlins said. "I knew Ned had a bit of a crush on Blaine, but not like you're talking about. He's just a kid!"

"He's twenty-five, Mr. Rawlins. Hardly a kid, although maybe Blaine made him feel like that if he told her how he felt. And then when he couldn't have her, he didn't want anyone else to have her. It's also why he decided to take photos of Blaine with her own camera afterwards and then hire a homeless drug addict to pose as a FedEx guy to bring them to me, in an attempt to make me part of the investigation. Then he planted the memory card from Blaine's camera in Avery's apartment after he killed him."

"I can't believe I'm hearing this," Rawlins said, clearly dumbfounded. "Especially about this homeless man you're talking about. How do you know about him?"

As Joplin explained about identifying James Corcoran, Rawlins' expression became more and more bewildered. Finally, he said, "But why would Ned want to involve *you*?"

"Because I once dated her. More to the point, I slept with her."

"But that was before Ned even began working at the *AJC*!" Rawlins sputtered.

"Didn't matter. Not to Beeson. He was jealous of anyone who'd ever been that close to Blaine. I had to be punished and made to suffer. And Winston Avery would become the prime suspect. We focused almost exclusively on him during the investigation. It would have worked, too, except for two things. First, Dr. Salinger was able to detect at the autopsy that Avery was murdered. He didn't count on that."

"What was the second thing?" Rawlins asked.

"That I have this weird kind of memory, and can recall everything I see and everything someone tells me," he said, then took another sip of his beer, knowing he looked a little smug.

Rawlins was silent again and seemed lost in thought. Then he swallowed the last of his drink and set it down on the table and sat up straighter in his chair. "Okay, tell me what it was that Ned has said or done to make you believe he killed three people? I'm not saying *I'll* believe it, but at least tell me. Maybe I can convince you otherwise. I'm very involved with the reporters I supervise; they're like family to me. Maybe because Emily and I could never have kids."

"Blaine felt that from you, Mark. And your wife. She talked about the Christmas and Fourth of July parties and the support you always gave her."

A wistful smile played across the editor's face. "Then I guess I'd better listen to what you have to say."

Joplin finished off his beer and sat back in his chair. "At first, it wasn't what Ned said, so much as what he *didn't* say. Unlike Lucy, he had only good things to say about Winston Avery—that he took the time to talk to him at your Christmas party; that he didn't seem arrogant, like everyone else thought; that he didn't seem possessive of Blaine. That he loved her. But Ned gave himself away: He couldn't hide his own feelings for Blaine. It was pretty obvious to me."

"But isn't that something that would make you *doubt* his guilt?" Rawlins insisted. "That he's so transparent, I mean? Subtlety isn't one of Ned's strong points."

"I disagree with you there, Mark," Joplin said and told him about Maggie Halloran's analysis of the photos the killer took of Blaine with the platinum ring on her right hand. "If it weren't for Maggie, we never would have gotten the message he was sending: That Blaine might have been wearing Winston Avery's engagement ring, but she was wearing *his* wedding band and would always belong to him."

"Or maybe that's just what Maggie Halloran was reading into it," said Rawlins, still looking credulous. "I know she's a well-known photographer, but isn't this out of her area of expertise? What was she doing looking at crime scene photos?"

"She's been a consultant for us a few times, actually. And I think she's right. Because when I went to the *AJC* offices and showed the pictures of the ring to you three, Ned couldn't help himself. He pointed out that it looked like a wedding band. 'One that a woman would wear by itself, without an engagement ring, I mean,' he said. Remember? He also suggested that it might have belonged to Blaine's grandmother or another relative."

"Yes, I remember his saying that," said Rawlins. "But why is that important?"

"Because he was making Winston Avery's ring seem insignificant, in a way. Saying that the plain silver band was more meaningful. And I think we'll find that the ring *did* belong to someone's grandmother—his. But if I can't get enough evidence to qualify as probable cause for an arrest warrant, I don't think that lead will be followed up. I've been able to get Sarah Petersen, the Chief Investigator, and Ike Simmons to *listen* to my theory, but they'll drop it if nothing pans out. If you won't help me, I mean. I'm pretty desperate to solve this case, Mark. For a lot of reasons."

Mark Rawlins frowned. "You sounded like you had a whole team behind you when you first got here, Hollis. But now it sounds like it's just *you* who's asking for my help. I assumed Ike Simmons and the APD were involved with this, too."

"They are," Joplin said quickly. "I mean, they *will* be, once you're on board."

Rawlins seemed to relax a little. "Okay, I get it. What is it you want me to do? What *can* I do?"

"I want you to call Ned Beeson. Right now. Tonight. And invite him over here. Tell him your wife is out for the night, and you need to talk to him.

That you've been thinking about Blaine's murder. And you've thought of some things that maybe hadn't occurred to the police—things that could make a good story for the paper. I'll tell you what to say to him before he gets here—like some of the things I've told you tonight. You can say you have a source at APD. And maybe he'll slip up. Say more than he means to say, and I can take him into custody."

"Yeah, and maybe he'll try to kill *me*," Mark Rawlins said. "According to you, he's already killed three people to cover his tracks. Why not me, too?"

"Because *I'll* be here," said Joplin. "I'll be close enough to listen in on the conversation, but I won't let him hurt you."

"I see," said Rawlins, but without much certainty. He stood slowly, with a distracted expression on his face, and Joplin hoped he hadn't said the wrong thing. But then Rawlins said, "I'm going to fix myself another drink and think about everything you've told me. Can I bring you another beer?"

"Why not?" Joplin said, sounding a little reckless.

Rawlins grabbed the empty beer bottle and headed for the kitchen. While he was gone, Joplin went over what he'd say next. He wasn't sure he'd gotten the right message to the editor. But when Rawlins returned a few minutes later carrying both drinks, his expression had lost its uncertainty. He handed the beer bottle to Joplin and sat down again.

"I've thought about it, and I feel I owe it to Blaine to help you," he said. "I'm not sure this...scheme of yours will work, but I guess all we can do is try. Should I go ahead and call Ned now or wait until you've told me what to say when he gets here?"

"Go ahead and call him now," Joplin said, lifting the beer bottle to his mouth and bringing it to his lips. "I'll tell you what to say while he's on his way."

"You're a lot more confident about getting Ned over here than I am. He could be out with friends."

"Or celebrating the fact that Winston Avery is dead. It's been all over the news. But you're his boss, and I'm sure it's not the first time you've called him at night when a hot story came up, right?"

"No, it's not," Rawlins said. "I'll get my phone." With a sigh, he set his drink down and walked over to his desk to retrieve the portable phone Joplin had seen earlier. But when he turned around, it wasn't a phone he was holding.

It was a small handgun.

CHAPTER FIFTY-TWO

"You should be feeling a little sleepy by now, Hollis," Mark Rawlins said, smiling again. "And just so you know, it was GHB, not Rohypnol that I put in Avery's drink last Friday. And in your beer a few minutes ago. Dr. Salinger's a pretty smart gal, I have to say. Maybe too smart. You wouldn't be here tonight if she hadn't ruled Avery's death a homicide. And pretty soon you'll be as dead as he is."

Joplin stared at him, a look of stark disbelief freezing on his face. He swallowed, then said, haltingly, slurring his words a little, "This…isn't…isn't—"

"Happening?" Rawlins said. "But it is. Not the way you thought it would. Or the way *I* thought it would either, actually. I had gotten Winston just about ready to go after you himself. Gotten him to believe that *you* had murdered Blaine, and you were going to get away with it by implicating him. But then I had to tweak the plan a bit."

"But…how? And, why, for God's sake?"

Rawlins looked at his watch. "My wife won't be home for at least another hour, so I'll tell you. But only if you do exactly as I say." When Joplin nodded, he said, "With one hand, reach into your jacket and pull out your gun by the barrel. Slowly."

"What makes you think I *have* a gun?" Joplin asked.

"Please. The games are over." He watched carefully as Joplin did as he said. "Okay, hand it to me, butt first. Thanks," he added, taking the gun and setting it on his lap. "Now, to answer your first question: It wasn't easy getting Winston to believe that Blaine was cheating on him. With you. But as I told you, we'd gotten close over the last year. So I told him something that was actually the truth, something he could confirm by asking her. And it was devastating to him. And to Blaine, of course."

"What?" Joplin asked.

"That the reason Blaine had broken up with you was because she was pregnant. With your child. And that she'd had an abortion. Her career was too important to her, and she wasn't ready to be a mother. But she couldn't tell you, so she just stopped seeing you after that."

"No," said Joplin, but even as he denied it, his mind flashed on the time that Blaine had mentioned that she wasn't sure if she wanted children. Not just because of her diabetes, but because of her career. It hadn't bothered him, because they weren't at the stage in their relationship where he would need to give it some thought. But his dreams had been trying to tell him what his conscious mind hadn't considered, and he knew what Mark Rawlins was saying was true.

There had been something abrupt and unfinished about the way his affair with Blaine had ended, and the knowledge that she'd been pregnant when she died had struck some inner chord that kept nagging at him. It was also why Winston Avery had said, "Did *you*?" when Joplin had asked if Avery knew Blaine was pregnant. He'd meant had *Joplin* known that Blaine was pregnant before she stopped seeing him.

"How... did you...know?" he managed to say, overwhelmed by what he'd been told.

"From Lucy, of course, our little gossip girl. She came to me when Blaine was recovering from the abortion, to explain why she wasn't up to going on a trip for a story she was working on. Lucy could never keep a secret. Anyway, when Winston confronted Blaine with it, she admitted it, thinking it was Lucy who'd told him. After that, it was pretty easy to convince him that she'd started seeing you again, Hollis. To make sure marrying him was what she wanted. And then he called off the engagement."

"I still don't get it, Mark." Joplin asked. "Why would he believe Blaine would cheat on him, even knowing about the abortion?"

"Because I'd been playing on his only real weakness: his doubt that Blaine loved him. Despite all his accomplishments and his wealth and prestige, deep down he still felt like the poor black kid raised by a rich family's maid. Oh, yes, he told me all about his upbringing," Rawlins added, when Joplin must have shown his surprise. "And how the General tried to make him feel like nothing when they met. We were such good friends by then." Rawlins smiled to himself, as if savoring the memory. "I managed to suggest that perhaps Blaine—without realizing it, of course—was using him to get at her father. Thumb her nose at everything the General stood for. And that ate away at him. So it wasn't hard to get him to believe that she'd never really gotten over you, Hollis."

Joplin's head was reeling from everything he'd heard, but he wanted to keep Rawlins talking. "And when you saw that your plan was working, you offered Blaine a shoulder to cry on, told her maybe breaking off the engagement with Avery was for the best. Maybe even told her how you'd felt about her all these years. Because that's really what this was all about, right, Mark? You loved Blaine, and hated it when she was with me. Hated that I could make her pregnant. Hated it even more when she fell in love with Winston Avery and was going to marry him. So you finally told her."

Mark Rawlins eyes glistened with tears. "She thanked me. *Thanked* me! That was all I got from her! She told me she cared about me deeply, but that she loved Winston and was going to do everything she could to get him back. To find out who had been telling lies about her." He looked up at Joplin, a wistful expression on his face. "It never even occurred to her that it was me. So I just told her I'd help her find out who had poisoned Winston's mind."

"You were in the car with Blaine…when she went home that Friday," Joplin said. "Mrs. Marlow admitted to me today that she'd only heard Blaine's car in the driveway that night, she hadn't actually seen her. You must have met her somewhere and asked for a ride. Told her your car wouldn't start or something and that your wife would pick you up at her place."

"Score one for you!" Rawlins said bitterly. "Yeah, I had already arranged to meet her at the Starbucks in Brookhaven the day before. To find out what she'd learned from Reginal Davis. That's how I got into her apartment without anyone seeing me."

"So you had already decided to kill her that night, because you knew that she wasn't going to give up. That she'd at least gotten Avery to talk to her again. They had dinner together two nights before she died. He told me. And you knew that sooner or later they would have realized your role in trying to break them up."

"I would have lost her forever," Rawlins said sadly.

"You *did* lose her, for Christ's sake—you murdered her!"

Rawlins' eyes glittered as he stared at Joplin, but Joplin couldn't tell whether it was from tears or madness. Or something else, deep inside his soul.

"I didn't want to kill her, Hollis," he said, seeming to get hold of himself. "You, of all people should be able to understand why I had to: The thought of Winston Avery's hands on her. It made me sick to my stomach every time I thought of them together. It wasn't right, and I couldn't stand it anymore. I even gave her a chance that night to come to her senses. But she told me again that she loved him. Said she'd just found out she was pregnant with his child. Can you believe it? She flushed your child down the drain, but she was going to have *his* child! I couldn't let that happen."

Joplin was dumbstruck for several seconds,. "You mean, this was all because he was *black*?"

Rawlins seemed to realize what he'd said and straightened in his chair. "Of course not. I'm as liberal as the next guy. But I just never thought that Blaine…I mean, even her family objected to the relationship. Her father—"

"Is a racist," Joplin said coldly. Then he took a deep breath, trying to calm down. "But I *do* know that you really didn't want to kill her. I do. You cried as you were strangling her, didn't you? Because you still loved her."

"I still do," Rawlins said. "I'll never stop loving her."

"But if you couldn't have her, no one could. Everything I said about Ned Beeson a little while ago applies to you, Mark. I realize that now. And I bet we'll find out that that platinum ring belonged to someone in *your* family. It was your way of showing that she belonged to you. Speaking of which, how did you know I'd be on the job the next morning? So you could send those photos to me?"

"Now, that's where Ned *does* come into this, Hollis. He's a genius when it comes to anything digital. A cyber whiz kid. And he was flattered when I asked him to show me how to get information from the Internet that most people can't get. 'Course *he* would never use it illegally; he's such a Boy Scout. But without realizing it, Ned gave me a lot of information about how to hack into computer websites—like the ME's office, for instance—and I took it from there. I was never a Boy Scout myself. Blaine had told me all about the 'menstrual Cycle' when she was writing that article about the ME"s office. When she met you. So I was able to find out exactly when you'd be on call. I didn't decide to take those photos until…until she was dead. Until I noticed the camera in the kitchen."

Joplin closed his eyes, sickened by what Rawlins had told him. "You wanted to twist the knife a little more, I suppose. Making sure I'd be the one to investigate the scene wasn't enough. And then, somehow, you got Avery to believe that I had killed her. But how?" When Rawlins just smiled at him, he made the connection. "You convinced him that Blaine had dumped me again, and this time I went ballistic."

The editor nodded, still smiling. "I made him believe there was no way of proving it. That you had made sure you'd be one of the first people on the scene, and that you'd have the whole police force on your side. He was almost ready to go after you and avenge Blaine's murder—but as the investigation went on, I could tell he was having doubts. And you were getting too close to the truth, Hollis. So I paid him a visit the night before the funeral. Hopped on the elevator as he was going up to his apartment and told him I didn't want him to be alone that night. The rest you already know."

Joplin knew he should keep his mouth shut and not provoke the bastard, but he couldn't help himself. "But you had to knock him out before you could even get close enough to stab him with his own knife, didn't you, you little shit? Winston Avery was more man than you'll ever be, Mark, and you knew it. He could have torn you apart with one hand tied behind his back."

Rawlins simply stared at him and then sighed. "I don't think you quite understand the gravity of your situation, Hollis. I've got *two* guns now, and you have a beer laced with GBH that you're going to finish drinking. Then before it kicks in completely, we're going to walk out to your car."

"Let me guess," said Joplin. "You're planning a fatal car accident for me, right?"

"Something like that. I'm not sure yet. But having you dead was always part of the plan, and letting Ned be the new fall guy is a great idea. And I always intended to kill you sooner or later. You just made it easier for me. Now drink up. It's getting late."

Reluctantly, Joplin brought the bottle up to his mouth and tilted his head back to finish off the beer. When Mark Rawlins stood up and motioned for him to do the same, he felt a little unsteady as he got to his feet. Rawlins pocketed Joplin's service weapon, then jerked his own gun towards the door. They reached the entry hall, and Joplin began to feel the effects of the GHB, but he made it to the front door.

"Open it," Rawlins said. "I'll be right behind you."

The night air revived him a bit, but Joplin wasn't sure how long he would be able to stay on his feet. Luckily, he didn't have to, because as soon as Rawlins came outside, he was ambushed by Simmons and Ricky Knox, who'd been standing on either side of the front door.

"That was...cutting it a little...too close, Ike," Joplin was able to say, before lurching down the walkway and pitching head first onto the Rawlins' beautifully manicured lawn.

CHAPTER FIFTY-THREE

Joplin came to in what looked like an ER, with an IV in his arm, oxygen tubes in his nose, and Carrie sitting next to his bed. A monitor on his left middle finger was connected to a machine that beeped steadily. His head hurt like hell, and he didn't remember how he'd gotten there or why.

Carrie gripped his hand and smiled. "You're in the ER at St. Joseph's, Hollis. Do you remember anything that happened?"

He searched his aching brain, but the only thing he could think of was that he must have had too much to drink and then passed out. Or blacked out, which terrified him. "Too much Yuengling?" he finally said. "Did I have a car accident?"

"Well, from what Ike told me, that's evidently what was planned for you tonight," Carrie said. "Luckily, he and Ricky rescued you in time. That was about three hours ago."

A few images filtered through his mind, but they made no sense. "But why am I here?"

"You're being given fluids to bring your blood pressure back up and oxygen to address your low respiration. It's about all that can be done for a GHB overdose. Oh, and the two beers you drank didn't help, either. That heightened the effects of the GHB."

"I have no idea what you're talking about, Carrie, but I'm glad you're here. When can we go home?"

"Not until we're sure you're stable. And don't worry if you can't piece everything together right away. The effects of the GHB will linger a while. What *do* you remember, though?"

Joplin sighed and closed his eyes, trying to bring up images to help him. "Not anything about drinking beer. I remember realizing that I didn't see Mark Rawlins' phone number on Blaine's phone records when she was pulling into her driveway, even though he'd told me she called him then. And that's when I began to suspect he was the killer. I remember a meeting in Dr. Minton's office with you and Sarah and Ike… where we planned my wearing a wire and going to Rawlins' house… I think I was supposed to pretend Ned Beeson was our chief suspect and ask him for his help in getting Ned to…confess. Then somehow try to get him to say something incriminating about…Blaine's murder." He shook his head, trying to dispel the cobwebs in it. "I think I was also supposed to admit that I had no evidence to support what everyone else thought was a crazy theory… hoping to get him to try to eliminate *me*." Joplin opened his eyes and looked at the beeping machine next to his bed. "I take it I was wildly successful."

As if on cue, the door opened, and Ike Simmons walked in. "You're awake," he said happily.

"And alive," Joplin said. "No thanks to you, Ike."

Carrie stood up and gave him a quick kiss. "I'm going to go talk to the doctor and see when I can take you home. I think your memory's coming back just fine."

Joplin waited until she'd gone, then said, "Why didn't you rush the house before I had to drink that second beer? I was just pretending to drink it before he pulled the gun on me."

"Believe me, we wanted to," Simmons said, coming closer to the bed. "But it was because of the gun that we didn't. Especially when we heard him get *your* gun, too. We were afraid he'd shoot you or take you hostage before we could get to you, so we decided to wait till you both came outside. It was a tactical decision, Hollis. And it worked."

"I guess," Joplin said begrudgingly. "Just tell me the bastard's in a cell and officially charged with all three murders."

"We're still workin' on that, but we're close. We couldn't get warrants to search his house and office for the GHB and evidence linking him to James Corcoran until we took what we had on tape to the DA's office. Judge Markham signed them immediately. CSU is still working both scenes, but I got word that they found the GHB in his refrigerator first thing."

"Well, that's good anyway. Has Rawlins said anything more?"

Simmons shook his head. "We Mirandized him as soon as we called the EMTs for you, and he asked us to call his lawyer, then clammed up. We took him to the station, and as soon as the lawyer finished talking to Rawlins he came out loaded for bear and said we couldn't use anything we had on tape, because you didn't read Rawlins his rights as soon as you got to his house. At which point, I told him we'd discussed this with Jeff Dillon at the DA's office before we even went to Rawlins' house and were informed that Rawlins could not be considered to be in custody, since he would be in his own house and could tell you to leave at any time. So we had no duty to read him his rights until we actually *did* take him into custody while he was attempting to walk you to your car at gun-point. He practically foamed at the mouth and said he'd see us in court. I don't think that will happen, though. With all we have on Rawlins, I think he'll go for a plea deal just to keep from getting the death penalty."

Joplin smiled for the first time since waking up. "Then the whole thing was worth it. And forget what I said, Ike, I know you did what you had to do. Thanks."

Simmons sat down in the chair Carrie had vacated. "One thing I didn't do is tell Carrie what Rawlins said about…you and Blaine. And the baby. I figured that was up to you, buddy."

The smile faded from Joplin's face as he remembered. "Thanks for that, too, Ike. I don't want any secrets from her, so I need to tell her. Just not here."

"I think that's a good idea," Simmons said.

"What's a good idea?" Carrie said, coming into the room. She was smiling.

"Taking tomorrow off," Simmons said, getting to his feet.

"That's exactly what his doctor recommended," she said. "As well as absolutely no alcohol for at least 48 hours."

"Believe it or not," Joplin said, "the way I feel, I'd even pass up one of Gerry's Dirty Martinis with blue cheese olives right now."

CHAPTER FIFTY-FOUR

When his cell phone rang at 10:45 p.m., Halloran was surprised to see Ike Simmons' name pop up.

"Ike!" he said. "You're the last person I expected to hear from tonight. Maggie and I have been following the news ever since Winston Avery passed away, and we were just waiting for the late news shows to hear more about Mark Rawlins' arrest. You must be knee-deep in all that."

"Well, I am, but there's more going on, and I didn't want you and Maggie to learn about it on the news, if there are more leaks to the press."

"Is Hollis alright?" Halloran said quickly. "Is this about him?"

"He's fine—now, anyway. He and Carrie left the ER just a little while ago and should be home by now, but I'd give them until tomorrow before you call."

"What happened?" Halloran asked tersely. "Do you mind if I put you on speaker, so Maggie can hear, too?" When Ike agreed, they listened as the detective gave a quick account of Avery's autopsy, as well as the plan hatched by Joplin to get evidence of Mark Rawlins' guilt in what had turned out to be three murders. A plan that had evidently almost gotten him killed, Halloran deduced, although Ike had assured them that he and Ricky had had everything under control.

"Did Carrie know he was going to do this?" Maggie asked.

"Oh, yes, although I think she had second thoughts. There were a lot of folks involved, including some from the DA's office. Anyway, I figured you knew why I couldn't meet with Cate Caldwell or get back with you about the Henry case, but I plan on ordering the investigation file first thing tomorrow."

"I appreciate that, Ike, especially with all you've got going on. I guess we can eliminate Winston Avery as a potential suspect, anyway."

"Yes, but I still want to look into the Henry case a little more." Ike said. "And I'm hoping we'll have another opportunity to talk to Rawlins, but his attorney's keepin' him on ice for now. We still don't know what his connection to James Corcoran was."

"We'll let you go now, Ike," Halloran said. "I know your night's not over. And thanks again."

"You bet," said Ike.

The 11 Alive News came on almost immediately, and Halloran agreed with Maggie's suggestion that they watch it for any updates on Rawlins' arrest before discussing what they'd just heard from Ike Simmons. In addition to earlier reports that recapitulated what had been known about Blaine Reynolds' murder and her editor's arrest, this broadcast contained footage of the Rawlins' house, as well as of the ER at St. Joseph Hospital. A reporter standing outside it told viewers that "our sources revealed that someone in law enforcement was injured during Mark Rawlins' arrest and is currently being treated here at St. Joseph's." Richard Danforth, a well-known criminal defense attorney, was identified as representing Rawlins, but had "no comment" as he was shown exiting the Atlanta Police station on Piedmont. There was no mention of James Corcoran's murder, or that Winston Avery hadn't committed suicide, but Halloran was sure that would change in the next twenty-four hours.

"Wow!" Maggie said when the broadcast went to a commercial. "This has been quite the day."

Halloran grabbed the remote and turned off the TV. "That's an understatement." He turned to look at Maggie. "I'm certainly glad Mark Rawlins has been arrested, but the best thing to come out of this whole sad story is that Winston Avery didn't kill Blaine. I hated to think that he had, and I know it will give Cate some comfort. She never believed that he was guilty."

"Just like Jayla Henry doesn't believe that her father is guilty," Maggie said. "I know there's nothing more we can do right now, but I'm still hoping that case might have a happier ending, too."

Halloran squeezed her hand and said, "I do, too. But we're just going to have to wait for Ike to see what's in the case file and take it from there. In the meantime, we need to think about Thanksgiving. We have twelve guests— including Jayla—coming to our house, in case you've forgotten."

"How could I?" she said, smiling. "I have a whole day of shopping and errands planned for tomorrow."

"I'm taking off Wednesday afternoon, so I'll be able to help then."

"Good," said Maggie. "Because I've got you down for a lot of chopping and cleaning up."

———

On Tuesday afternoon, Ike Simmons got back from a quick lunch to find a message from the Records Retention officer that he could pick up the Henry murder investigation file any time. He was back at his desk with the bound notebook in ten minutes and decided to give it a quick once-over before getting back to the mountain of paperwork generated by Mark Rawlins' arrest and the events of the night before. So far, Rawlins had followed his attorney's instructions not to talk, but Simmons had gotten word from the DA's office that Danforth had requested a meeting with the ADA assigned to the case.

The APD had adopted the highly structured "Murder Book" format devised by the LAPD several years ago, which had a Table of Contents allowing Simmons to quickly access the section that held warrants and subpoenas. He saw search warrants for both the crime scene, Will Henry's car, and his apartment and trailer on the set of *The Undead Zone,* all issued at the time of his arrest. There was also a previous warrant to seize Henry's cell phone that Halloran had said was so controversial in his trial. He flipped to the section entitled "Property and Evidence Reports" which showed both phones in the list of property seized at the crime scene and on Will Henry's person, a week prior to his arrest. The SIM cards of the phones, usually removed for examination, were also listed.

So far, it looked like Bill Riker had done everything by the book, and Simmons felt a little guilty for thinking the worst of the man. He moved on to Section 11, which contained personal and official information about the murder victim. As he'd expected, Daisy Henry had no arrests or convictions, not even a traffic ticket. A list of friends, family members, co-workers, and neighbors, generated within the first 48 hours, with marks to show they'd been contacted and/or interviewed, as well as places she frequented, such as a local spa, her hairdresser, the nearby Starbucks, etc. came next. Simmons expected that Daisy's activities on the day of her death had been pieced together with these lists and would be in the section containing a chronological report of the investigation, as well as the sections giving the witness list and statements and any elimination of suspects. The examination of her cell phone and the phone records from AT&T came next.

Again, Riker seemed to have done a thorough job of checking out numbers on the contacts, call logs, texts messages, and emails on the cell phone itself. There was a list of names corresponding to the phone numbers which was similar to the list of family, friends, co-workers, etc. Daisy had had frequent contact with Will Henry, even during the time they were estranged, including a call from him in the afternoon before she'd been killed. After Will Henry's number, the next most frequent number belonged to the show's director, Nate Mauldin, and had increased in frequency in the two months before her death.

There were only two surprises in the call log list and the corresponding phone records that Simmons saw: Daisy and Trina Daily, the woman Will had left her for, had contacted each other often before Will had moved out, and Daisy had made several calls to her mother in the months after Will had left her. He guessed the two actresses had been friendly before the affair, but it was puzzling that Daisy had repeatedly called a woman who, by all accounts, had cut off all contact with her daughter because she'd married a black man. And the phone records showed that the calls had each lasted several minutes. The last one had been placed by Daisy soon after the call from Will that afternoon.

Still turning this over in his mind, Simmons locked the file in his bottom drawer, but decided to put off doing paperwork for a little while longer to make another trip to the Evidence Room.

———

By one p.m., Maggie had unloaded everything from the cleaners, and all the food and decorations she'd bought for Thanksgiving dinner at Swoozie's and Whole Foods. After grabbing a vanilla yogurt from the refrigerator, she sat down to go over the list of things she still needed to do. Only going to Maggiano's to pick up dinner for Carrie and Hollis was still on the list. As she finished the yogurt, an idea came to her, and after making a quick call to her mother, she grabbed her car keys.

Ten minutes later, Maggie turned out of Ansley Park onto Piedmont; traffic would be bad everywhere, and she figured it would be worse on Peachtree. But she'd already made up her mind to go see the Bullochs one more time. She could go to Maggiano's on the way home. Tom had told her the day before that Ike didn't think he could get a warrant for Daisy's phone records, and that there was no guarantee they were in the murder case file. Daisy's parents, he'd said, as next of kin, could give permission to get the records, even though Maggie's encounter with them indicated that probably wouldn't happen.

But in the past few weeks, Maggie had been thinking about that afternoon. She was sure she'd seen a look of intense regret on Jeremiah Bulloch's face when she'd told him about the cross Daisy had given Jayla. Maybe he and Rachel had even talked about it after she'd left, despite the way they'd driven her out of the church. And maybe they'd be willing to give their permission about the phone records if she stopped by to see them again and appealed to whatever feelings they still had for their daughter. She knew Tom wouldn't be happy about what she was doing, but she decided it was worth trying, even if Rachel Bulloch made good on her threat to call the police.

It took another thirty minutes to reach the church, which seemed even more forlorn-looking than a few weeks earlier. The church doors were locked, and no one responded to her knocking. Maggie started walking slowly back to her car, then, squaring her shoulders, she turned and headed for the small, gray house next to the church.

CHAPTER FIFTY-FIVE

Tom Halloran listened intently as Ike told him what he'd discovered that afternoon while going through the investigation case file.

"Well, I agree with you that it's not too strange that Daisy and Trina Daily might have been friends before the affair, but the phone calls to her mother are puzzling, to say the least," he said. "If Daisy Henry was trying to fix her relationship with her parents, it must not have been successful, given the way the Bullochs acted after her death."

"I don't know that yet. But I'm gonna find out. In the meantime, you need to know that Winston Avery's name *wasn't* on any of the call logs on Daisy's phone, and he was never eliminated as a suspect, because he wasn't on any list of Daisy's friends or even aquaintances. But the thing we really need to discuss—if you believe in Will Henry's innocence—is this: Who would Daisy Henry have let in her house after Will left? No one called her after that, and from the crime scene photos, I could tell that there wasn't a window near the back door or even a peephole."

"And she'd already gotten ready for bed by then, which meant that a little time had elapsed since Will had been there."

"Well, if Daisy *was* having an affair of her own, she might have arranged earlier to have the guy come by—maybe to break things off if she and Will were talking about gettin' back together," Ike said. "Or he mighta just knocked on the back door and said it was him, and she let him in. I doubt she woulda let Trina Daily in, especially if she thought Trina knew Will was coming back home."

"Yeah, that doesn't seem likely," said Halloran. "It had to be someone she knew well and trusted."

"Like her own mother?" Ike suggested. "Especially if they'd been talking recently. And the last call between them was on the afternoon of the day Daisy was murdered."

"I hate to think that Daisy's mother could've killed her, but it's certainly a possibility. According to Maggie, she still seemed to have a lot of anger toward Daisy when she talked to her a few weeks ago. But it makes more sense to me that a rejected lover—like Mark Rawlins turned out to be— would be able to get Daisy to let him in so they could talk. "

"Well, you think on it some more. I've gotta return a call to the DA's office about Rawlins, and then I think I'll have a little prayer meetin' with Detective Riker."

But the longer Halloran thought about it, he decided that Ike's suggestion was more than just a possibility. What if Daisy's mother had begun to believe that Daisy and Will were getting a divorce, then found out that wasn't going to happen? Maybe Daisy had called her after Will left that night and told her what happened. And maybe she'd rushed over to see her daughter, to convince her that she couldn't let her husband come back. Maggie had told him that Rachel Bulloch seemed…unhinged. "Fanatical" was the word she'd used. Had that all-consuming fanaticism driven her to kill Daisy? It had certainly driven both parents to disown her when she married Will Henry, as well as to reject their only grandchild. And yet, Ike had said that Daisy had talked to her mother in the afternoon, *before* Will had been to see her, so that scenario didn't work.

Pulling his thoughts from questions he had no way of answering, Halloran turned his attention back to preparing for his next appointment. He'd just have to wait until Ike got back to him.

———

The door was opened by Rachel Bulloch, who must have seen Maggie through one of the glass panels on either side of it, because her expression was anything but welcoming. Her clothes were as plain and drab as the last time Maggie had seen her, but there were darker circles under eyes, and her face seemed thinner.

"What are you doing back here?" she asked, her voice full of hostility. "I told you never to bother us again. Do I need to call the police?"

"Of course not," Maggie said, trying to sound soothing. "I'll leave if you want me to. I just came here to ask if you and your husband would agree to let the police investigate Daisy's cell phone. We really think her husband is innocent. That he didn't kill Daisy, and there might be evidence on the phone that proves that. As her next of kin, you could give permission, because the police don't have probable cause to open up the case again. So I thought that maybe—"

"You just won't listen, will you?" Rachel Bulloch said scornfully. "Daisy was dead to us before she died! Why can't you get that through your head!"

"What's going on here?"

Maggie whirled around and saw that it was Jeremiah Bulloch. There were dark circles under his eyes, too, and he seemed to be even thinner.

"I'm handling it," Rachel said. "You don't need to worry about it, Jeremiah."

"But, why have you been having words?" Daisy's father asked.

"It was a misunderstanding," Maggie said quickly, not wanting to explain. She didn't feel the same threatening vibes from Jeremiah Bulloch as she had from his wife, but he didn't know why she was there. Now all she could think of was how to get away from both of them. "I won't bother you again," she added, then started to walk past him.

"I think we need to talk first," Bulloch said, reaching out and grabbing her arm.

"I told you I was handling it, Jeremiah!" said Rachel, her voice rising.

And as Maggie looked at the woman's terrified expression and then into her husband's flat, dead eyes, she realized that she'd been afraid of the wrong Bulloch.

CHAPTER FIFTY-SIX

"Tom, I hate to bother you," Halloran heard his mother-in-law say.

"No problem, Colleen," he said. "By the way, we're really looking forward to seeing you and Kevin on Thanksgiving."

"We are, too," she said quickly. "But do you know where Maggie is? The school just called me when they couldn't get hold of her, so I'm on my way to pick up the kids. I told Maggie earlier I'd be happy to get them if she were running late, but I never heard from her."

Halloran was immediately alarmed. It wasn't like Maggie to be late to get the kids or forget to call her mother if she were going to be. "I know she said she was going to Whole Foods and Swoozie's, but I don't know where else, do you?"

"She's already been there," said Colleen. "I talked to her around one, and she said she had a few more errands to run. That's when I said to call if she needed me to get the kids for her. I'm worried, Tom."

"I'm sure there's an explanation, Colleen. Let me do some checking. Are you okay with the kids for a while?"

"Sure. Just keep in touch."

But despite his soothing words to Colleen, Halloran remained alarmed. His conversation with Ike had opened up the possibility of a new suspect in Daisy Henry's murder: her own mother. Maggie didn't know that, and Halloran remembered telling her about the problem Ike would have getting a warrant to search Daisy's cell phone. He'd also told her that the Bullochs, as next of kin, could authorize such a search.

Halloran first tried to reach Maggie, but when her phone went directly to voicemail, he left her a message urging her to call him, then jabbed at the icon near Ike's name. He'd rather make a fool of himself than risk Maggie's safety—or life. Thankfully, Ike answered right away, and instead of blowing off his concerns, asked for details about Maggie's car.

"It's a silver Mercedes ML 350—an SUV," Halloran said quickly. "License plate BWS 7209. And she's got an mbrace tracking device in the car."

"That'll help. We can get someone on that right away. I'll also get a uniform to go to the Bullochs' house. I don't like the sound of this at all."

———

"Jeremiah, we need to just let her be on her way," said Rachel Bulloch.

Maggie was sitting on the couch in the living room, where Jeremiah had placed her, after dragging her into the house. He was pacing back and forth in front of her, and she thought of making a dash for the door, but decided not to chance it. There was still a possibility that she could get out of there alive, that she'd jumped to the wrong conclusion when she thought he might have killed his own daughter. But that hope was dashed by his next words.

"She's not going to give up, Rachel, and you know it. She and her husband are going to keep at it and at it and at it until they find out what happened. I was only doing God's will, but they won't care about that. The police will lock me up, and then what will happen to our church?" He stopped pacing and turned to look at his wife. "None of this would have happened if you hadn't started talking to Daisy again. She was *dead* to us. And then he left her, and we got our hopes up when we thought she was going to divorce him."

"And she was, Jeremiah." Rachel insisted. She was standing behind her husband, close to the small dining room. "She was! But then she called me that afternoon and said they'd talked. That he was coming over that night, and she was going to agree to let him come home. She hoped we could still keep in touch, maybe meet Jayla. Maybe even meet *him*. I shouldn't have told you. I know that now. But I didn't know how upset you'd be. That you would rush out of here and go to see her. You're right—it was all my fault. My fault! Not yours."

He sighed and said, "It doesn't matter now. What matters is that the Lord still has work to do. He doesn't want our church to be destroyed." Jeremiah looked at Maggie. "Not by this woman. A daughter of Eve, if I ever saw one. Just like Daisy. A daughter of Eve and the Whore of Babylon combined. I brought her into this world, and it was up to me to take her out of it."

"You can't kill her!" Rachel said. "I've already got one death on my soul. I can't let you do this, Jeremiah!"

"Killing me won't stop the new investigation into Daisy's death," said Maggie, trying to sound calm. "And my husband knows I intended to come by and see you today. To ask about permission for the cell phone to be examined," she added, hoping he believed her. "I should have picked my kids up from school fifteen minutes ago, and they'll be looking for me soon."

Jeremiah began pacing again. "I can't think. I can't think! *God* will tell me what to do. I just have to listen. But I can't think with all the talking going on."

Maggie looked past him to where Rachel stood, pity and terrible remorse playing across her face. And then it changed to fear as Jeremiah suddenly turned and walked over to where Maggie was sitting. She stood up, determined not to let him kill her without putting up some kind of fight. His hands reached out and grabbed her by the throat. Maggie tried to break his grip on her, but whatever madness had overtaken him had also given him a kind of strength that was almost superhuman. His eyes had no emotion in them as he stared down at her. They were the eyes of bishops and judges who had ordered the burning of heretics and witches, and she realized this was how he had looked to Daisy as he killed her. And this was how Daisy had felt as she was dying.

Maggie's vision began to dim, and there was a roaring in her ears. And then she heard Rachel screaming at Jeremiah and felt something warm spatter on her face and hair. His hands lost their grip on her throat, and they both fell to the floor as sirens blared from somewhere outside.

EPILOGUE

Carrie and Maggie were in the kitchen setting up trays of Champagne flutes and appetizers, so Tom Halloran ushered Hollis into his study before the other guests arrived. They hadn't had a chance to process everything since Tuesday afternoon, when two police officers had burst into the Bulloch house and found Maggie half dead and Rachel Bulloch standing over her husband with a fire extinguisher in her hands. Although Ike Simmons had appeared on the scene minutes later, calling the EMTs and more officers, it had been complete chaos for several hours. Halloran's first sight of Maggie at the hospital had been one of the hardest things he'd ever had to go through. It was still haunting him.

The next day had been taken up with Jeremiah Bulloch's interrogation at Northside Hospital, as well as interviews with Rachel and Maggie. Then came all the paperwork dealing with the petition to have Will Henry's conviction vacated, which both the DA and Damon Copeland handled, and an indictment on murder charges for Jeremiah. Halloran had dogged Ike and Damon every step of the way, until he'd been summarily ordered out of both the APD and the DA's office. He'd finally gone to his in-laws' house, where Maggie was resting and being given TLC by her mother, by late afternoon. Only talking to Maggie, who'd insisted she was fine, and being with his kids, had finally calmed him down. And Frank O'Connell's liberal applications of Jameson whiskey.

"Maggie seems fine," Hollis said to him now.

"No thanks to me," Halloran said. "I had my head in some kind of legal cloud while my wife was in danger. And I was the one who put her there by talking about getting a relative's permission to search Daisy Henry's phone. What the fuck was I thinking?"

"It wasn't your fault, Tom. That's what you told me when Carrie was kidnapped last year, remember? And when I realized that I had no idea that my best friend was a sociopath."

Halloran shook his head. "Yeah, but this was different. Part of me was still convinced that Will Henry had killed his wife. And before that, I thought Winston Avery had done it."

"We were both guilty of that, Tom. For a long time, we each thought the two cases might be connected, and that Winston was that connection."

"Yes, but because of Carrie's work on the autopsy, you figured out that he was innocent. And you put your own life on the line to prove it. All I did was call Ike, when Maggie went missing. He's the one who put the pieces together."

"What can I say, Tom? You're not law enforcement. You're a hell of a lawyer, but you need to leave the cop stuff to the cops," Hollis said. "But Ike told me you're the one who figured out where Maggie might have gone that day. The uniforms wouldn't have gotten there as quickly, even with the tracking system on her car."

Halloran sighed. "Even so, it was Rachel Bulloch who kept Jeremiah from killing her. Ike told me she might face some charges, too, but they're taking that into consideration. I don't think she realized her husband would end up killing Daisy when she told him Will was moving back home, but when she did know, she couldn't turn him in. Jeremiah exercised a lot of patriarchal control—and not just in his church. His wife and daughter were little more than chattel to him, and only he and God knew best."

"Well, at least Jayla will have her father back soon, once all the bureaucratic tape is untangled," said Hollis. "He'd still be in prison if you and Maggie hadn't gotten involved."

"It turns out he thought Trina Daily had killed Daisy, and his own guilt over his affair with her kept him from letting Jayla testify," Halloran said. "Damon told me Will was also afraid Trina might try to harm Jayla in some way, if she found out Jayla knew Will had left the house before Daisy was killed. That was also why he didn't want Cate and me to go looking for other suspects." Halloran shook his head, still amazed by what he'd learned. "He was willing to rot in prison rather than take that chance. I think Trina genuinely believed Will was guilty, but I also think there was some basis for Will to think she could be pretty ruthless. If she had known he intended to go back to Daisy, Trina might have dealt with her before Elder Bulloch got there. I don't think that romance will be rekindled."

Hollis gave him a wistful smile. "But all things considered, your case had a better outcome than mine. I didn't put the pieces together until it was too late for Winston Avery, something I'll always regret. He was someone I wish I'd gotten to know—as he really was. But there was so much misinformation being thrown at us that we couldn't see the actual man behind all of it."

The doorbell rang, and Halloran heard the sound of excited children as they rushed to answer it. He stood up and looked at Hollis. "I guess we better join the others, but thanks for talking to me, Hollis. It helped."

"Don't go getting all mushy on me, Tom," he said, standing up, too. "I'm liable to think aliens have taken over your body."

———

Hollis Joplin stood up and looked around at the large group gathered in the Hallorans' living room, then hoisted his Champagne glass. "I'd like to make a toast." When all the others had raised their own glasses, he said, "To Maggie Halloran, the newest member of a very special club: the Survivors' Club. You can only join it if you've almost been killed by a raving-lunatic murderer."

"Hollis!" said Carrie. "How can you joke about that?"

"I'm not joking!" he insisted. "Tom and I both almost got killed during the Carter case, and after Libba Woodridge died, you got kidnapped and almost killed, right? And Maggie was almost killed by an honest-to-God, fire and brimstone preacher! We've got a lot to celebrate: Elder Jeremiah Bulloch is in custody while he recuperates from being hit over the head by his wife with a fire extinguisher, and Will Henry is being released tomorrow."

"To Maggie!" they all said in unison, when Joplin finished his speech and took a long sip of his wine.

Maggie stood as Joplin sat down. She was wearing a pretty scarf around her neck to hide the bruises Joplin knew were there. There were tears in her eyes, but she was smiling. "I am honored to be a member of the Survivors' Club and appreciate everything you said, Hollis. I truly have a lot to be thankful for this year. But I'd rather that we remember three people who weren't so lucky and can't be here with us tonight: Daisy Henry, Blaine Reynolds, and Winston Avery. They will always be in our hearts, though," she added, looking across the entry hall into the den, where Jayla Henry was playing with Megan and Tommy, then at Joplin. "Always."

This toast was a somber one, and Joplin glanced at Carrie as he raised his glass again. He had finally been able to talk to her the night before about Blaine's brief pregnancy during their relationship, and she'd held him tightly as he mourned the child he'd never known about and the woman who had lost much more than that. It would hurt him for a long time that she'd gone through that alone. It also hurt that when Blaine had finally been ready for a child, that one, too, had been taken from her, as well as the man she would have married if Mark Rawlins hadn't been so consumed by jealousy and his obsession with her. And the devil who lived inside him.

On Tuesday morning, Rawlins and his attorney had met with Simmons and Danny Akron, Fulton County's senior prosecutor, to hammer out the plea bargain that would take the death penalty off the table. Answers to some of the questions that had plagued them during the investigation were finally given. Rawlins' own days as an investigative reporter, for example, had led to his acquaintance with James Corcoran, when he'd worked on a story about homeless vets. And the ring he'd placed on Blaine's finger had belonged to his own grandmother. He'd posed her, just as Maggie had theorized, to draw attention to it. Then he'd covered her face with her hair to keep Joplin from knowing she was the victim until he turned her over, hoping to ratchet up the pain a little more.

The only pleasant information to come out of that meeting with Mark Rawlins, in Joplin's opinion, was that the man would be in prison for the rest of his life. No chance of parole. He usually didn't find it productive to examine the concept of evil and whether it existed as an entity or only within human beings, but he found himself thinking about that as he held Carrie's hand and sipped his Champagne. The last time had been while he was recuperating from the knife wounds Jack Tyndall had inflicted on him. Joplin had seen true evil looking at him through Jack's eyes then, and he'd seen the same thing in Mark Rawlins' expression as he talked about why he'd had to kill Blaine.

Joplin's attention was suddenly claimed by the three children as they came into the living room.

"We're hungry!" Tommy Halloran announced. "Is it time to eat yet?"

And so they all laughed and then headed for the big kitchen to help Maggie and Tom unload warming ovens and unwrap tightly foiled casserole dishes. Maggie's father, the surgeon, carved the Turducken and a small turkey for those with less adventurous palates; Carrie's father took wine bottles to the table; and Carrie's mother gave Joplin a a clumsy hug as she teetered on her crutches.

"Maybe next year at your new house?" she whispered, raising her eyebrows. "The condo just isn't big enough for grandchildren."

"No, it isn't," Joplin whispered back. "I'll work on that."

ACKNOWLEDGEMENTS

Writing is a necessarily solitary occupation and takes place in my mind, on long walks, and in front of a computer screen. But I'm lucky to be able to rely on good friends, both personal and professional, to collaborate with me along the way. To all of them I offer my heartfelt gratitude and appreciation.

John Martucci, of Martucci Designs, created the amazing cover for *The Devil's Bidding*. It provides not only the lure to attract a reader from a bookshelf or an Internet seller, it also sets the tone of the book itself. He's done this for my previous books, and I will count on him to work his magic for those that follow.

Jarell Jones, a long-time friend, is an attorney whom even Hollis Joplin would like: a Southern boy, former Duke basketball player, accomplished cook, and a good shot. He took the time to read several of the chapters dealing with legal issues, as well as to send me reams of information on the 4th Amendment. Any mistakes that Tom Halloran makes in the book are mine alone.

I could not have written any of my books without my faithful manuscript readers: Nicole and Tom Armentrout, Sue Crawford, and Bill Donovan. They are all perceptive, meticulous, and fearless in their quest to provide me with the objectivity needed to create the best book I can. From the most basic things, like finding typos and missing or added words that are beyond Spellcheck, to alerting me to outright mistakes and character or plot deviations, they have saved my derriere on too many occasions to mention.

Next comes Morgana Gallaway, designer and editor of both the print and digital versions of the books. It's always a jolt when I have to finally release the manuscript and then go through the line-by-line process with her as it reaches publication. Her patience, expertise, and gentle suggestions make it much easier to bear.

I could not do without Jane Ryder, of Ryder Author Resources. I am an uneasy denizen of the cyber world, competent only at word processing, and that none too well. Jane is a marketer *extraordinaire,* who handles my Facebook account and its monthly posts, as well as my website. She is supremely competent at what she does and always available to provide support, both technical and personal. We share a love of cats, perverse humor, and interesting insomnia solutions.

The fun part of writing is going to book signings, events, and, especially, the many book clubs who invite me to attend their meetings as a guest author. They encourage me to keep writing and impress me every time with their insights and suggestions. The food and wine aren't bad either.

Finally, my heartfelt gratitude to those of you reading this book. If you enjoyed it, I hope you'll tell your friends and consider writing a review on Amazon, Goodreads, or Barnes and Noble. I'd also love to hear from you, and I promise to respond to any questions, suggestions, or constructive criticism. You can contact me at **www.pldoss.com.**

AUTHOR'S NOTES

As mentioned in the previous books, there is currently no Milton County in Georgia. But, up until 1932, it did exist, having been created in 1857 from bits and pieces of Cobb, Cherokee, and Forsyth Counties. It was then merged with Fulton County to save it from bankruptcy during the Depression. My Milton County extends much further south than the original, but, in my opinion, reflects the current racial, political, and financial concerns of its residents. My main intention in bringing it back to life, however, was to have more creative control over the medical examiner's office where Carrie Salinger and Hollis Joplin work, as well as to differentiate it from the ME offices in Fulton, Cobb, Dekalb and Gwinnet Counties.

Blaine Reynolds is fictional and had nothing to do with the comprehensive coverage of what is known as the Atlanta Schools Scandal by the *Atlanta Journal-Constitution,* but she stands in for the many reporters who did. The *AJC* was also instrumental in getting an official investigation launched when it reported the results of its own investigation of suspicious test results on standardized test results in city schools. Reginal Dukes is an actual investigator hired to look into cheating at one such school. Everything I wrote about him is taken from newspaper and television broadcasts.

We have all become so dependent on cell phones in this day and age, that it was a real eye-opener for me when I began researching certain legal aspects of Will Henry's murder trial and conviction for Halloran to explore. I was surprised to find out how little protection there was in 2013 for Georgia citizens with regard to their 4th Amendment rights and their cell phones. *Riley v, California,* the landmark U.S. Supreme Court decision in 2014, which held that the warrantless search and seizure of cell phones, which have become so much more than merely a means of communication, is unconstitutional, changed all that. I found it fascinating, and although this book is meant to entertain, and I didn't want to hit the reader over the head with case law, I hope I shed a little light on the subject.

About the Author

Photo by John Martucci

While completing a Master of Science degree in Criminal Justice at Georgia State University in 1987, P. L. Doss served a graduate internship at the Fulton County Medical Examiner's Office. Assigned to the investigative division, she discovered how important the duties of the investigators were in helping the forensic pathologists determine cause and manner of death. She was also able to observe many autopsies—an experience that proved to be invaluable in toughening her up for her career in law enforcement, first as a volunteer analyst in the Missing Children's Information Center at the Georgia Bureau of Investigation, and then as a probation officer and supervisor of officers at the Georgia Department of Corrections. She currently lives in the North Georgia mountains with her husband and cat and is hard at work on her fourth Joplin/Halloran mystery.